TOPSIDE

"An intriguing mix of adventure and wonder and the mundane, both quietly epic and very personal. Wonderful art. Highly recommended."

–Jeff VanderMeer, *Annihilation*

"*Topside* is an engrossing adventure buoyed by lush sci–fi landscapes and unlikely friendships. Monk and Bogosian have crafted an imaginative odyssey that calls to mind the works of Hayao Miyazaki."

–Kristen Gudsnuk, *Making Friends*

"Thoughtful, woke, and enjoyably propulsive. The world Monk and Bogosian describe is terrible, but such an enjoyable place to spend an afternoon."

–Zander Cannon, *Kaijumax*

"Vibrant and fun, *Topside* blasts off on a colorful journey across an alien world."

–Katie Shanahan, *Silly Kingdom*

TOP

SIDE

J. N. Monk

Harry Bogosian

Graphic Universe™ • Minneapolis

Graphic Universe™
An imprint of Lerner Publishing Group, Inc.
241 First Avenue North
Minneapolis, MN 55401 USA

For reading levels and more information, look up this title at www.lernerbooks.com.

Main body text set in CCDaveGibbonsLower.
Typeface provided by Comicraft.

Library of Congress Cataloging-in-Publication Data

Names: Monk, J. N., 1986–author. | Bogosian, Harry, 1987–illustrator.
Title: Topside / J.N. Monk ; Harry Bogosian.
Description: Minneapolis : Graphic Universe, [2019] | Summary: Sixteen-year-old
   Jo, a maintenance technician in an underground society, makes a massive error
   during a routine repair and to set things right, must journey above ground, to
   a dangerous area swarming with alien life. | Identifiers: LCCN 2018038299
   (print) | LCCN 2018043374 (ebook) | ISBN 9781541561120 (eb pdf) |
   ISBN 9781512445893 (lb : alk. paper)
Subjects: LCSH: Graphic novels. | CYAC: Graphic novels. | Mechanics (Persons)—
   Fiction. | Extraterrestrial beings—Fiction. | Science fiction.
Classification: LCC PZ7.7.M643 (ebook) | LCC PZ7.7.M643 Top 2019 (print) |
   DDC 741.5/973—dc23

LC record available at https://lccn.loc.gov/2018038299

Manufactured in the United States of America
1-42519-26195-3/13/2019

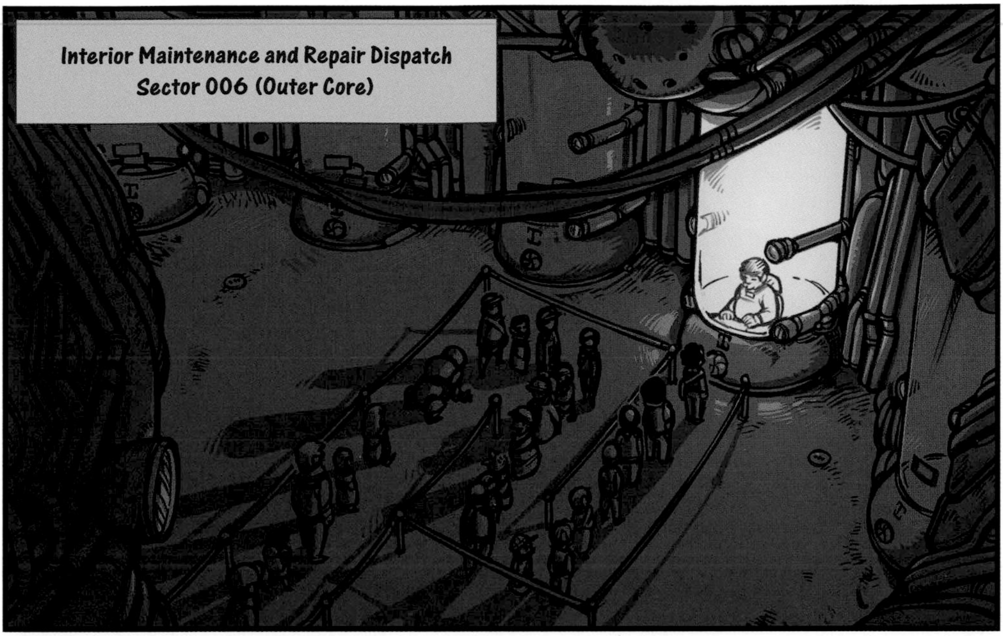
Interior Maintenance and Repair Dispatch
Sector 006 (Outer Core)

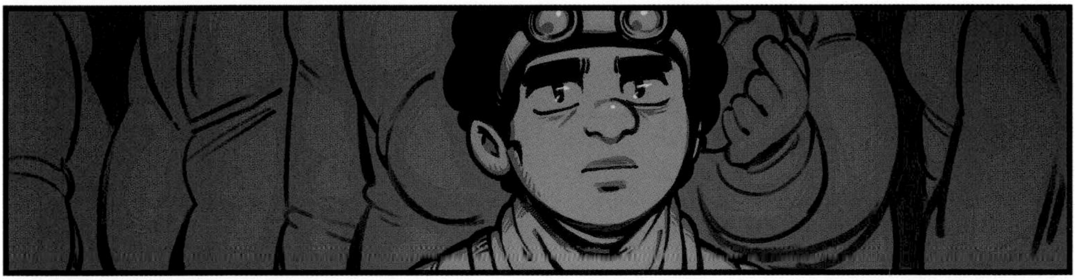

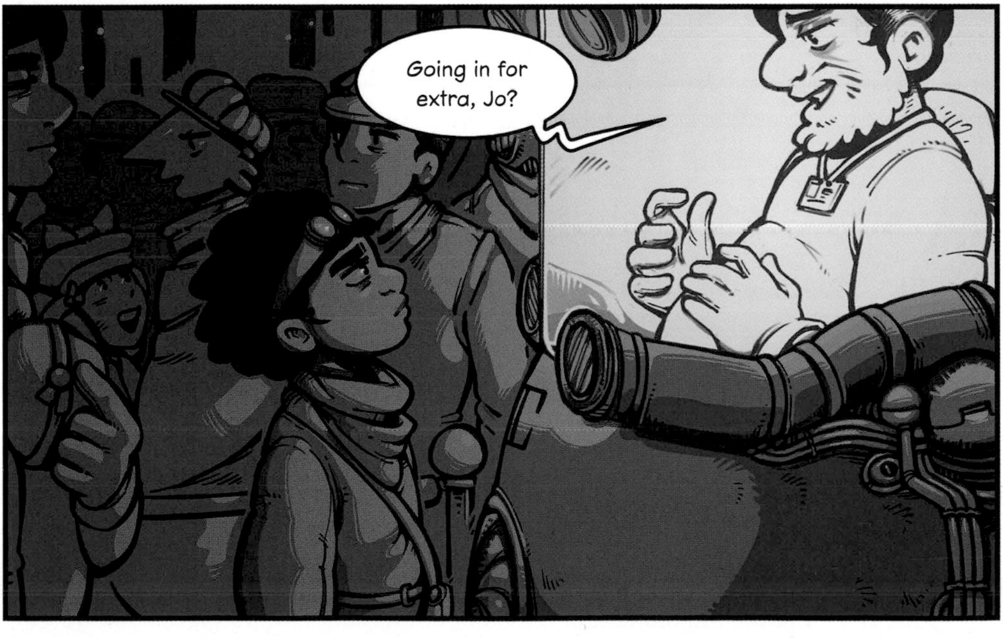
Going in for extra, Jo?

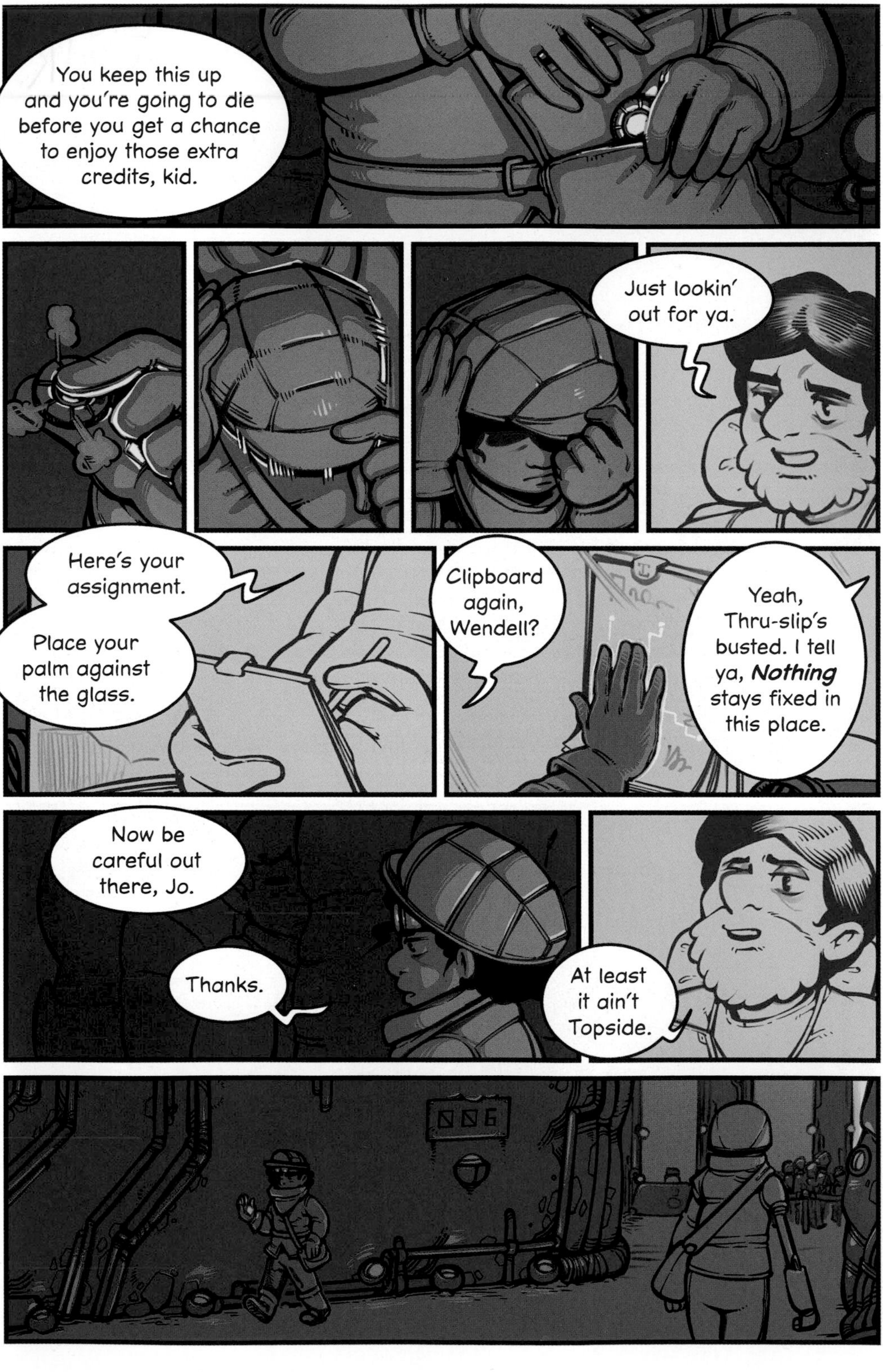
You keep this up and you're going to die before you get a chance to enjoy those extra credits, kid.
Just lookin' out for ya.
Here's your assignment.
Place your palm against the glass.
Clipboard again, Wendell?
Yeah, Thru-slip's busted. I tell ya, **Nothing** stays fixed in this place.
Now be careful out there, Jo.
Thanks.
At least it ain't Topside.
006

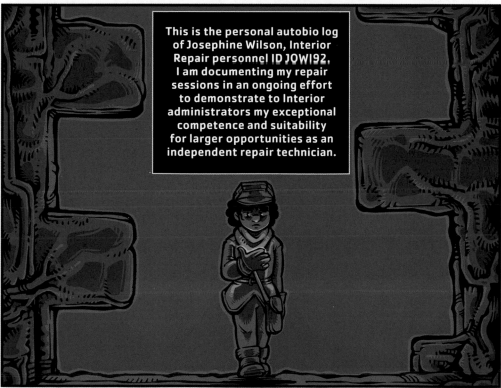

This is the personal autobio log of Josephine Wilson, Interior Repair personnel ID JOWl92. I am documenting my repair sessions in an ongoing effort to demonstrate to Interior administrators my exceptional competence and suitability for larger opportunities as an independent repair technician.

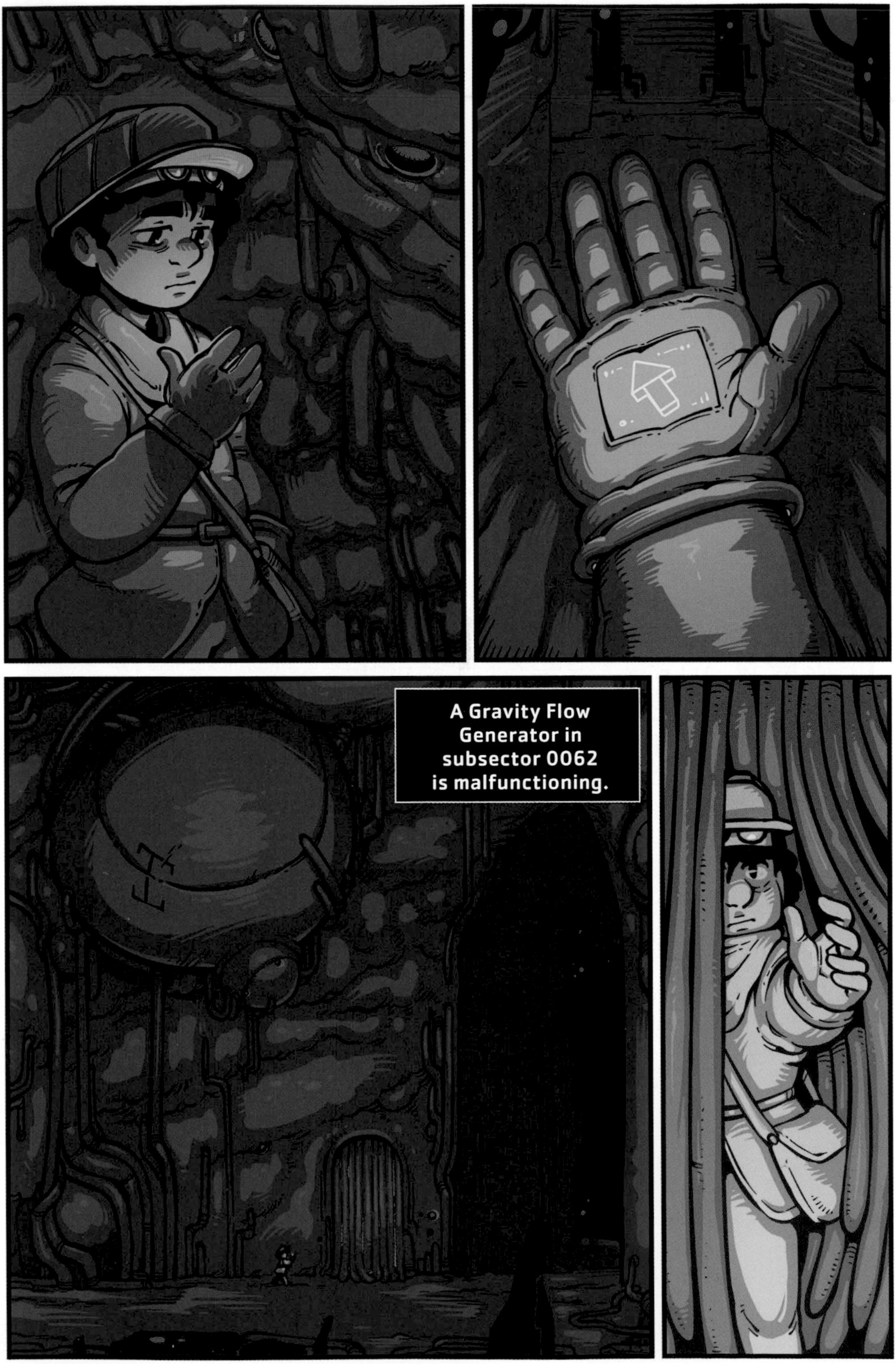
A Gravity Flow Generator in subsector 0062 is malfunctioning.

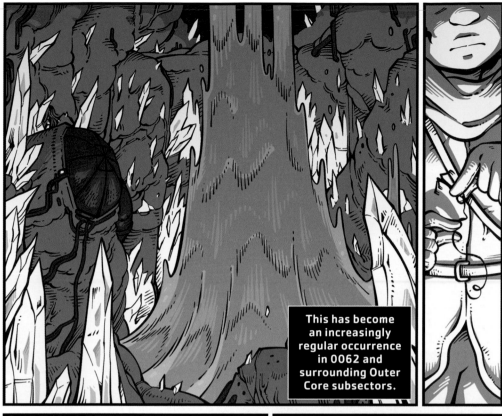

This has become an increasingly regular occurrence in 0062 and surrounding Outer Core subsectors.

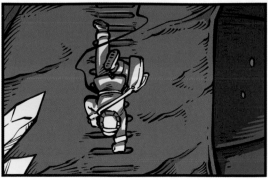

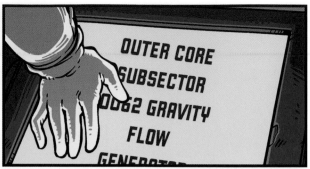

OUTER CORE
SUBSECTOR
0062 GRAVITY
FLOW
GENERATOR

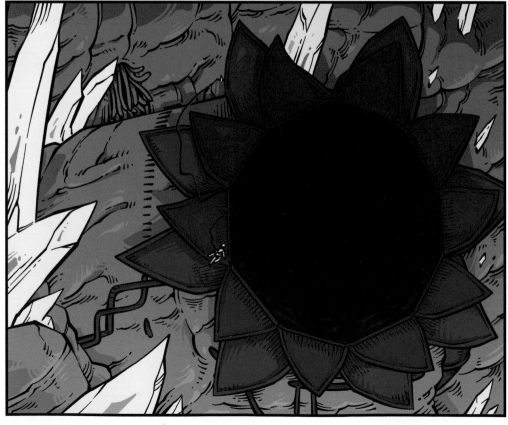

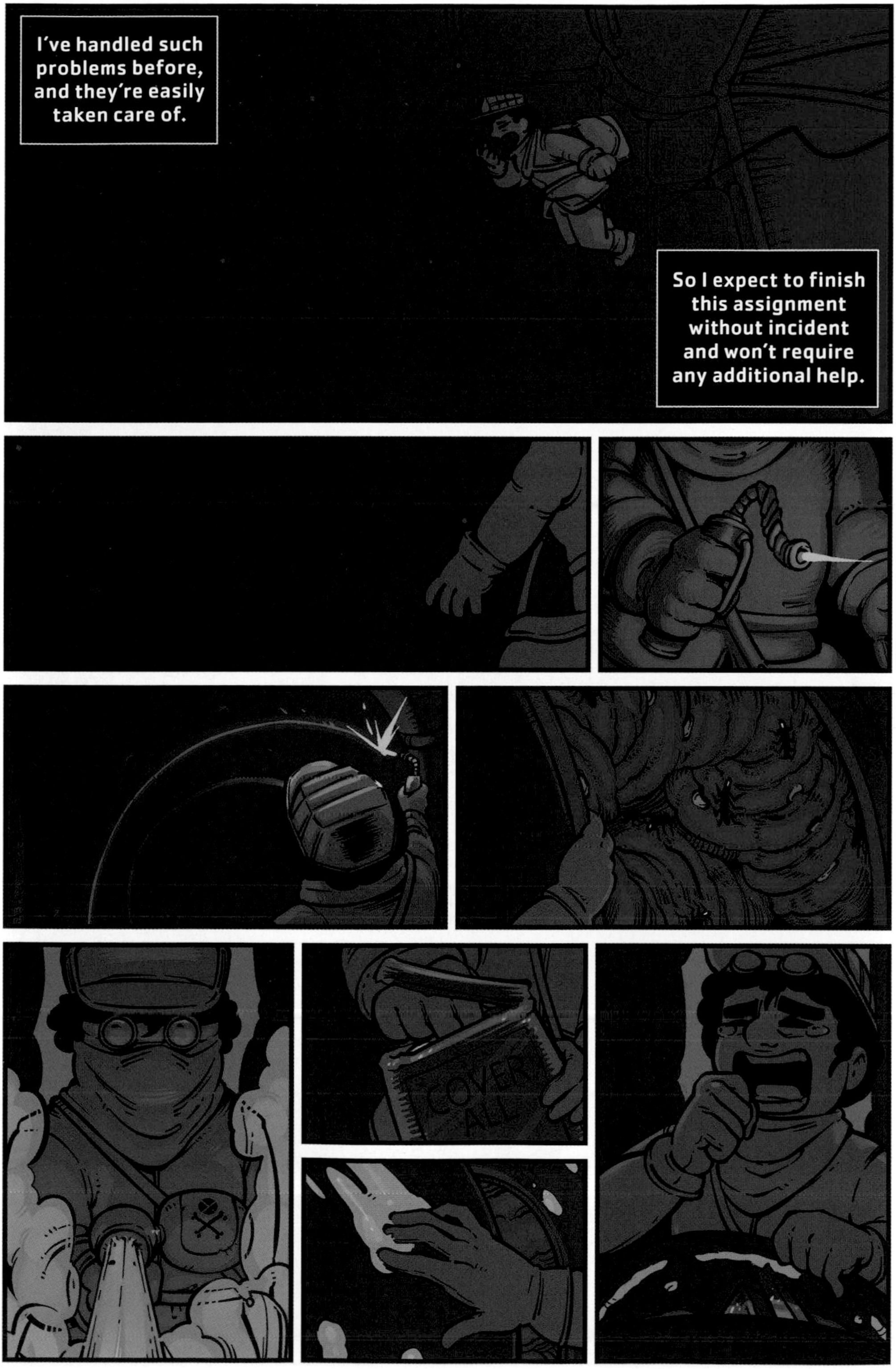
I've handled such problems before, and they're easily taken care of.
So I expect to finish this assignment without incident and won't require any additional help.
COVER ALL

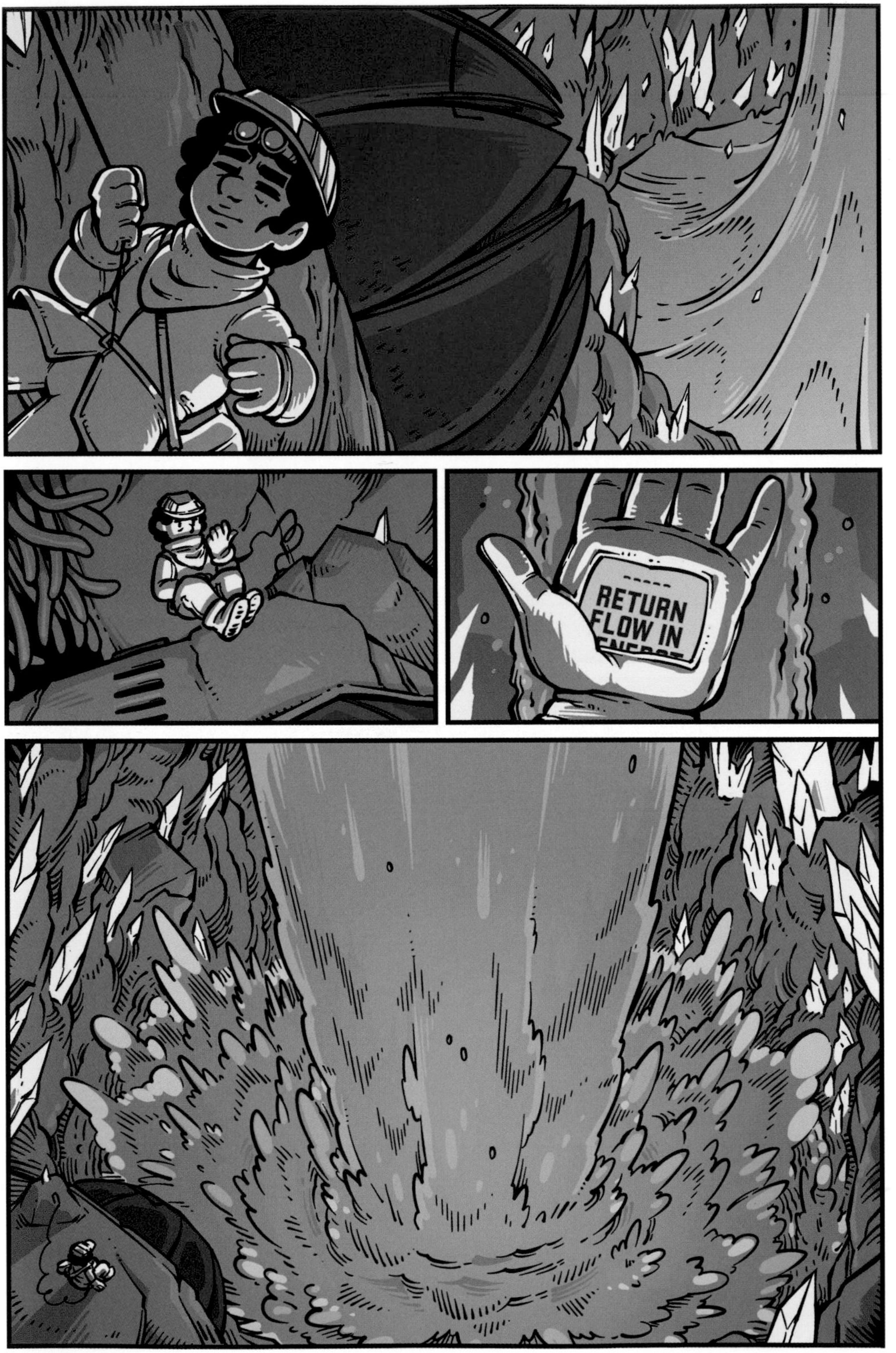
RETURN
FLOW IN

OST REPAIR ASSESMEN
REPAIRS COMPLETED
DEVICE REQUIRING REPAIR
GRAVITY FLOW GENERATOR
EQUIPMENT UTILIZED:
-CUTTER TORCH
-BIO SPRAY
-COVER ALL
FLUID PATCH...
Fluid Patch?
THE COVER ALL!
I should still have the packaging!
Wai—
WWHOOOOOMMPH

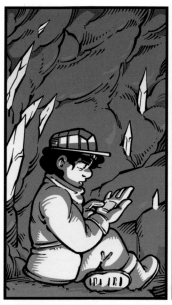

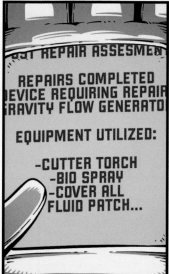

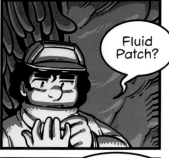

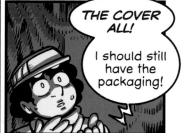

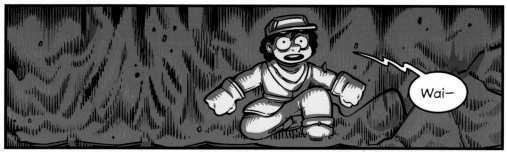

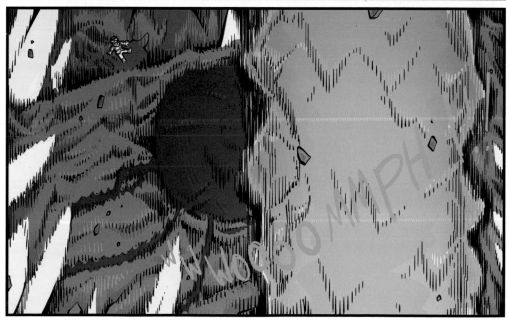

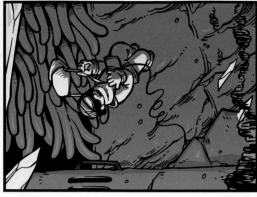

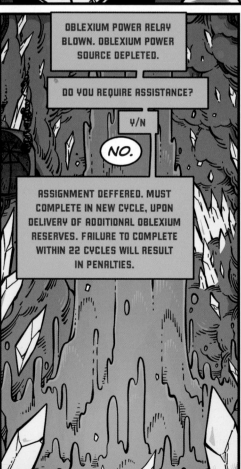

OBLEXIUM POWER RELAY BLOWN. OBLEXIUM POWER SOURCE DEPLETED.

DO YOU REQUIRE ASSISTANCE?

Y/N

NO.

ASSIGNMENT DEFFERED. MUST COMPLETE IN NEW CYCLE, UPON DELIVERY OF ADDITIONAL OBLEXIUM RESERVES. FAILURE TO COMPLETE WITHIN 22 CYCLES WILL RESULT IN PENALTIES.

Time of arrival for new Oblexium reserves?

PROJECTED DELIVERY DATE: 21 CYCLES-35 CYCLES.

21 to 35 cycles? What if it doesn't—

PLEASE REPORT DEFERRAL TO DISPATCH.

...

Wendell's gonna kill me.

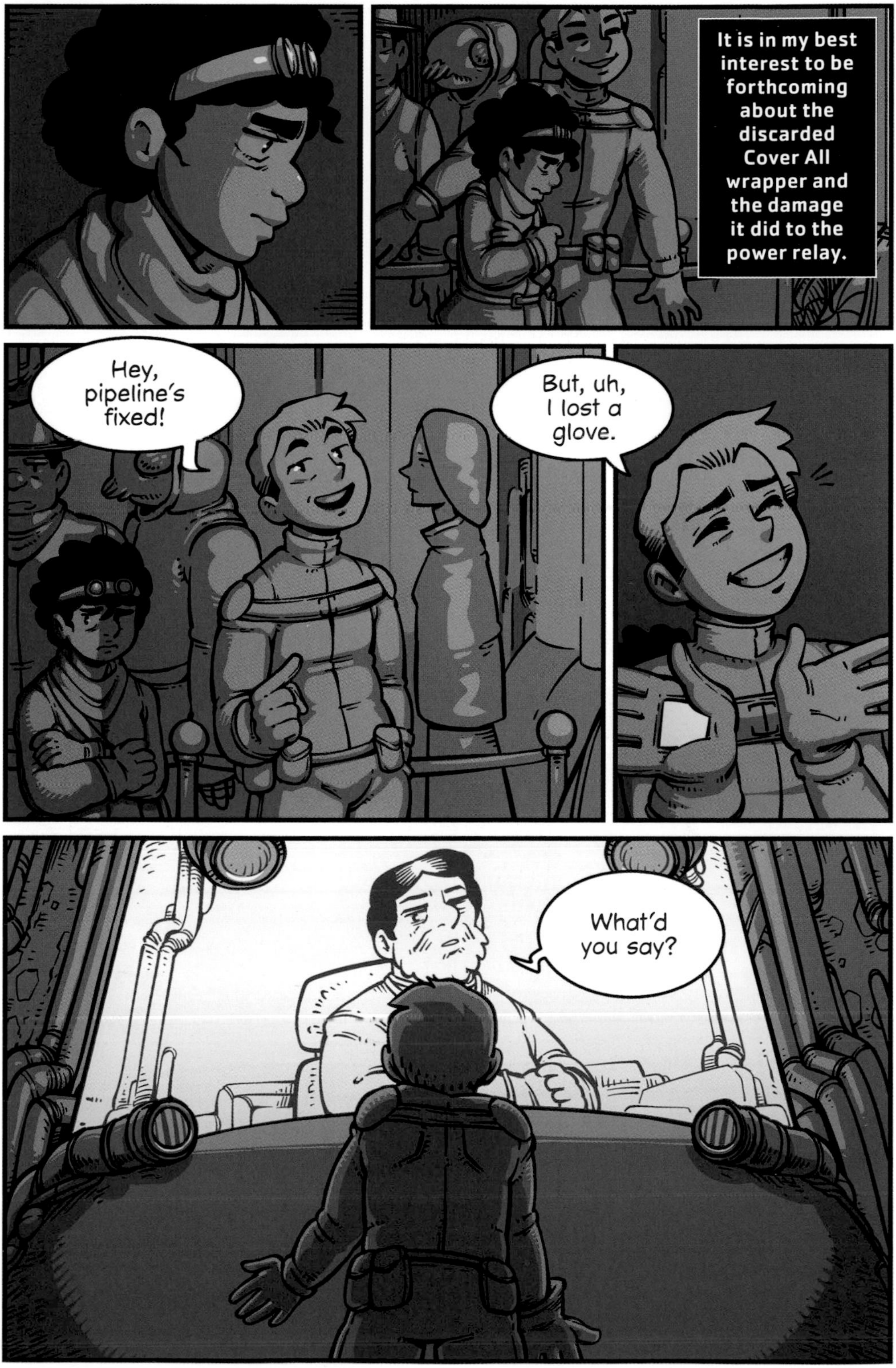
It is in my best interest to be forthcoming about the discarded Cover All wrapper and the damage it did to the power relay.
Hey, pipeline's fixed!
But, uh, I lost a glove.
What'd you say?

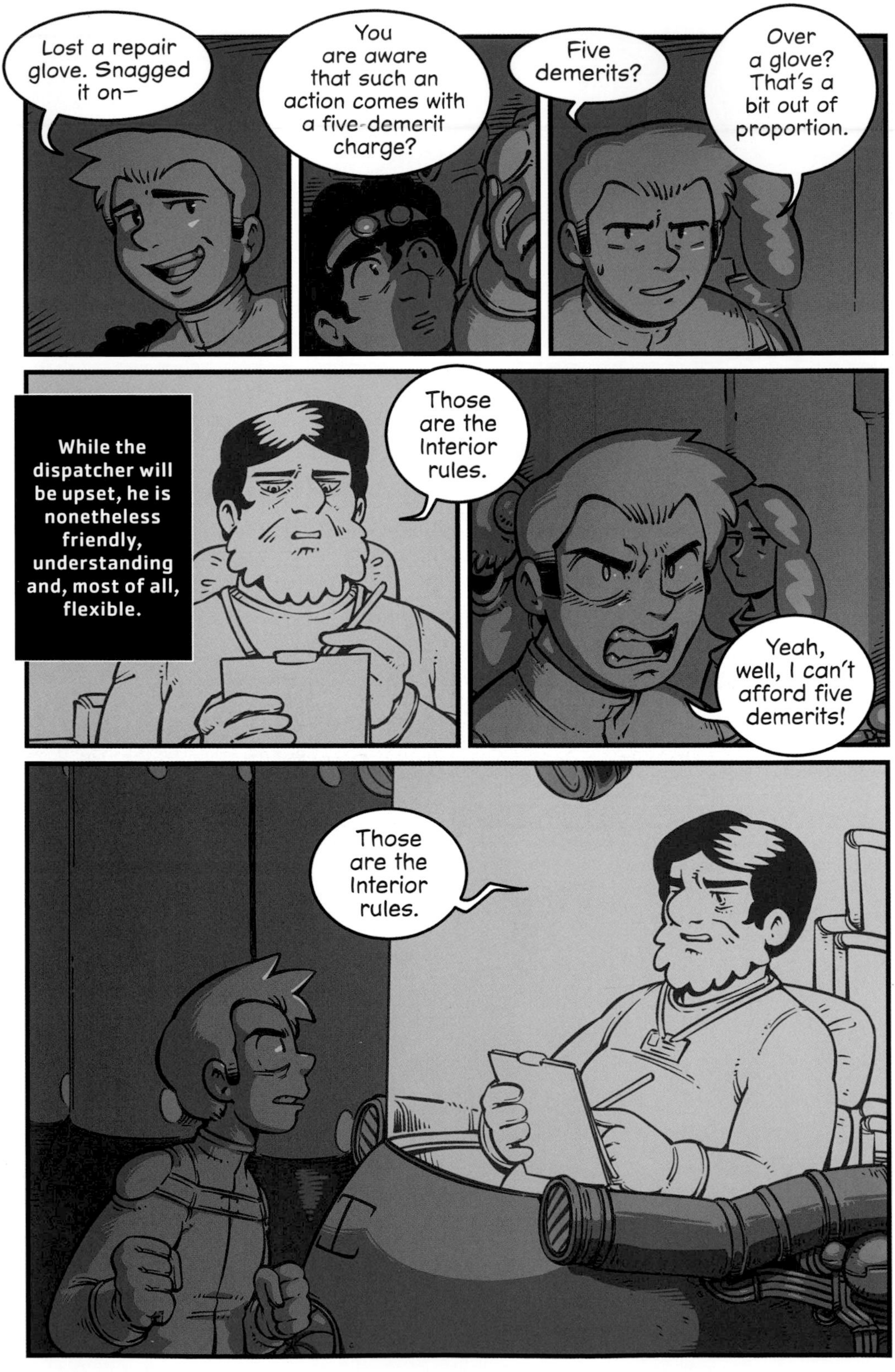

Lost a repair glove. Snagged it on—
You are aware that such an action comes with a five-demerit charge?
Five demerits?
Over a glove? That's a bit out of proportion.
While the dispatcher will be upset, he is nonetheless friendly, understanding and, most of all, flexible.
Those are the Interior rules.
Yeah, well, I can't afford five demerits!
Those are the Interior rules.

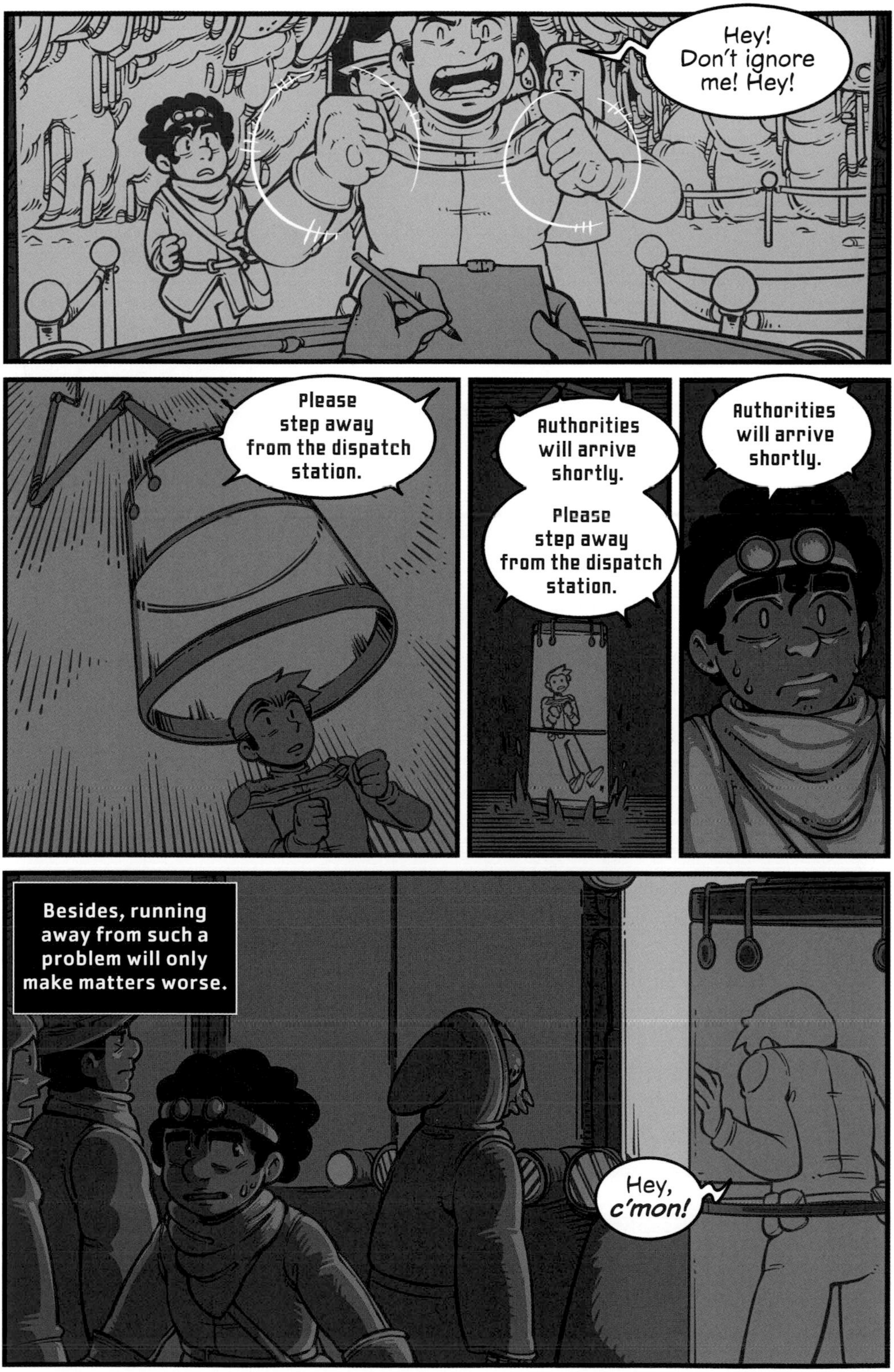
Hey!
Don't ignore
me! Hey!
Please
step away
from the dispatch
station.
Authorities
will arrive
shortly.
Please
step away
from the dispatch
station.
Authorities
will arrive
shortly.
Besides, running
away from such a
problem will only
make matters worse.
Hey,
c'mon!

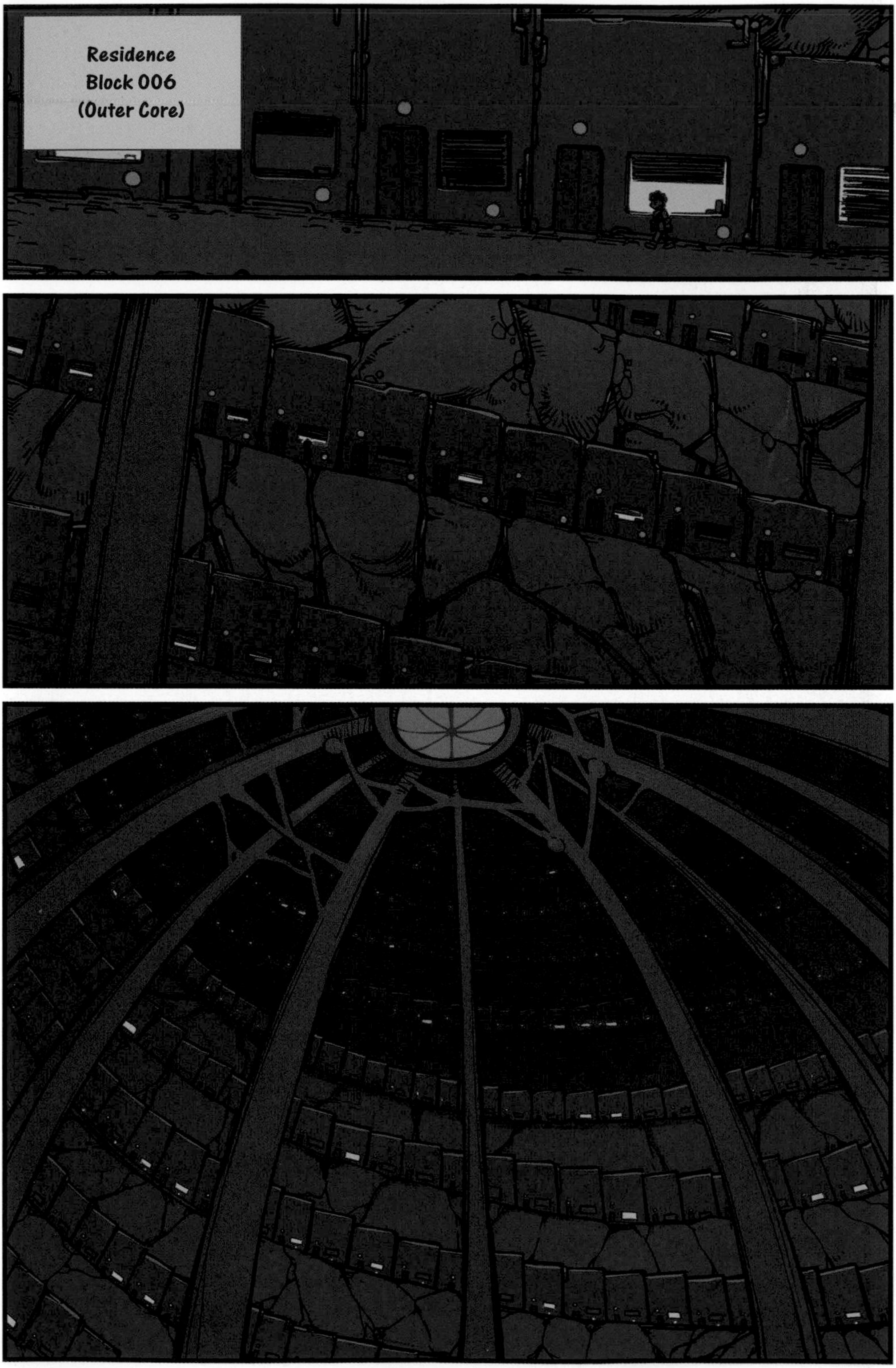
Residence
Block 006
(Outer Core)

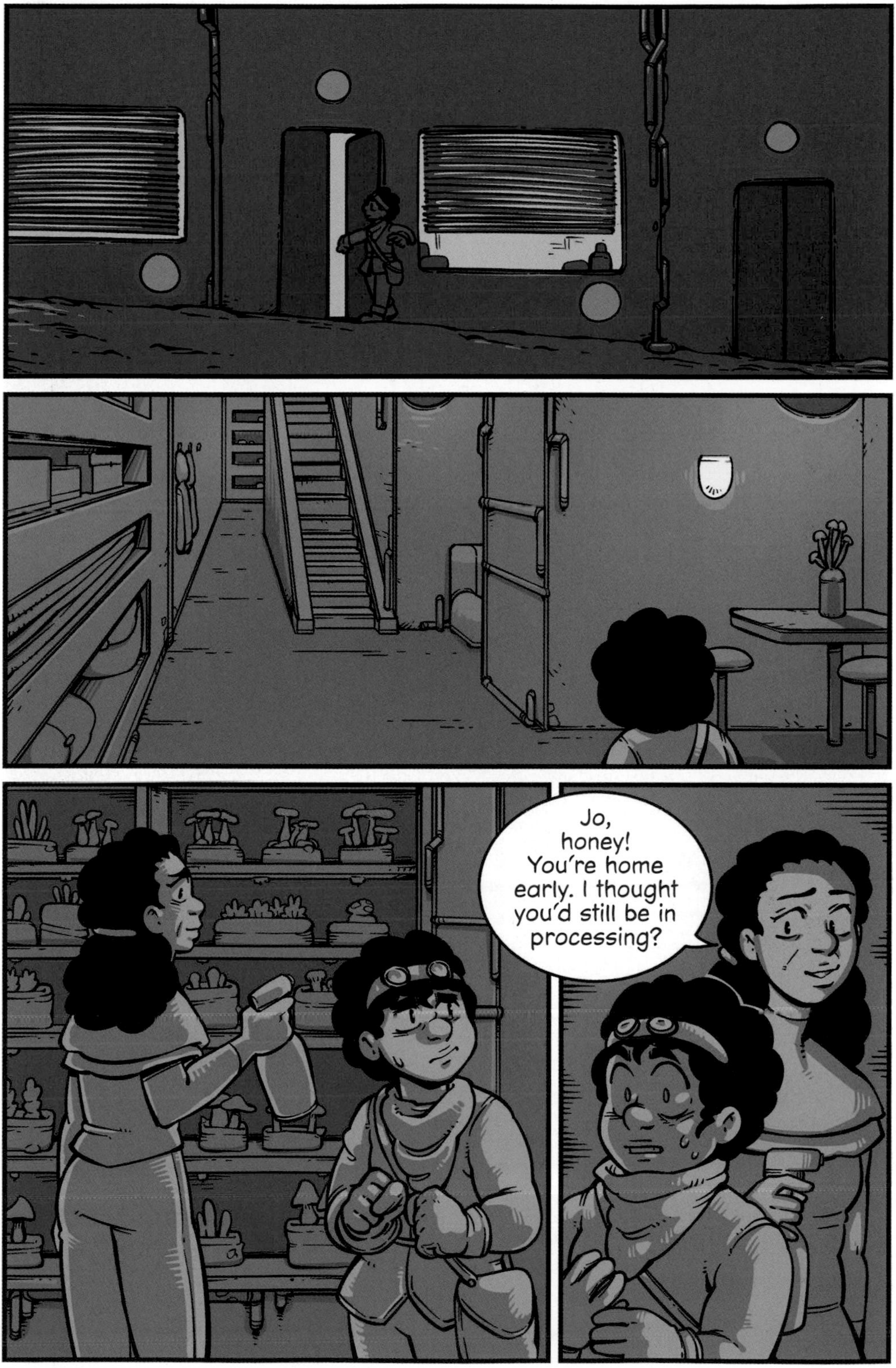
Jo, honey! You're home early. I thought you'd still be in processing?

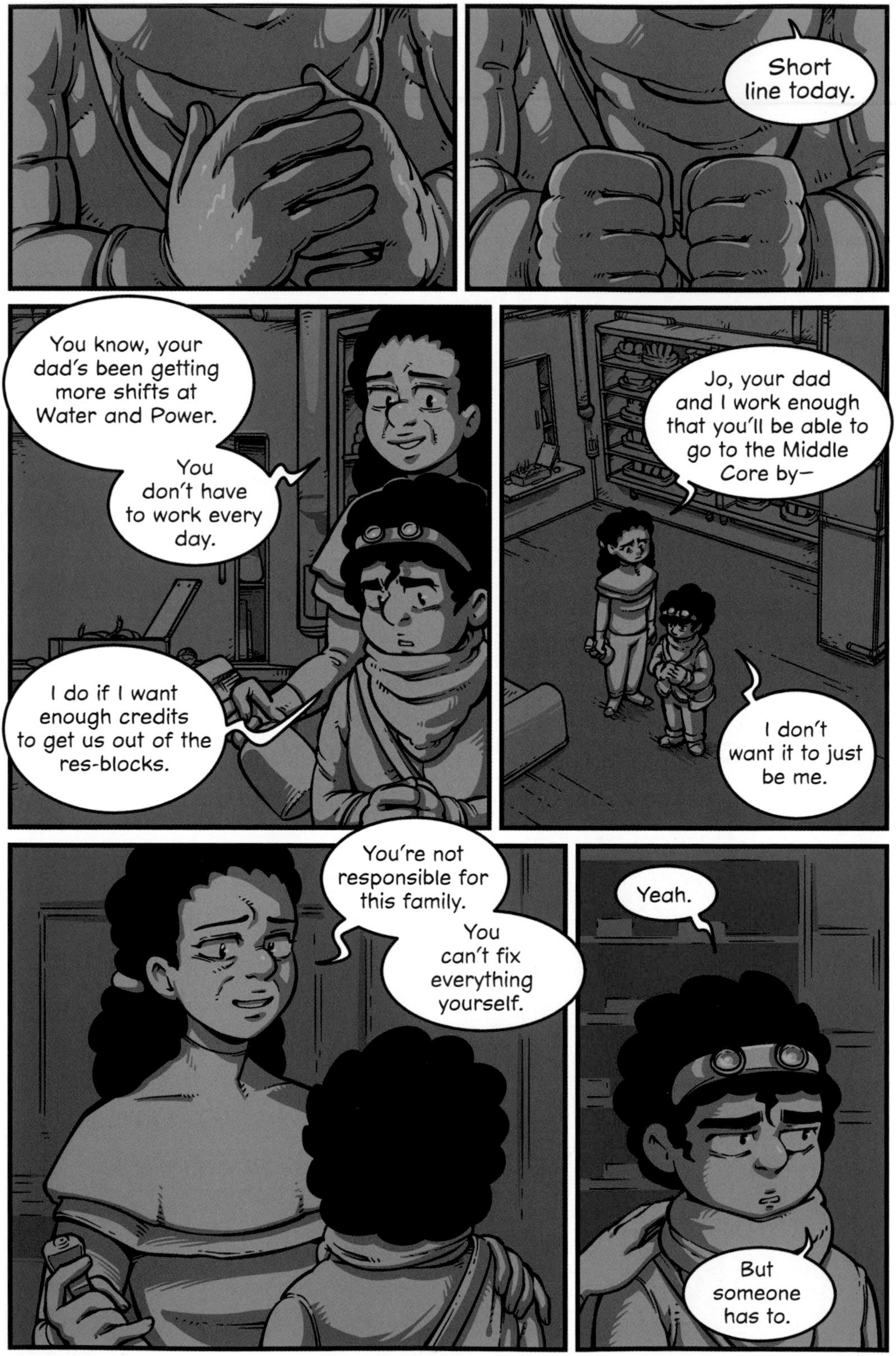
Short line today.
You know, your dad's been getting more shifts at Water and Power.
You don't have to work every day.
I do if I want enough credits to get us out of the res-blocks.
Jo, your dad and I work enough that you'll be able to go to the Middle Core by—
I don't want it to just be me.
You're not responsible for this family.
You can't fix everything yourself.
Yeah.
But someone has to.

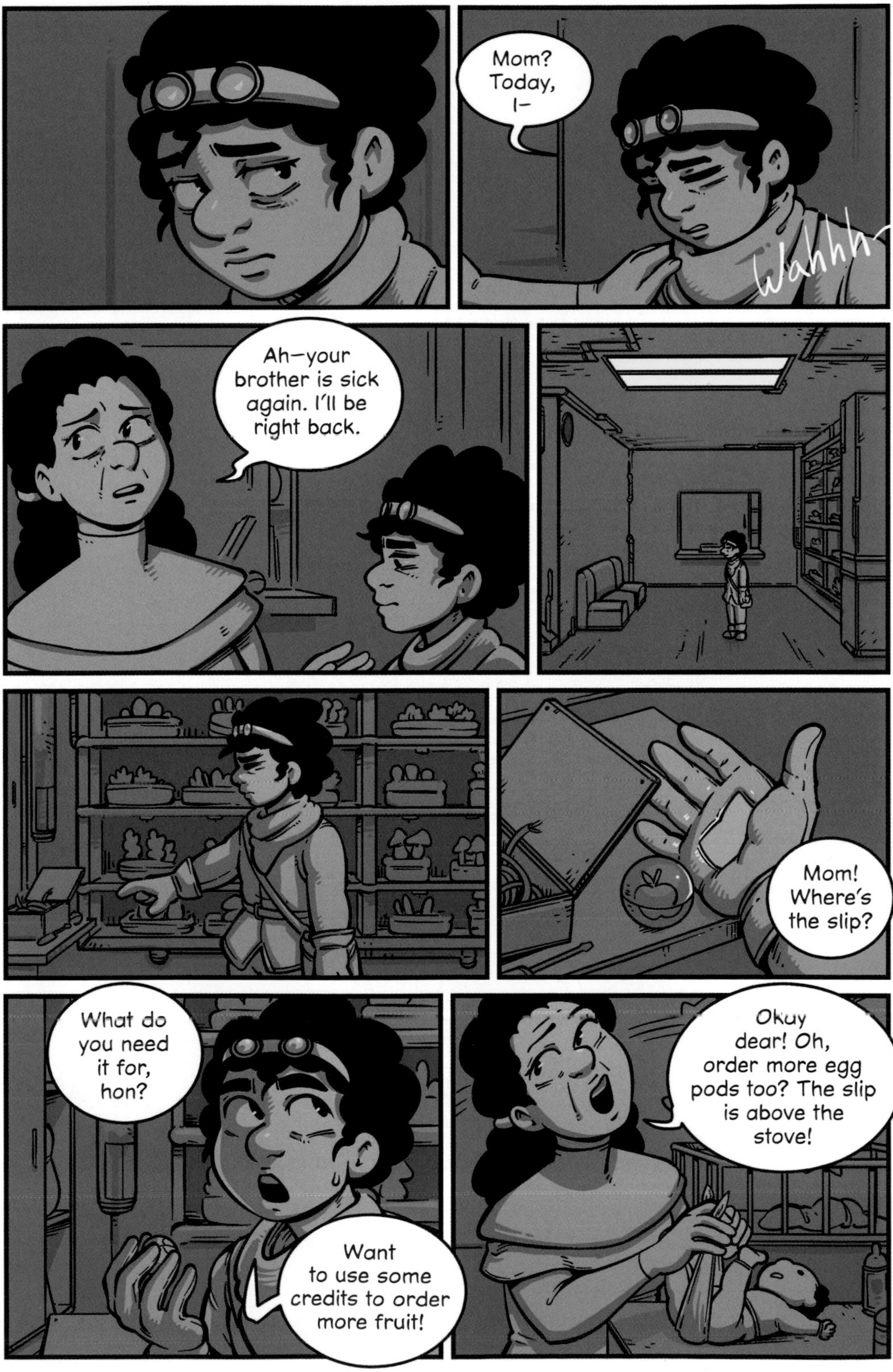
Mom?
Today,
I–
Wahhh–
Ah—your brother is sick again. I'll be right back.
Mom! Where's the slip?
What do you need it for, hon?
Want to use some credits to order more fruit!
Okay dear! Oh, order more egg pods too? The slip is above the stove!

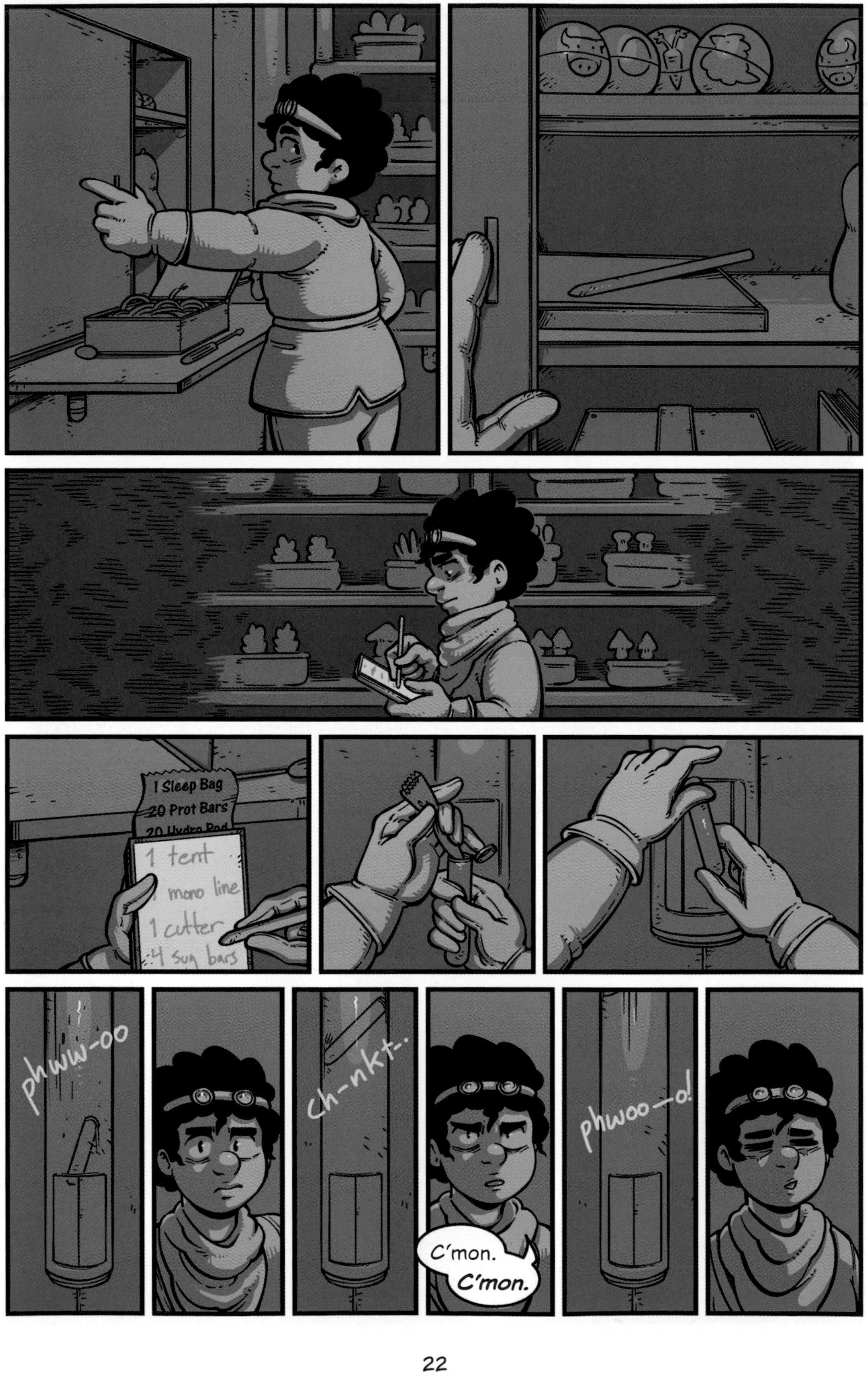
1 Sleep Bag
20 Prot Bars
1 tent
mono line
1 cutter
4 sun bars
phww-oo
ch-nkt..
C'mon.
C'mon.
phwoo-o!

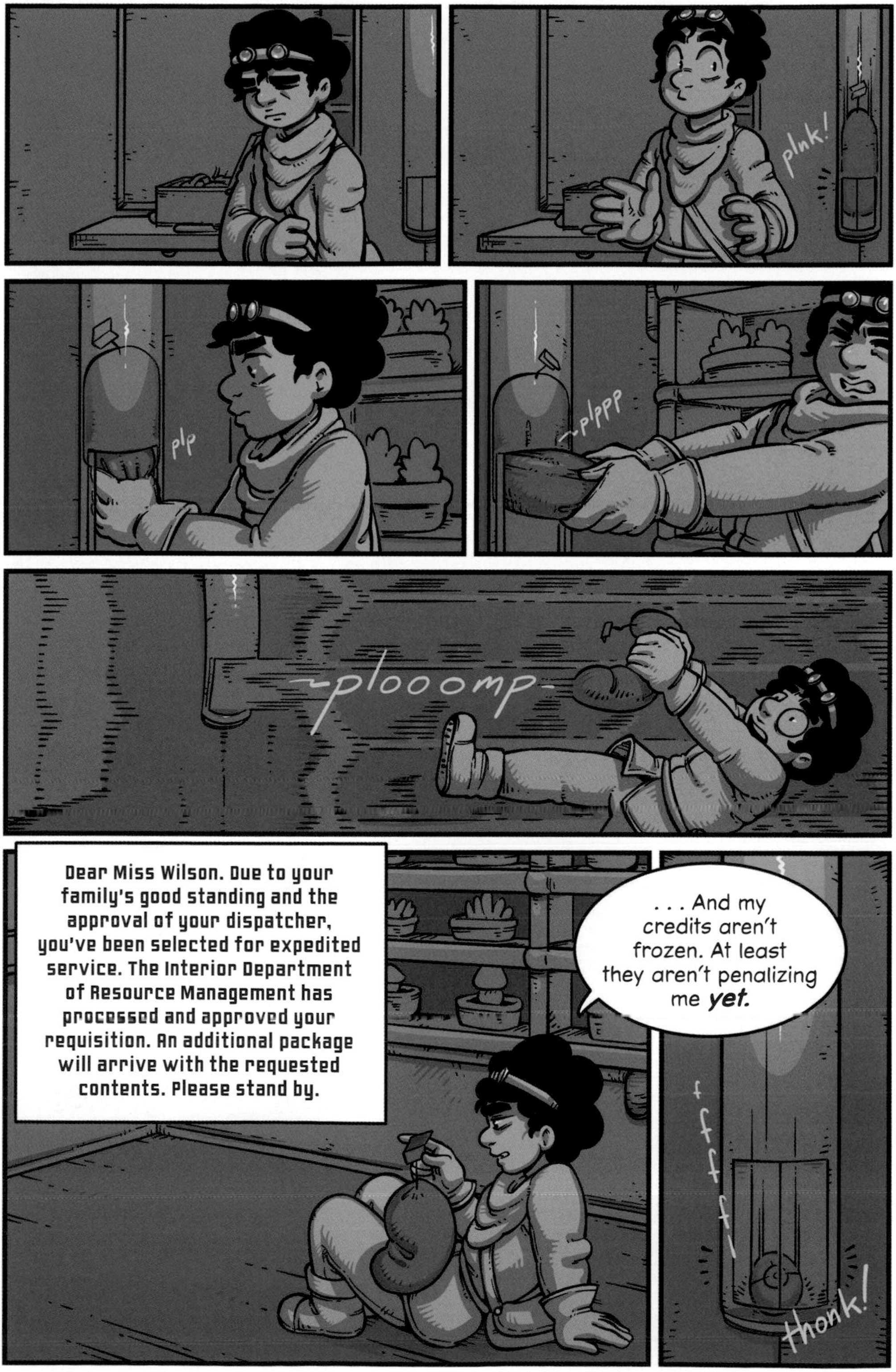
plnk!
plp
~plppp
~plooomp~
Dear Miss Wilson. Due to your family's good standing and the approval of your dispatcher, you've been selected for expedited service. The Interior Department of Resource Management has processed and approved your requisition. An additional package will arrive with the requested contents. Please stand by.
. . . And my credits aren't frozen. At least they aren't penalizing me *yet.*
thonk!

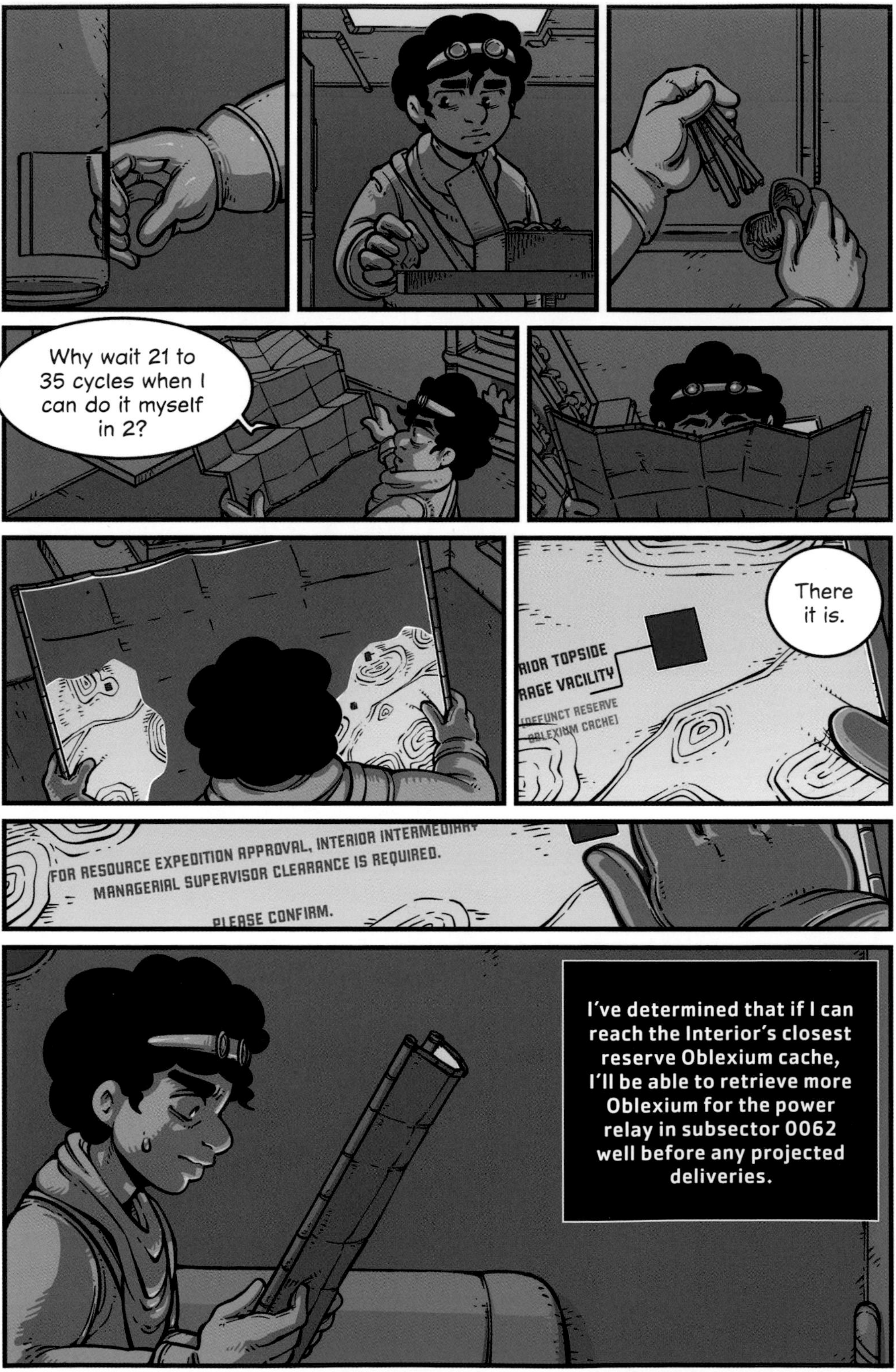
Why wait 21 to 35 cycles when I can do it myself in 2?
There it is.
RIOR TOPSIDE
RAGE VACILITY
[DEFUNCT RESERVE
OBLEXIUM CACHE]
FOR RESOURCE EXPEDITION APPROVAL, INTERIOR INTERMEDIARY
MANAGERIAL SUPERVISOR CLEARANCE IS REQUIRED.
PLEASE CONFIRM.
I've determined that if I can reach the Interior's closest reserve Oblexium cache, I'll be able to retrieve more Oblexium for the power relay in subsector 0062 well before any projected deliveries.

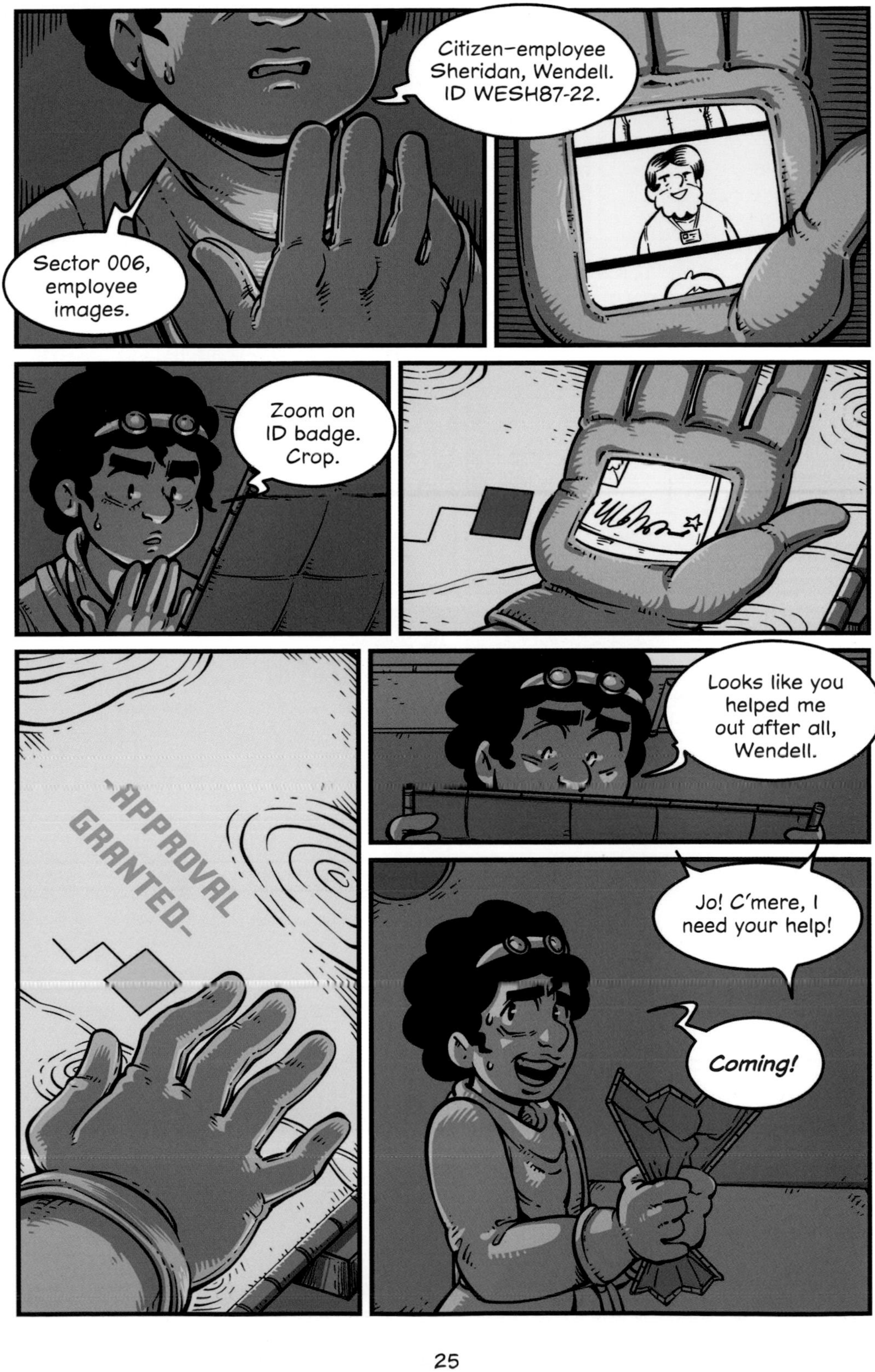
Sector 006, employee images.
Citizen-employee Sheridan, Wendell. ID WESH87-22.
Zoom on ID badge. Crop.
-APPROVAL GRANTED-
Looks like you helped me out after all, Wendell.
Jo! C'mere, I need your help!
Coming!

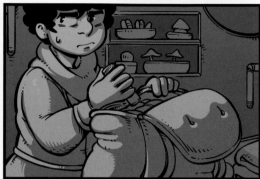

Away on
deep mine
work —
Love, J

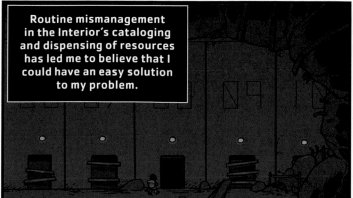

Routine mismanagement in the Interior's cataloging and dispensing of resources has led me to believe that I could have an easy solution to my problem.
AUTHORIZED PERSONNEL ONLY
Although the reserve Oblexium cache has been labeled as defunct, Interior personnel have been wrong many times before, and that margin of error has only increased.

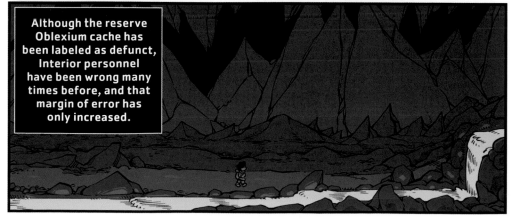

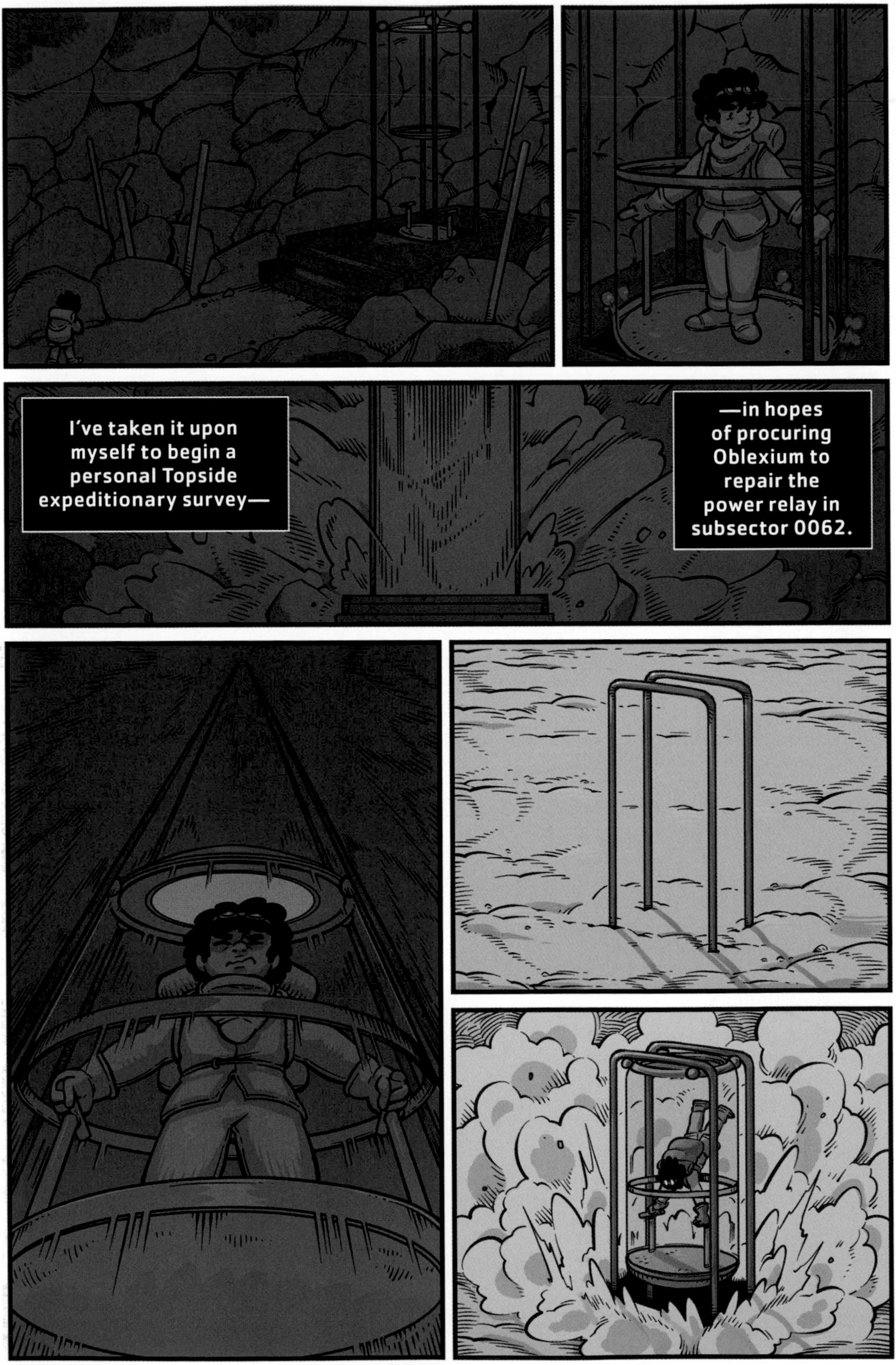
I've taken it upon myself to begin a personal Topside expeditionary survey—
—in hopes of procuring Oblexium to repair the power relay in subsector 0062.

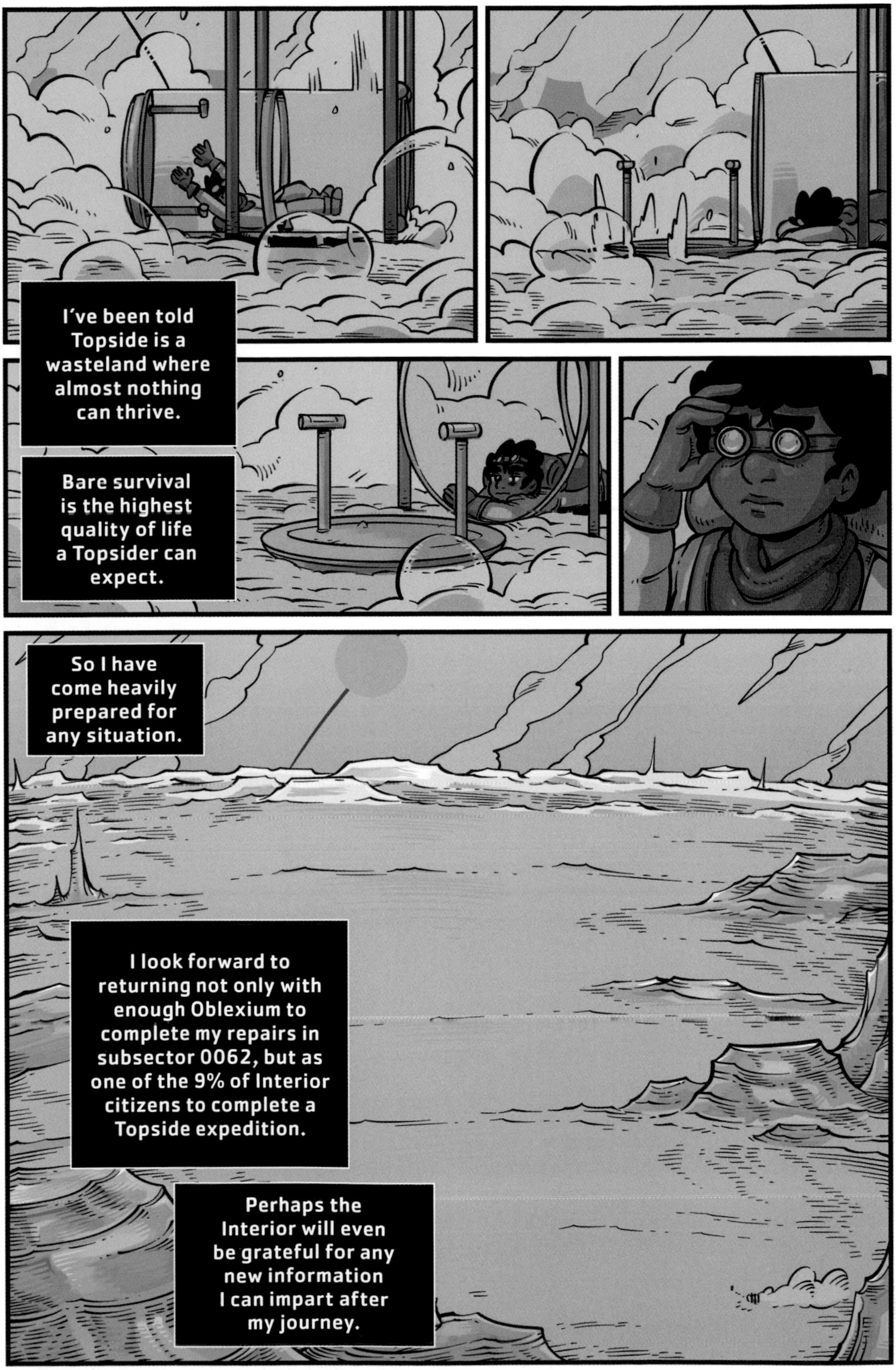

I've been told Topside is a wasteland where almost nothing can thrive.
Bare survival is the highest quality of life a Topsider can expect.
So I have come heavily prepared for any situation.
I look forward to returning not only with enough Oblexium to complete my repairs in subsector 0062, but as one of the 9% of Interior citizens to complete a Topside expedition.
Perhaps the Interior will even be grateful for any new information I can impart after my journey.

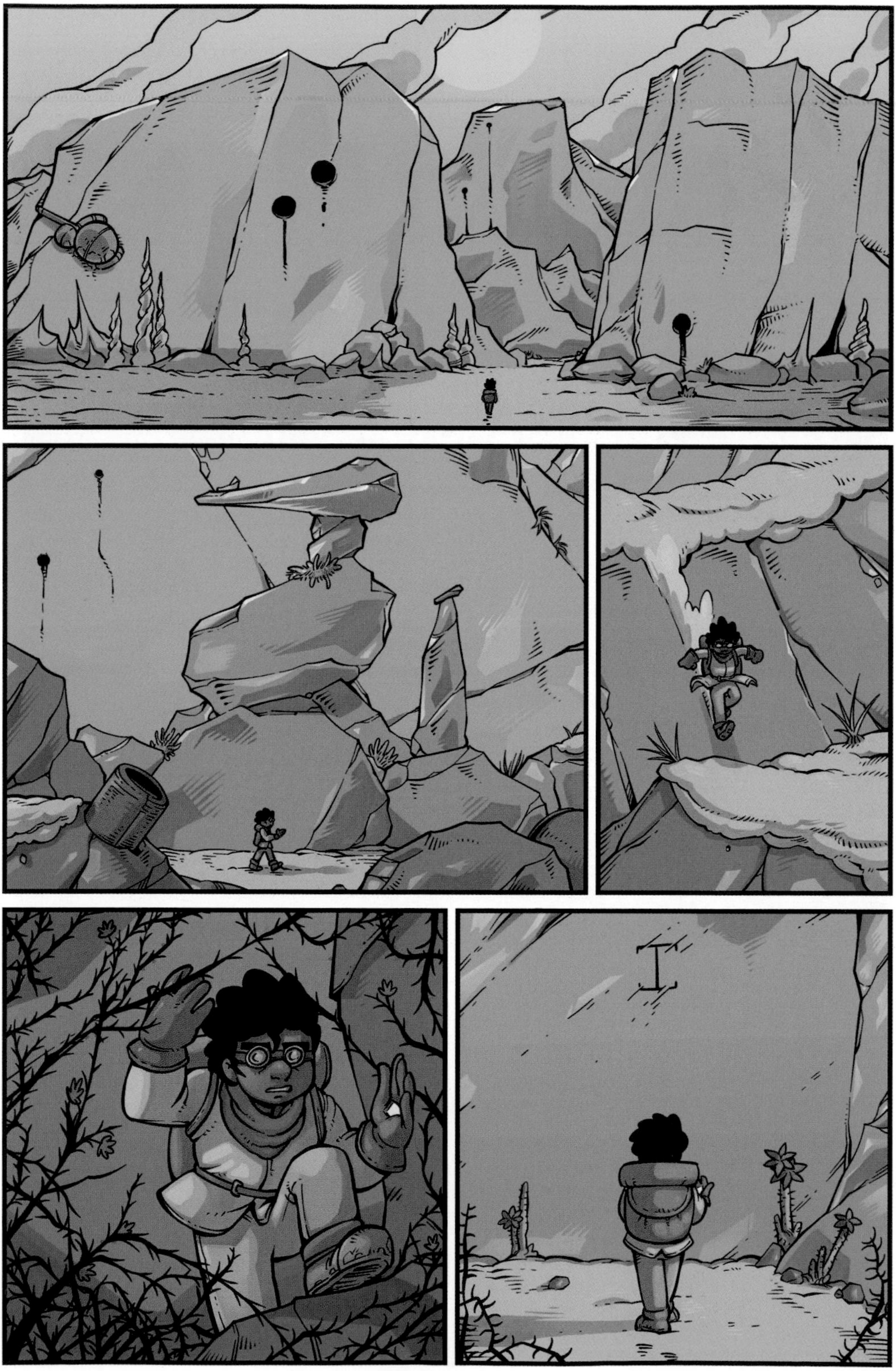

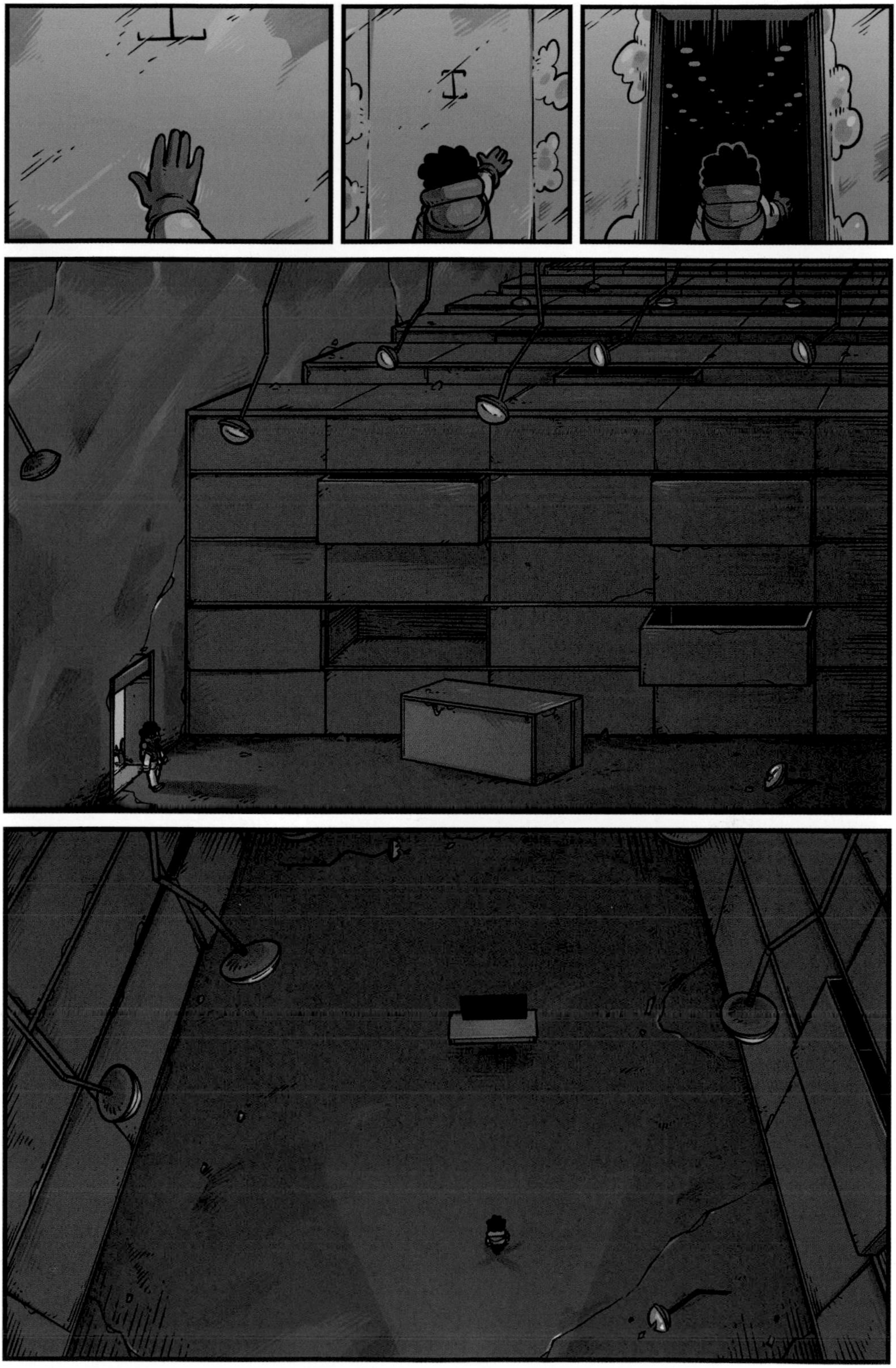

OBLEXIUM
X
X
X

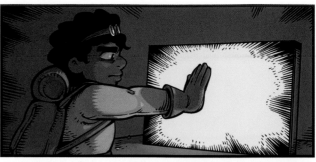

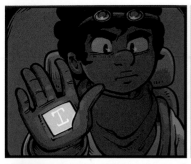

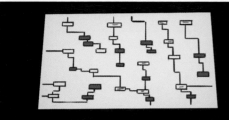

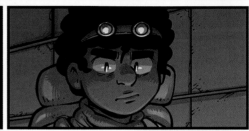

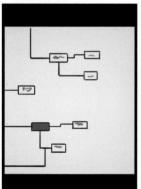

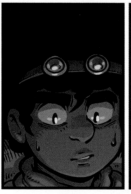

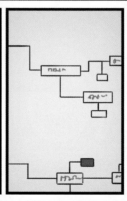

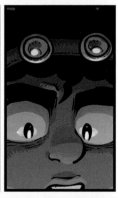

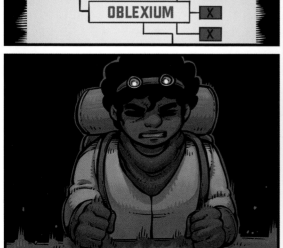

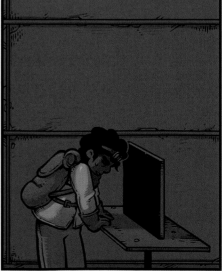

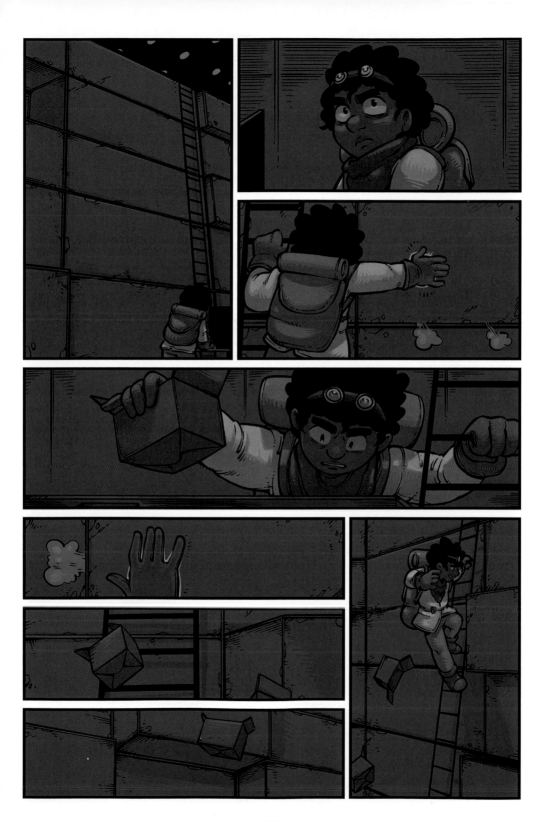

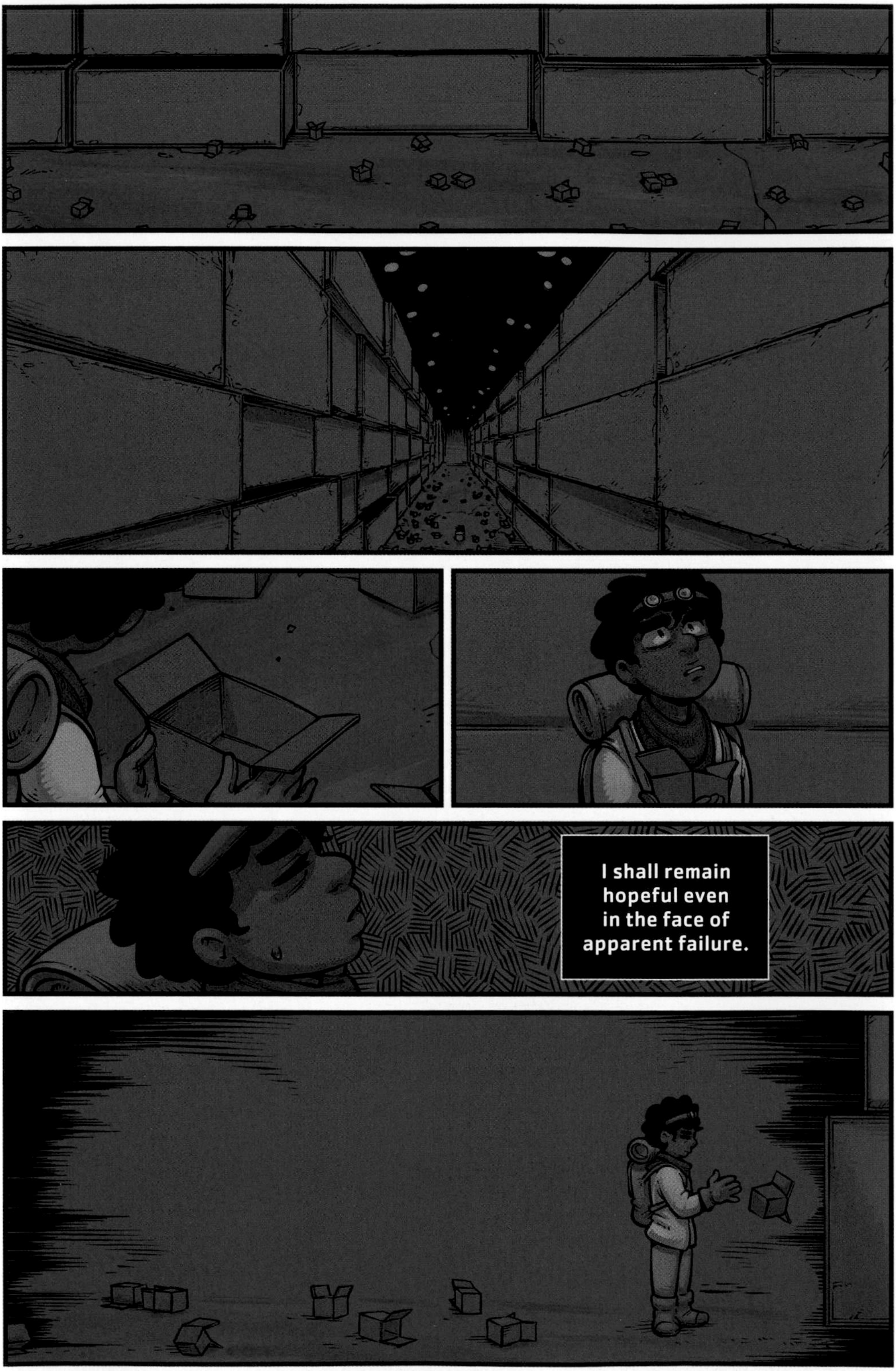
I shall remain hopeful even in the face of apparent failure.

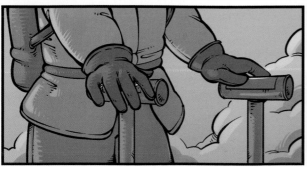
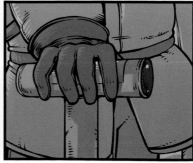

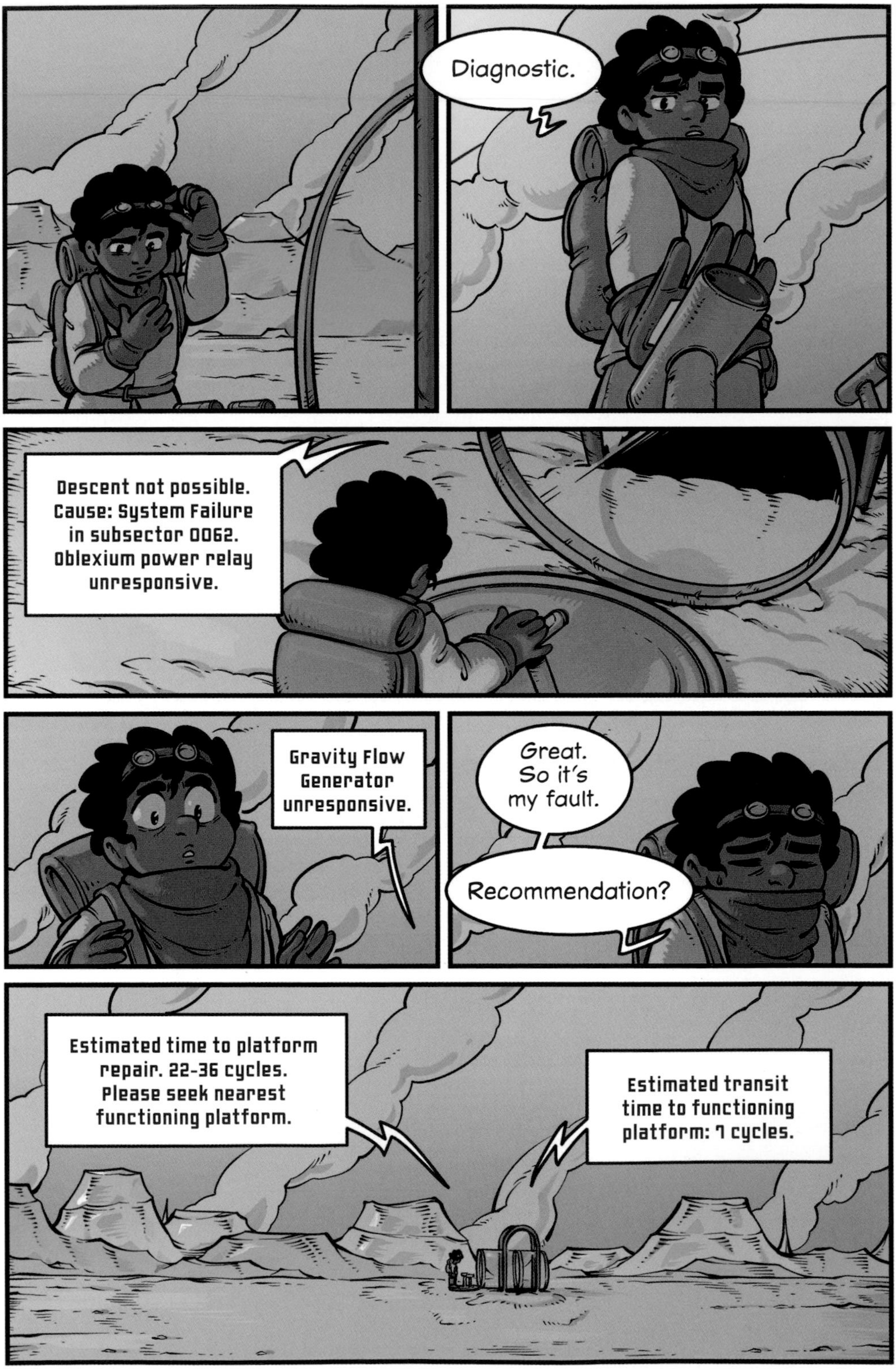
Diagnostic.
Descent not possible. Cause: System Failure in subsector 0062. Oblexium power relay unresponsive.
Gravity Flow Generator unresponsive.
Great. So it's my fault.
Recommendation?
Estimated time to platform repair. 22-36 cycles. Please seek nearest functioning platform.
Estimated transit time to functioning platform: 7 cycles.

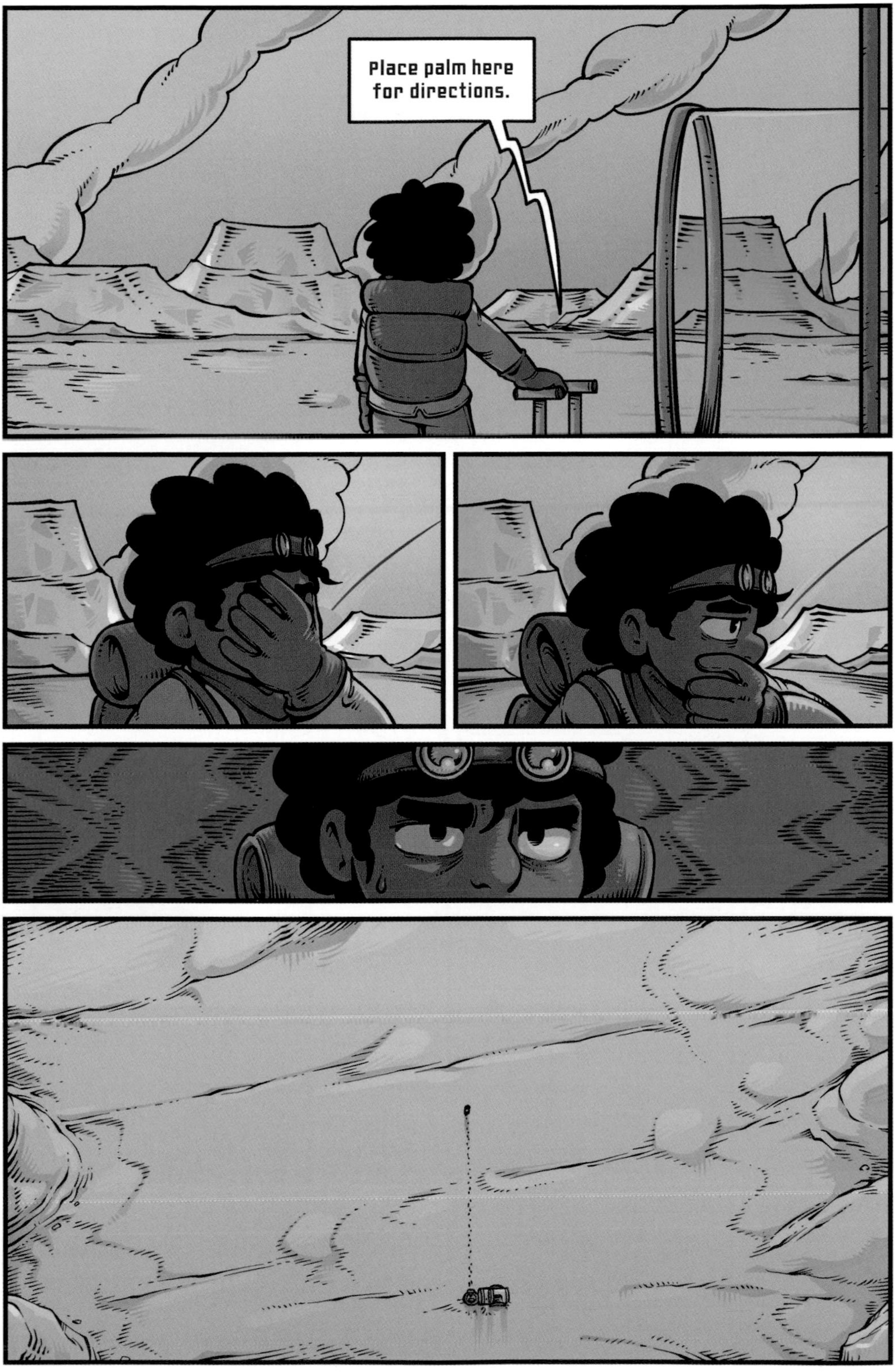
Place palm here for directions.

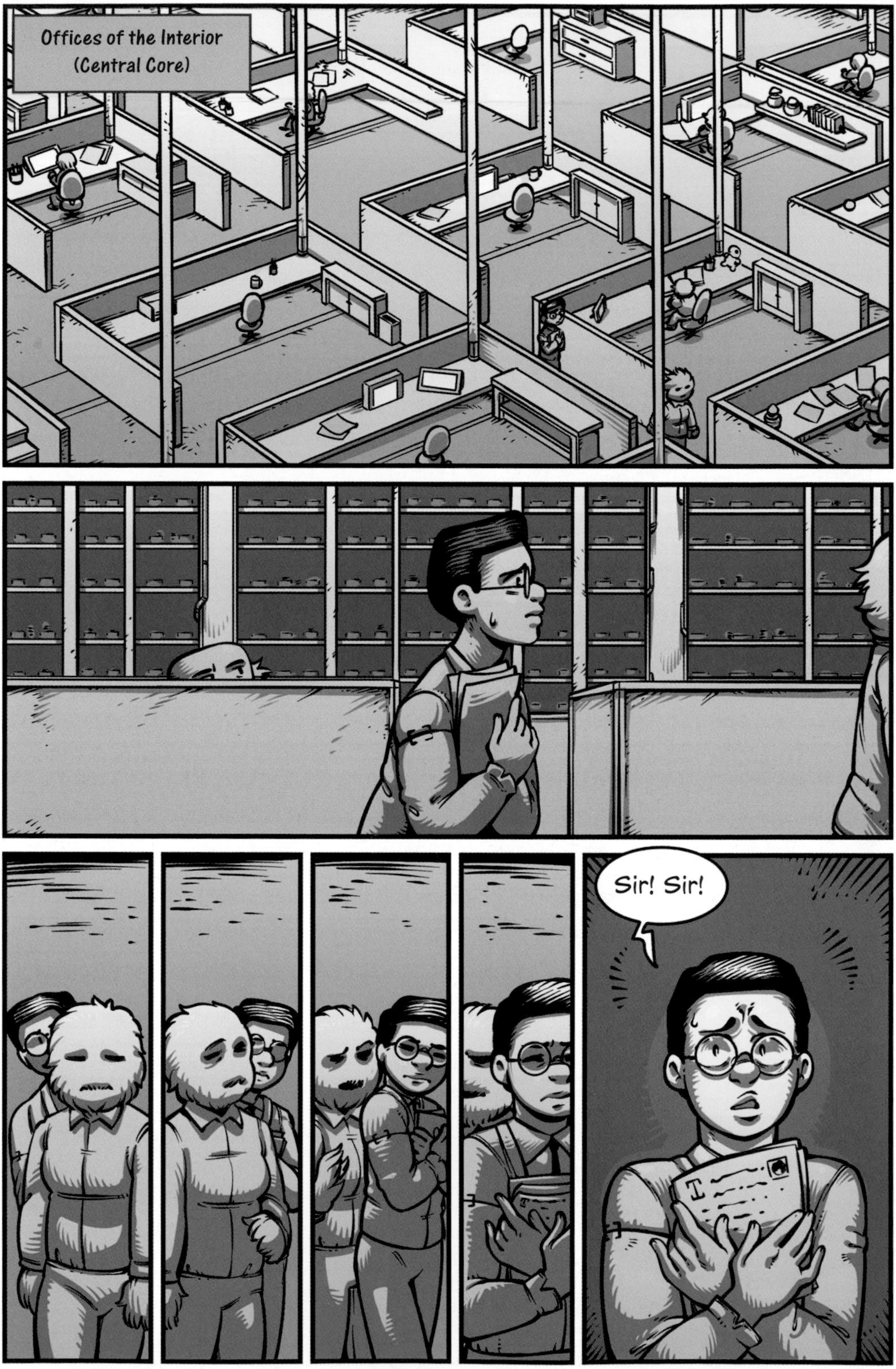
Offices of the Interior
(Central Core)
Sir! Sir!

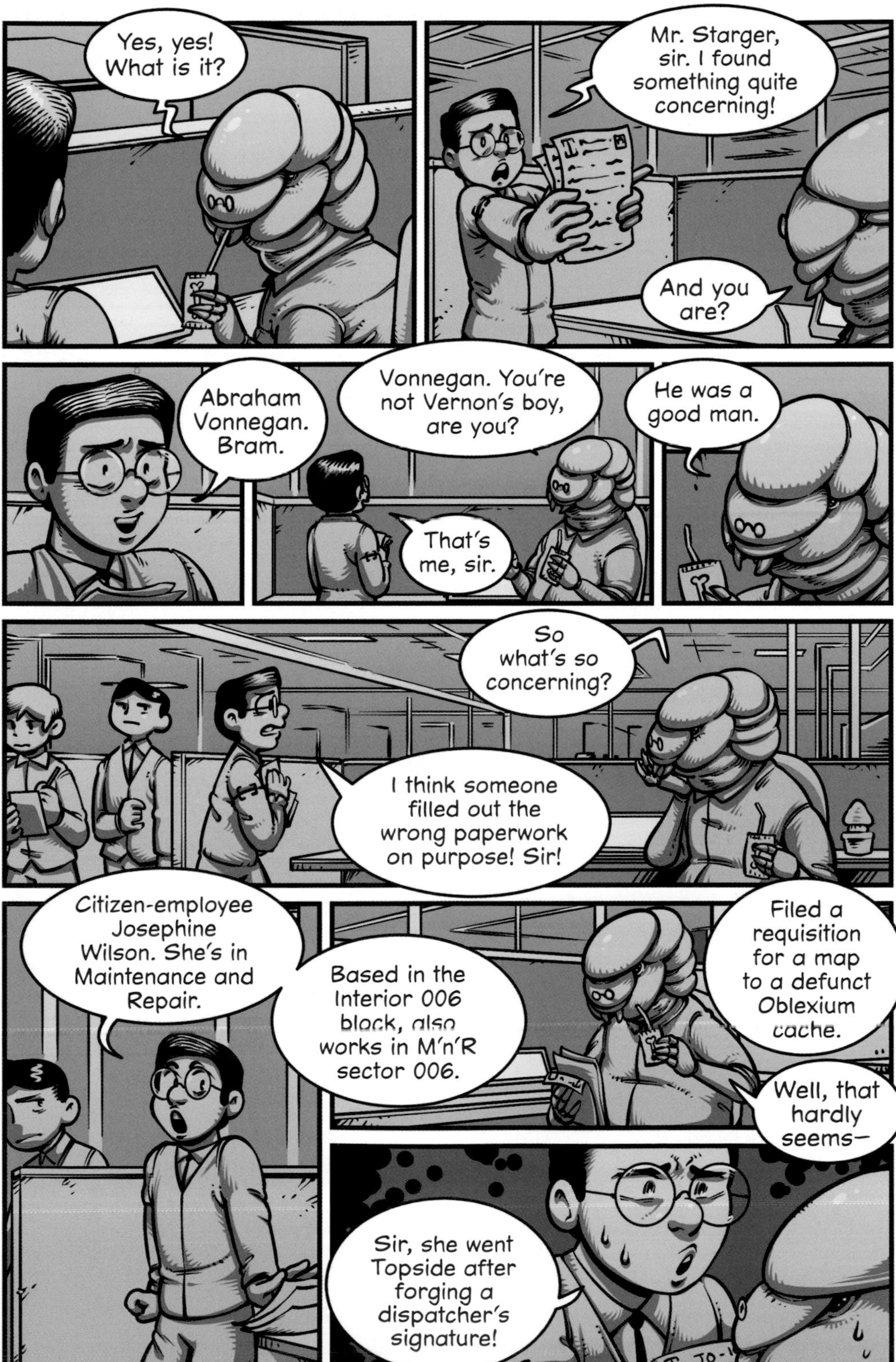
Yes, yes! What is it?
Mr. Starger, sir. I found something quite concerning!
And you are?
Abraham Vonnegan. Bram.
Vonnegan. You're not Vernon's boy, are you?
That's me, sir.
He was a good man.
So what's so concerning?
I think someone filled out the wrong paperwork on purpose! Sir!
Citizen-employee Josephine Wilson. She's in Maintenance and Repair.
Based in the Interior 006 block, also works in M'n'R sector 006.
Filed a requisition for a map to a defunct Oblexium cache.
Well, that hardly seems—
Sir, she went Topside after forging a dispatcher's signature!

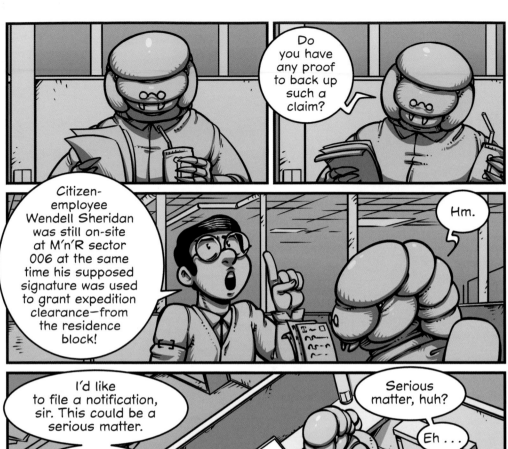

Do you have any proof to back up such a claim?

Citizen-employee Wendell Sheridan was still on-site at M'n'R sector 006 at the same time his supposed signature was used to grant expedition clearance—from the residence block!

Hm.

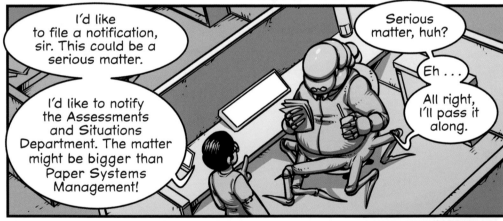

I'd like to file a notification, sir. This could be a serious matter.

I'd like to notify the Assessments and Situations Department. The matter might be bigger than Paper Systems Management!

Serious matter, huh?

Eh . . .

All right, I'll pass it along.

And Vonnegan?

Yes, sir?

Keep up the good work.

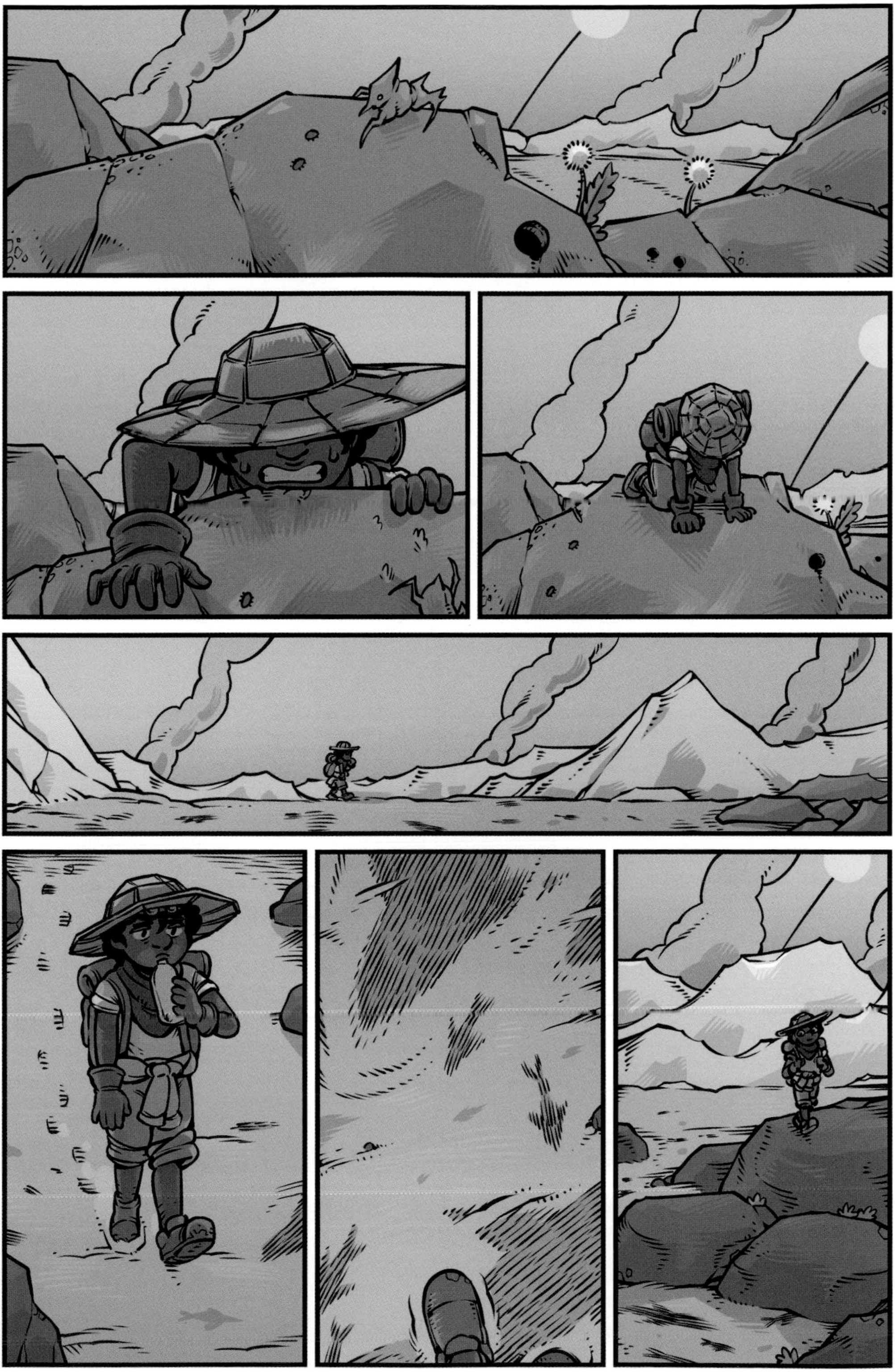

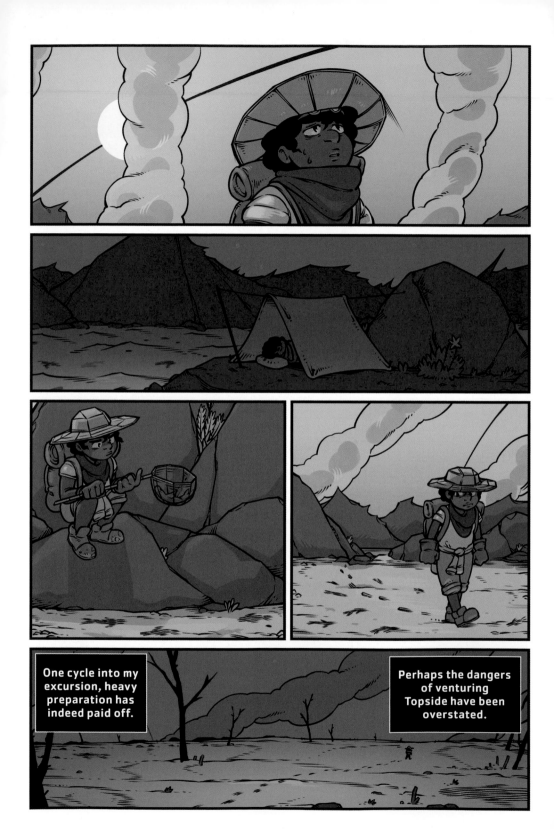

One cycle into my excursion, heavy preparation has indeed paid off.

Perhaps the dangers of venturing Topside have been overstated.

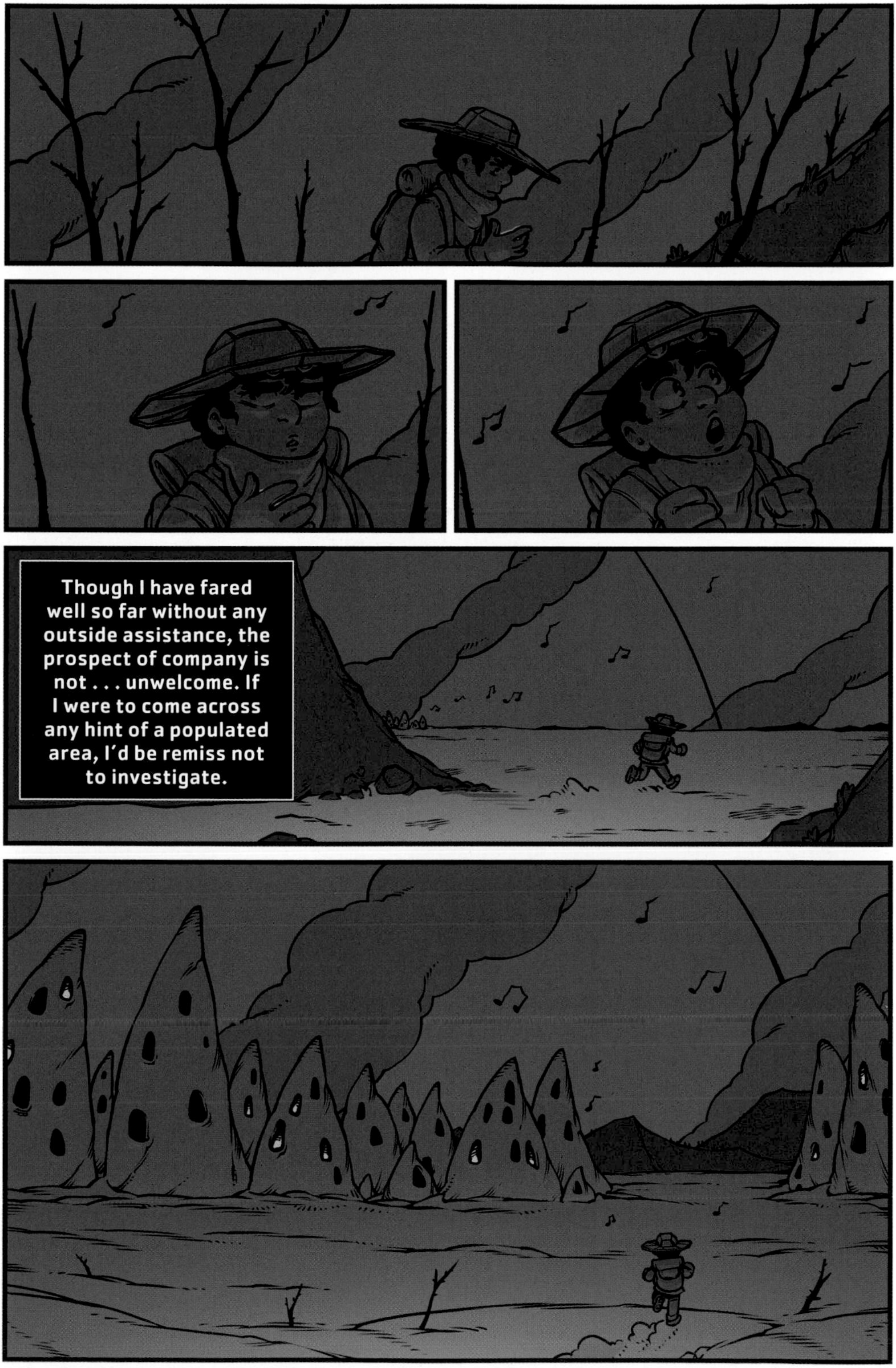
Though I have fared well so far without any outside assistance, the prospect of company is not . . . unwelcome. If I were to come across any hint of a populated area, I'd be remiss not to investigate.

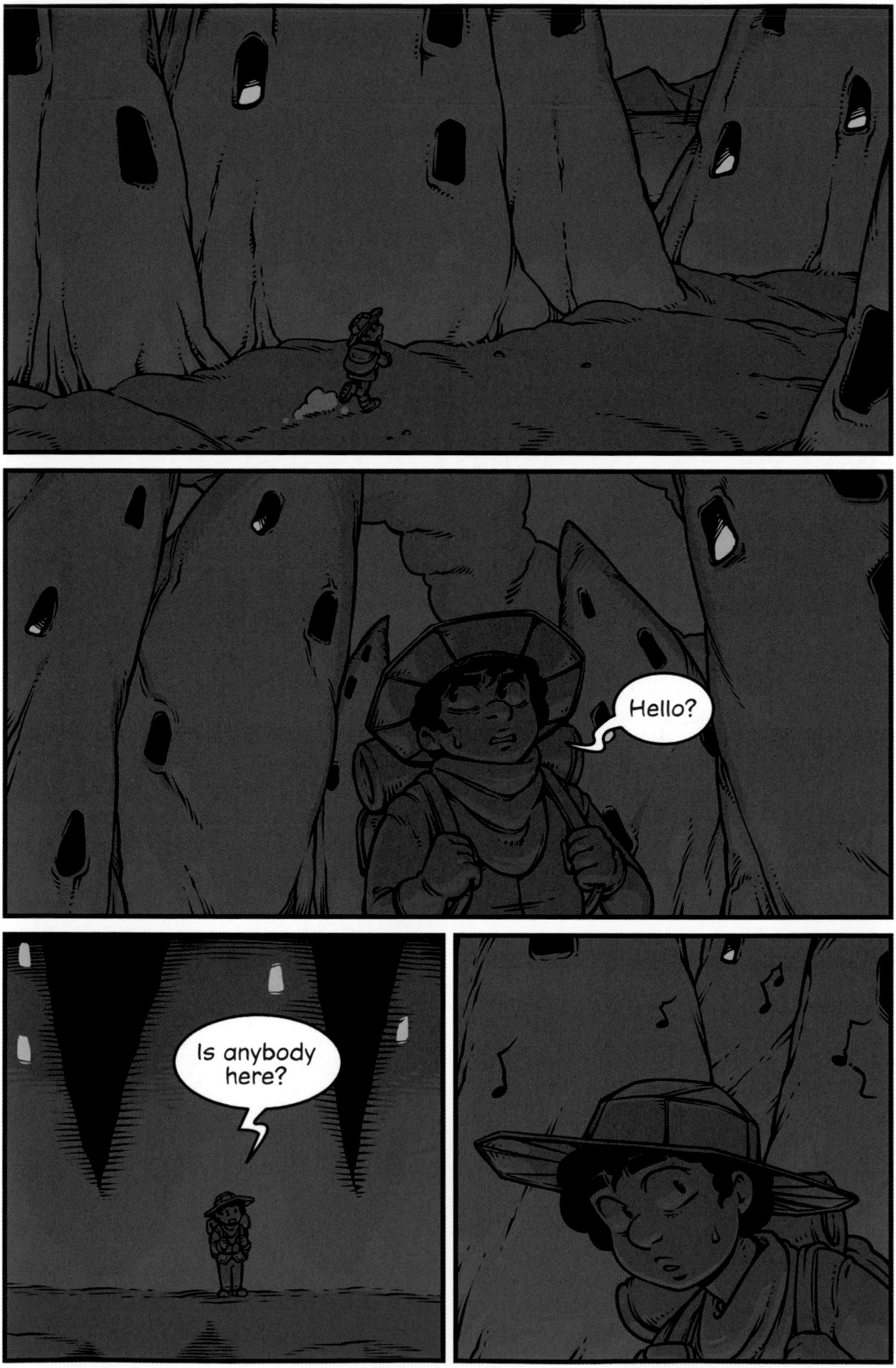
Hello?
Is anybody here?

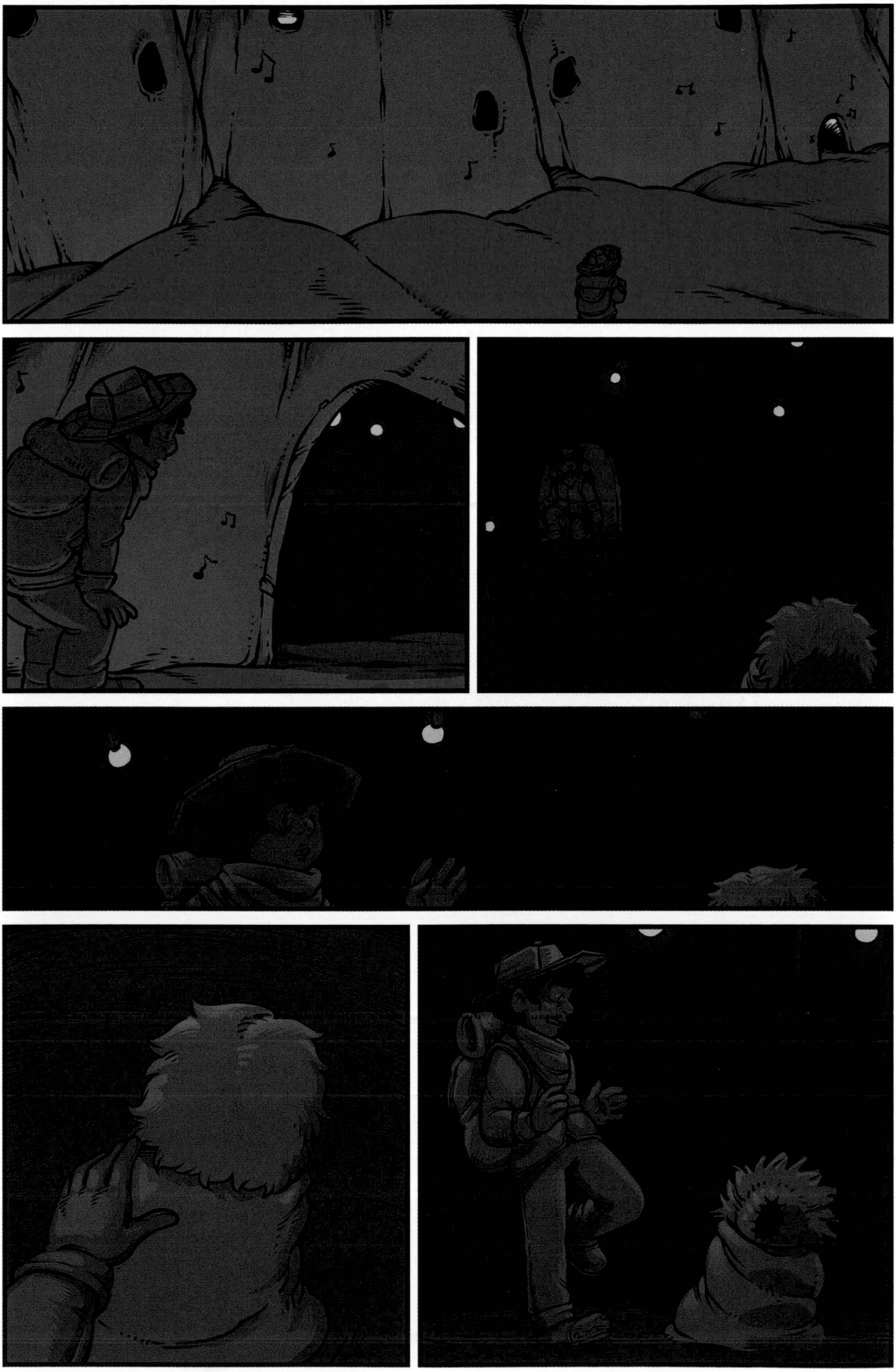

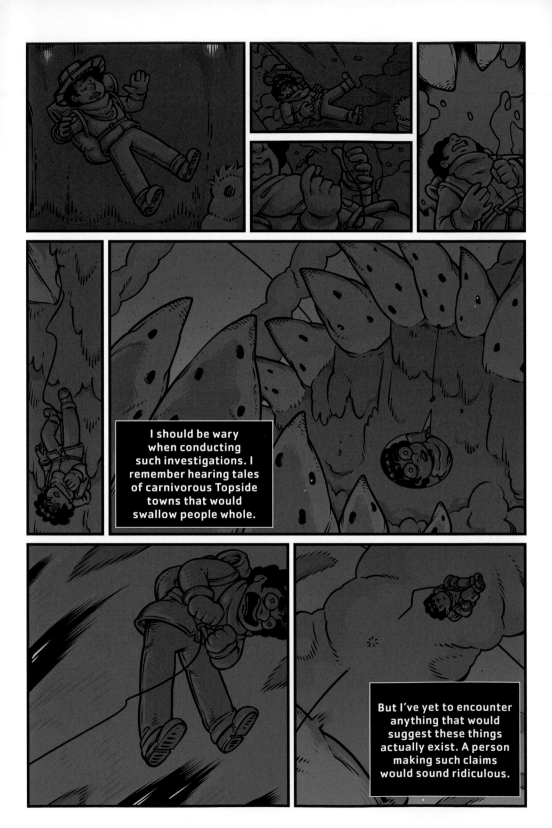

I should be wary when conducting such investigations. I remember hearing tales of carnivorous Topside towns that would swallow people whole.

But I've yet to encounter anything that would suggest these things actually exist. A person making such claims would sound ridiculous.

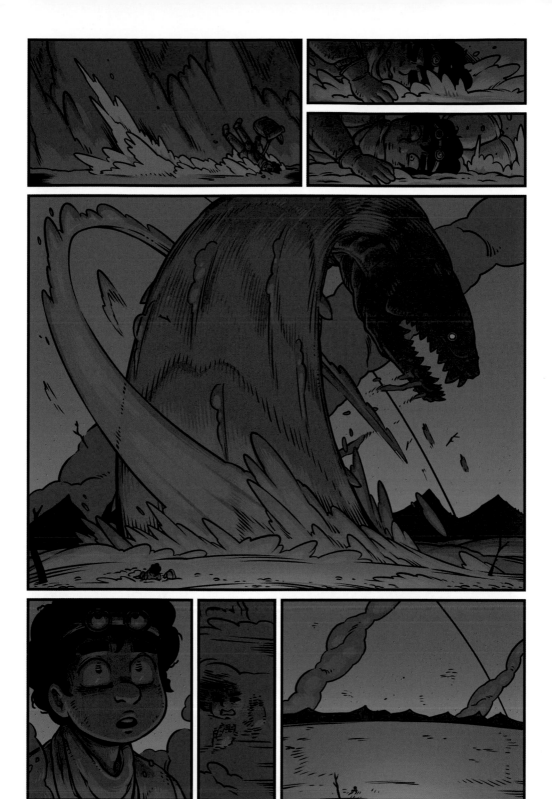

I have awakened this morning with the suspicion that system failures at the previous platform compromised the directions I received there. Despite careful adherence to these directions, my surroundings no longer match the map.

Fortunately, it won't be long until I reach civilization, as I appear to be approaching a Topsider hub.

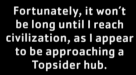

If one could call such disorder "civilization."

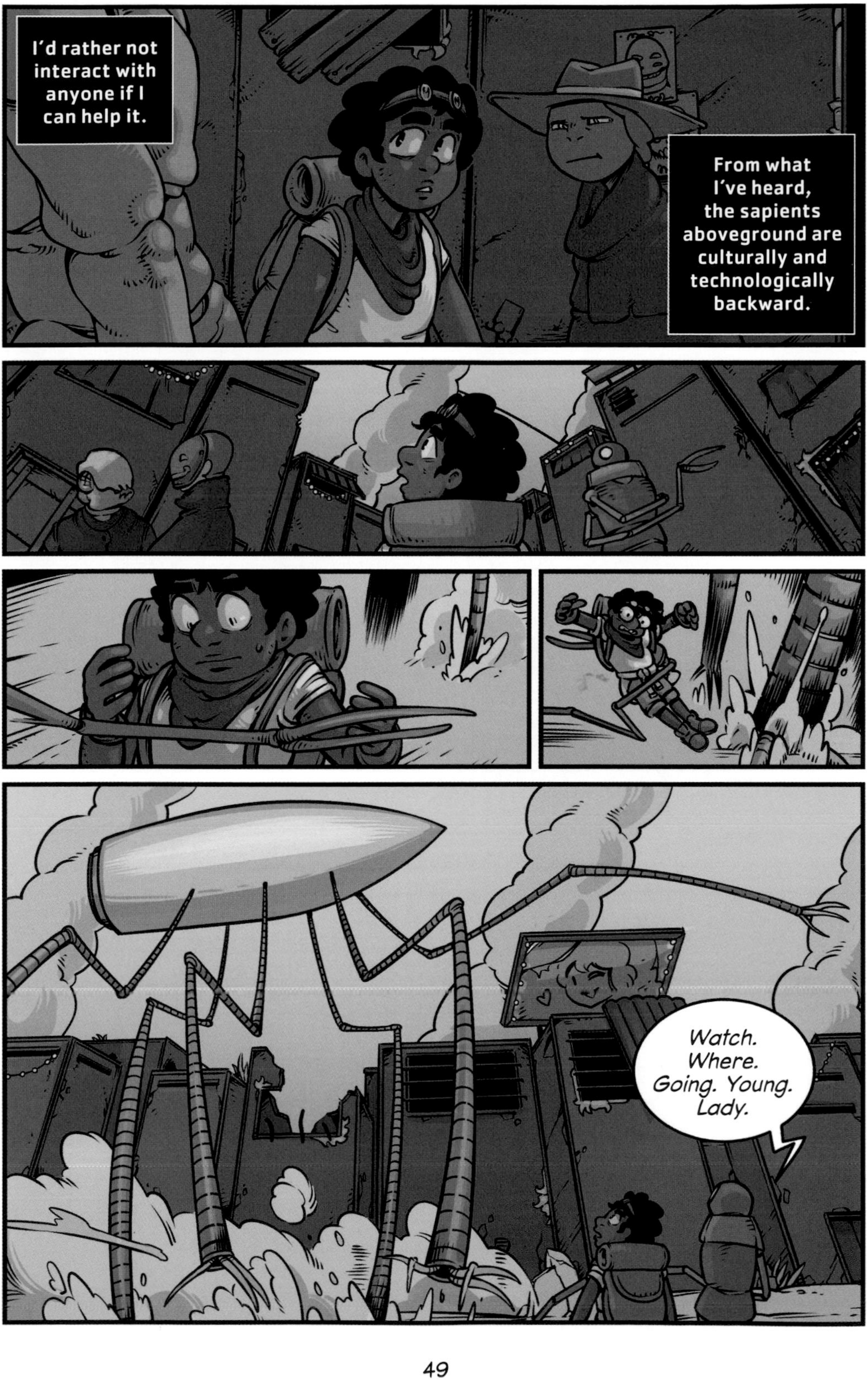
I'd rather not interact with anyone if I can help it.
From what I've heard, the sapients aboveground are culturally and technologically backward.
Watch. Where. Going. Young. Lady.

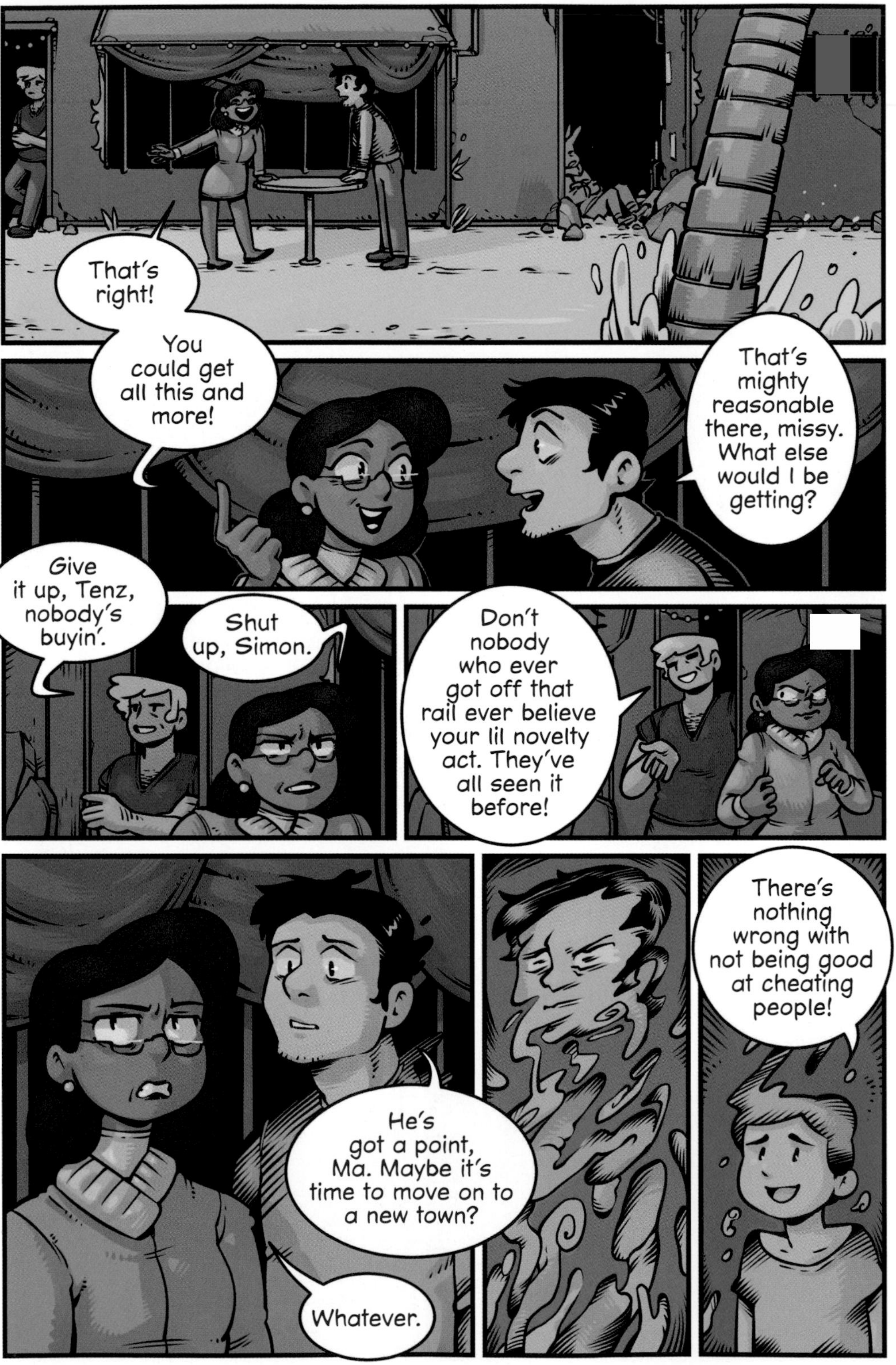
That's right!
You could get all this and more!
That's mighty reasonable there, missy. What else would I be getting?
Give it up, Tenz, nobody's buyin'.
Shut up, Simon.
Don't nobody who ever got off that rail ever believe your lil novelty act. They've all seen it before!
He's got a point, Ma. Maybe it's time to move on to a new town?
Whatever.
There's nothing wrong with not being good at cheating people!

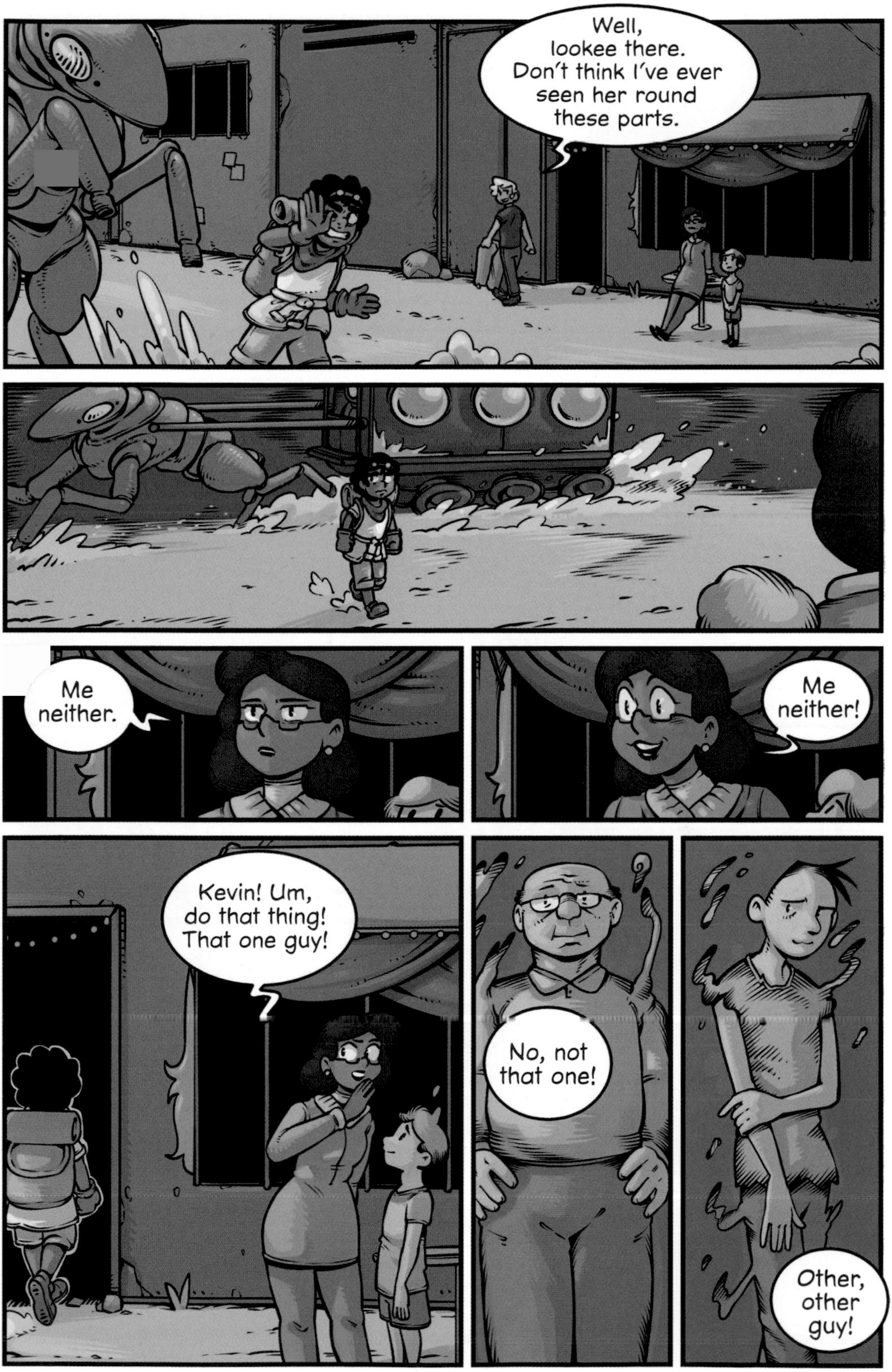
Well, lookee there. Don't think I've ever seen her round these parts.
Me neither.
Me neither!
Kevin! Um, do that thing! That one guy!
No, not that one!
Other, other guy!

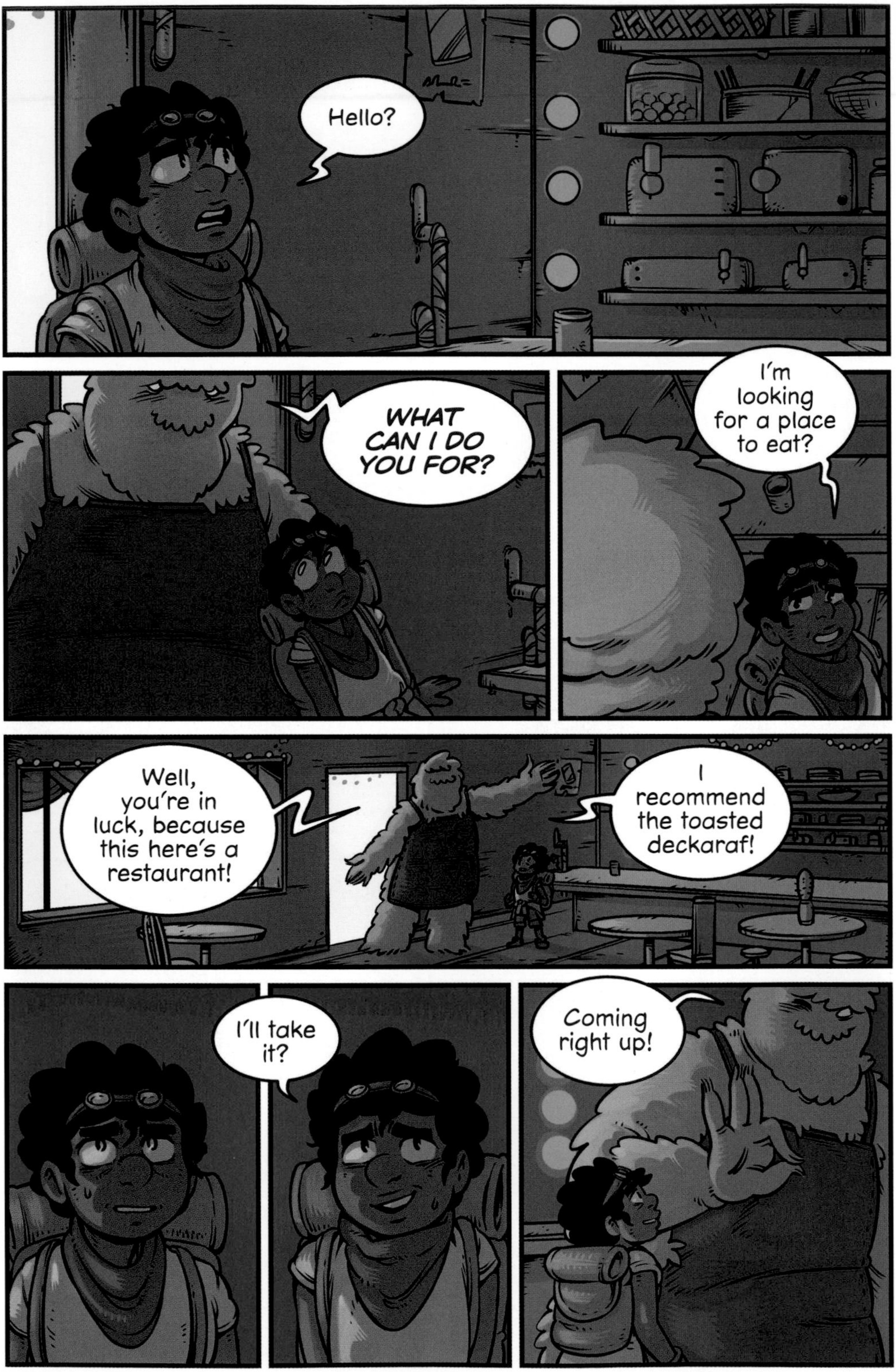
Hello?
WHAT CAN I DO YOU FOR?
I'm looking for a place to eat?
Well, you're in luck, because this here's a restaurant!
I recommend the toasted deckaraf!
I'll take it?
Coming right up!

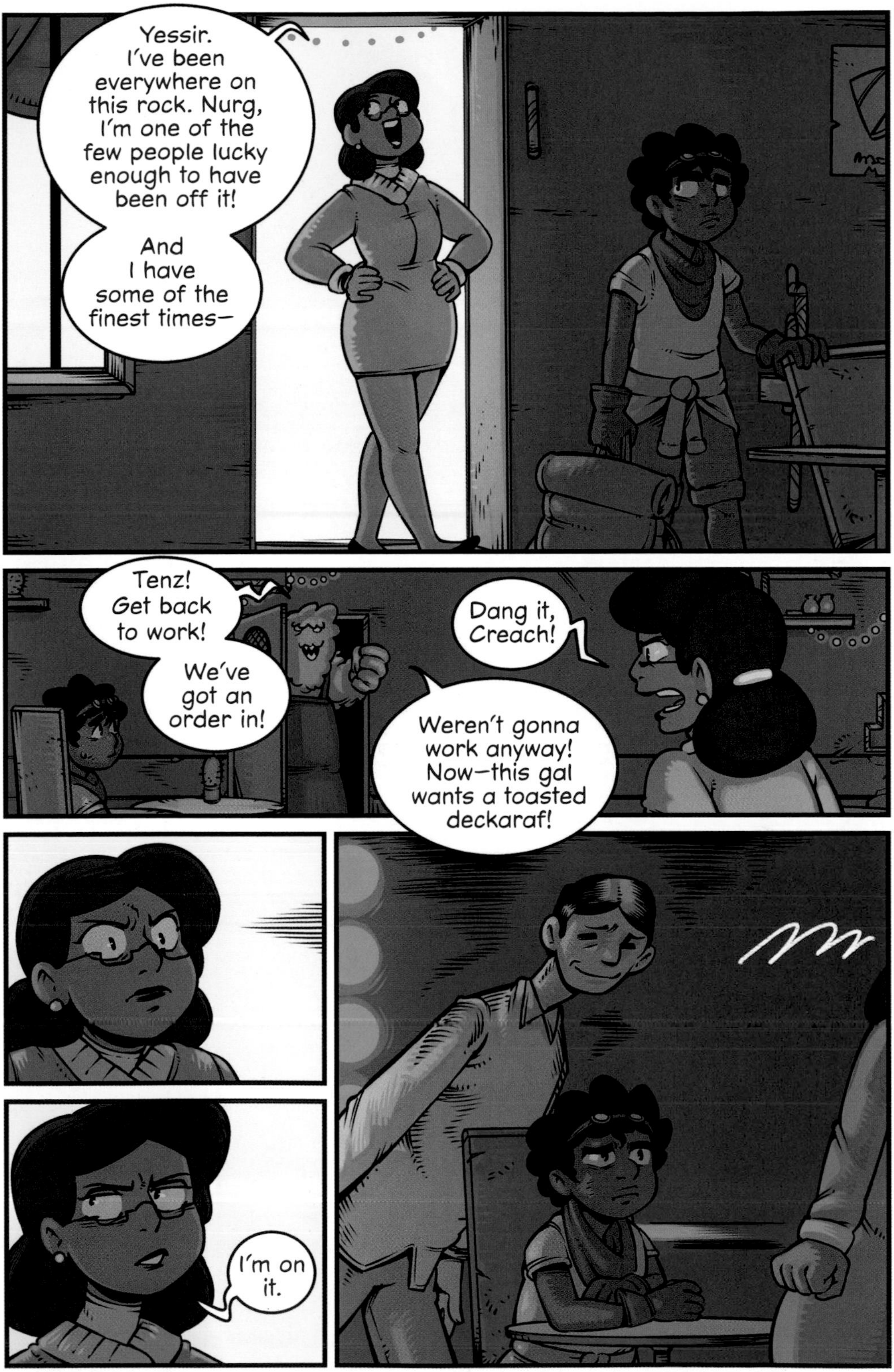
Yessir. I've been everywhere on this rock. Nurg, I'm one of the few people lucky enough to have been off it!
And I have some of the finest times—
Tenz! Get back to work!
We've got an order in!
Dang it, Creach!
Weren't gonna work anyway! Now—this gal wants a toasted deckaraf!
I'm on it.

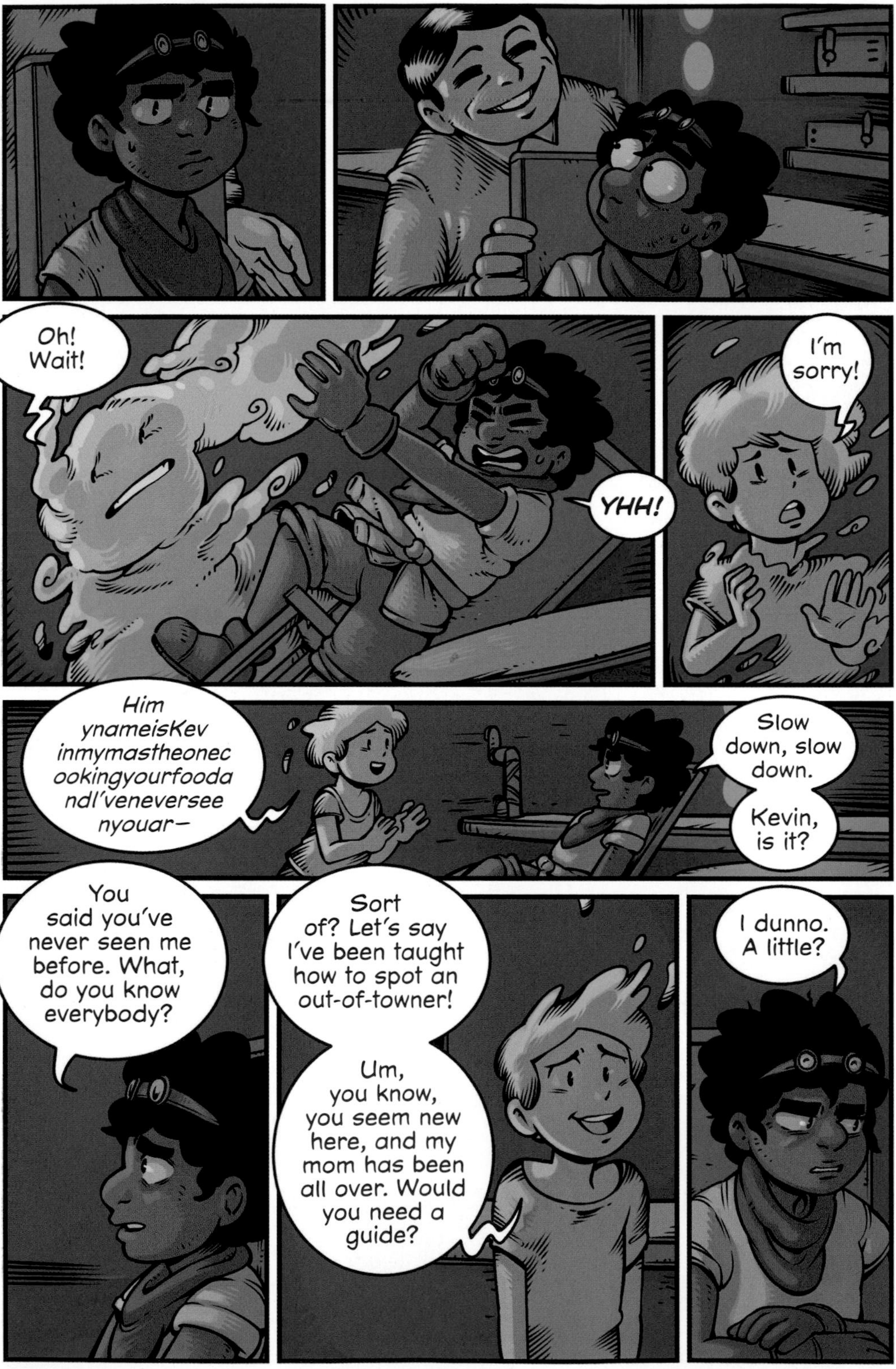

Oh! Wait!
YHH!
I'm sorry!
Him ynameisKev inmymastheonec ookingyourfooda ndl'veneversee nyouar—
Slow down, slow down.
Kevin, is it?
You said you've never seen me before. What, do you know everybody?
Sort of? Let's say I've been taught how to spot an out-of-towner!
Um, you know, you seem new here, and my mom has been all over. Would you need a guide?
I dunno. A little?

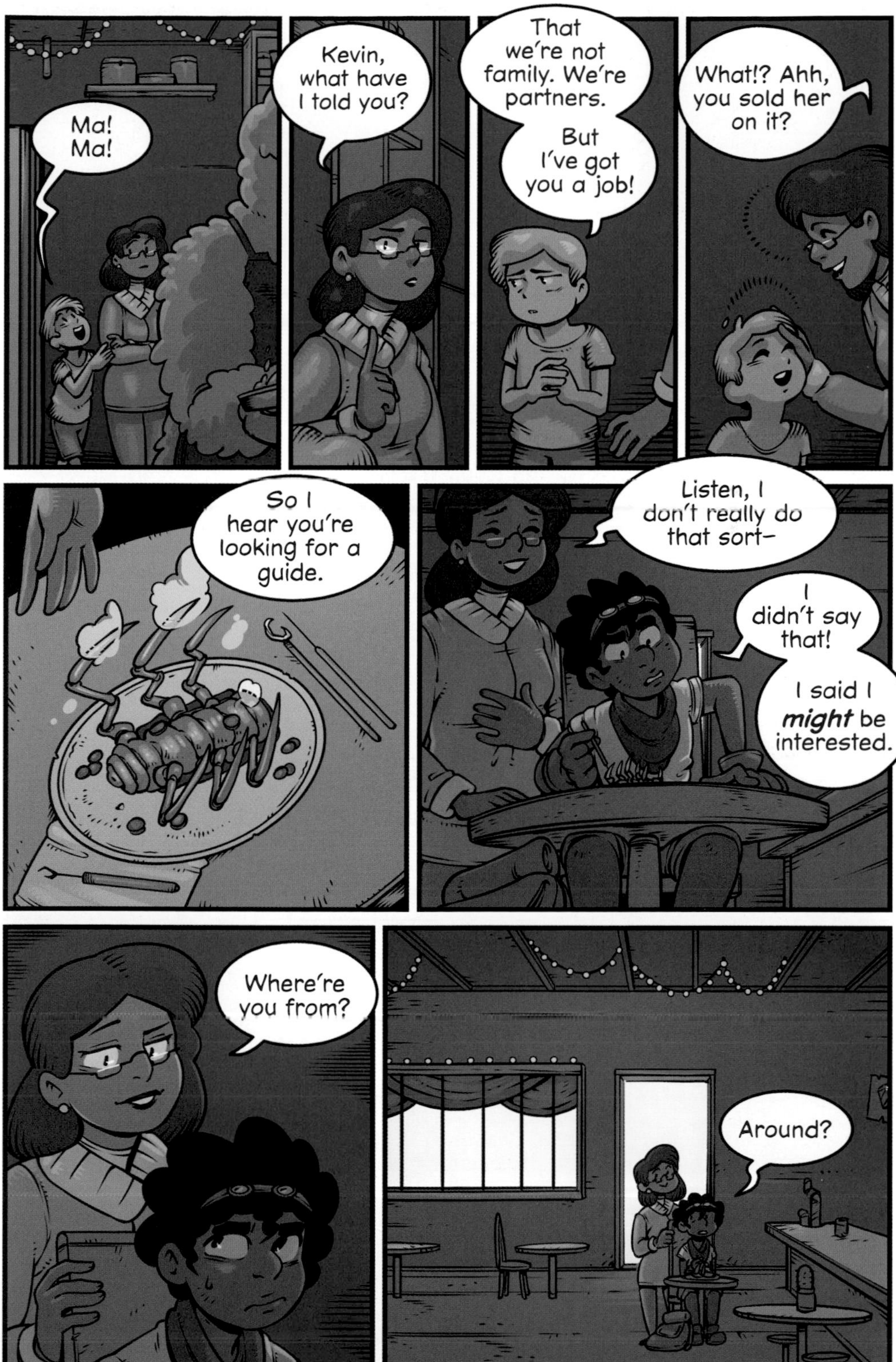
Ma! Ma!
Kevin, what have I told you?
That we're not family. We're partners.
But I've got you a job!
What!? Ahh, you sold her on it?
So I hear you're looking for a guide.
Listen, I don't really do that sort–
I didn't say that!
I said I *might* be interested.
Where're you from?
Around?

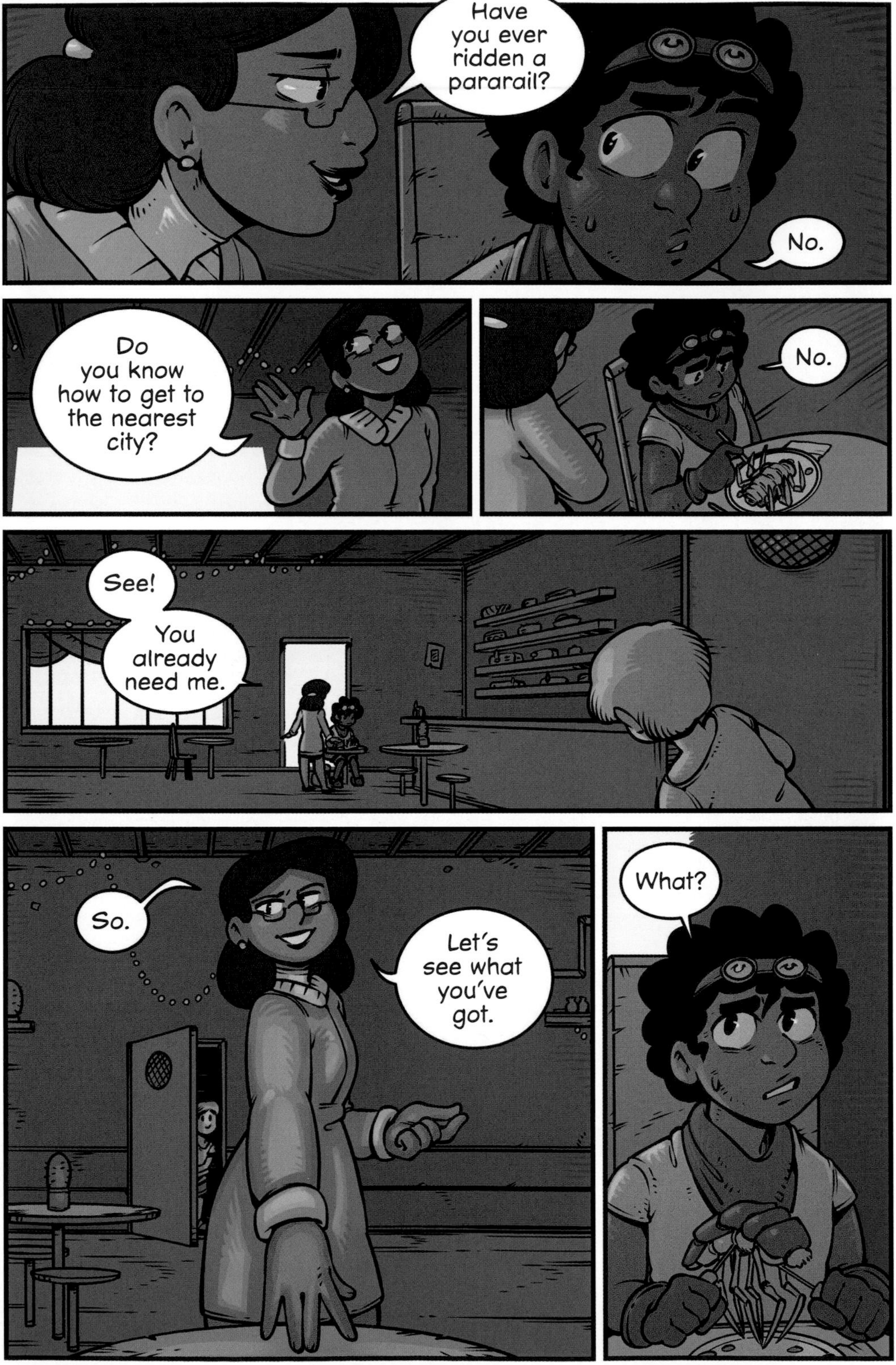
Have you ever ridden a pararail?
No.
Do you know how to get to the nearest city?
No.
See!
You already need me.
So.
Let's see what you've got.
What?

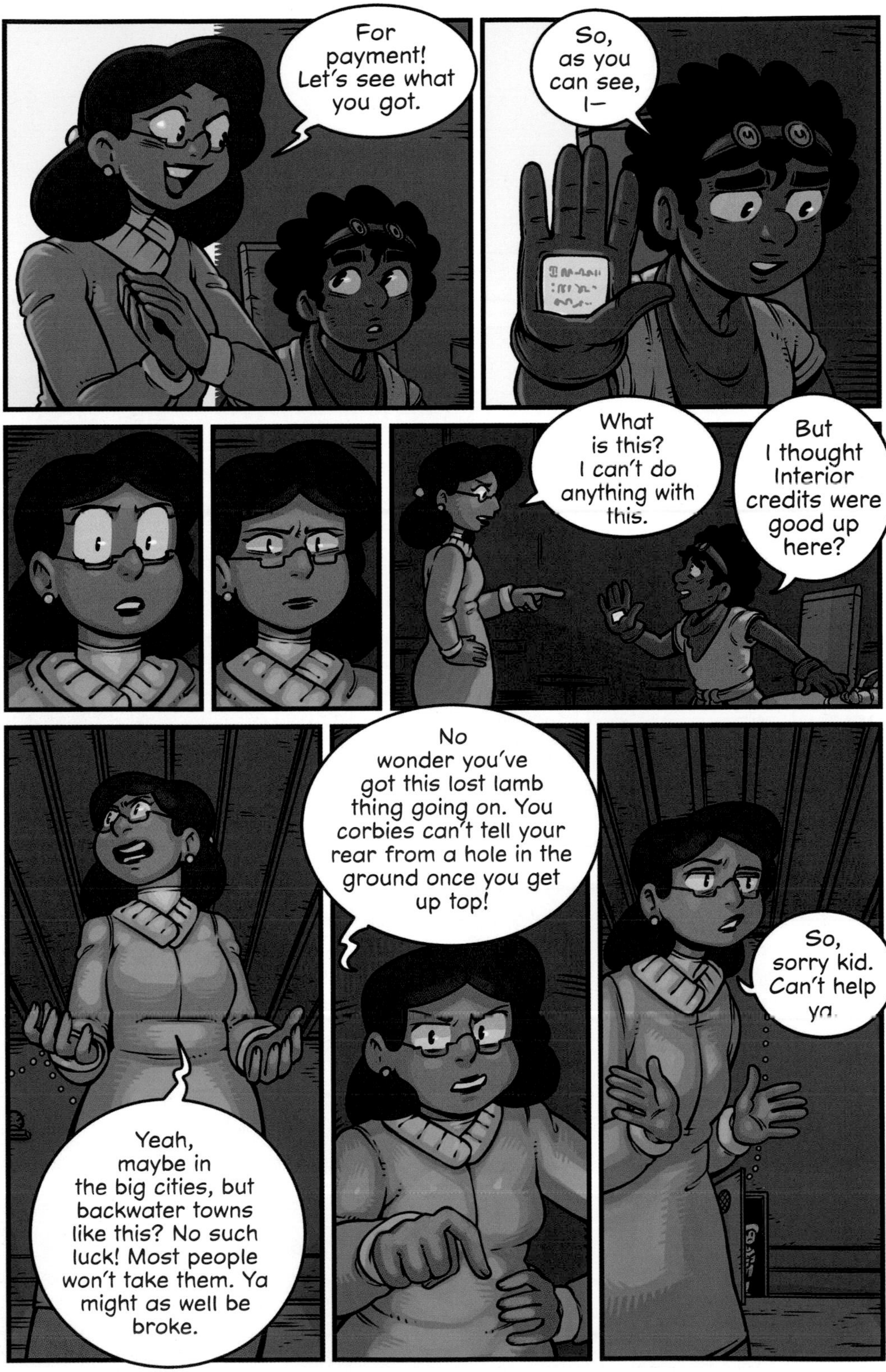
For payment! Let's see what you got.
So, as you can see, I—
What is this? I can't do anything with this.
But I thought Interior credits were good up here?
Yeah, maybe in the big cities, but backwater towns like this? No such luck! Most people won't take them. Ya might as well be broke.
No wonder you've got this lost lamb thing going on. You corbies can't tell your rear from a hole in the ground once you get up top!
So, sorry kid. Can't help ya.

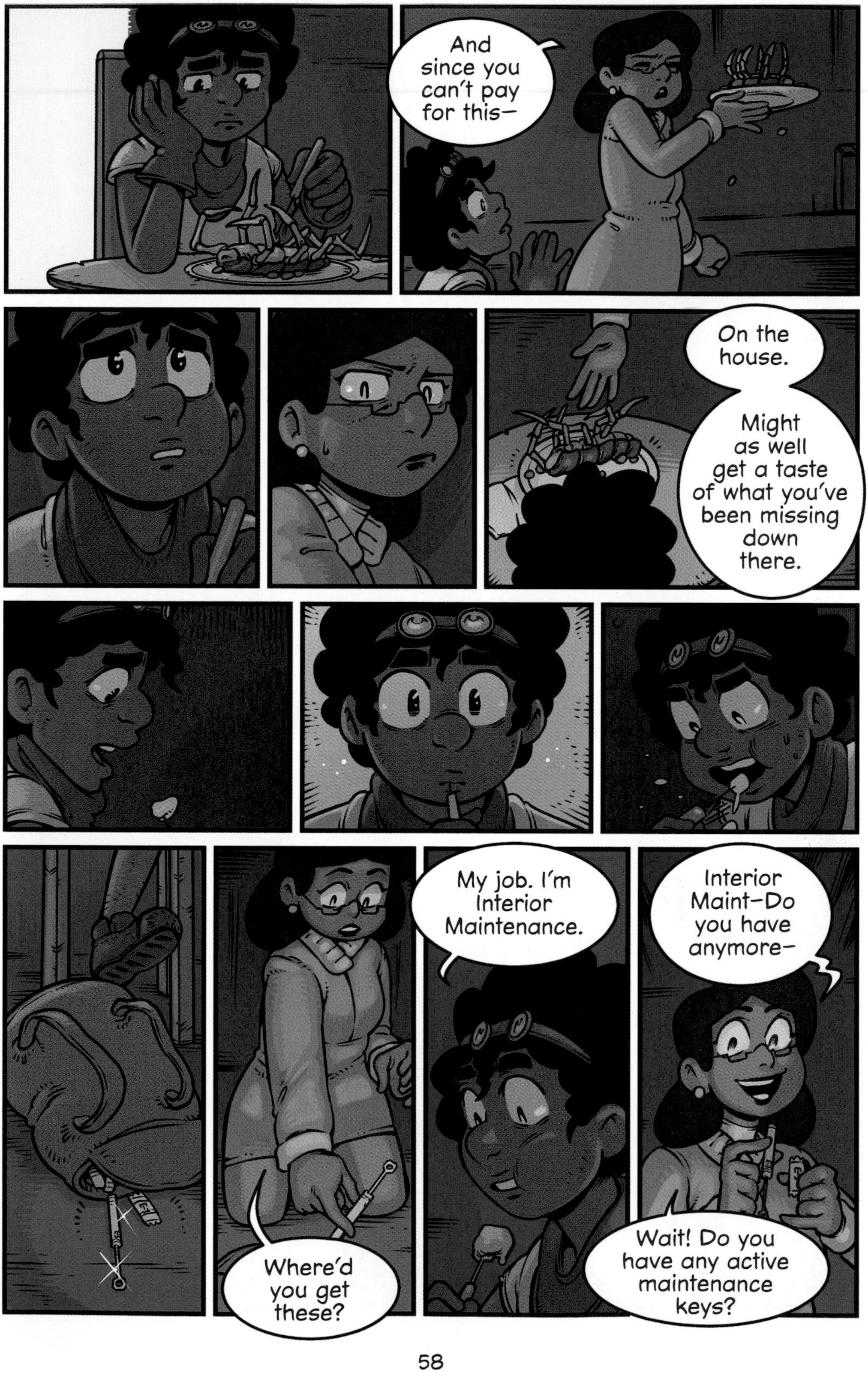
And since you can't pay for this—
On the house.
Might as well get a taste of what you've been missing down there.
My job. I'm Interior Maintenance.
Interior Maint—Do you have anymore—
Where'd you get these?
Wait! Do you have any active maintenance keys?

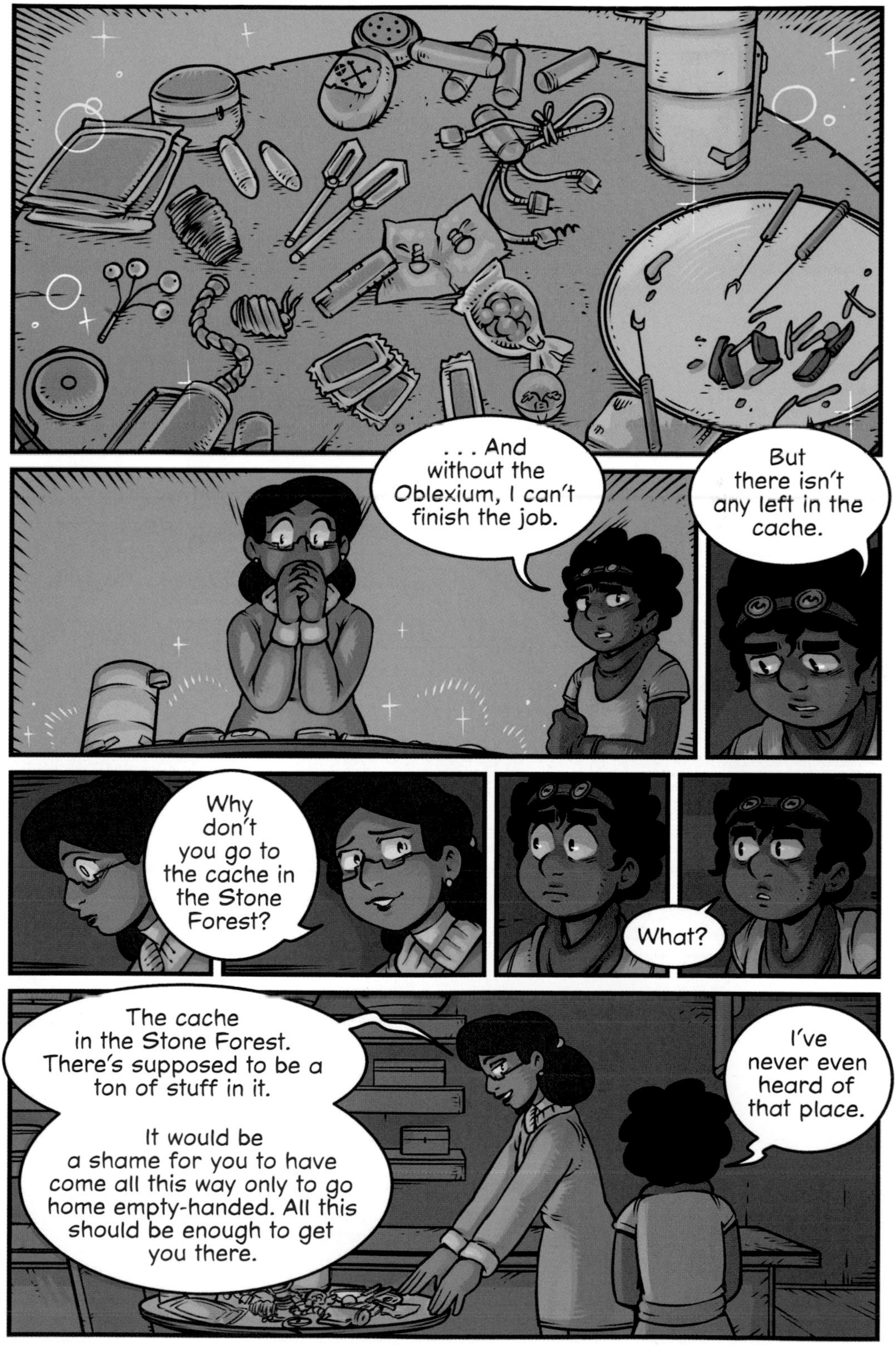
. . . And without the Oblexium, I can't finish the job.
But there isn't any left in the cache.
Why don't you go to the cache in the Stone Forest?
What?
The cache in the Stone Forest. There's supposed to be a ton of stuff in it.
It would be a shame for you to have come all this way only to go home empty-handed. All this should be enough to get you there.
I've never even heard of that place.

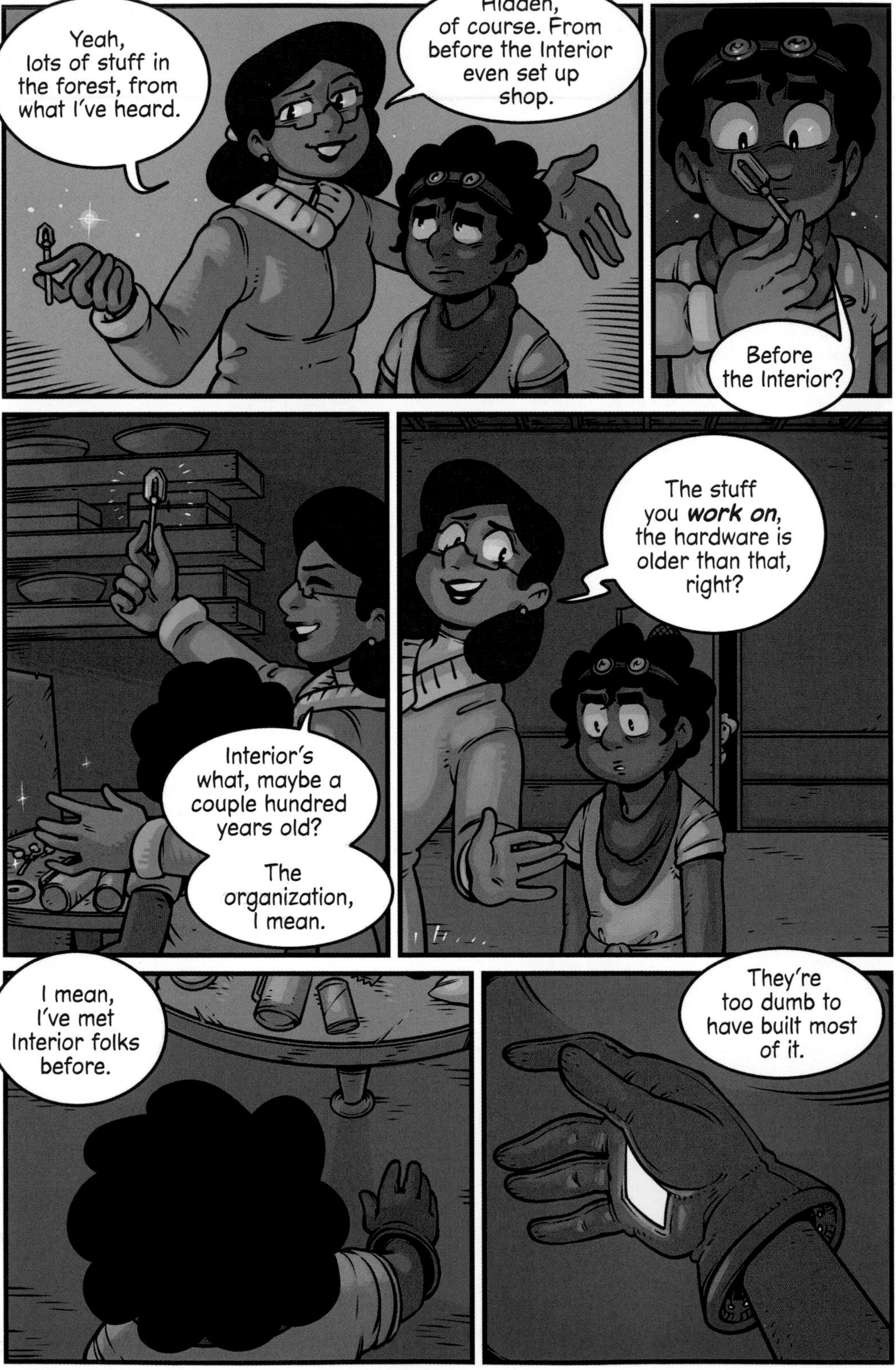
Yeah, lots of stuff in the forest, from what I've heard.
Hidden, of course. From before the Interior even set up shop.
Before the Interior?
Interior's what, maybe a couple hundred years old?
The organization, I mean.
The stuff you ***work on***, the hardware is older than that, right?
I mean, I've met Interior folks before.
They're too dumb to have built most of it.

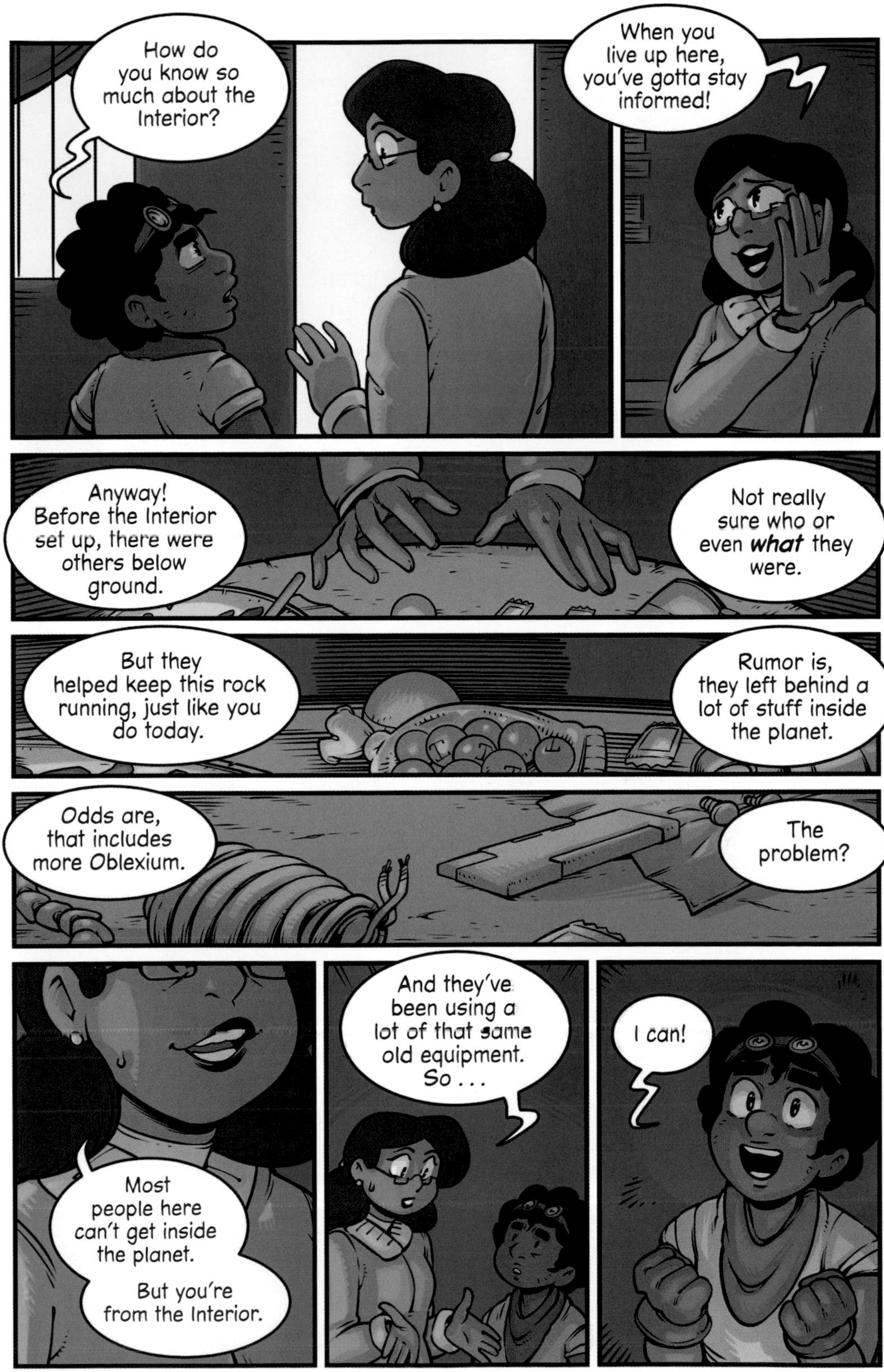
How do you know so much about the Interior?
When you live up here, you've gotta stay informed!
Anyway! Before the Interior set up, there were others below ground.
Not really sure who or even *what* they were.
But they helped keep this rock running, just like you do today.
Rumor is, they left behind a lot of stuff inside the planet.
Odds are, that includes more Oblexium.
The problem?
Most people here can't get inside the planet.
But you're from the Interior.
And they've been using a lot of that same old equipment. So . . .
I can!

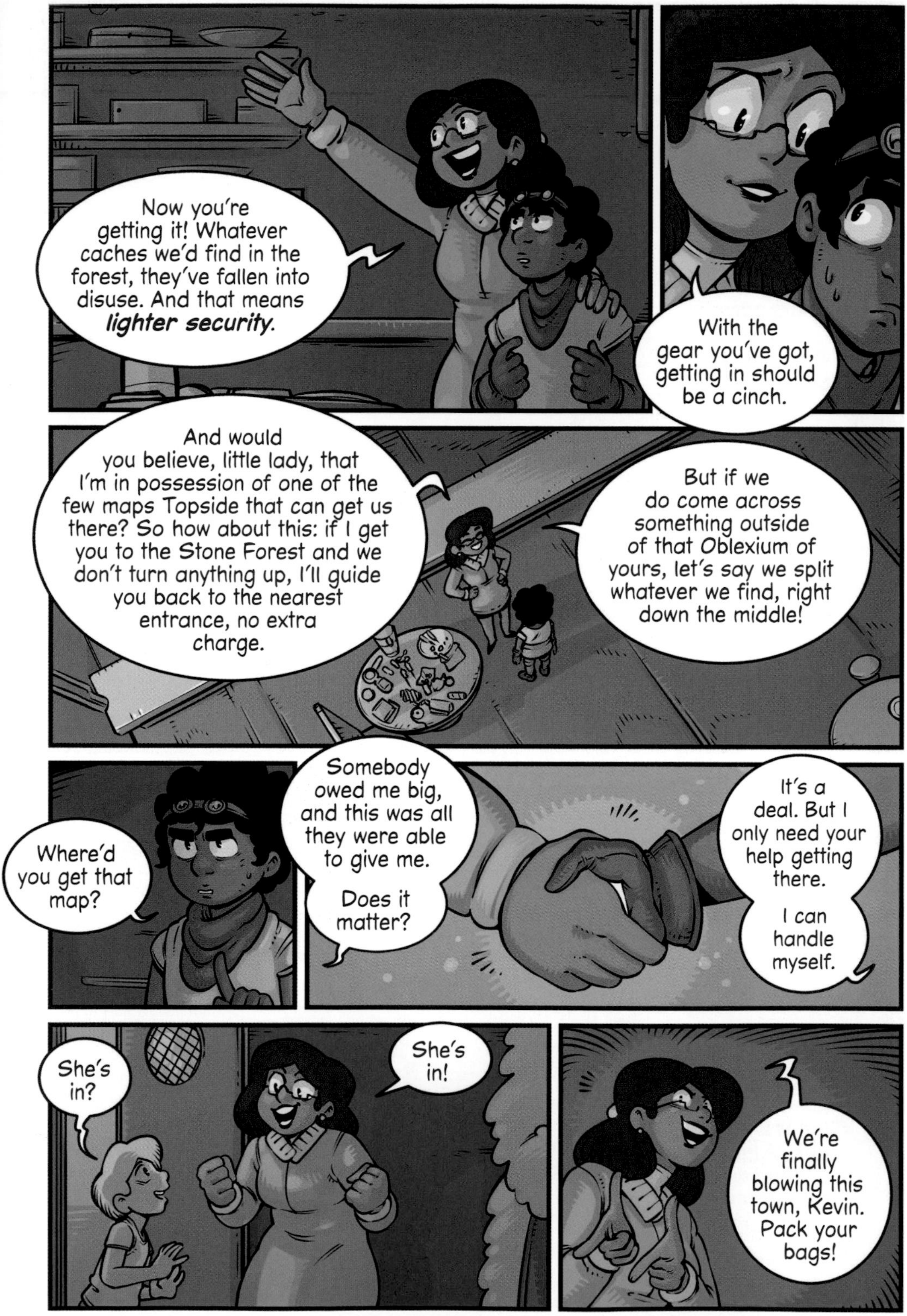

Now you're getting it! Whatever caches we'd find in the forest, they've fallen into disuse. And that means ***lighter security***.
With the gear you've got, getting in should be a cinch.
And would you believe, little lady, that I'm in possession of one of the few maps Topside that can get us there? So how about this: if I get you to the Stone Forest and we don't turn anything up, I'll guide you back to the nearest entrance, no extra charge.
But if we do come across something outside of that Oblexium of yours, let's say we split whatever we find, right down the middle!
Where'd you get that map?
Somebody owed me big, and this was all they were able to give me.
Does it matter?
It's a deal. But I only need your help getting there.
I can handle myself.
She's in?
She's in!
We're finally blowing this town, Kevin. Pack your bags!

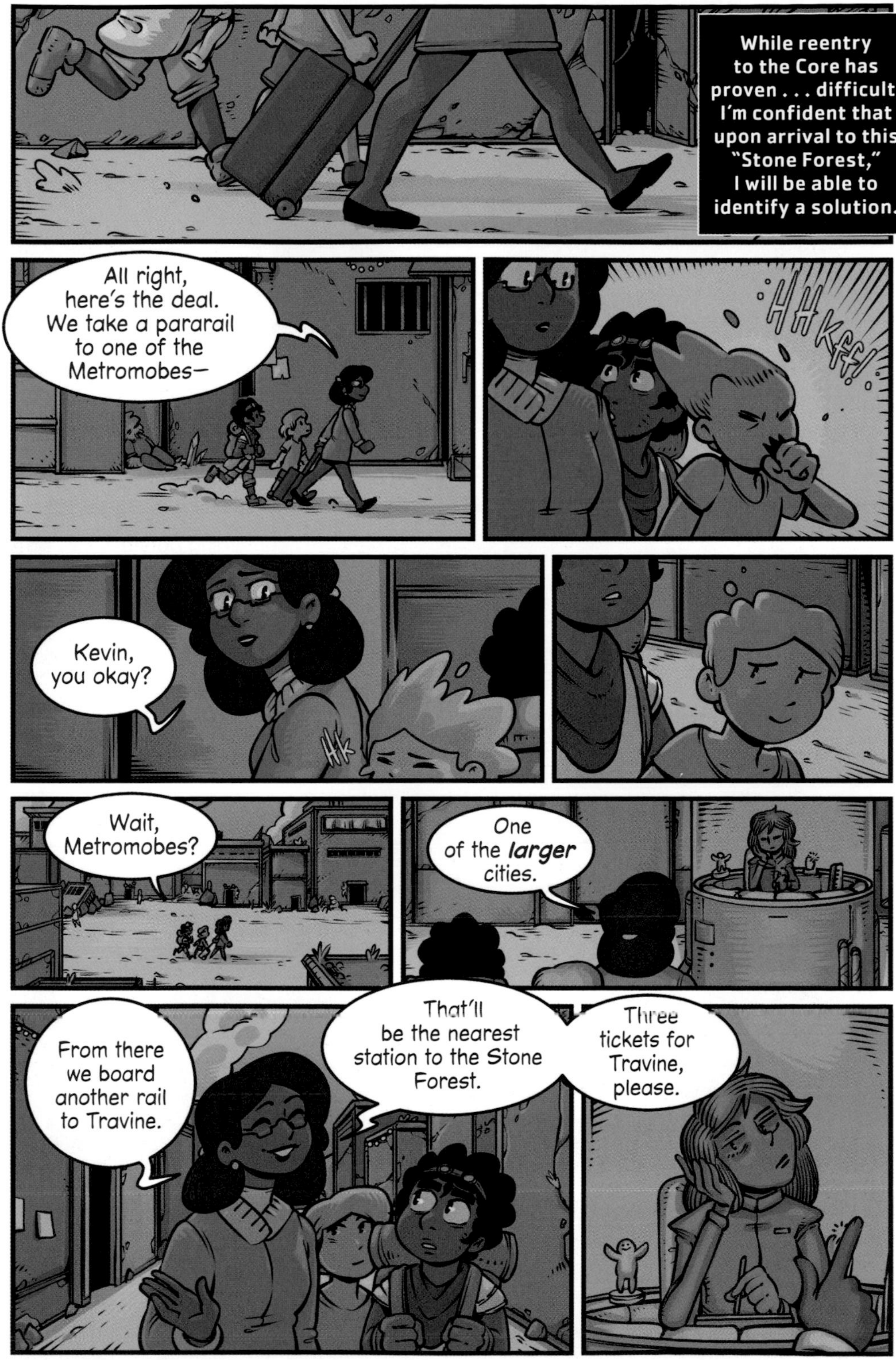

While reentry to the Core has proven . . . difficult, I'm confident that upon arrival to this "Stone Forest," I will be able to identify a solution.
All right, here's the deal. We take a pararail to one of the Metromobes—
HHKff!
Hk
Kevin, you okay?
Wait, Metromobes?
One of the *larger* cities.
From there we board another rail to Travine.
That'll be the nearest station to the Stone Forest.
Three tickets for Travine, please.

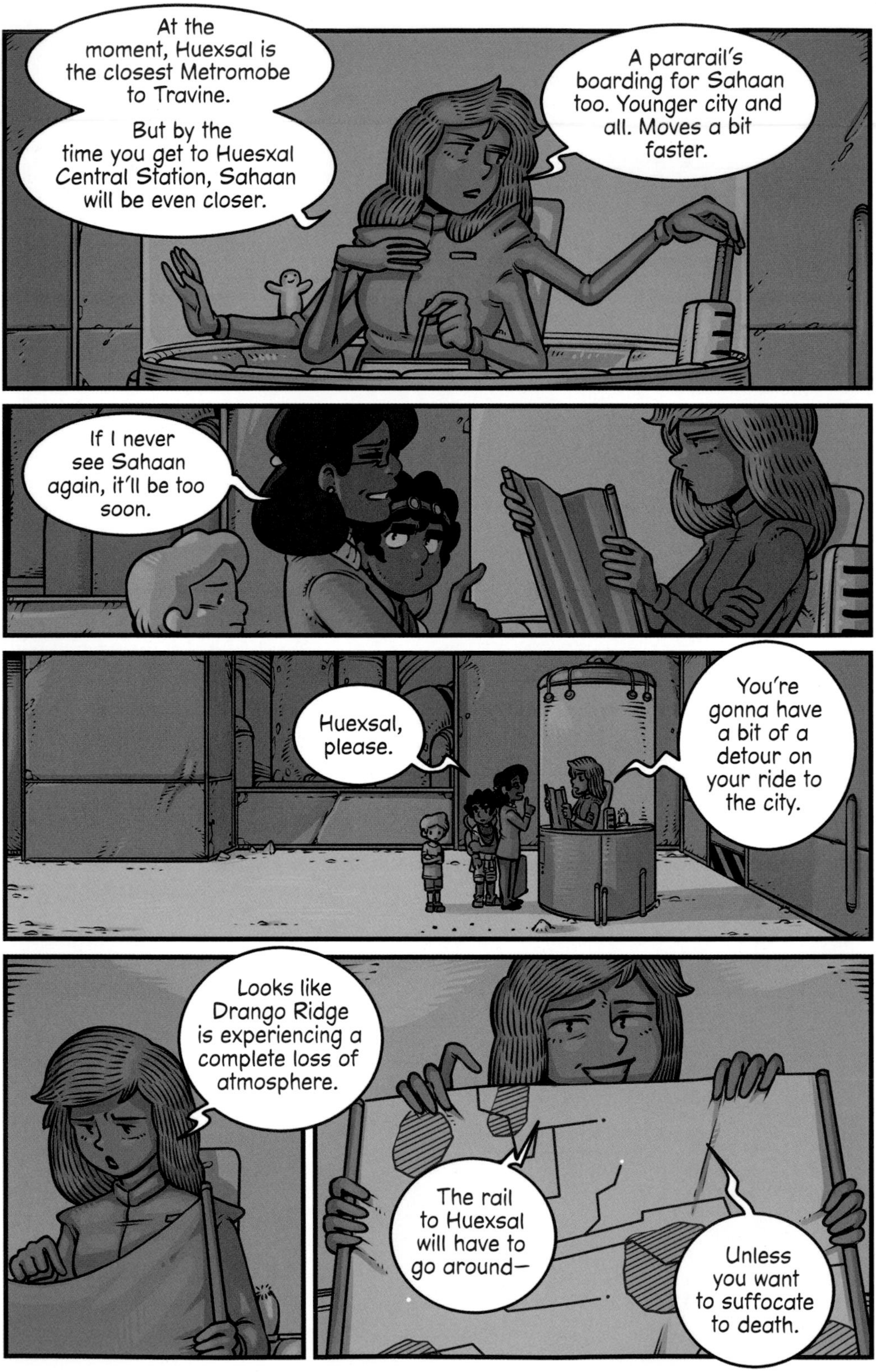
At the moment, Huexsal is the closest Metromobe to Travine.
But by the time you get to Huesxal Central Station, Sahaan will be even closer.
A pararail's boarding for Sahaan too. Younger city and all. Moves a bit faster.
If I never see Sahaan again, it'll be too soon.
Huexsal, please.
You're gonna have a bit of a detour on your ride to the city.
Looks like Drango Ridge is experiencing a complete loss of atmosphere.
The rail to Huexsal will have to go around—
Unless you want to suffocate to death.

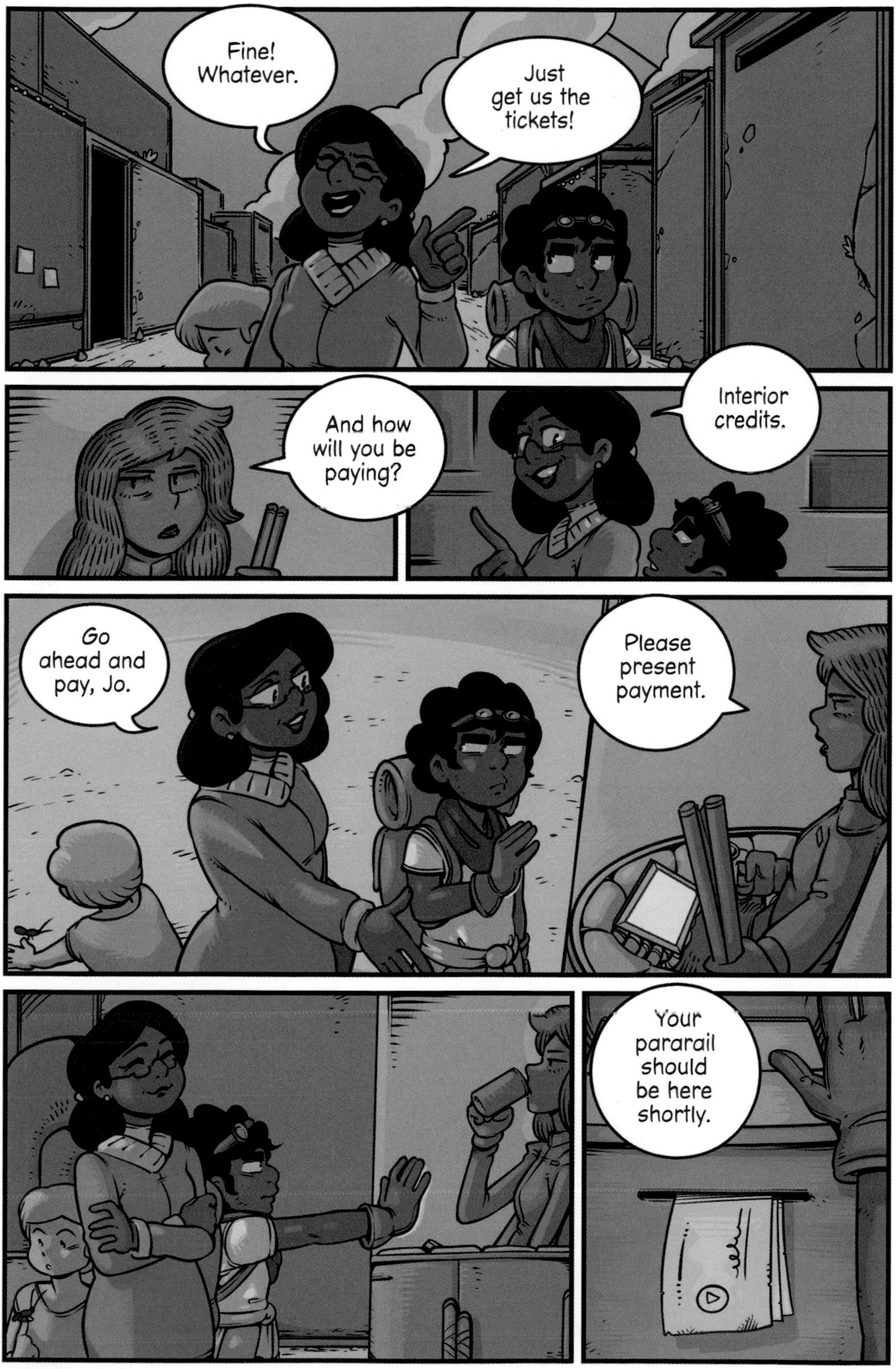
Fine! Whatever.
Just get us the tickets!
And how will you be paying?
Interior credits.
Go ahead and pay, Jo.
Please present payment.
Your pararail should be here shortly.

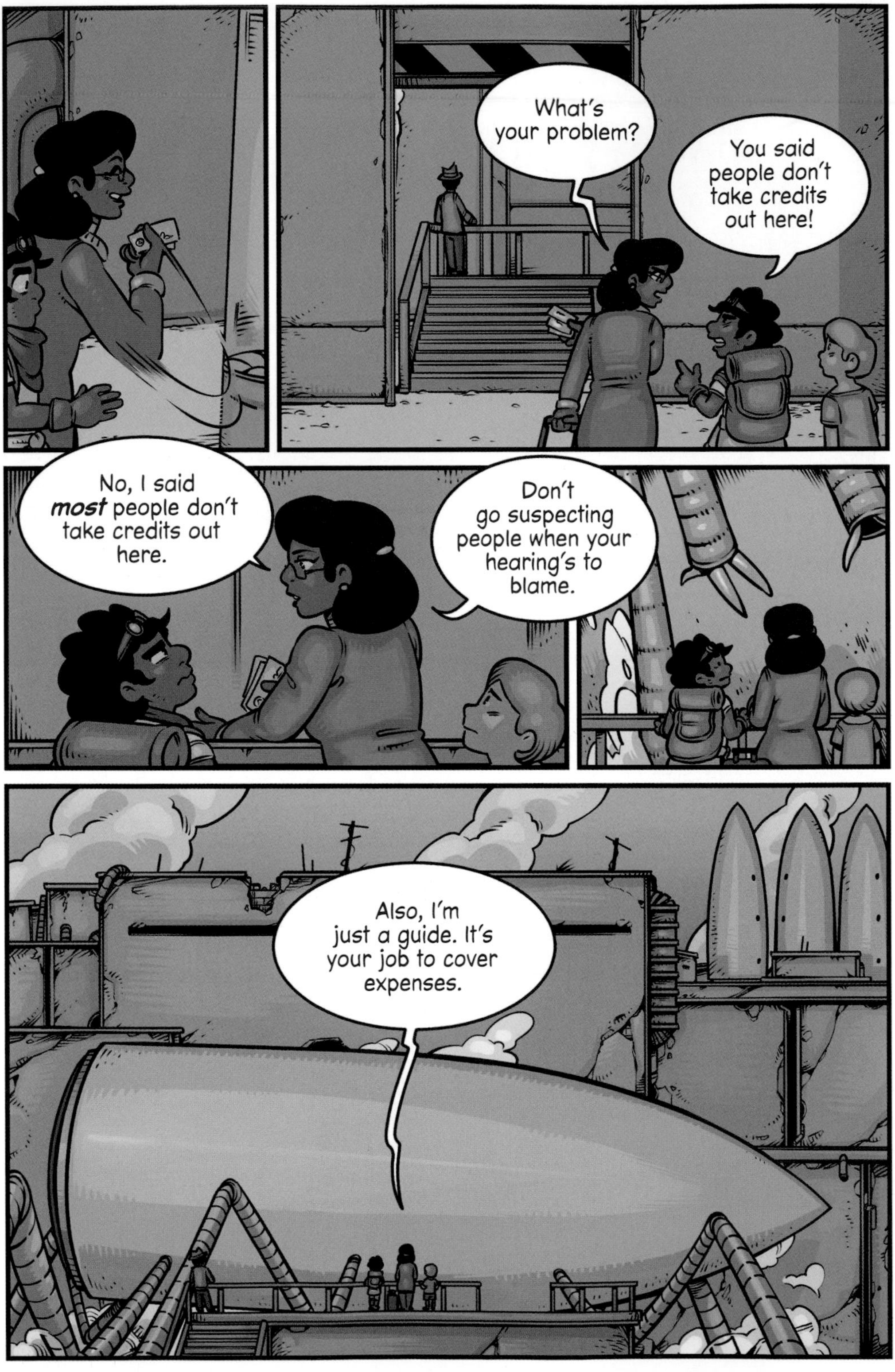
What's your problem?
You said people don't take credits out here!
No, I said ***most*** people don't take credits out here.
Don't go suspecting people when your hearing's to blame.
Also, I'm just a guide. It's your job to cover expenses.

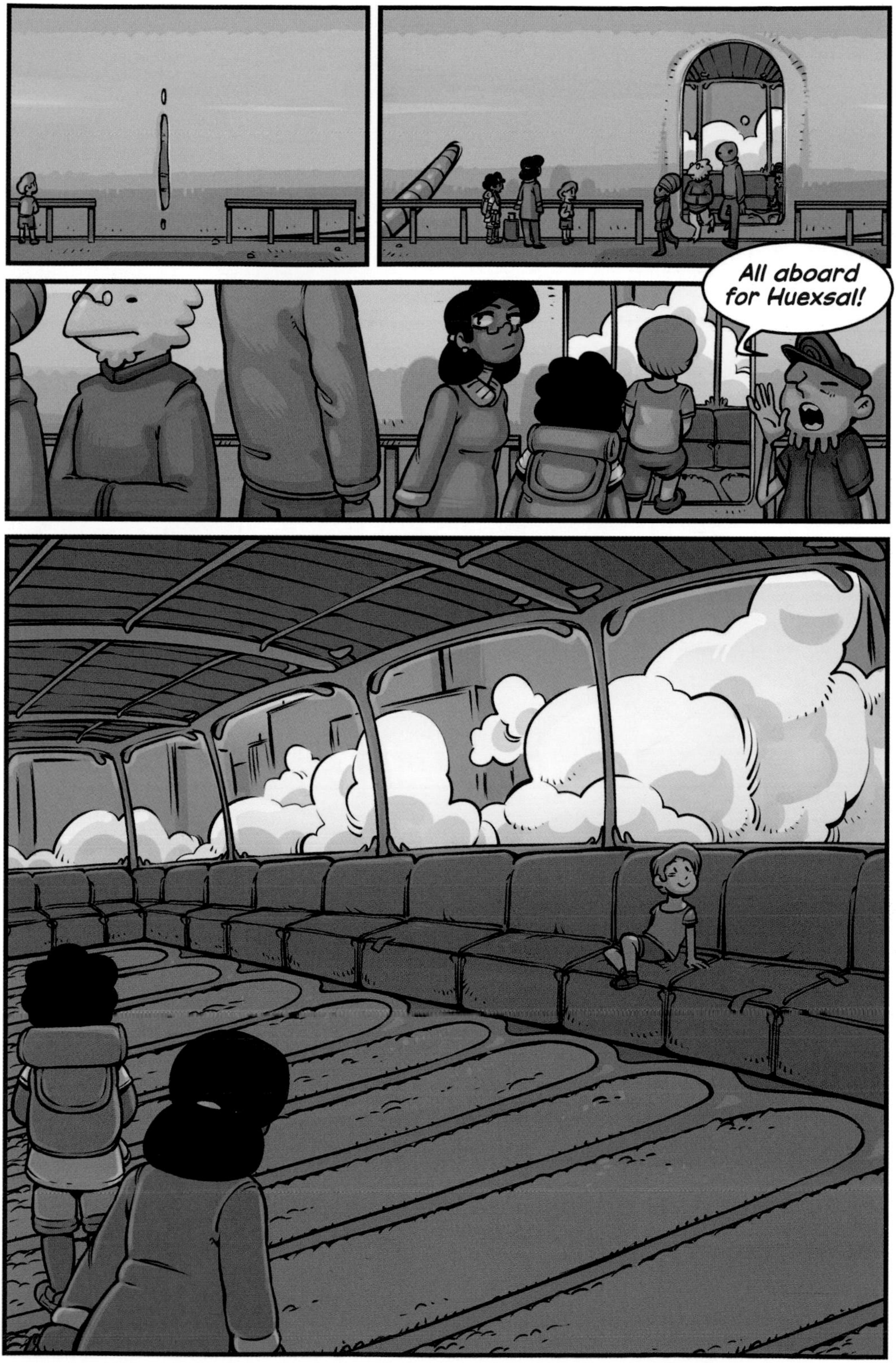
All aboard for Huexsal!

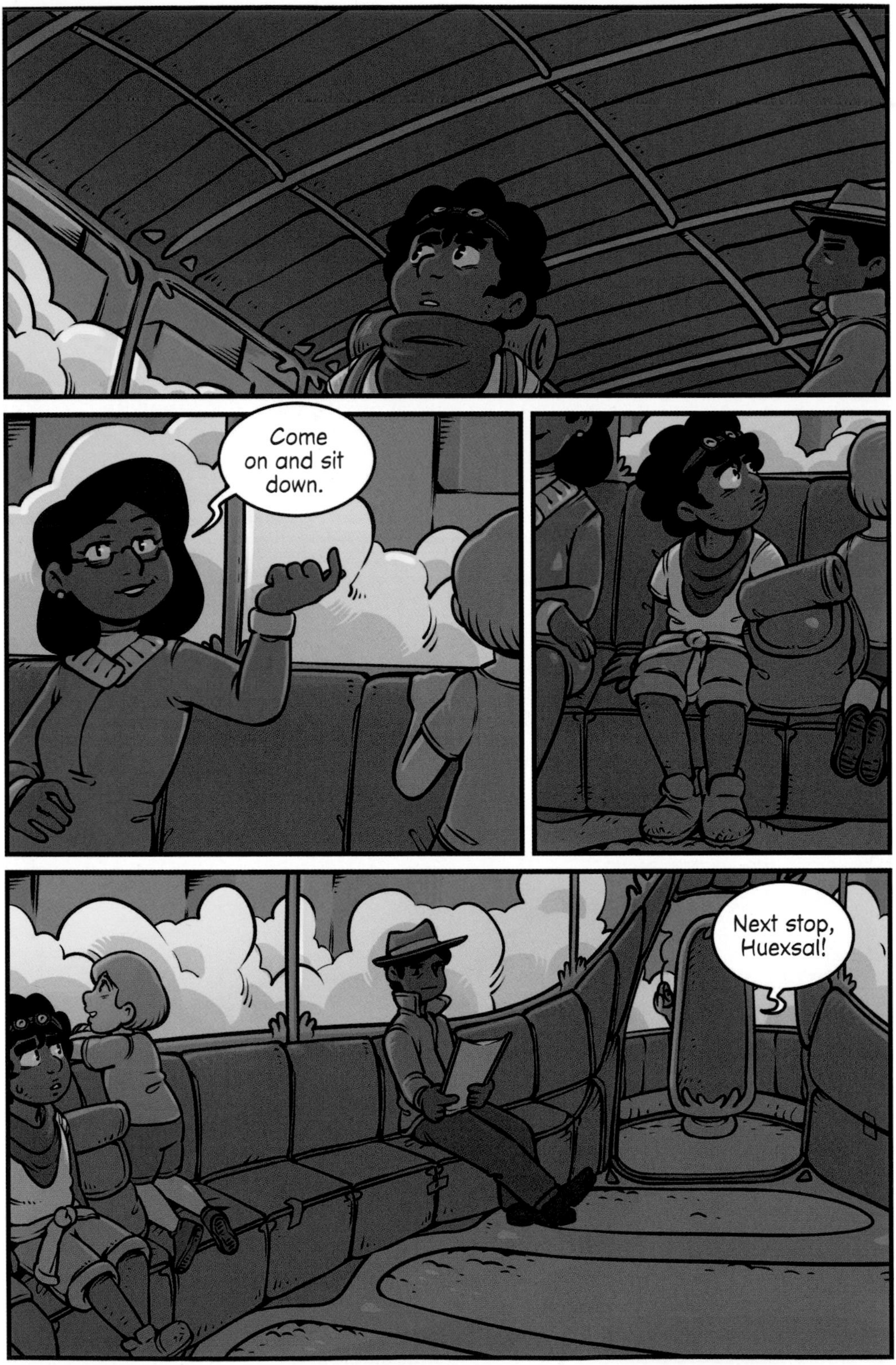
Come on and sit down.
Next stop, Huexsal!

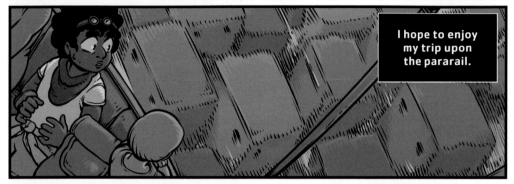

I hope to enjoy my trip upon the pararail.

But I cannot help but think that the journey will be thoroughly unmemorable.

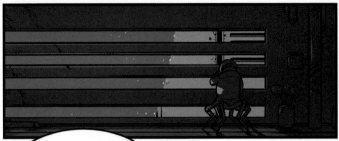

MR. STARGER, SIR! THERE'S BEEN AN UPDATE ON THE TECHNICIAN WHO DUPLICATED 006 DISPATCHER WESH87-22's SIGNATURE!

Connelly! You don't have to yell!

Sorry, sir!

What's that about the technician?

Josephine Wilson. Maintenance and Repair, 006 block. Reported missing—

She's Topside confirmed. Booked passage on a pararail to Huexsal. She's apparently accompanied by two Topsiders, sir.

Almost none, sir. Assessments and Situations is ruling this as an abduction.

Huexsal? What business could she possibly have on that route? And with two Topsiders?

70

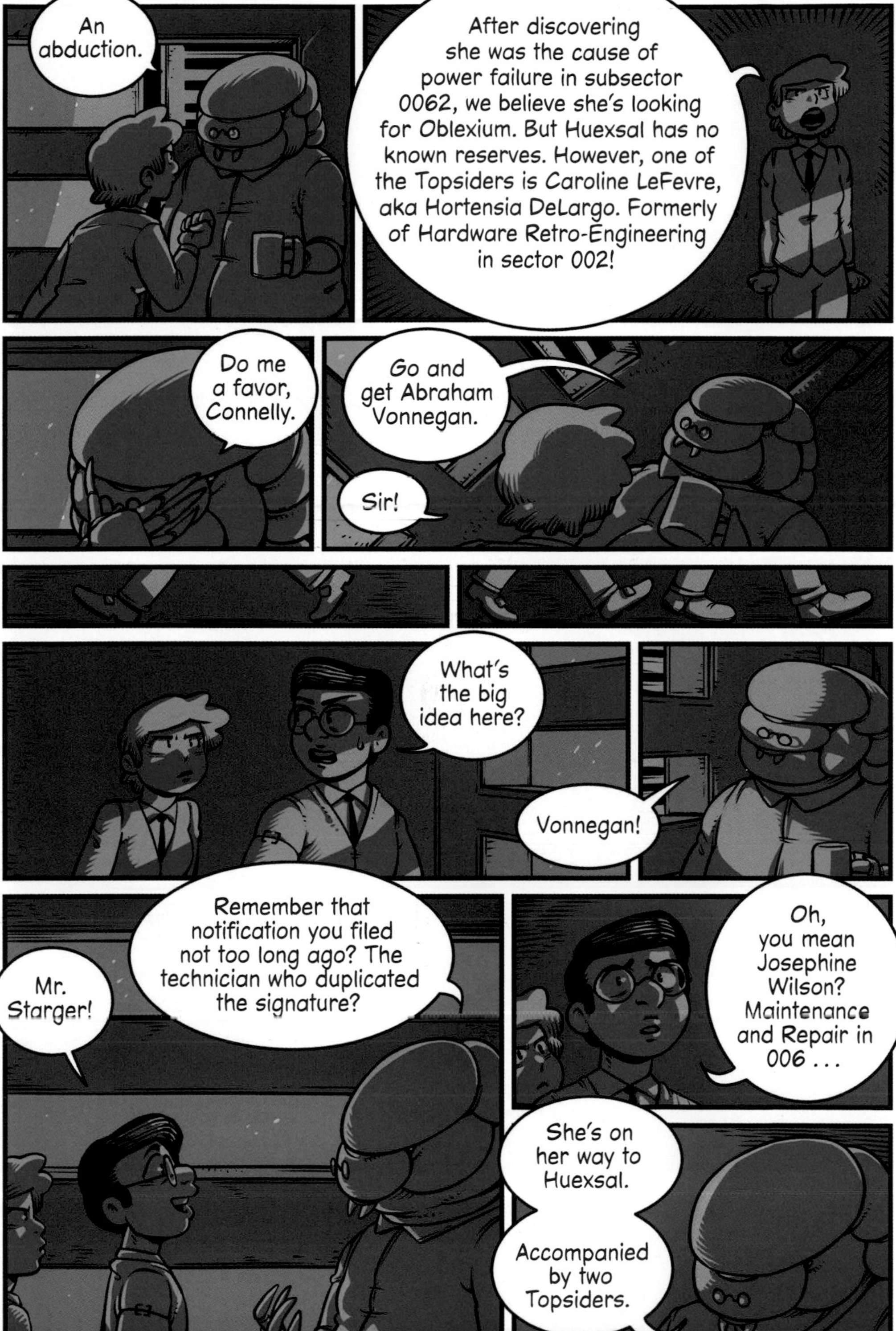
An abduction.
After discovering she was the cause of power failure in subsector 0062, we believe she's looking for Oblexium. But Huexsal has no known reserves. However, one of the Topsiders is Caroline LeFevre, aka Hortensia DeLargo. Formerly of Hardware Retro-Engineering in sector 002!
Do me a favor, Connelly.
Go and get Abraham Vonnegan.
Sir!
What's the big idea here?
Vonnegan!
Mr. Starger!
Remember that notification you filed not too long ago? The technician who duplicated the signature?
Oh, you mean Josephine Wilson? Maintenance and Repair in 006 . . .
She's on her way to Huexsal.
Accompanied by two Topsiders.

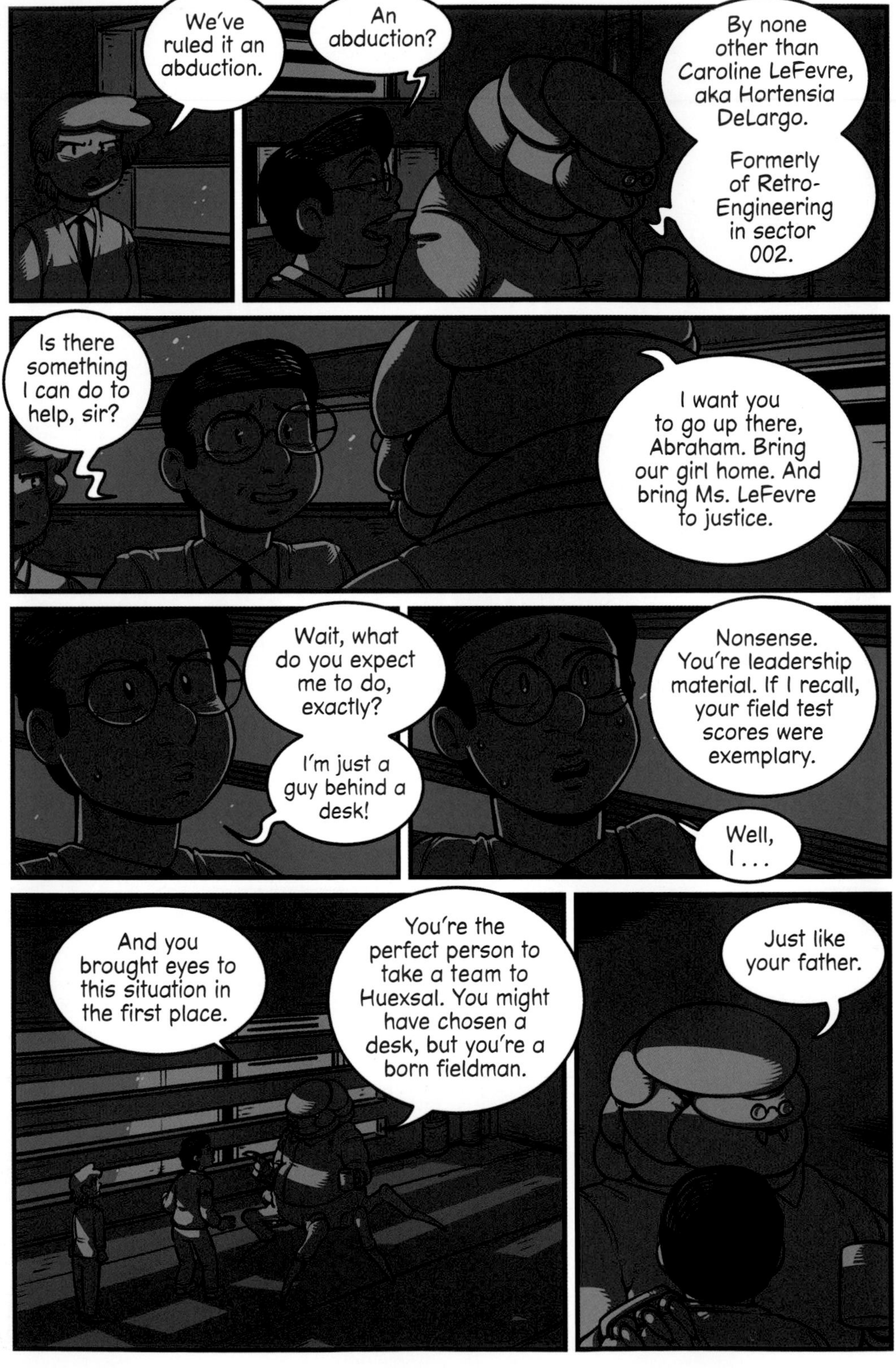
We've ruled it an abduction.
An abduction?
By none other than Caroline LeFevre, aka Hortensia DeLargo.
Formerly of Retro-Engineering in sector 002.
Is there something I can do to help, sir?
I want you to go up there, Abraham. Bring our girl home. And bring Ms. LeFevre to justice.
Wait, what do you expect me to do, exactly?
I'm just a guy behind a desk!
Nonsense. You're leadership material. If I recall, your field test scores were exemplary.
Well, I . . .
And you brought eyes to this situation in the first place.
You're the perfect person to take a team to Huexsal. You might have chosen a desk, but you're a born fieldman.
Just like your father.

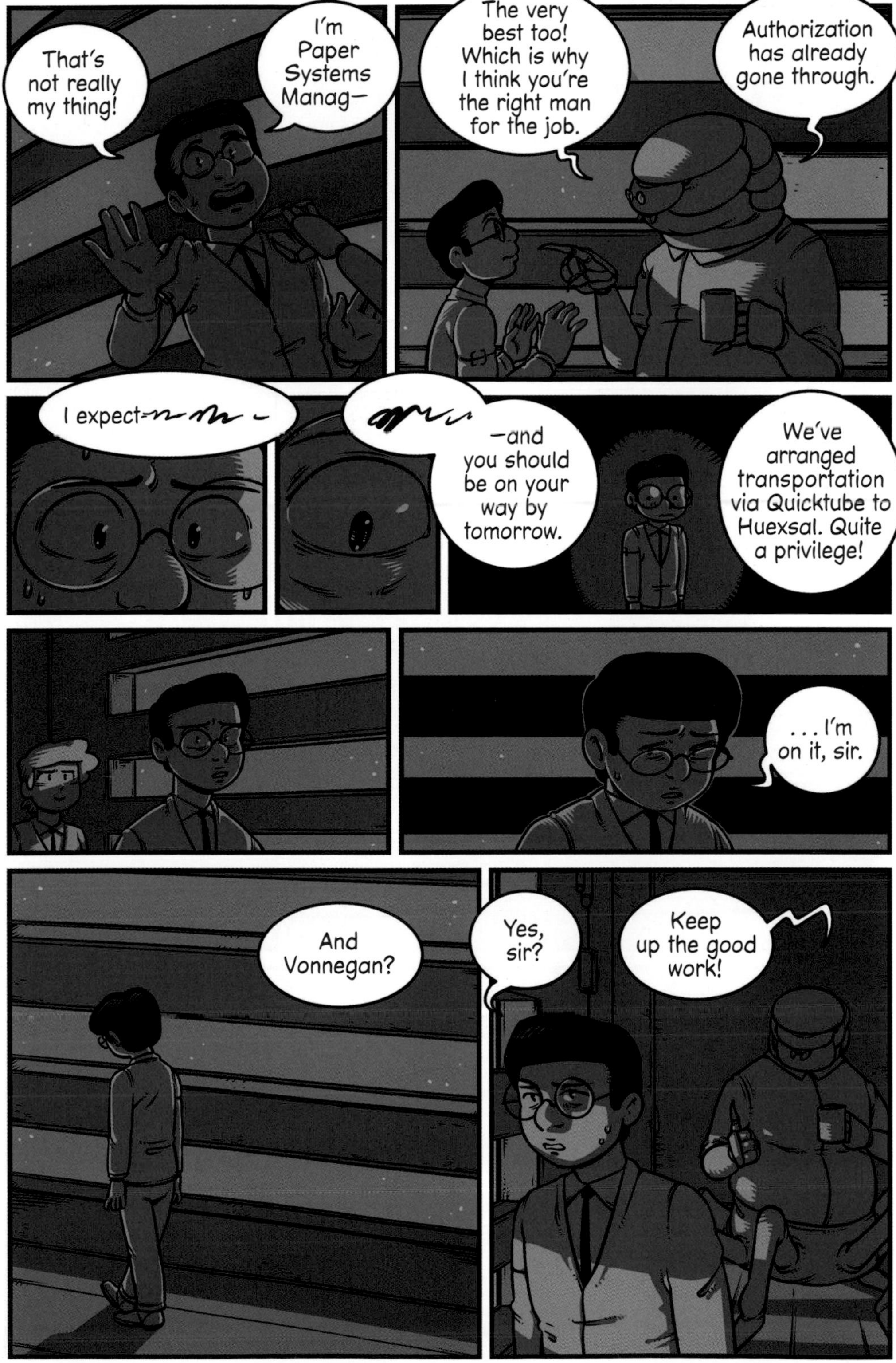
That's not really my thing!
I'm Paper Systems Manag—
The very best too! Which is why I think you're the right man for the job.
Authorization has already gone through.
I expect—
—and you should be on your way by tomorrow.
We've arranged transportation via Quicktube to Huexsal. Quite a privilege!
. . . I'm on it, sir.
And Vonnegan?
Yes, sir?
Keep up the good work!

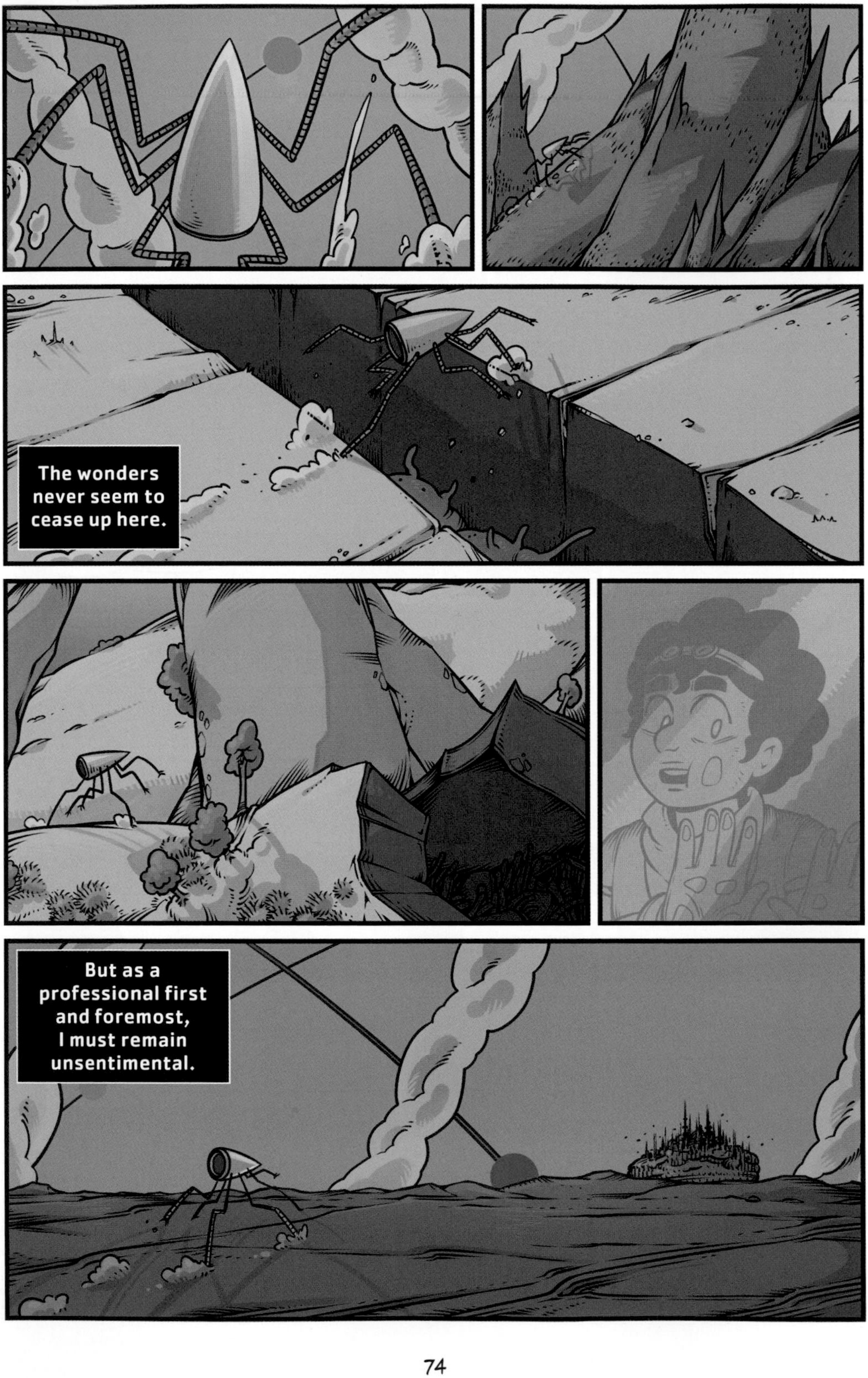
The wonders never seem to cease up here.
But as a professional first and foremost, I must remain unsentimental.

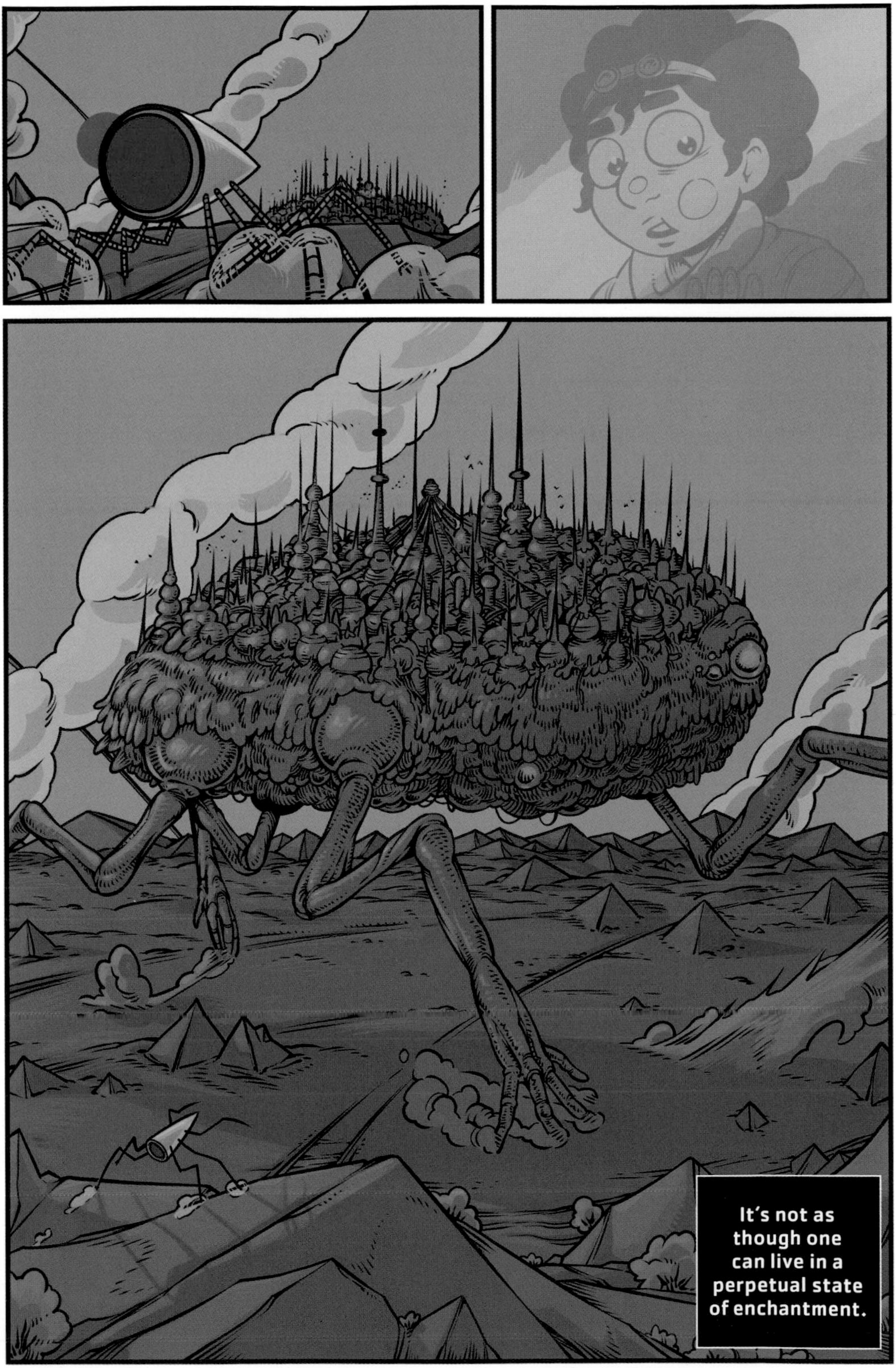
It's not as though one can live in a perpetual state of enchantment.

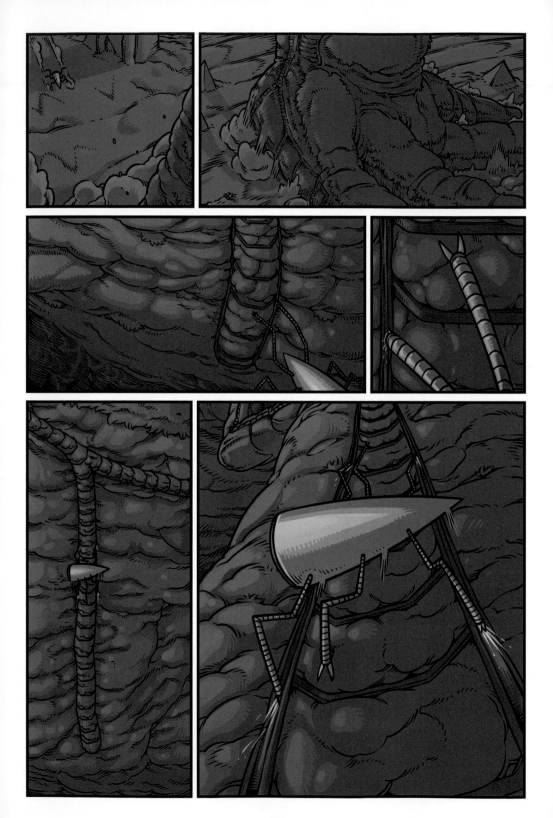

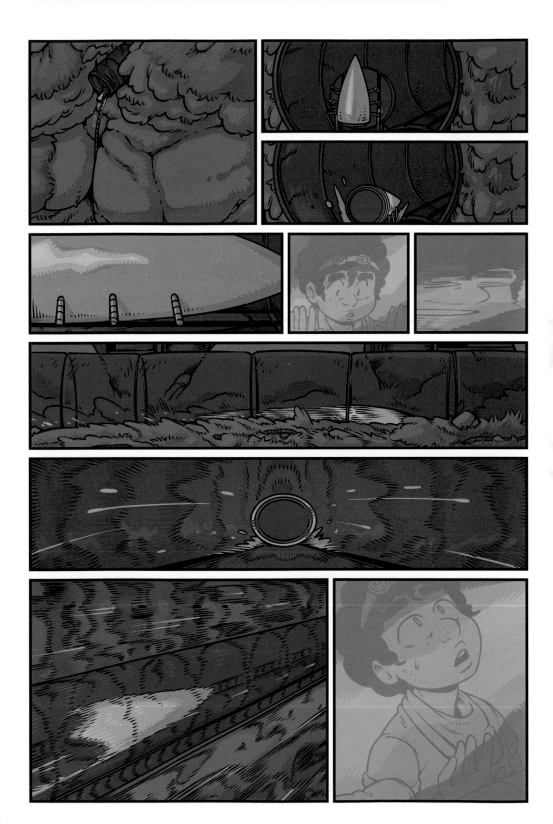

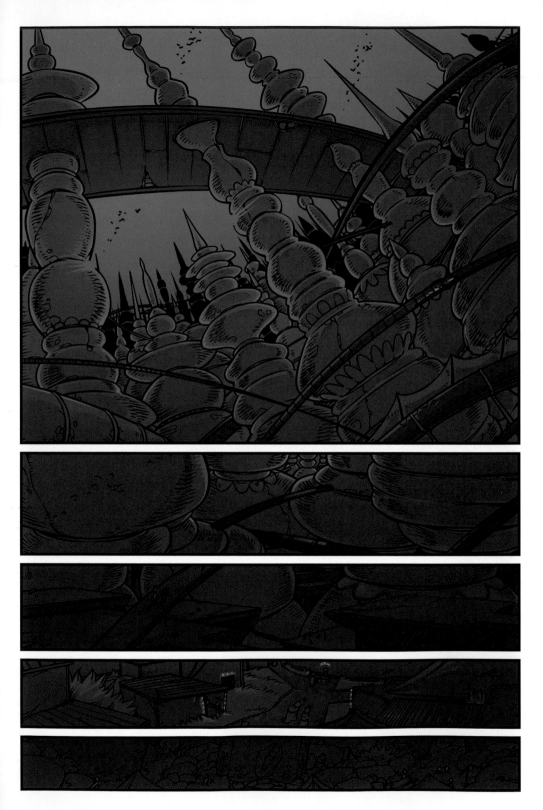

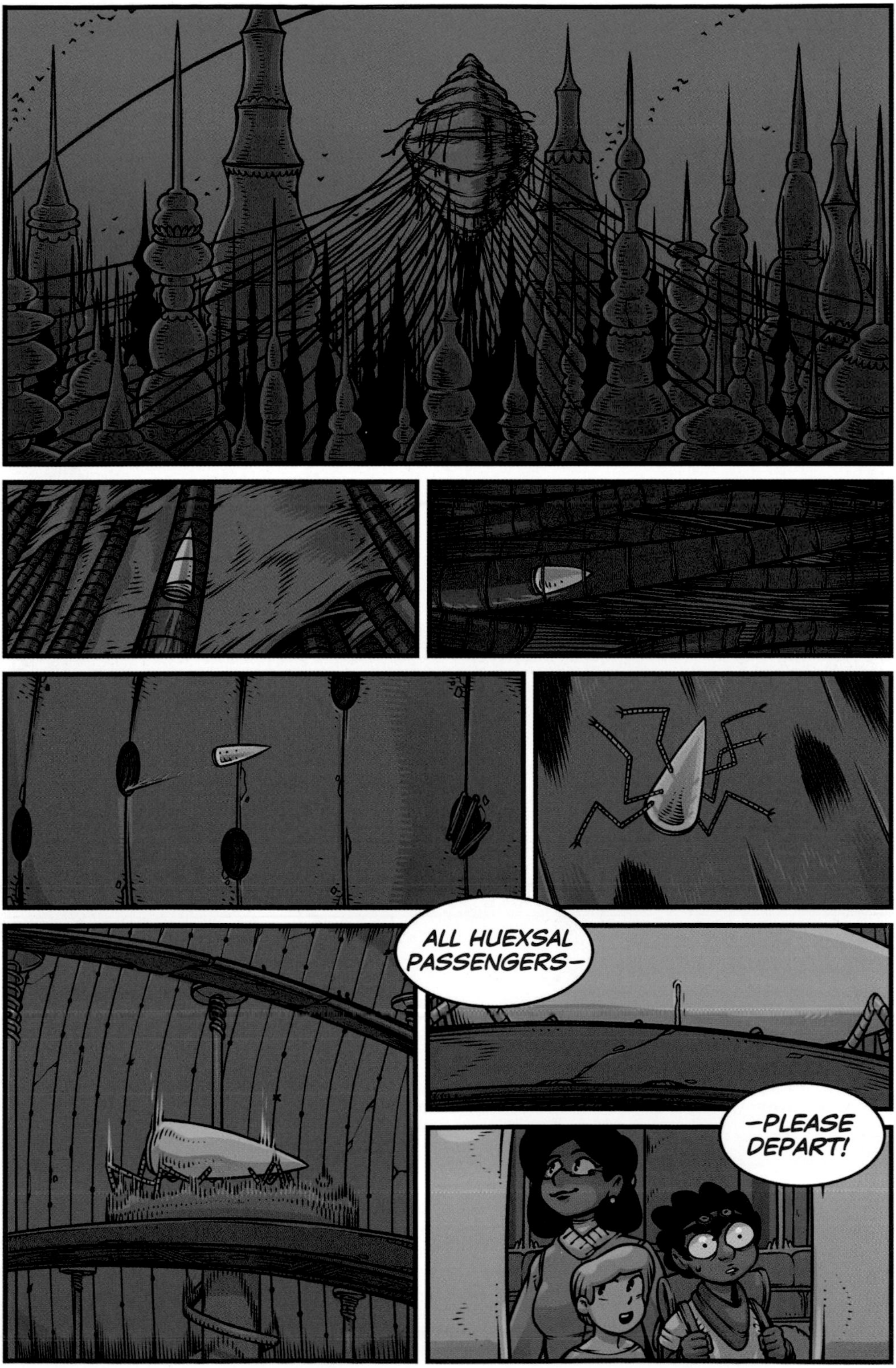
ALL HUEXSAL PASSENGERS—
—PLEASE DEPART!

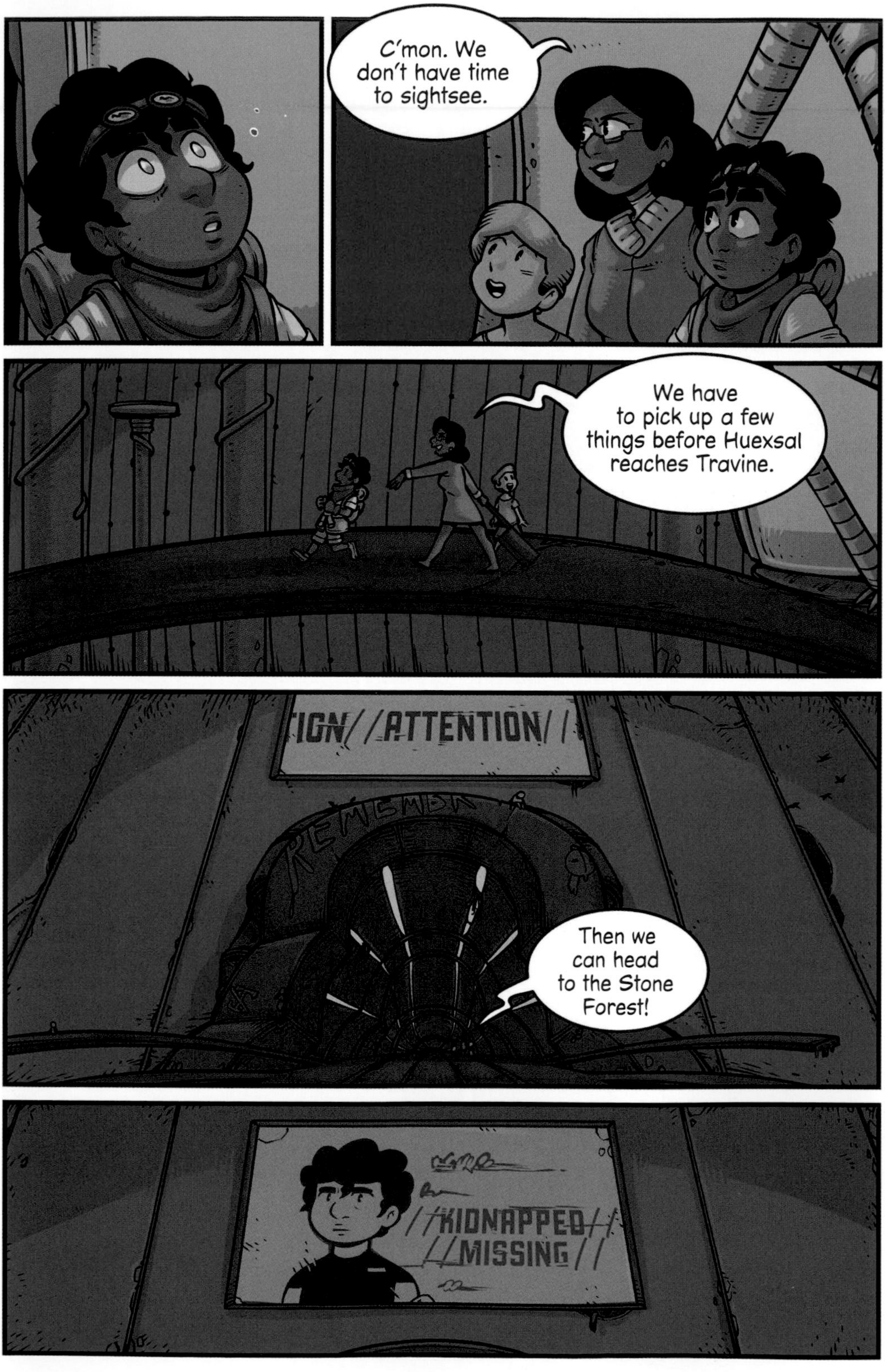

C'mon. We don't have time to sightsee.
We have to pick up a few things before Huexsal reaches Travine.
TION//ATTENTION//
Then we can head to the Stone Forest!
//KIDNAPPED//
//MISSING//

So, what are we looking at here?

Bzzt-bz!

Speak up, Lumi—I can't hear you.

An easy bounty, Karina!

Remember Tenz DeLargo?

Can't say it rings a bell. I don't have your head for names, hon.

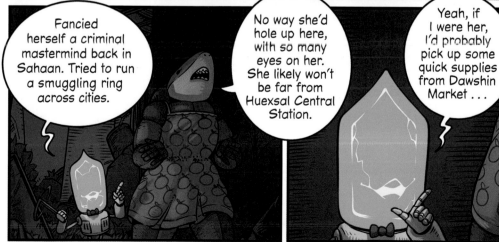

Fancied herself a criminal mastermind back in Sahaan. Tried to run a smuggling ring across cities.

No way she'd hole up here, with so many eyes on her. She likely won't be far from Huexsal Central Station.

Yeah, if I were her, I'd probably pick up some quick supplies from Dawshin Market . . .

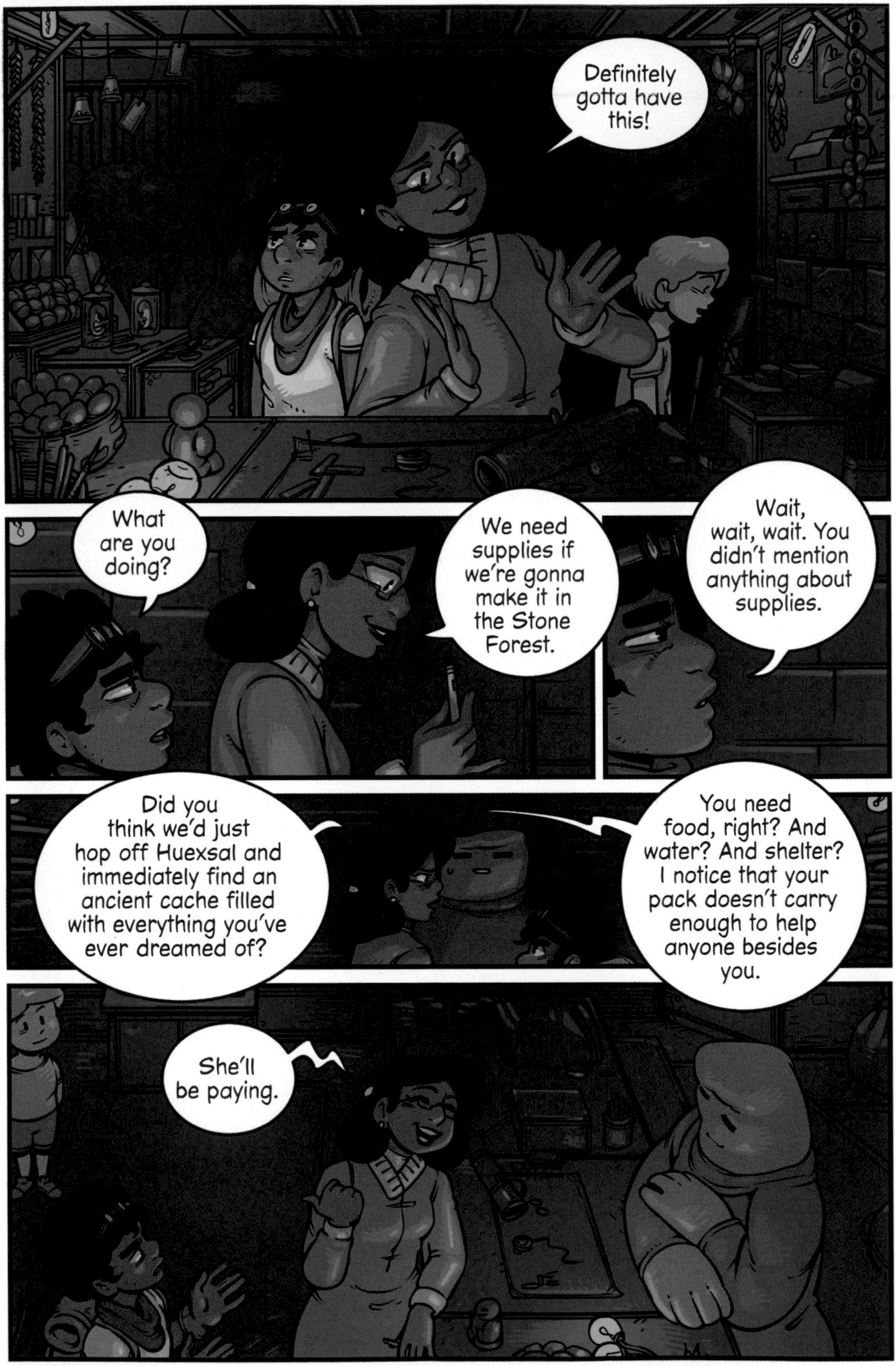
Definitely gotta have this!
What are you doing?
We need supplies if we're gonna make it in the Stone Forest.
Wait, wait, wait. You didn't mention anything about supplies.
Did you think we'd just hop off Huexsal and immediately find an ancient cache filled with everything you've ever dreamed of?
You need food, right? And water? And shelter? I notice that your pack doesn't carry enough to help anyone besides you.
She'll be paying.

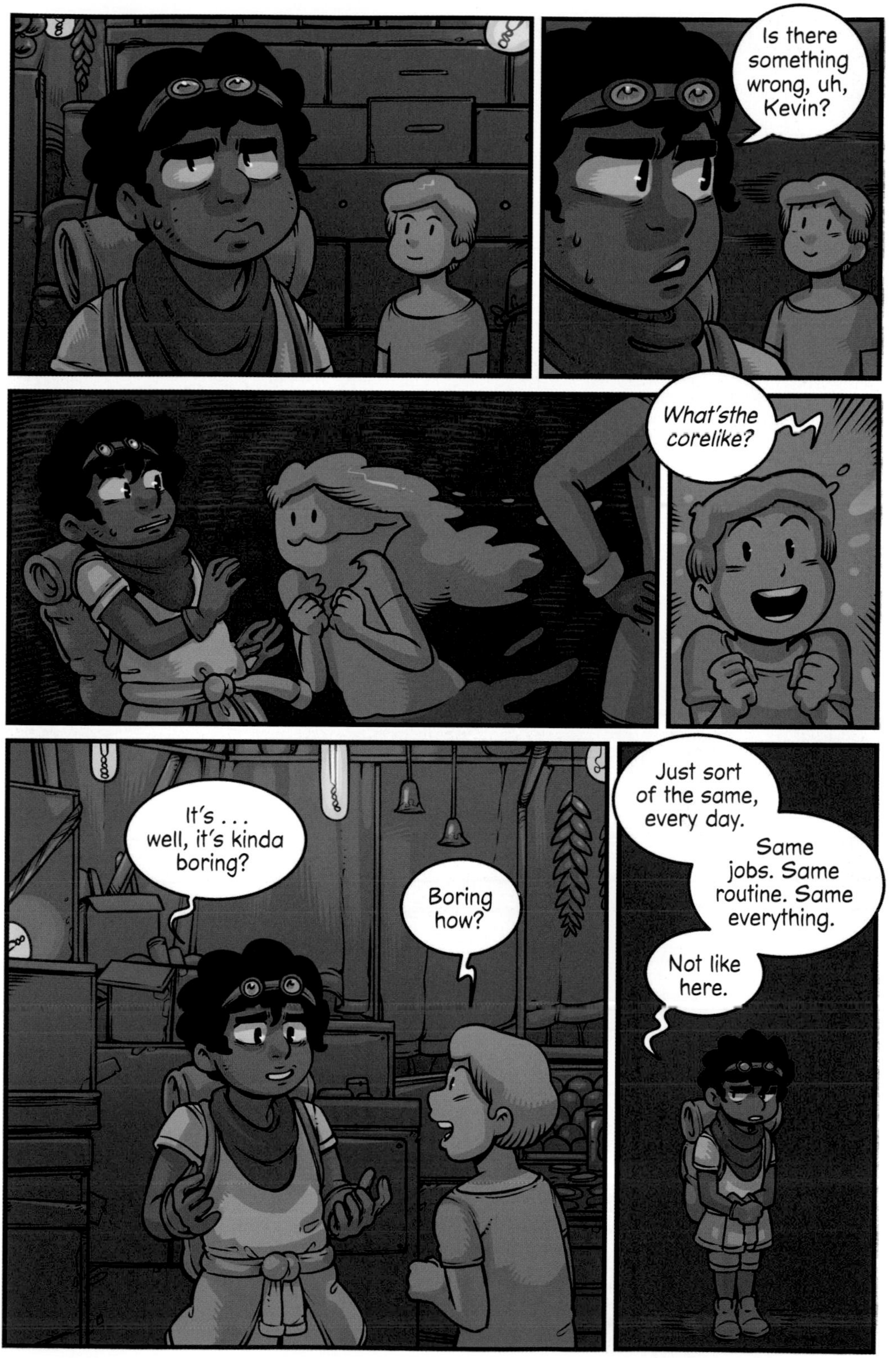
Is there something wrong, uh, Kevin?
What'sthe corelike?
It's . . . well, it's kinda boring?
Boring how?
Just sort of the same, every day.
Same jobs. Same routine. Same everything.
Not like here.

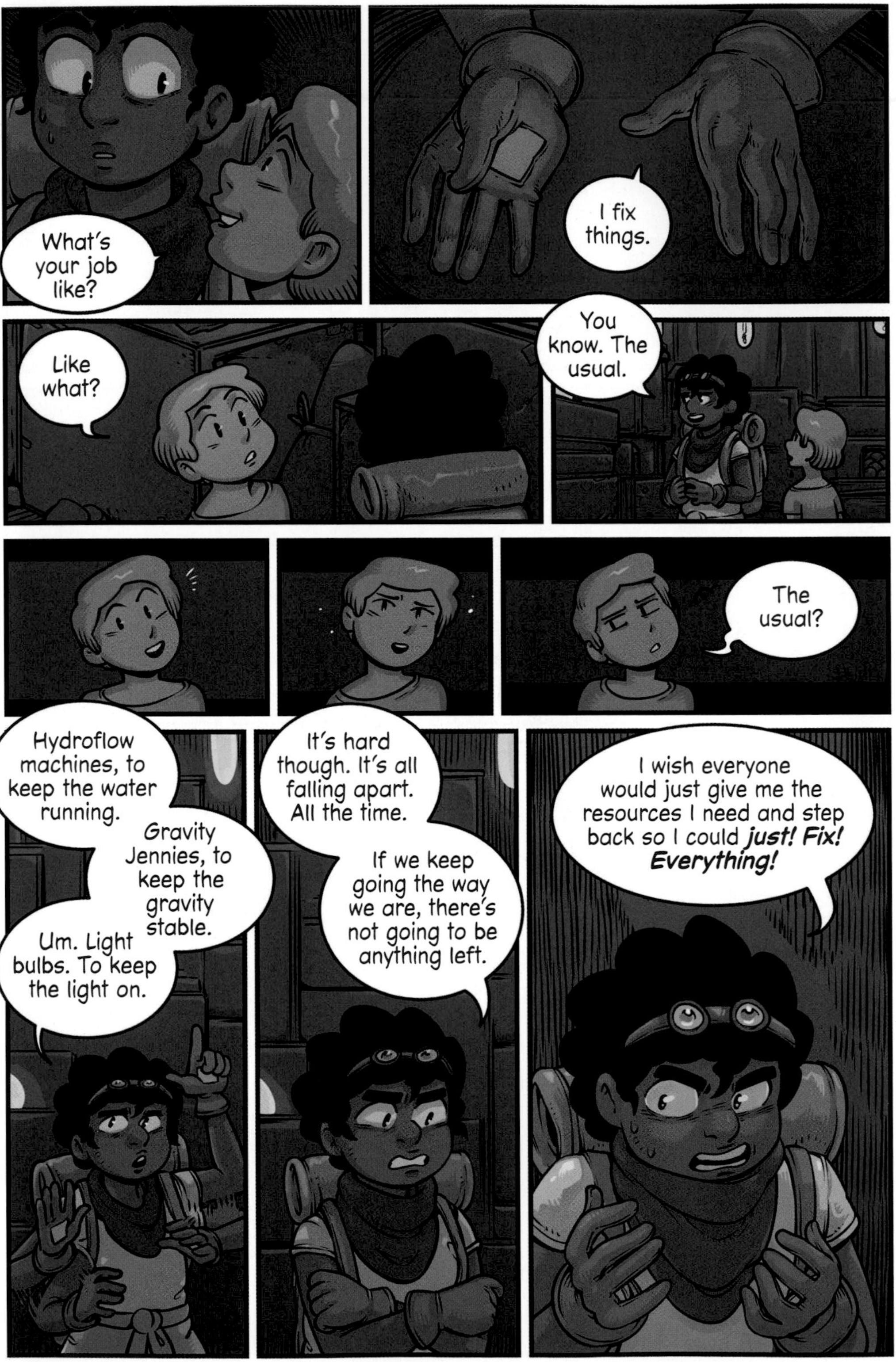
What's your job like?
I fix things.
Like what?
You know. The usual.
The usual?
Hydroflow machines, to keep the water running.
Gravity Jennies, to keep the gravity stable.
Um. Light bulbs. To keep the light on.
It's hard though. It's all falling apart. All the time.
If we keep going the way we are, there's not going to be anything left.
I wish everyone would just give me the resources I need and step back so I could ***just! Fix! Everything!***

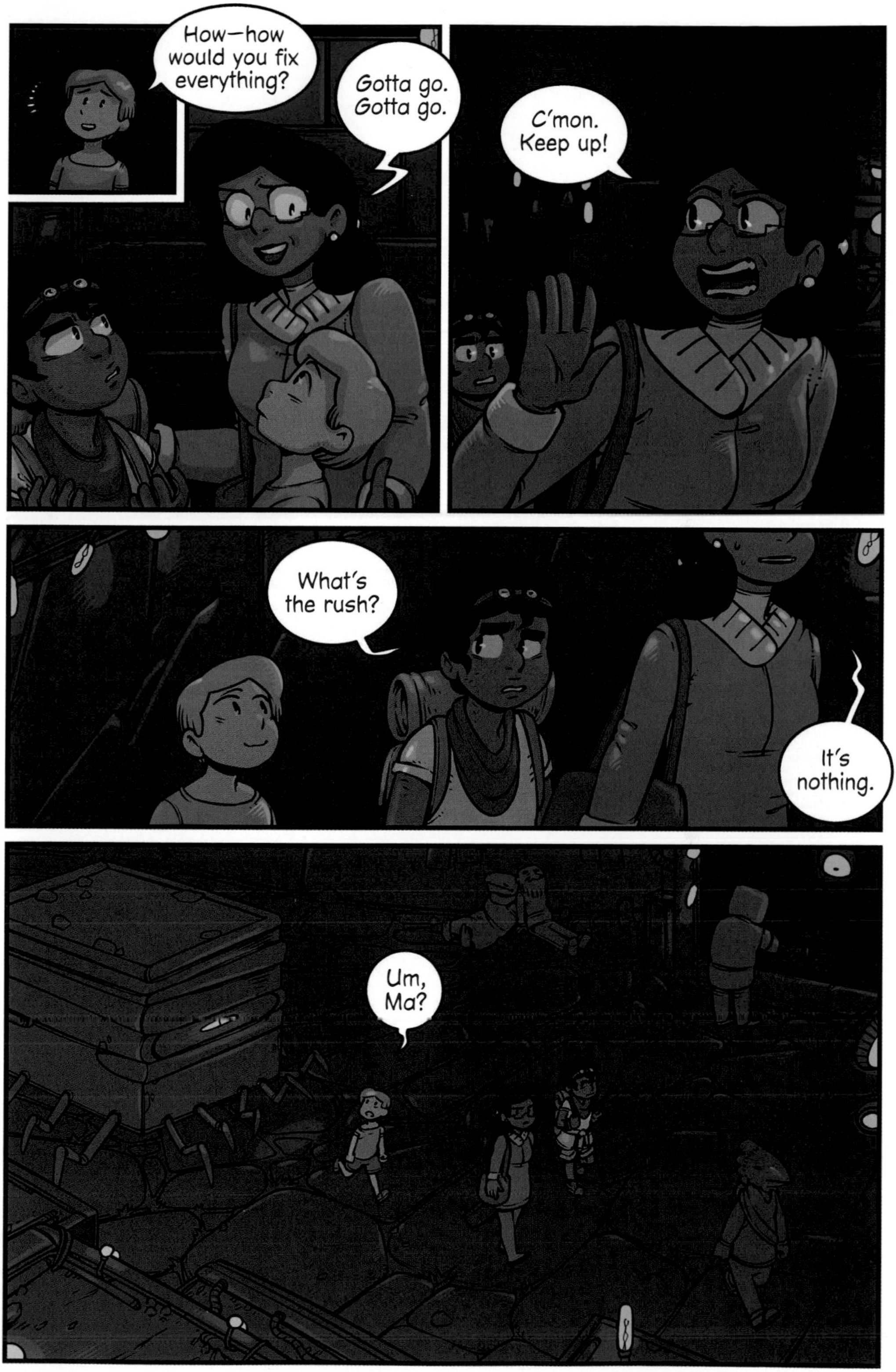
How—how would you fix everything?
Gotta go. Gotta go.
C'mon. Keep up!
What's the rush?
It's nothing.
Um, Ma?

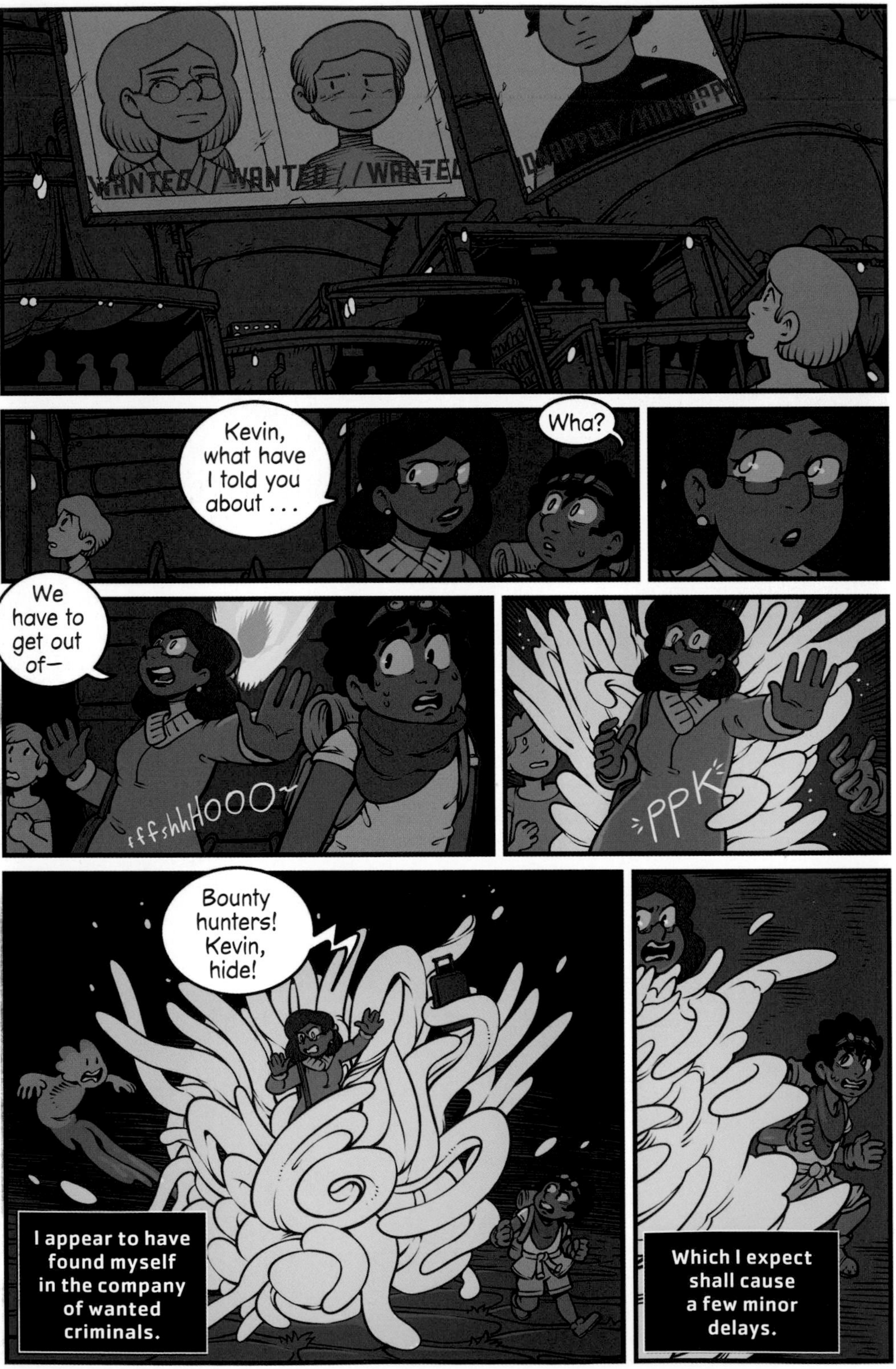
WANTED / WANTED / WANTED
KIDNAPPED / KIDNAPPED
Kevin, what have I told you about . . .
Wha?
We have to get out of—
ffshhHOOO~
PPK
Bounty hunters! Kevin, hide!
I appear to have found myself in the company of wanted criminals.
Which I expect shall cause a few minor delays.

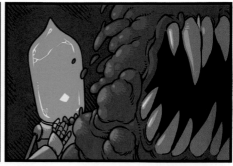

They said the kid was her accomplice, not a threat . . .

Careful with that shape-shifter!

Wait a second—

Karina, I don't want to alarm you, but I'm gonna take a swing at him!

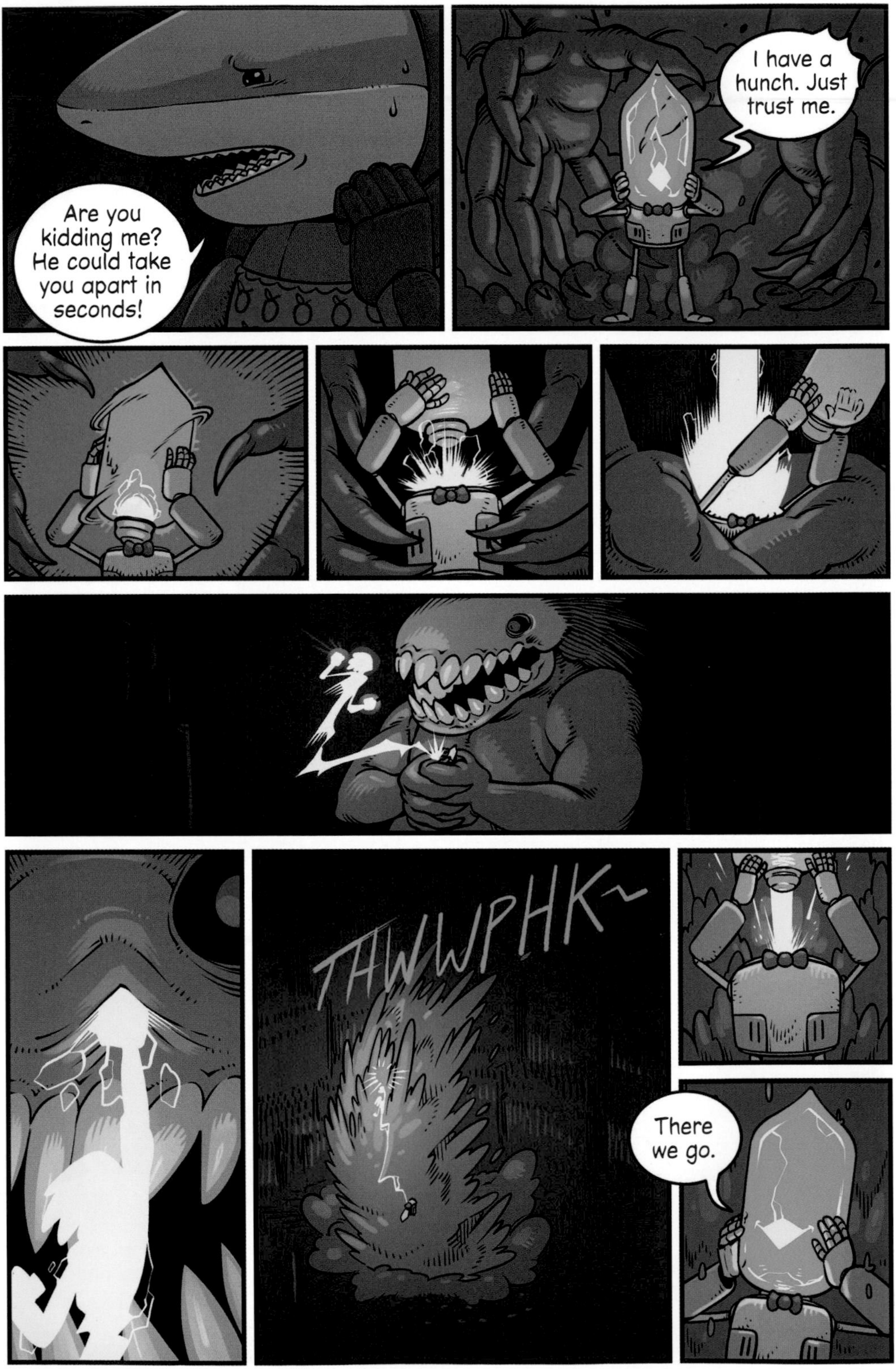

Are you kidding me? He could take you apart in seconds!
I have a hunch. Just trust me.
THWWPHK~
There we go.

All right. I'm coming down.

Hey. Hey! What's going on here?!

I *wasn't* abducted. I hired her to help me get to the Stone Forest!

You also splattered my kid. But more importantly, *let me out of this thing . . .*

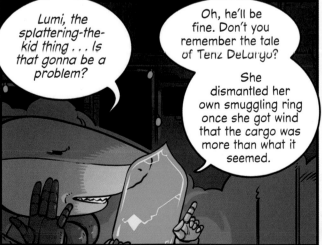

Lumi, the splattering-the-kid thing . . . Is that gonna be a problem?

Oh, he'll be fine. Don't you remember the tale of Tenz DeLargo?

She dismantled her own smuggling ring once she got wind that the cargo was more than what it seemed.

A Drevarian refugee.

Yeah, after seeing the kid transform . . .

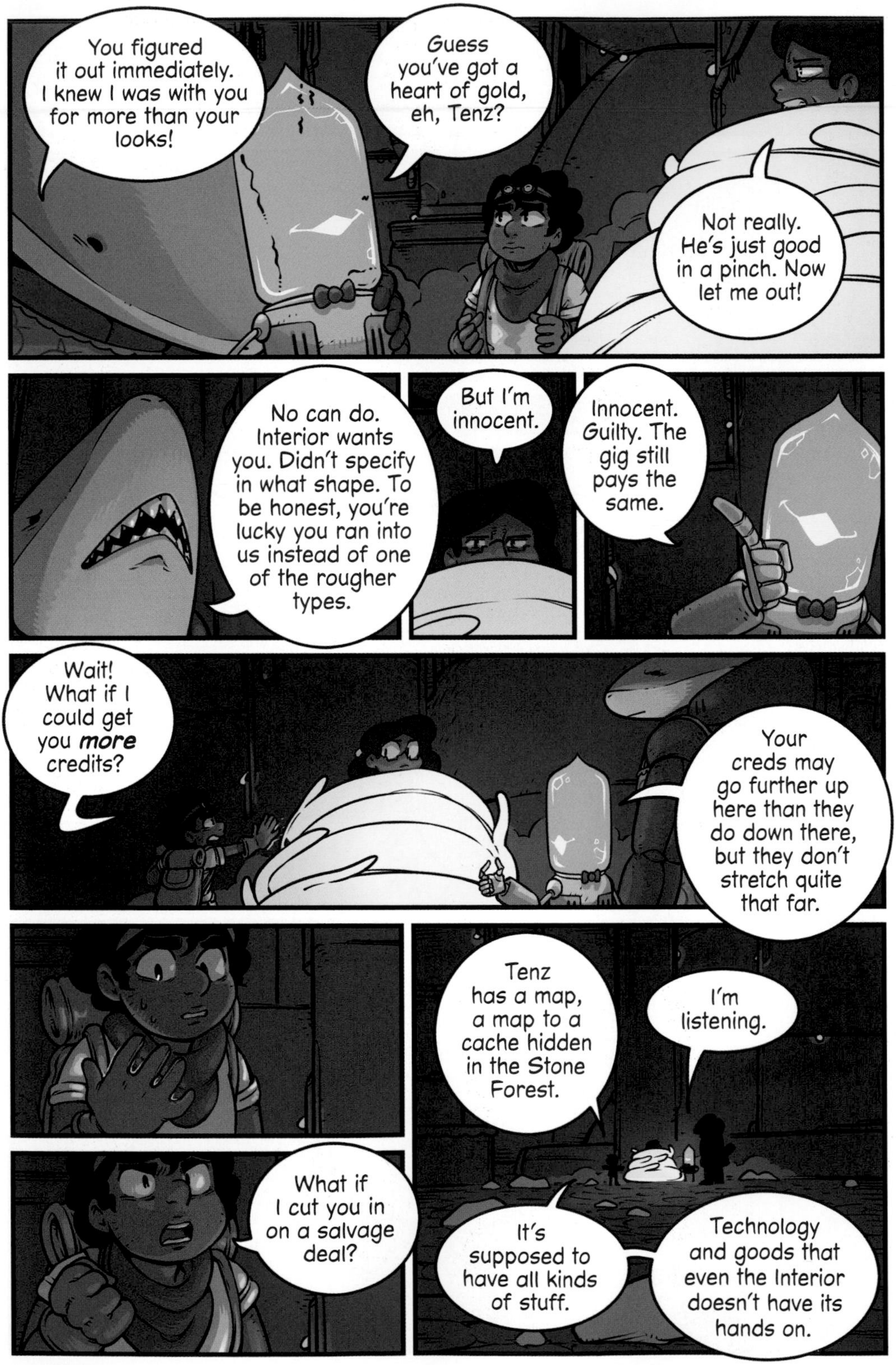
You figured it out immediately. I knew I was with you for more than your looks!
Guess you've got a heart of gold, eh, Tenz?
Not really. He's just good in a pinch. Now let me out!
No can do. Interior wants you. Didn't specify in what shape. To be honest, you're lucky you ran into us instead of one of the rougher types.
But I'm innocent.
Innocent. Guilty. The gig still pays the same.
Wait! What if I could get you ***more*** credits?
Your creds may go further up here than they do down there, but they don't stretch quite that far.
What if I cut you in on a salvage deal?
Tenz has a map, a map to a cache hidden in the Stone Forest.
I'm listening.
It's supposed to have all kinds of stuff.
Technology and goods that even the Interior doesn't have its hands on.

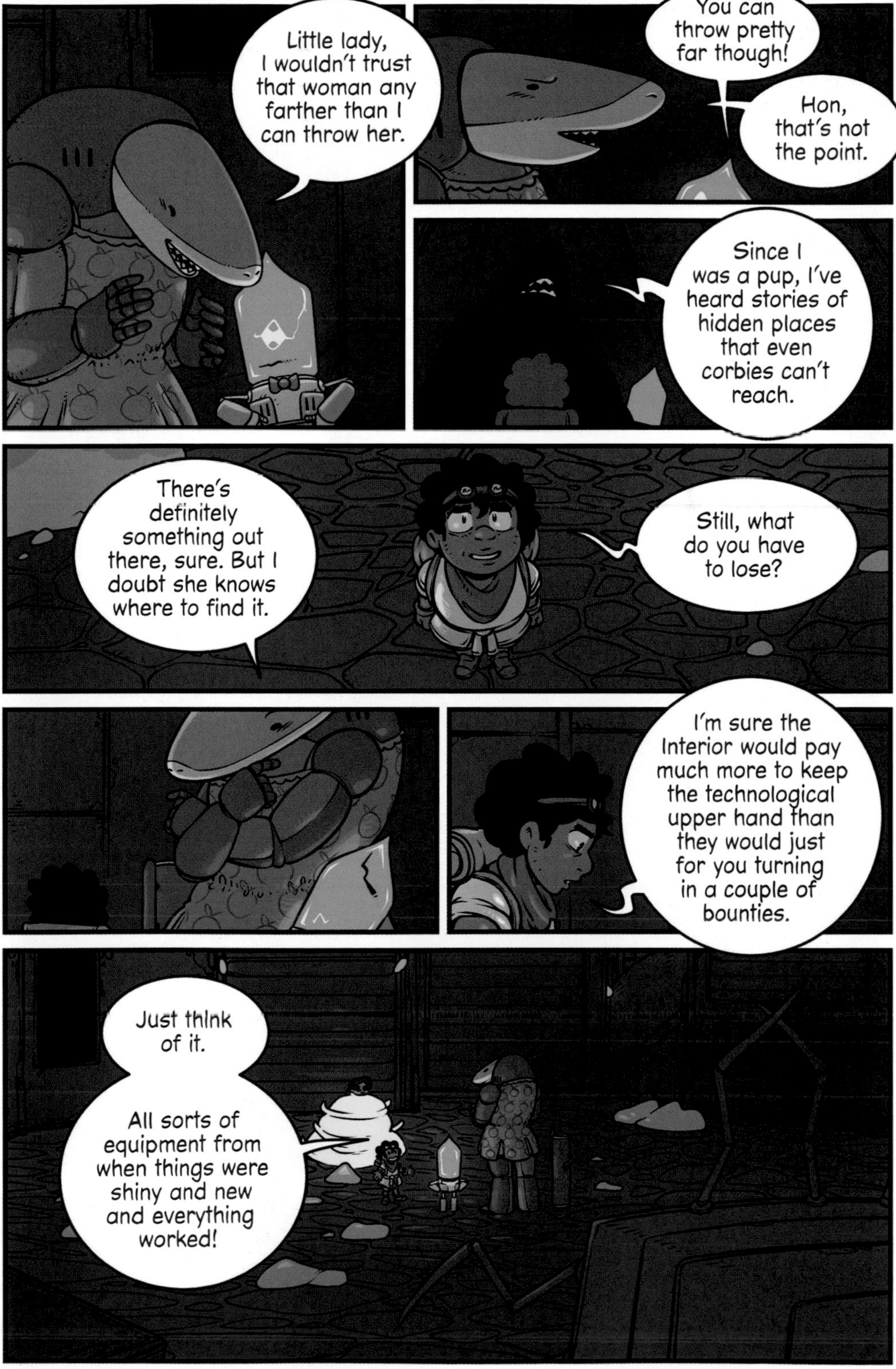
Little lady, I wouldn't trust that woman any farther than I can throw her.
You can throw pretty far though!
Hon, that's not the point.
Since I was a pup, I've heard stories of hidden places that even corbies can't reach.
There's definitely something out there, sure. But I doubt she knows where to find it.
Still, what do you have to lose?
I'm sure the Interior would pay much more to keep the technological upper hand than they would just for you turning in a couple of bounties.
Just think of it.
All sorts of equipment from when things were shiny and new and everything worked!

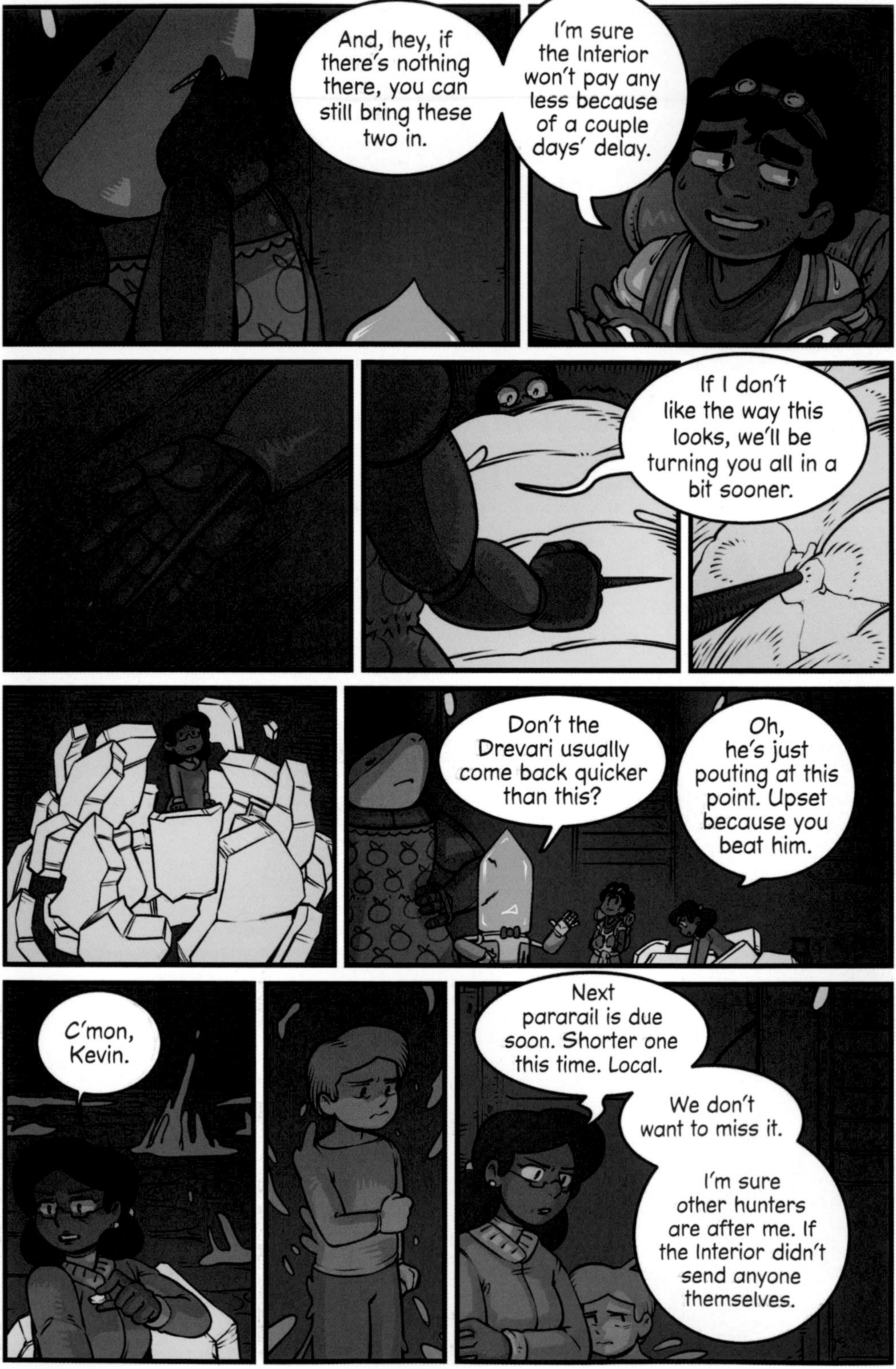
And, hey, if there's nothing there, you can still bring these two in.
I'm sure the Interior won't pay any less because of a couple days' delay.
If I don't like the way this looks, we'll be turning you all in a bit sooner.
Don't the Drevari usually come back quicker than this?
Oh, he's just pouting at this point. Upset because you beat him.
C'mon, Kevin.
Next pararail is due soon. Shorter one this time. Local.
We don't want to miss it.
I'm sure other hunters are after me. If the Interior didn't send anyone themselves.

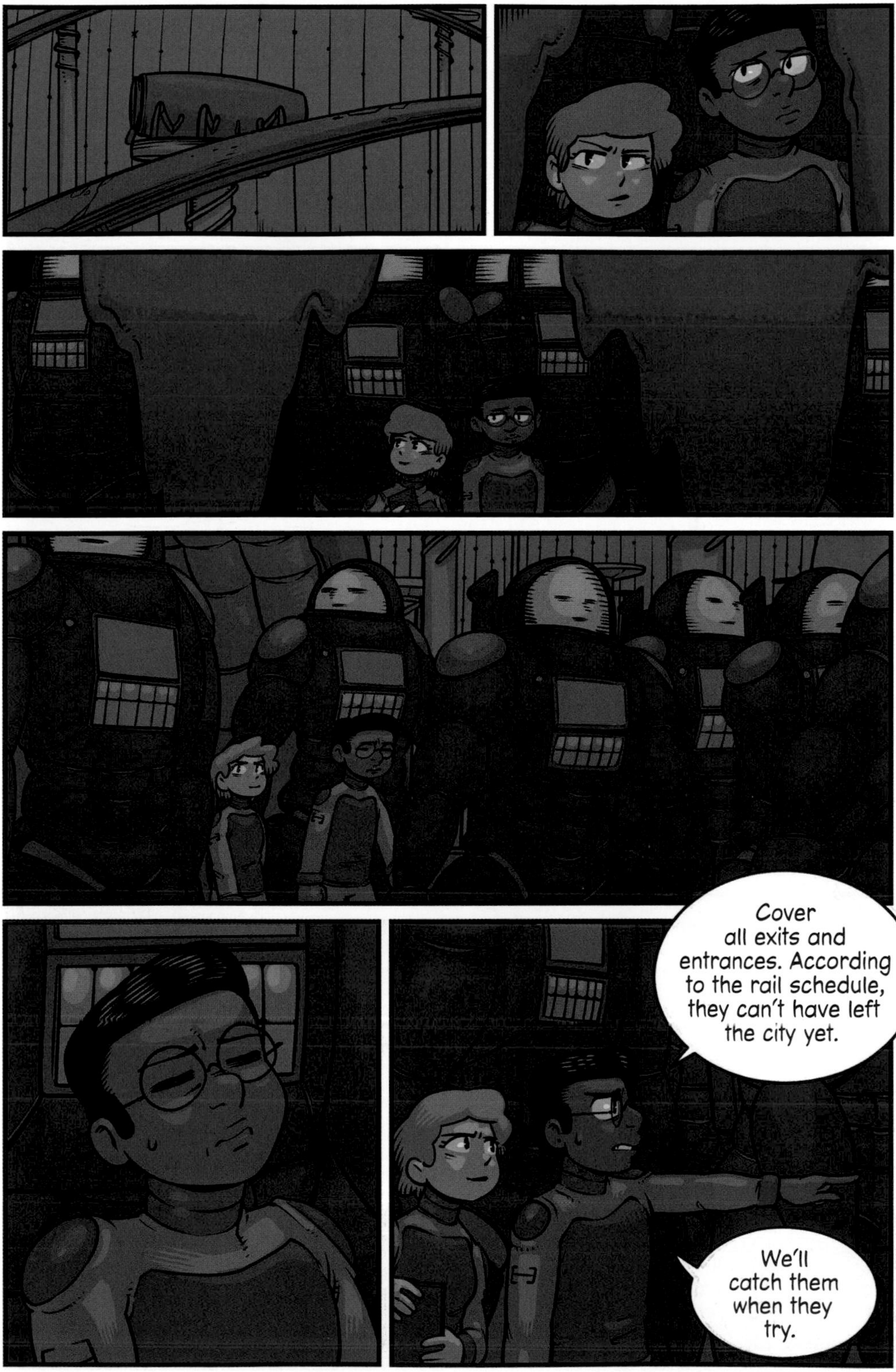

Cover all exits and entrances. According to the rail schedule, they can't have left the city yet.
We'll catch them when they try.

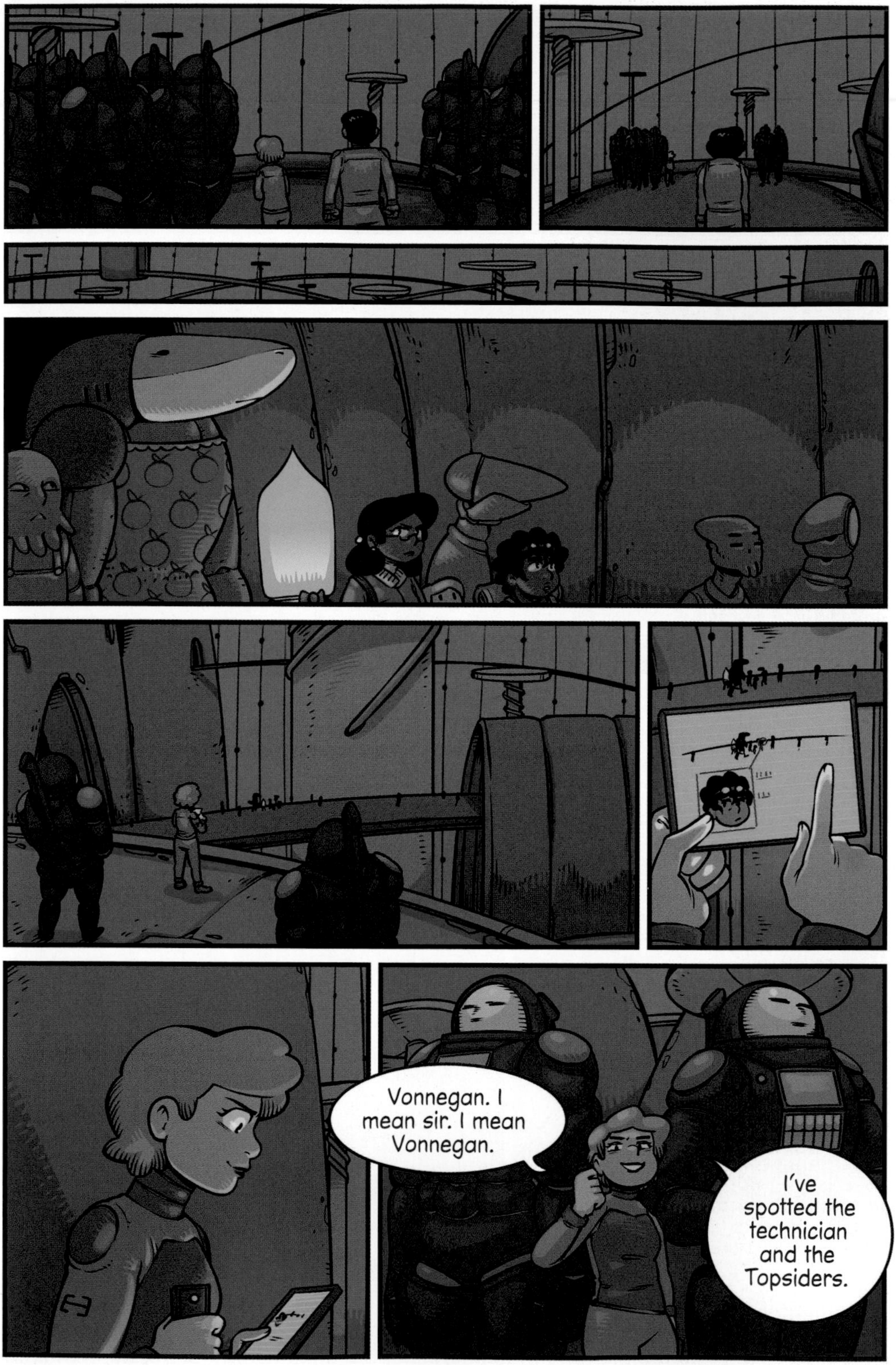
Vonnegan. I mean sir. I mean Vonnegan.
I've spotted the technician and the Topsiders.

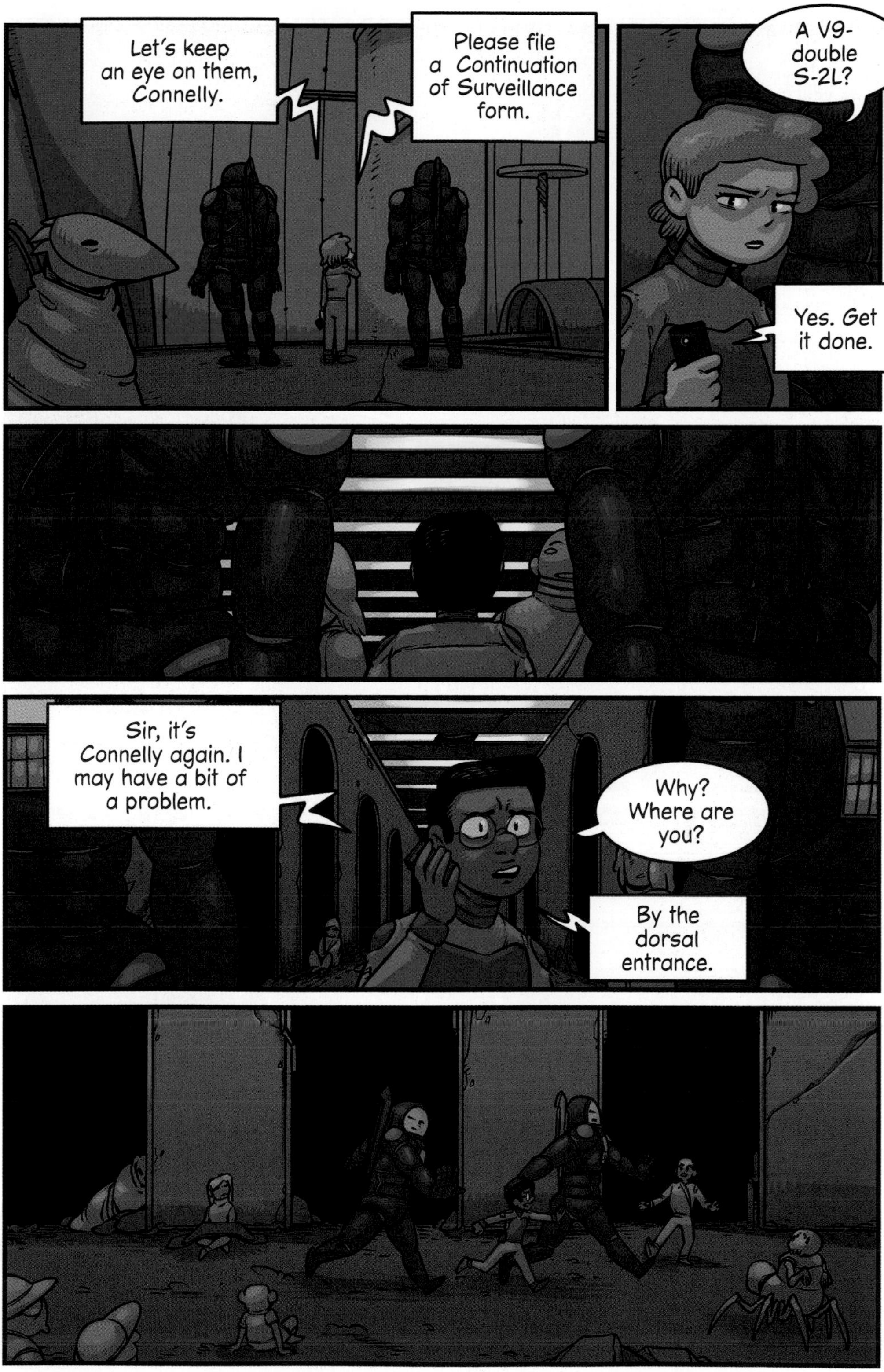
Let's keep an eye on them, Connelly.
Please file a Continuation of Surveillance form.
A V9-double S-2L?
Yes. Get it done.
Sir, it's Connelly again. I may have a bit of a problem.
Why? Where are you?
By the dorsal entrance.

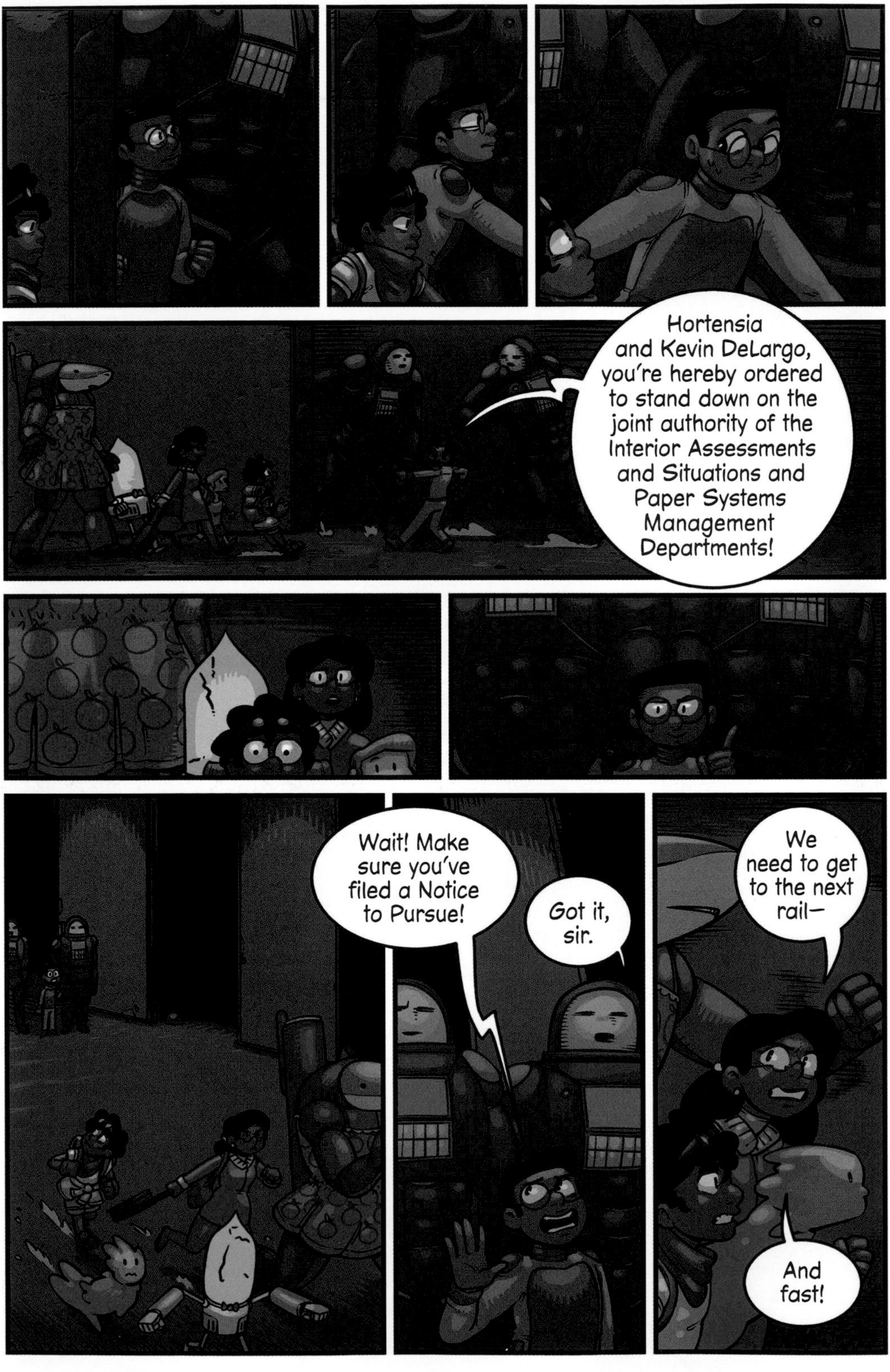
Hortensia and Kevin DeLargo, you're hereby ordered to stand down on the joint authority of the Interior Assessments and Situations and Paper Systems Management Departments!
Wait! Make sure you've filed a Notice to Pursue!
Got it, sir.
We need to get to the next rail—
And fast!

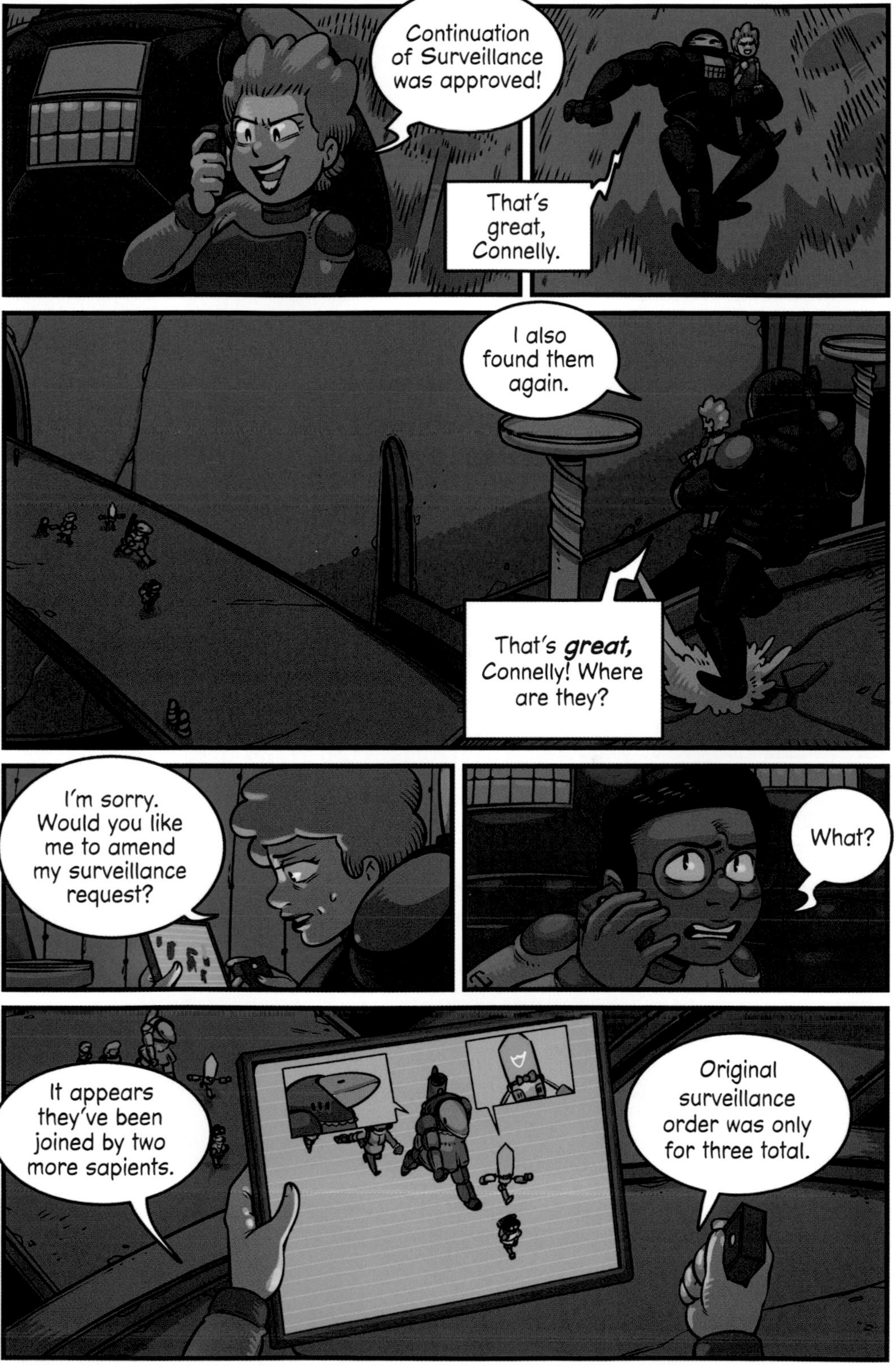

Continuation of Surveillance was approved!
That's great, Connelly.
I also found them again.
That's **great,** Connelly! Where are they?
I'm sorry. Would you like me to amend my surveillance request?
What?
It appears they've been joined by two more sapients.
Original surveillance order was only for three total.

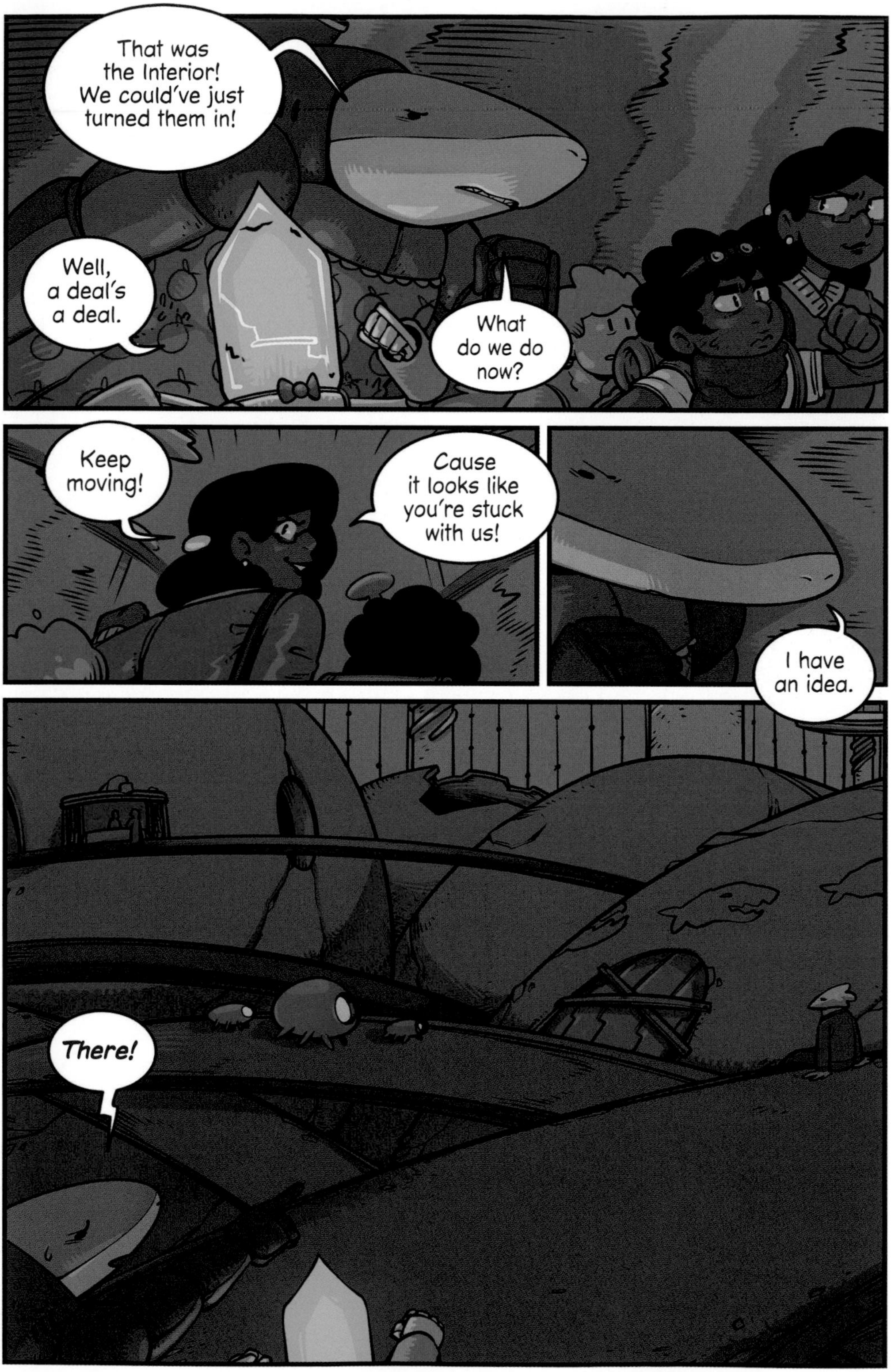
That was the Interior! We could've just turned them in!
Well, a deal's a deal.
What do we do now?
Keep moving!
Cause it looks like you're stuck with us!
I have an idea.
There!

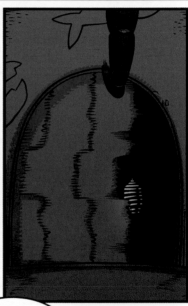

My amendment was approved, but I lost 'em.

Your attention to protocol is . . . duly noted. And don't worry.

I think I know where they're going.

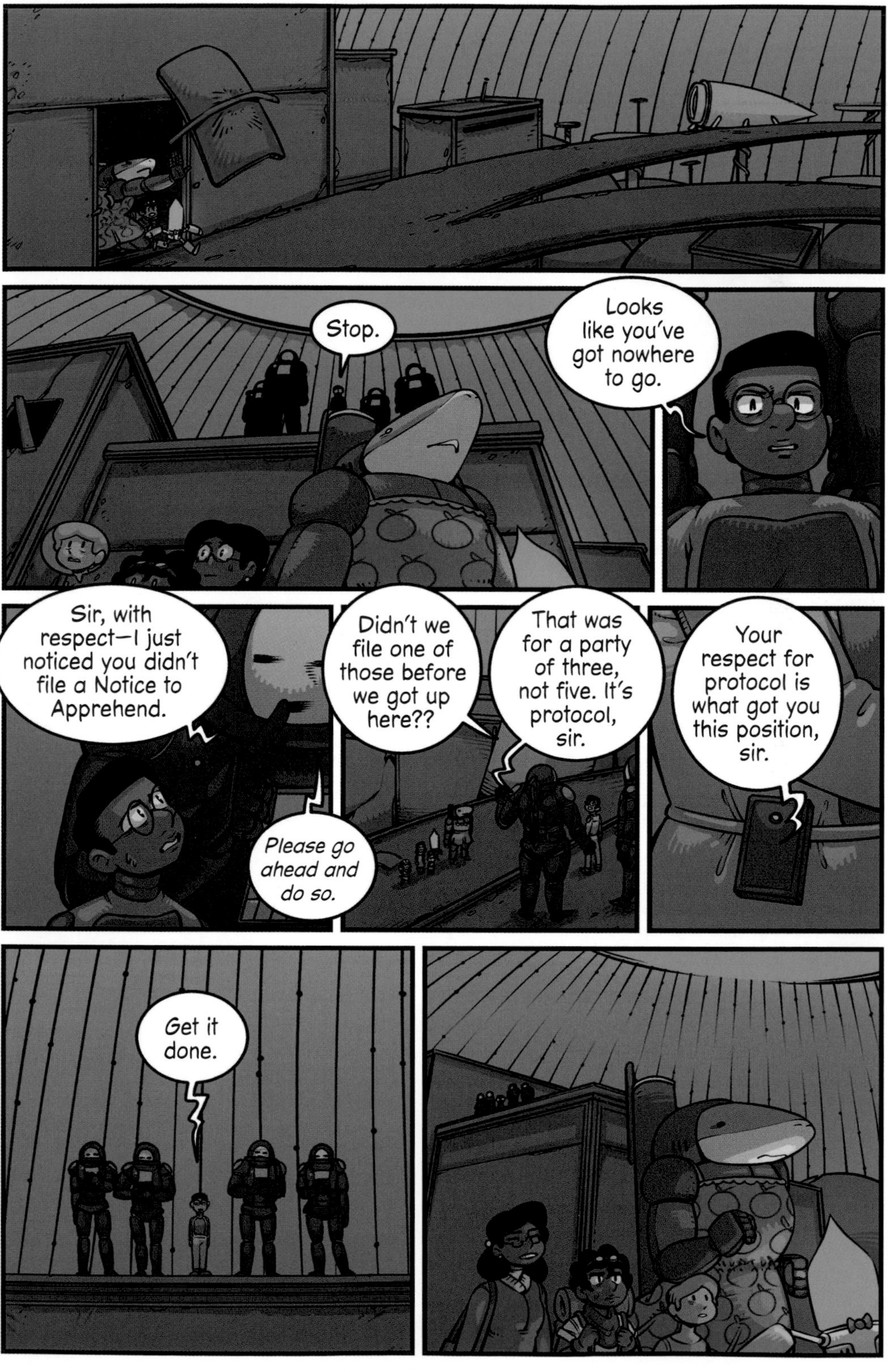
Stop.
Looks like you've got nowhere to go.
Sir, with respect—I just noticed you didn't file a Notice to Apprehend.
Please go ahead and do so.
Didn't we file one of those before we got up here??
That was for a party of three, not five. It's protocol, sir.
Your respect for protocol is what got you this position, sir.
Get it done.

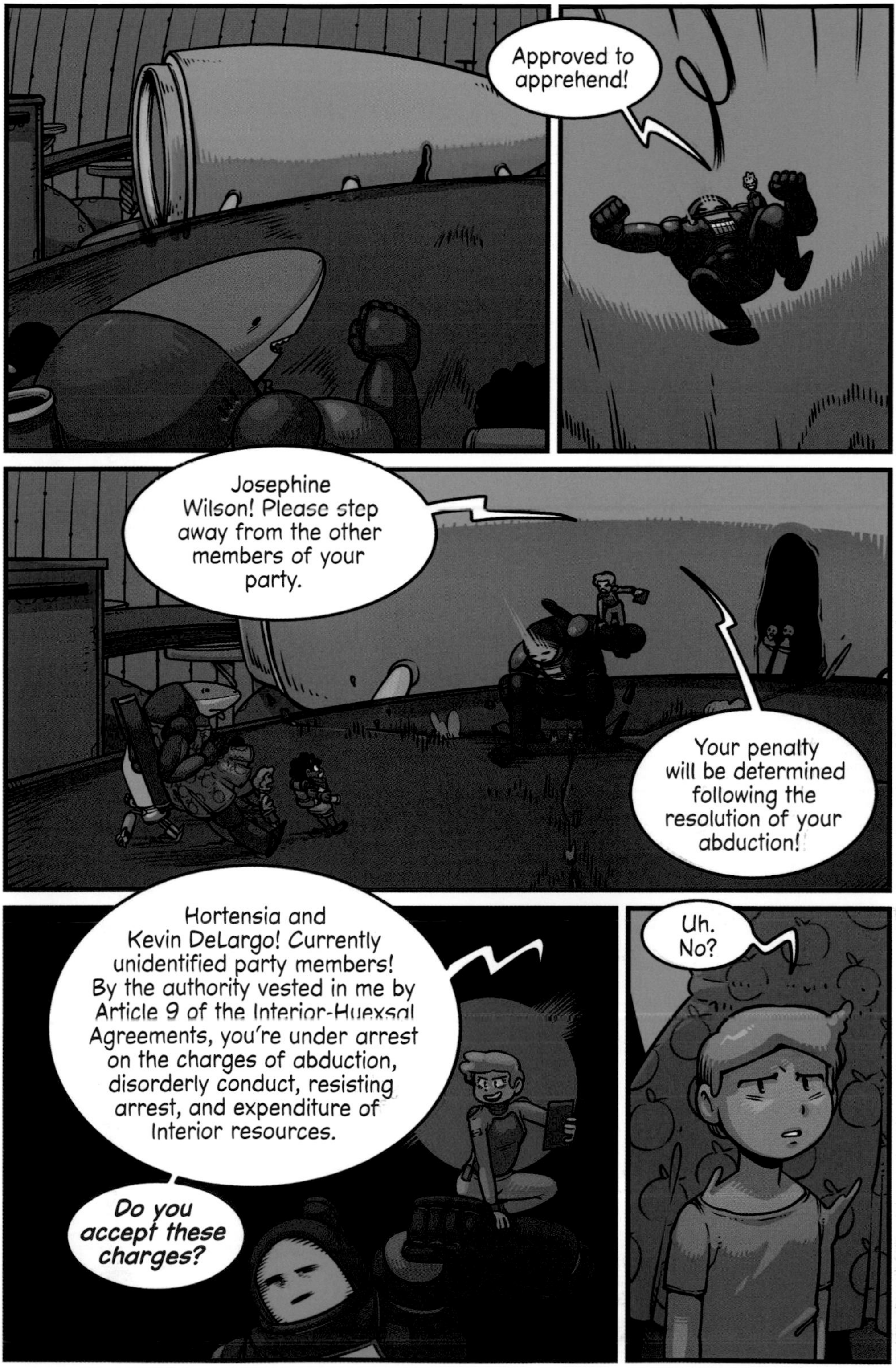
Approved to apprehend!
Josephine Wilson! Please step away from the other members of your party.
Your penalty will be determined following the resolution of your abduction!
Hortensia and Kevin DeLargo! Currently unidentified party members! By the authority vested in me by Article 9 of the Interior-Huexsal Agreements, you're under arrest on the charges of abduction, disorderly conduct, resisting arrest, and expenditure of Interior resources.
Do you accept these charges?
Uh. No?

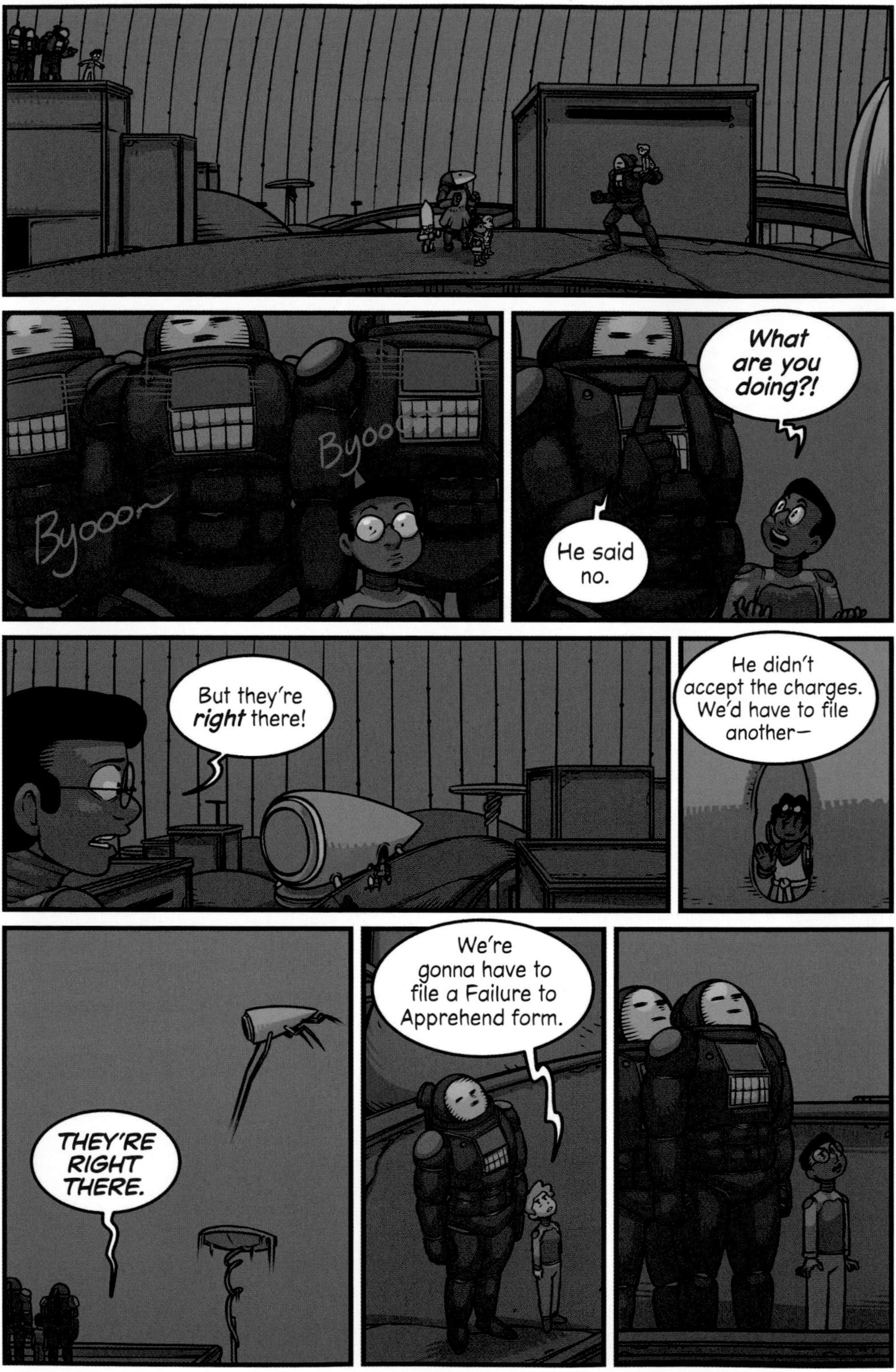
Byooon
Byooo
He said no.
What are you doing?!
But they're ***right*** there!
He didn't accept the charges. We'd have to file another—
THEY'RE RIGHT THERE.
We're gonna have to file a Failure to Apprehend form.

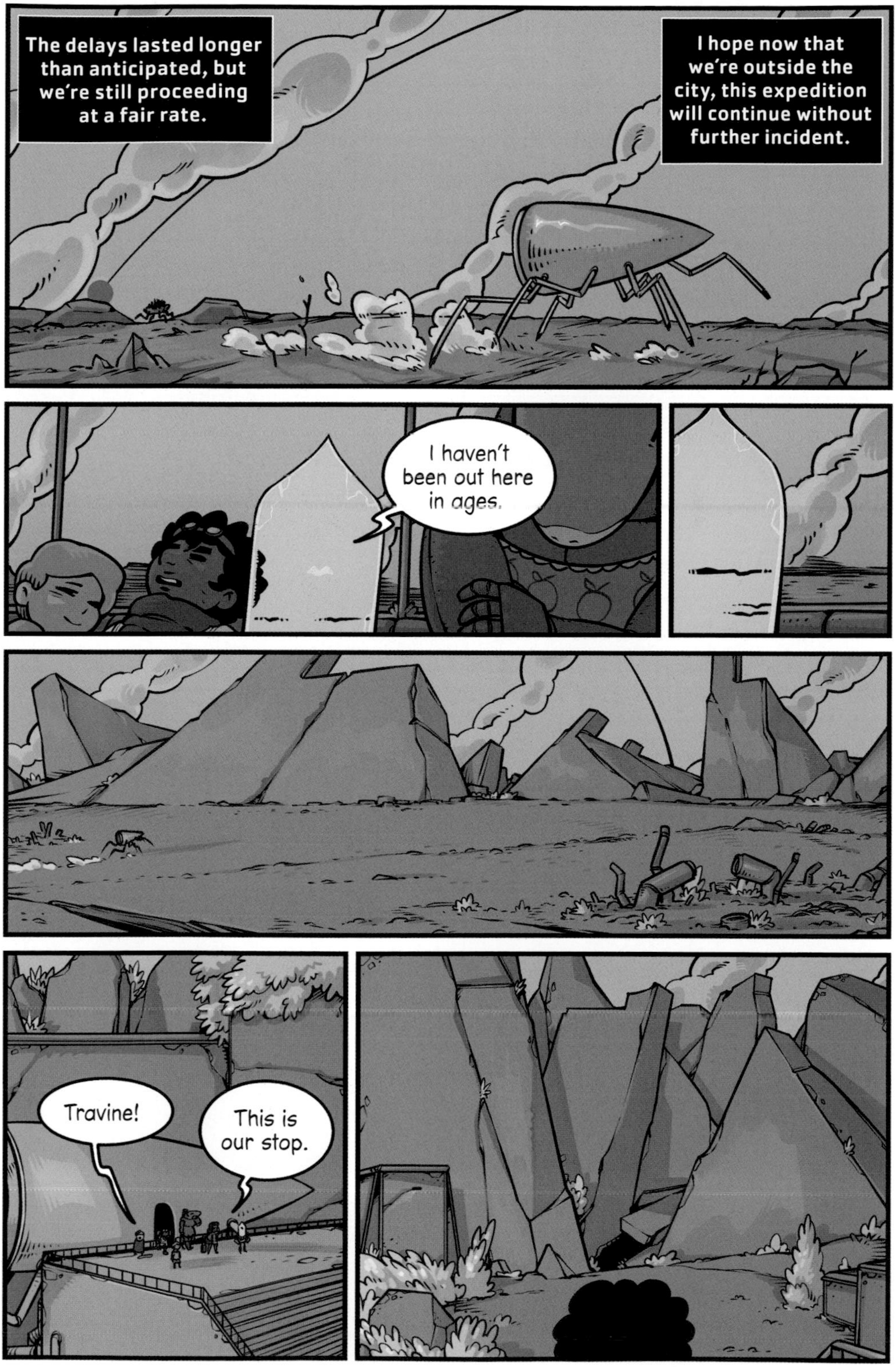
The delays lasted longer than anticipated, but we're still proceeding at a fair rate.
I hope now that we're outside the city, this expedition will continue without further incident.
I haven't been out here in ages.
Travine!
This is our stop.

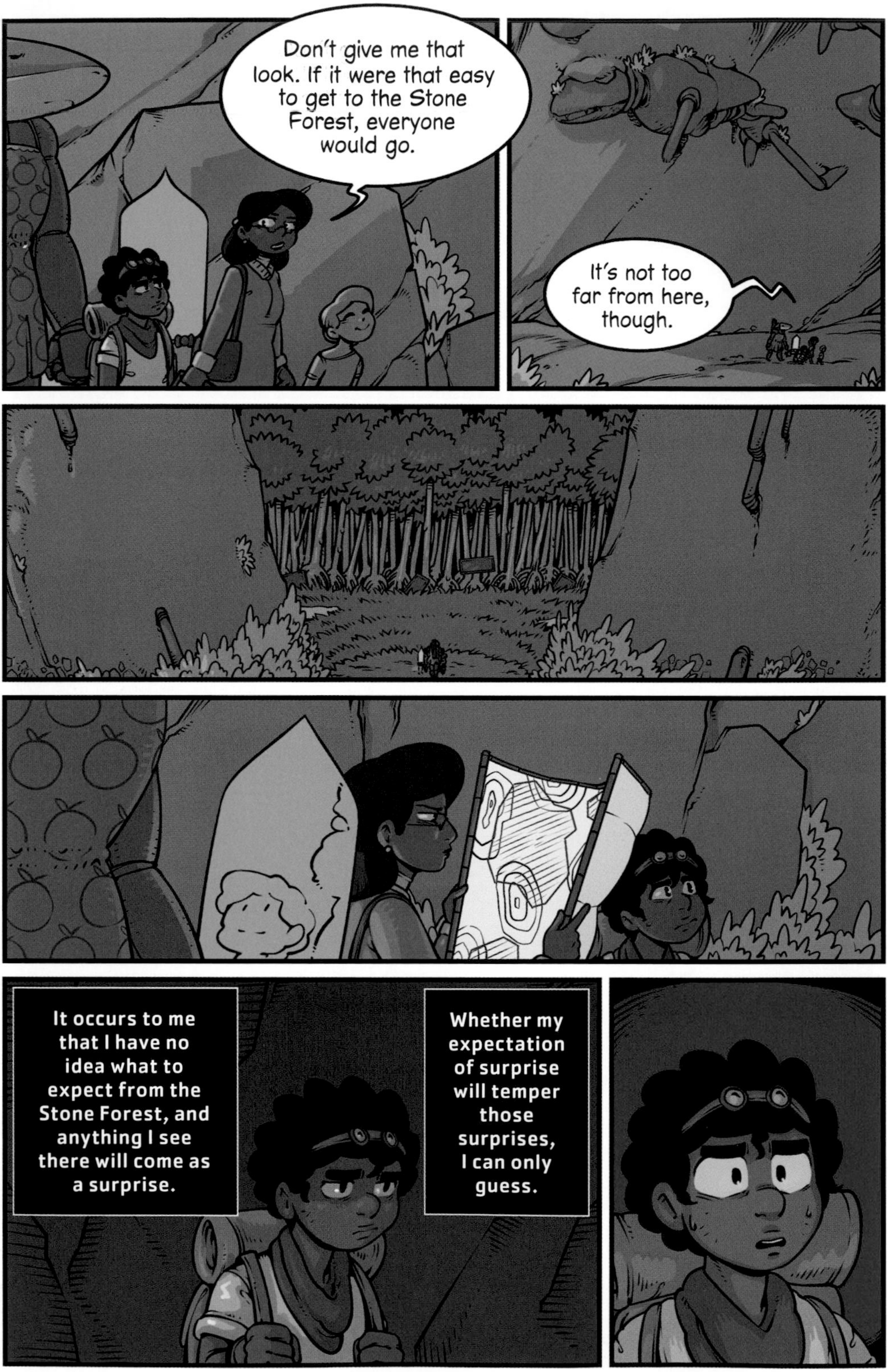
Don't give me that look. If it were that easy to get to the Stone Forest, everyone would go.
It's not too far from here, though.
It occurs to me that I have no idea what to expect from the Stone Forest, and anything I see there will come as a surprise.
Whether my expectation of surprise will temper those surprises, I can only guess.

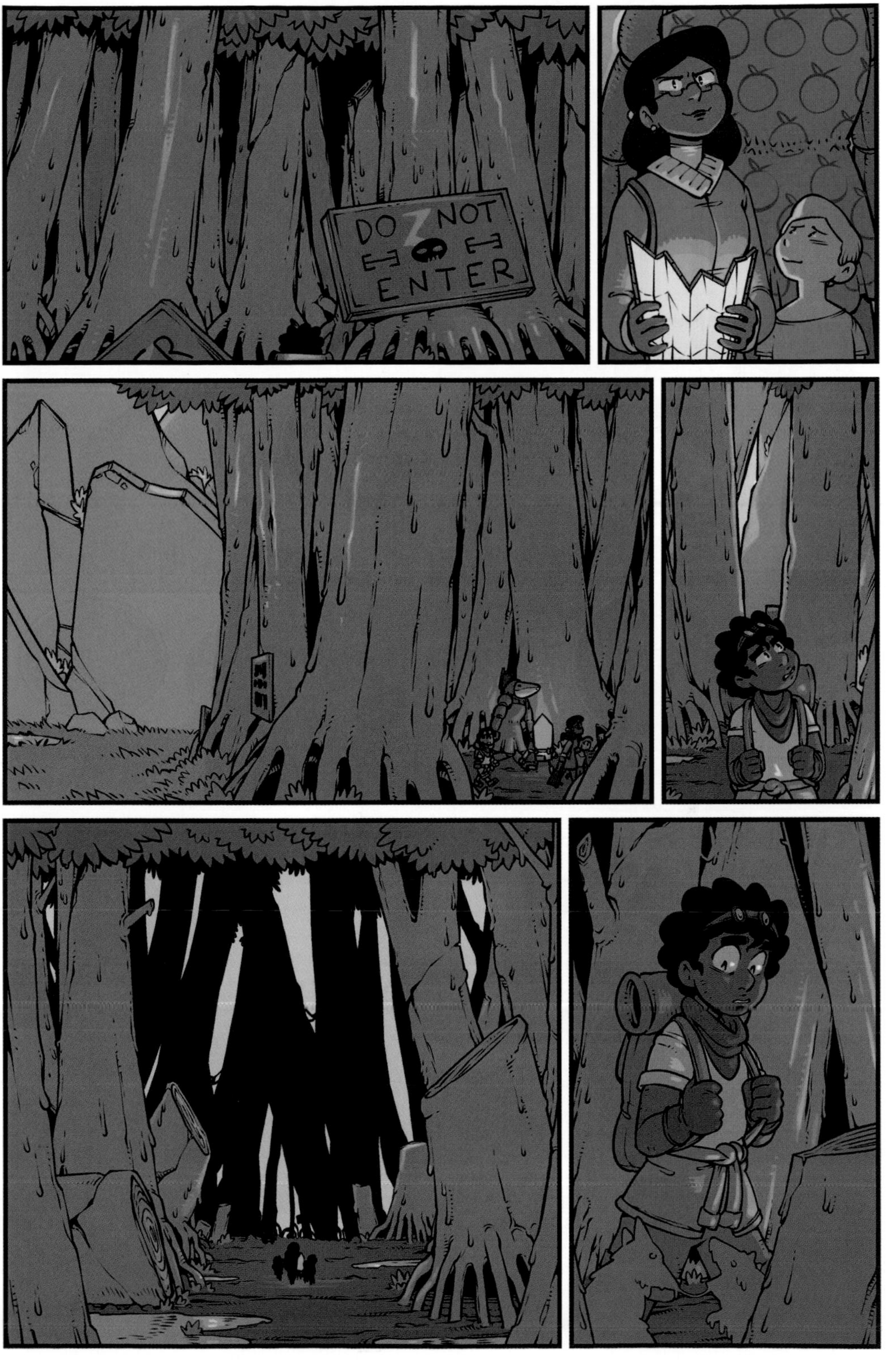
DO NOT ENTER

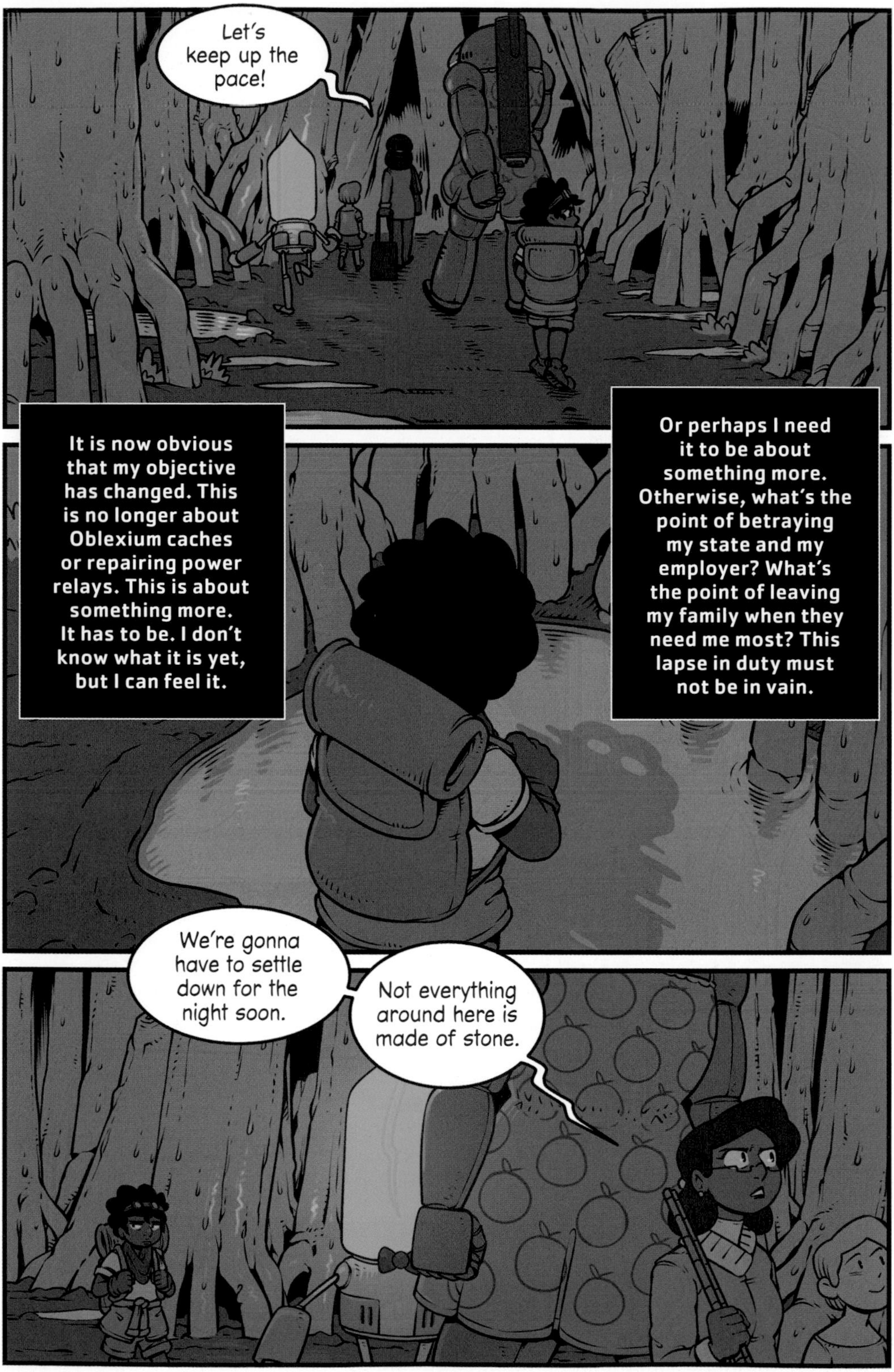
Let's keep up the pace!
It is now obvious that my objective has changed. This is no longer about Oblexium caches or repairing power relays. This is about something more. It has to be. I don't know what it is yet, but I can feel it.
Or perhaps I need it to be about something more. Otherwise, what's the point of betraying my state and my employer? What's the point of leaving my family when they need me most? This lapse in duty must not be in vain.
We're gonna have to settle down for the night soon.
Not everything around here is made of stone.

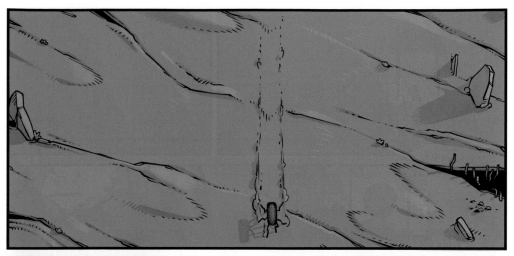

Two worlds that should never meet.

Huh?

Oh. My dad always said that desk and field are two worlds that should never meet.

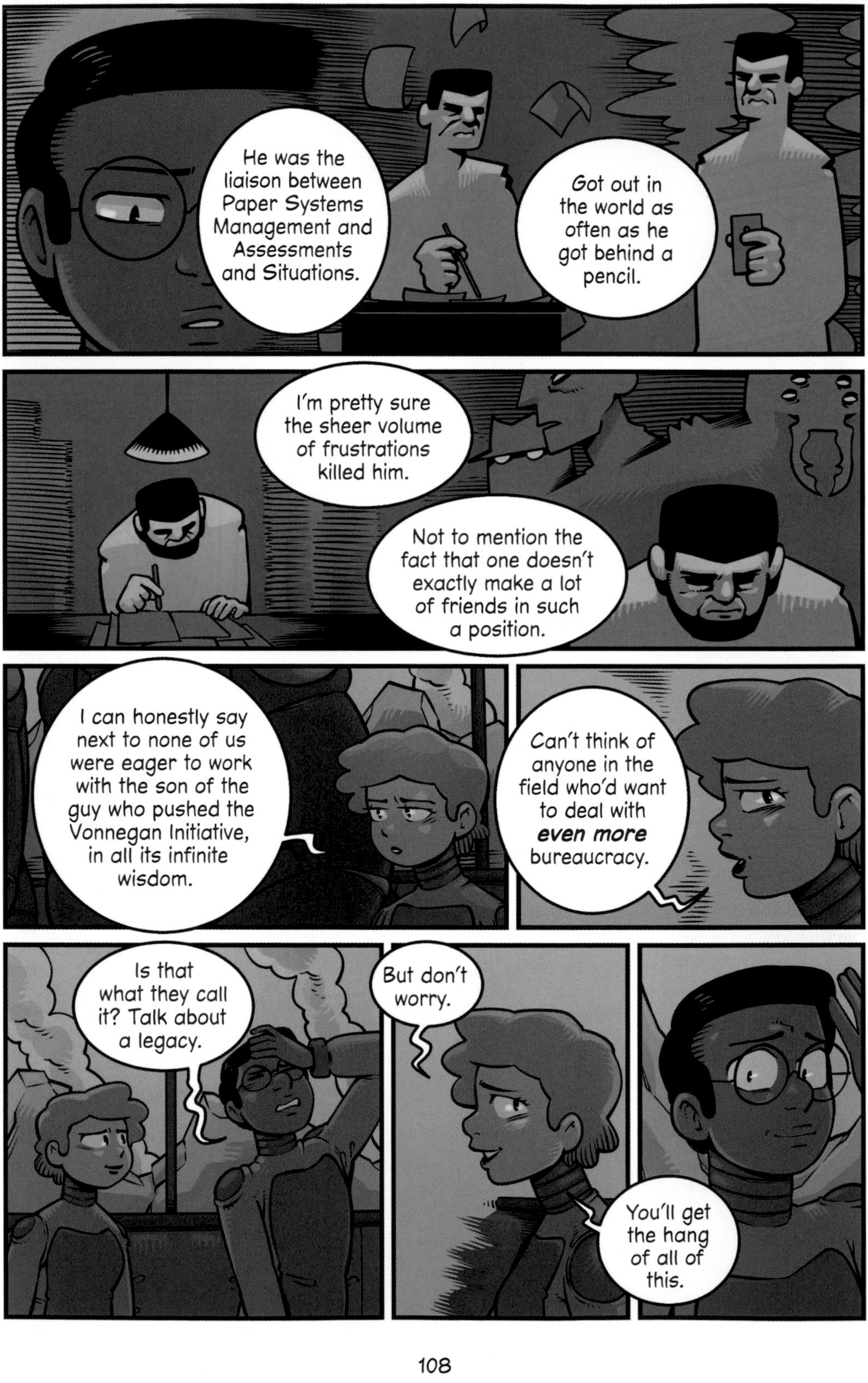
He was the liaison between Paper Systems Management and Assessments and Situations.
Got out in the world as often as he got behind a pencil.
I'm pretty sure the sheer volume of frustrations killed him.
Not to mention the fact that one doesn't exactly make a lot of friends in such a position.
I can honestly say next to none of us were eager to work with the son of the guy who pushed the Vonnegan Initiative, in all its infinite wisdom.
Can't think of anyone in the field who'd want to deal with ***even more*** bureaucracy.
Is that what they call it? Talk about a legacy.
But don't worry.
You'll get the hang of all of this.

I mean, you'd **better.** Somehow Starger thinks you're a master of two worlds.

It would be in your best interest to start acting like one.

You're going to have to file a requisition for irreverent insubordination if you want to continue this vein of conversation, Connelly.

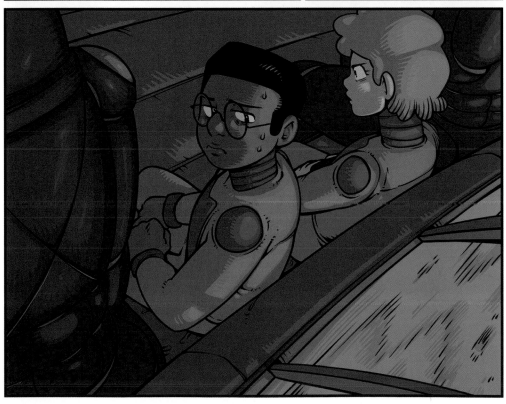

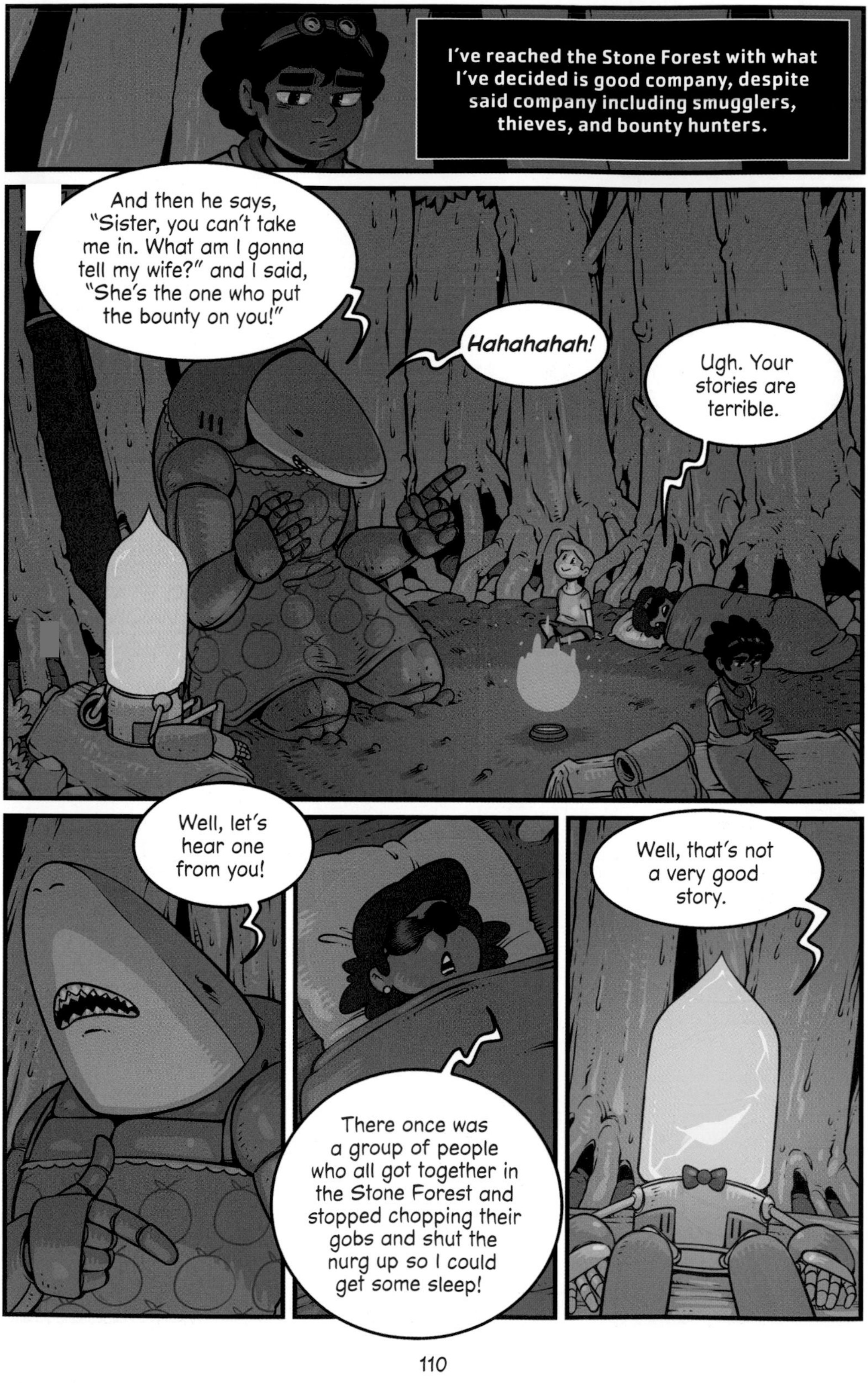
I've reached the Stone Forest with what I've decided is good company, despite said company including smugglers, thieves, and bounty hunters.
And then he says, "Sister, you can't take me in. What am I gonna tell my wife?" and I said, "She's the one who put the bounty on you!"
Hahahahah!
Ugh. Your stories are terrible.
Well, let's hear one from you!
There once was a group of people who all got together in the Stone Forest and stopped chopping their gobs and shut the nurg up so I could get some sleep!
Well, that's not a very good story.

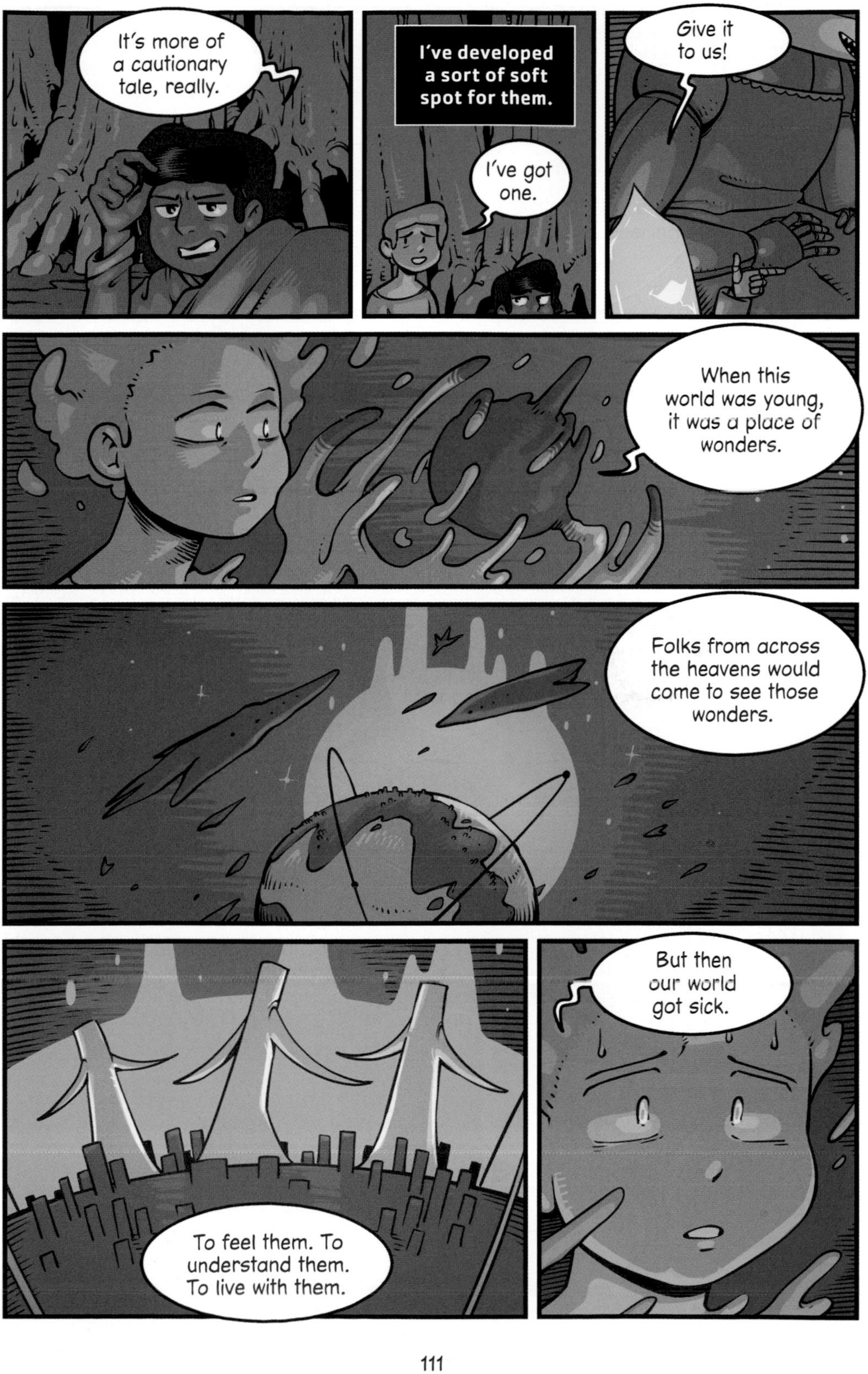
It's more of a cautionary tale, really.
I've developed a sort of soft spot for them.
I've got one.
Give it to us!
When this world was young, it was a place of wonders.
Folks from across the heavens would come to see those wonders.
To feel them. To understand them. To live with them.
But then our world got sick.

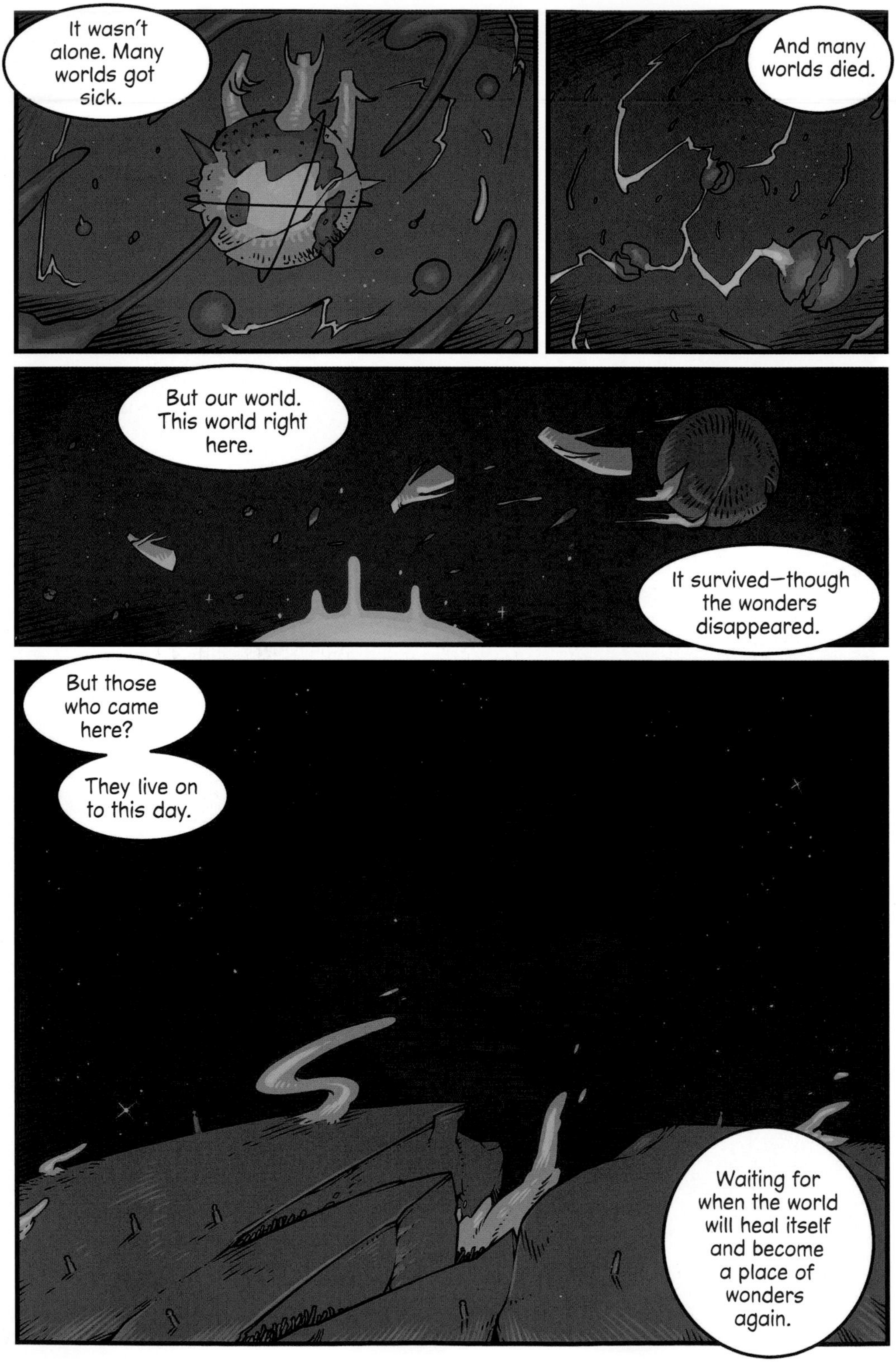
It wasn't alone. Many worlds got sick.
And many worlds died.
But our world. This world right here.
It survived—though the wonders disappeared.
But those who came here?
They live on to this day.
Waiting for when the world will heal itself and become a place of wonders again.

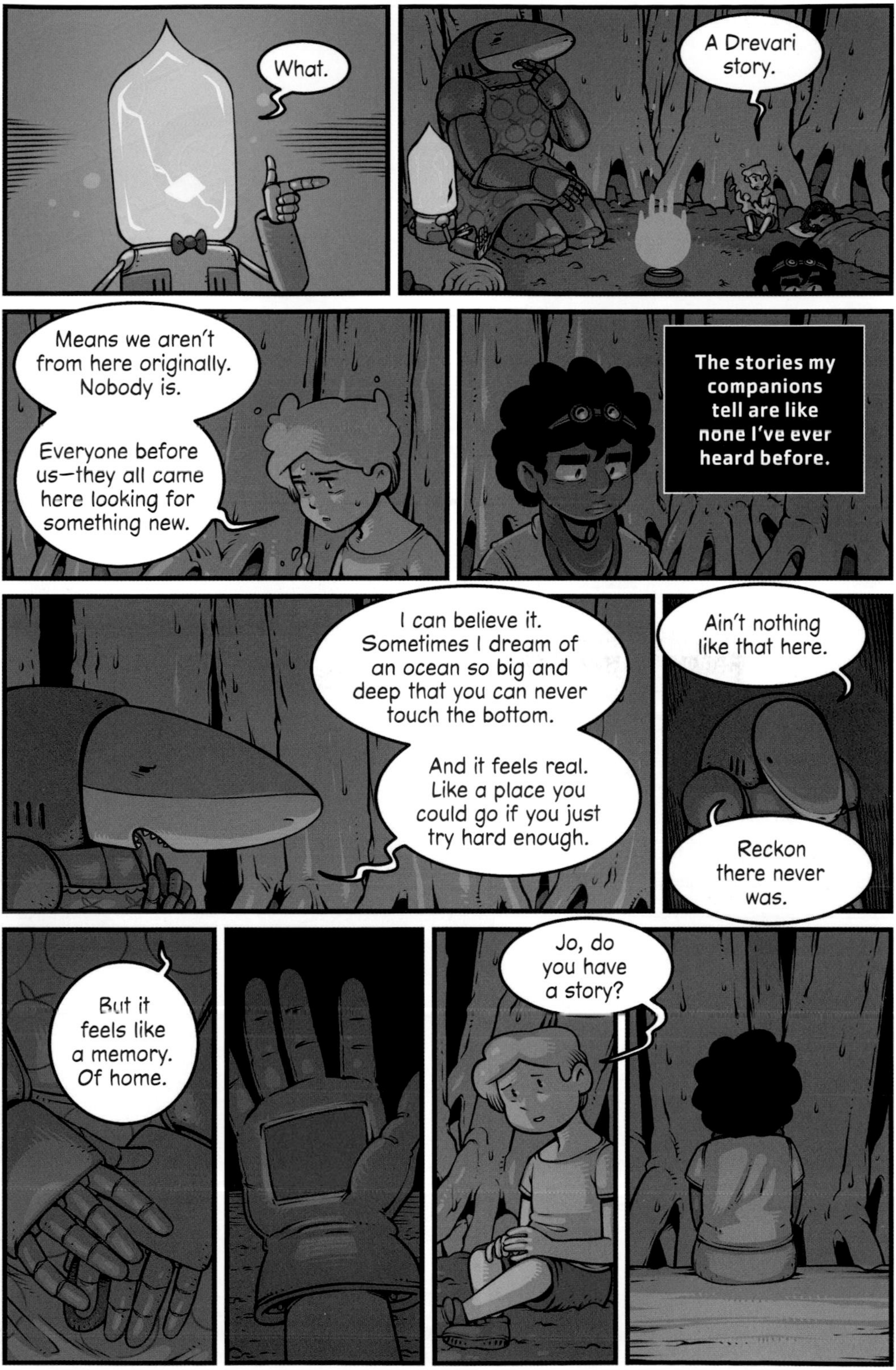
What.
A Drevari story.
Means we aren't from here originally. Nobody is.
Everyone before us—they all came here looking for something new.
The stories my companions tell are like none I've ever heard before.
I can believe it. Sometimes I dream of an ocean so big and deep that you can never touch the bottom.
And it feels real. Like a place you could go if you just try hard enough.
Ain't nothing like that here.
Reckon there never was.
But it feels like a memory. Of home.
Jo, do you have a story?

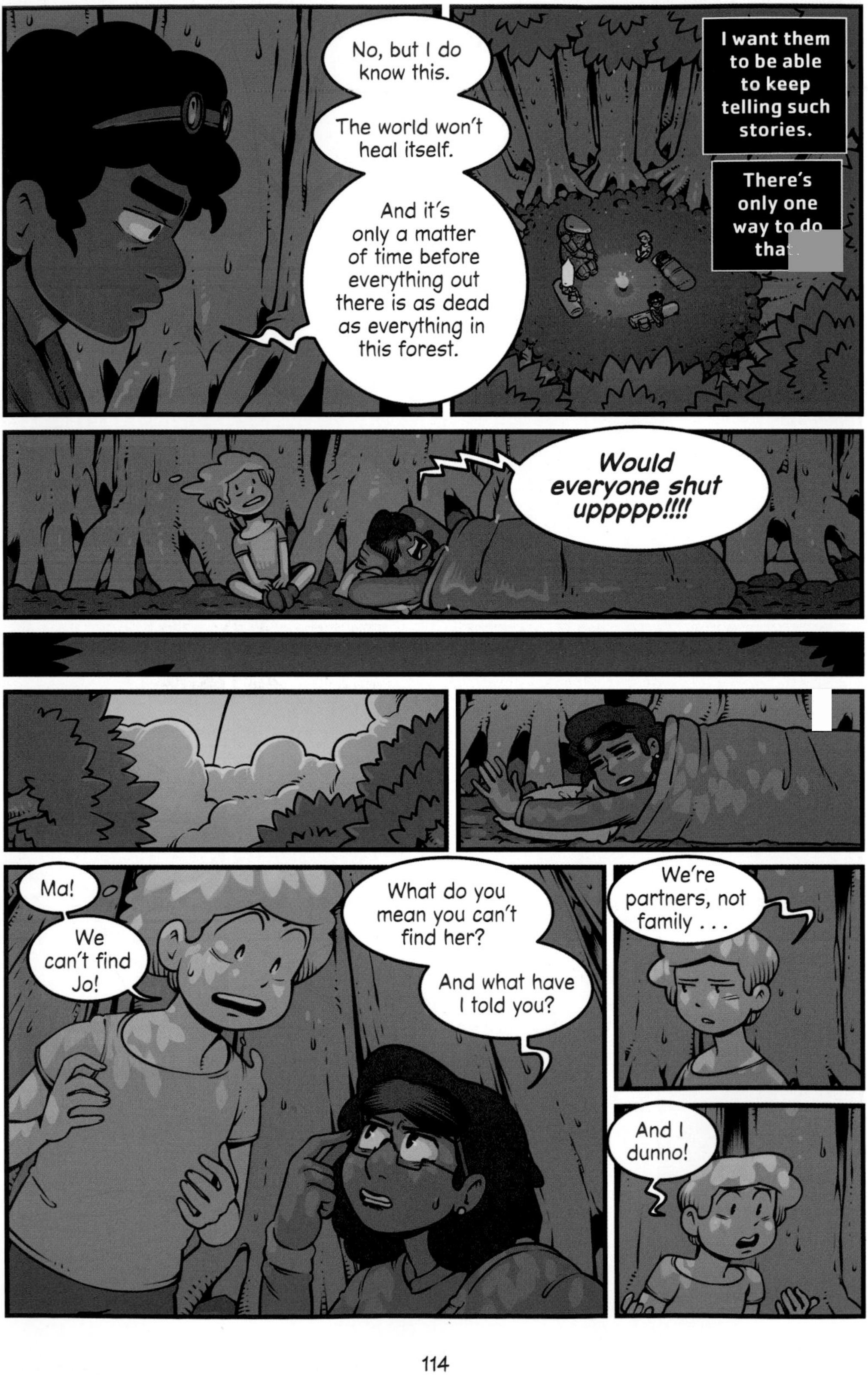
No, but I do know this.
The world won't heal itself.
And it's only a matter of time before everything out there is as dead as everything in this forest.
I want them to be able to keep telling such stories.
There's only one way to do that.
Would everyone shut uppppp!!!!
Ma!
We can't find Jo!
What do you mean you can't find her?
And what have I told you?
We're partners, not family . . .
And I dunno!

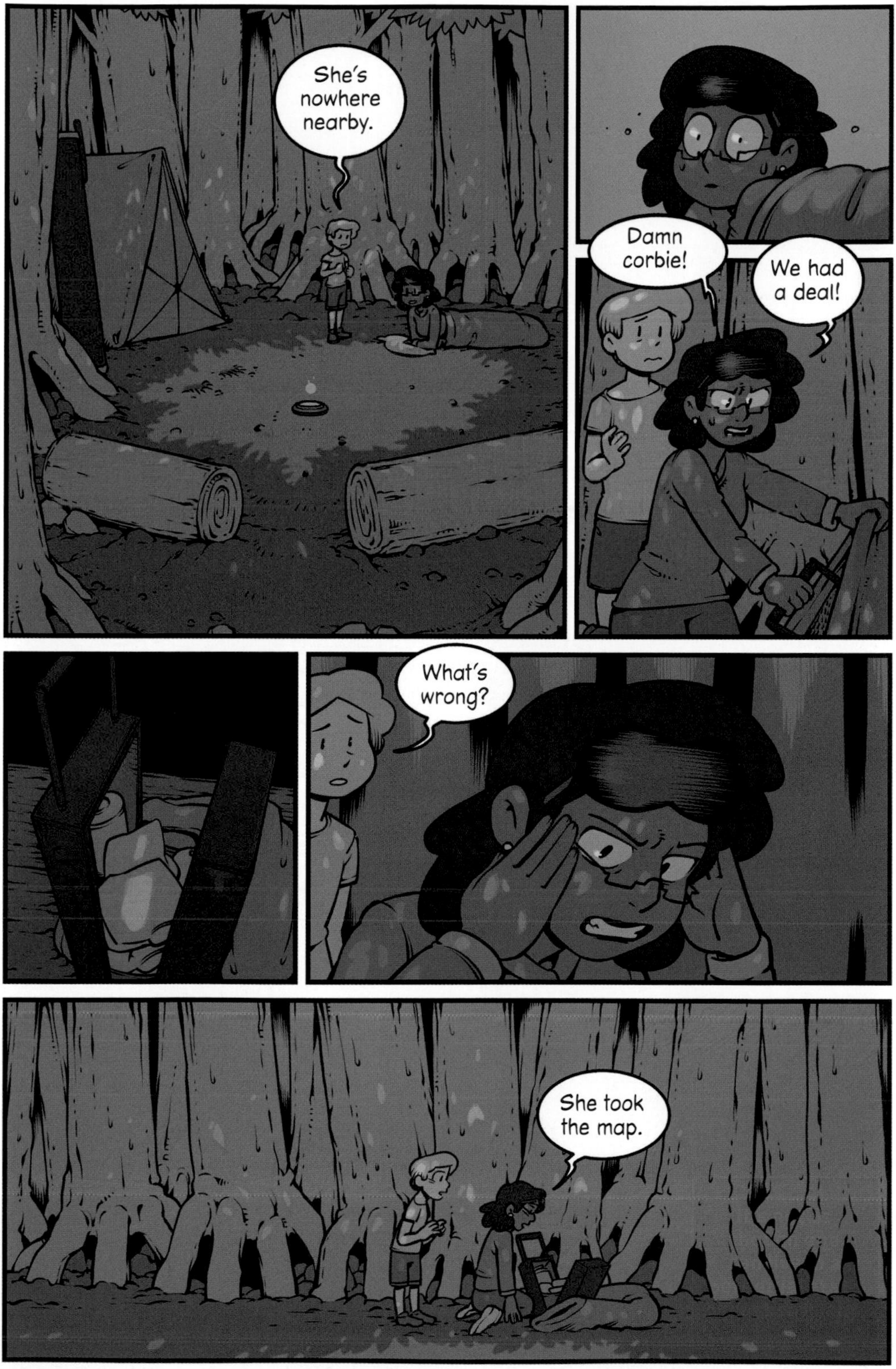
She's nowhere nearby.
Damn corbie!
We had a deal!
What's wrong?
She took the map.

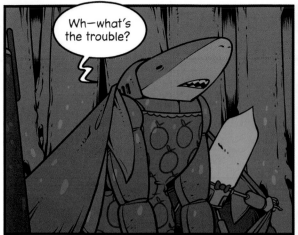

Wh—what's the trouble?

She took the map.

And you don't know where she is?

Does it *seem* like I know?

Hey now, let's all be calm here.

I'd be a lot calmer if I had access to the only reason why we're even here.

Wait a minute.

If she's gone, she can't pay us!

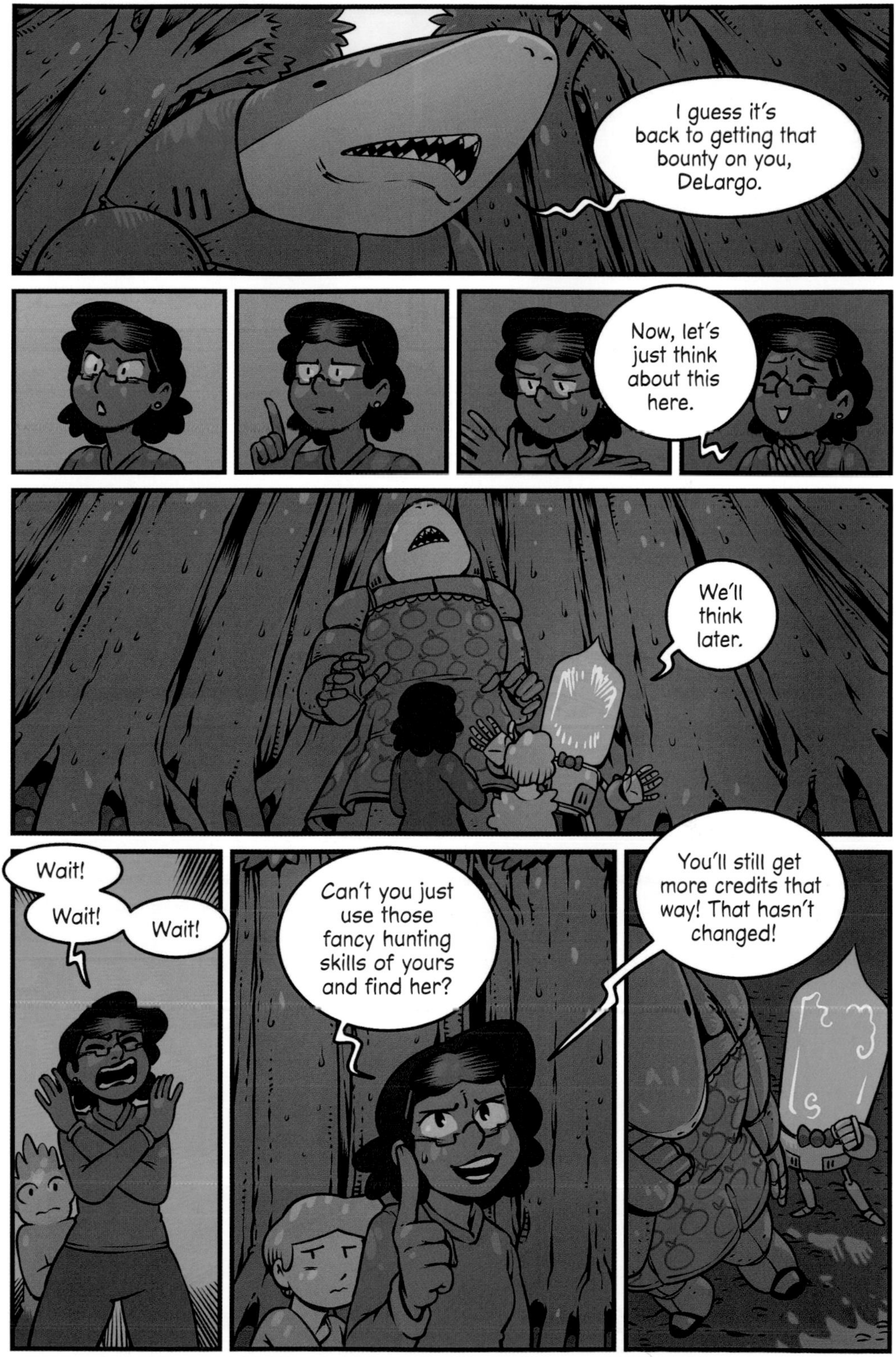
I guess it's back to getting that bounty on you, DeLargo.
Now, let's just think about this here.
We'll think later.
Wait!
Wait!
Wait!
Can't you just use those fancy hunting skills of yours and find her?
You'll still get more credits that way! That hasn't changed!

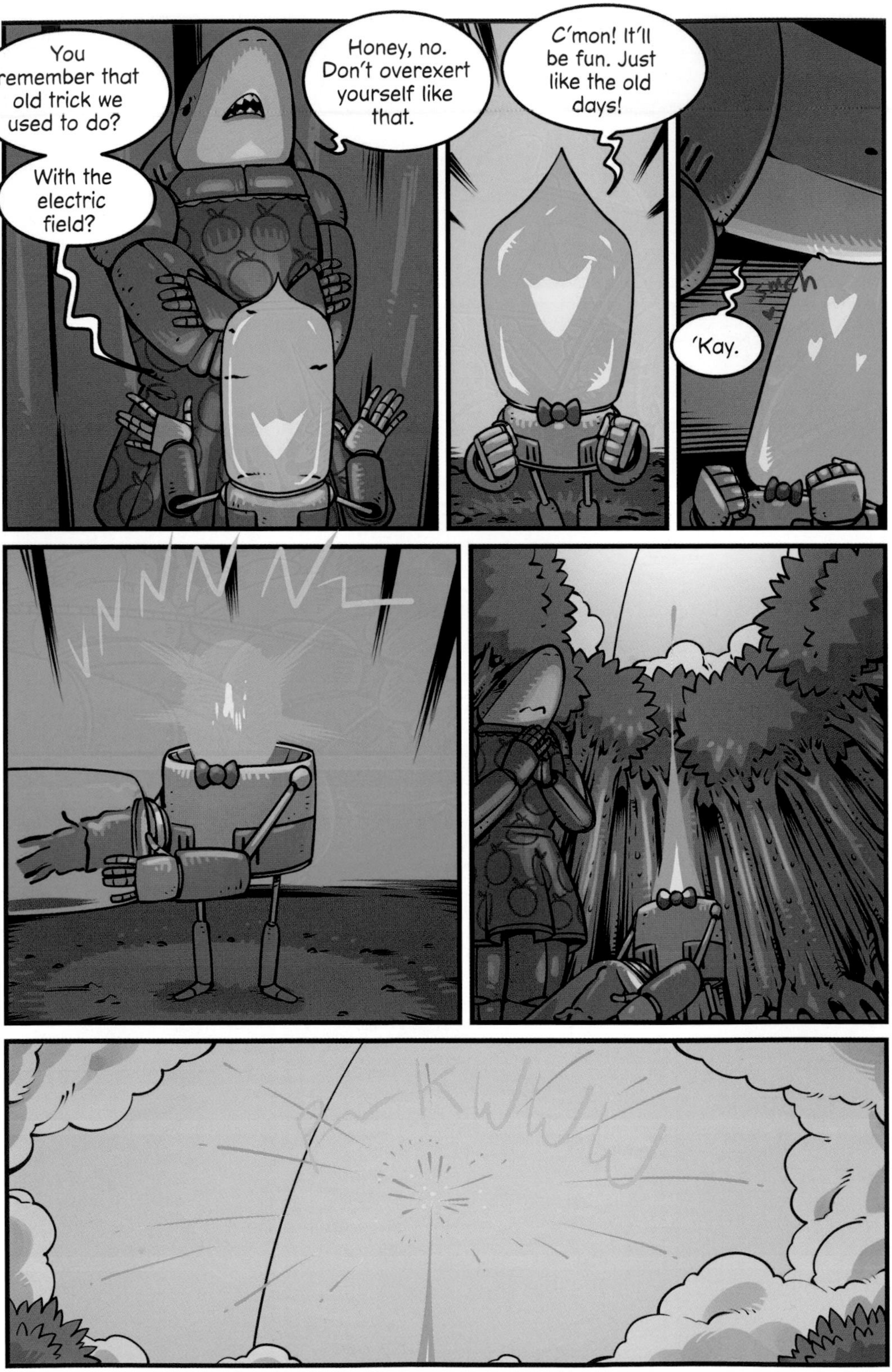
You remember that old trick we used to do?
With the electric field?
Honey, no. Don't overexert yourself like that.
C'mon! It'll be fun. Just like the old days!
smch
'Kay.
VNNN N
KWWW

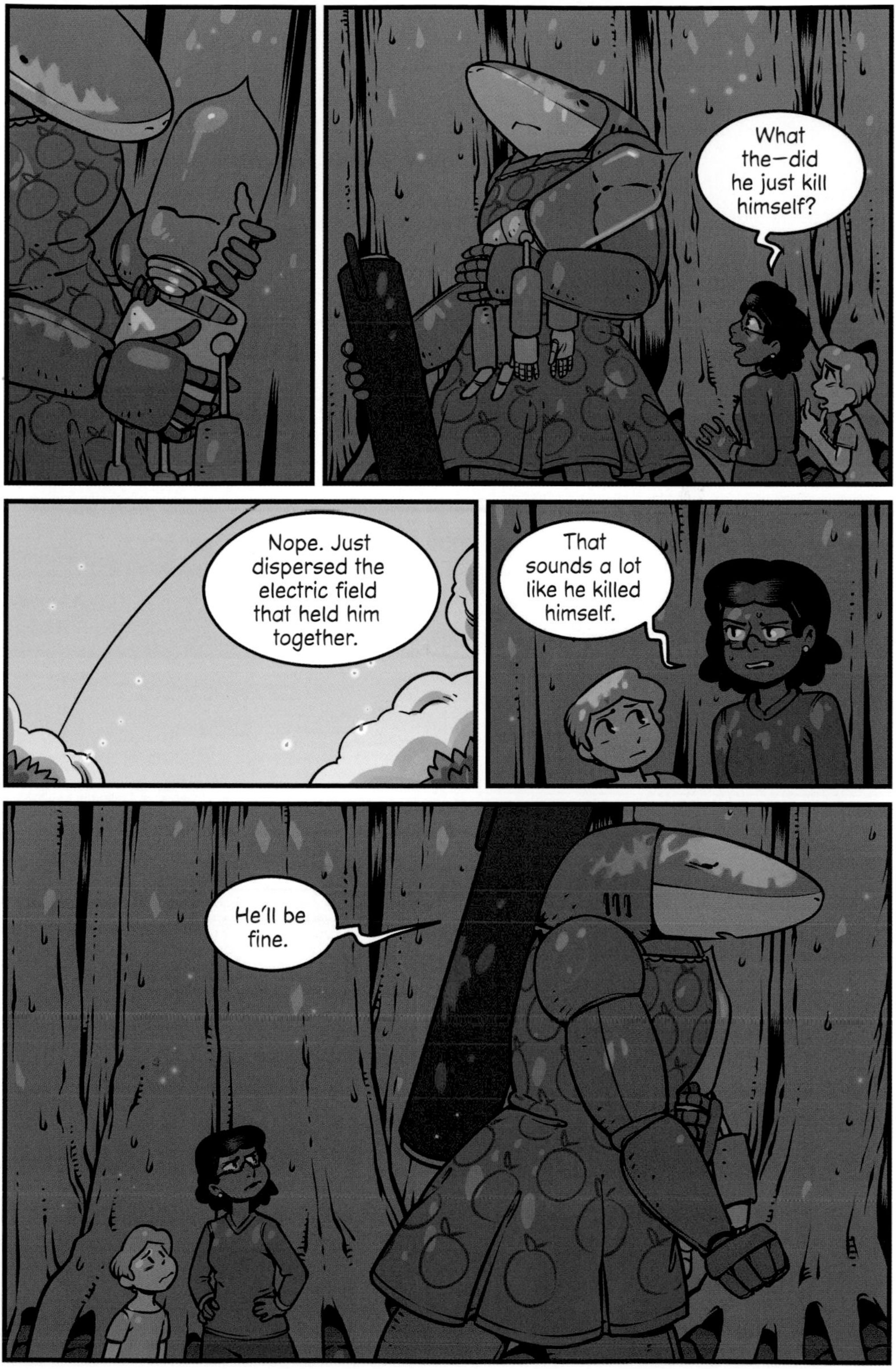
What the—did he just kill himself?
Nope. Just dispersed the electric field that held him together.
That sounds a lot like he killed himself.
He'll be fine.

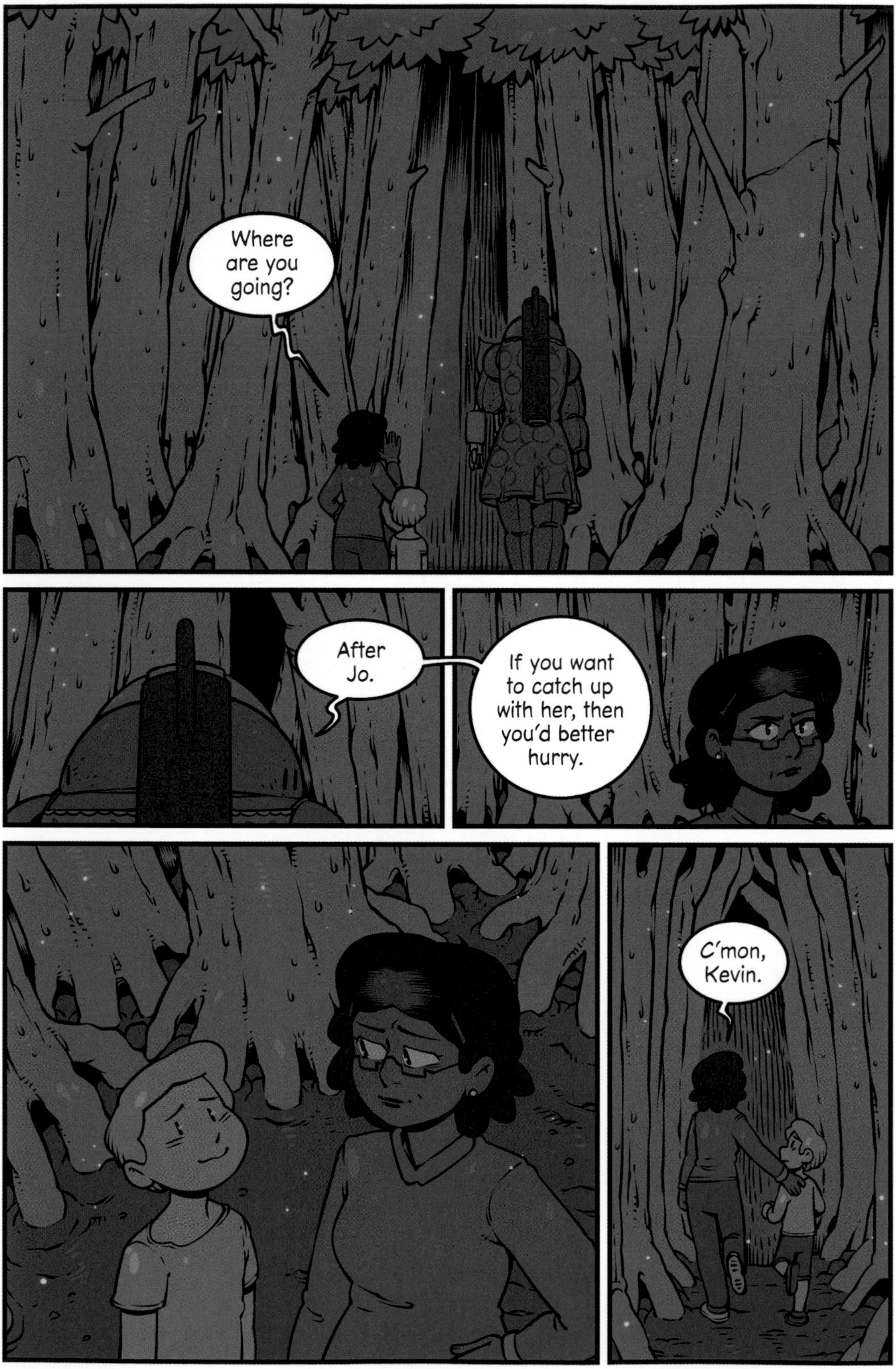
Where are you going?
After Jo.
If you want to catch up with her, then you'd better hurry.
C'mon, Kevin.

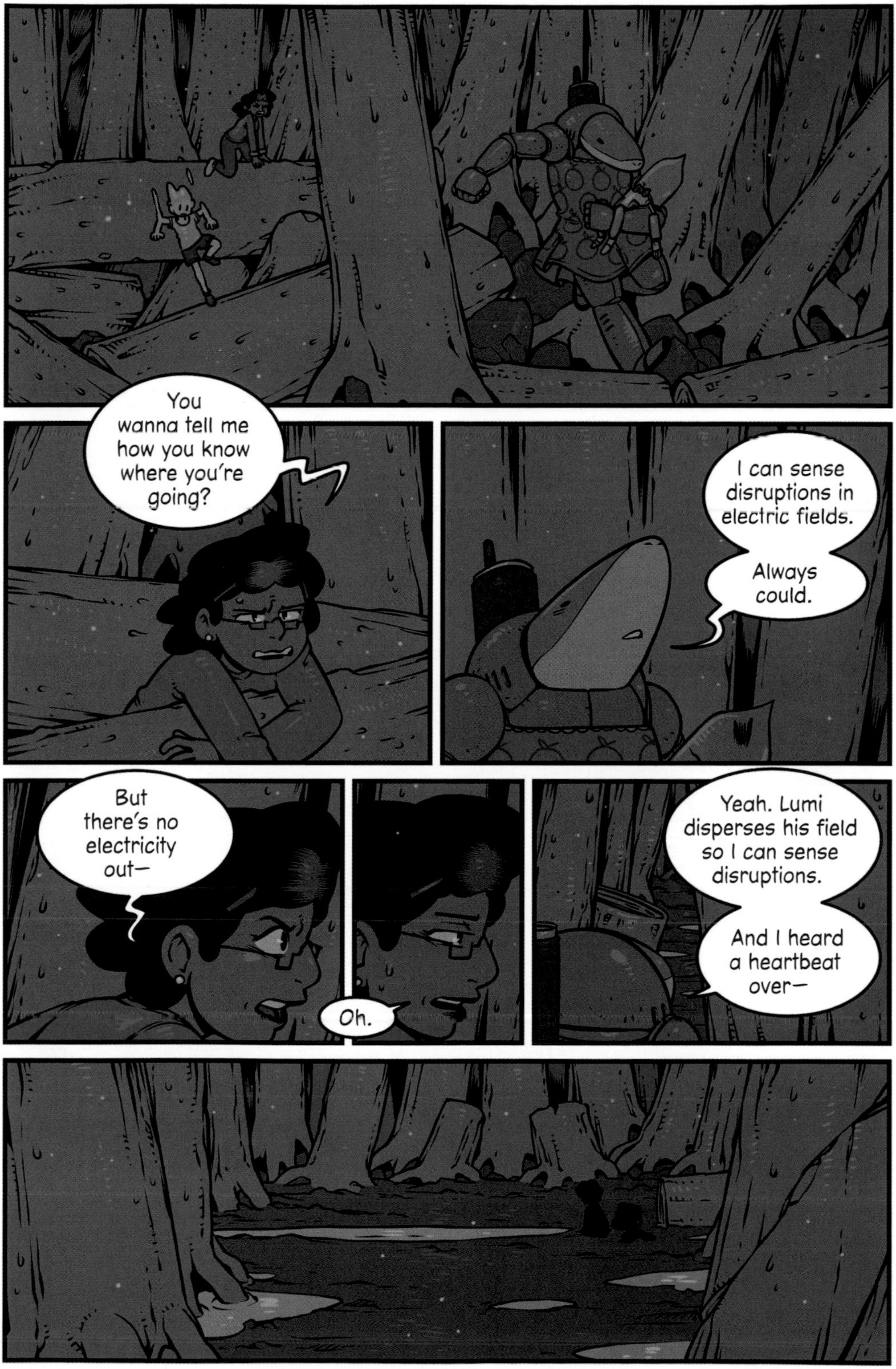
You wanna tell me how you know where you're going?
I can sense disruptions in electric fields.
Always could.
But there's no electricity out—
Oh.
Yeah. Lumi disperses his field so I can sense disruptions.
And I heard a heartbeat over—

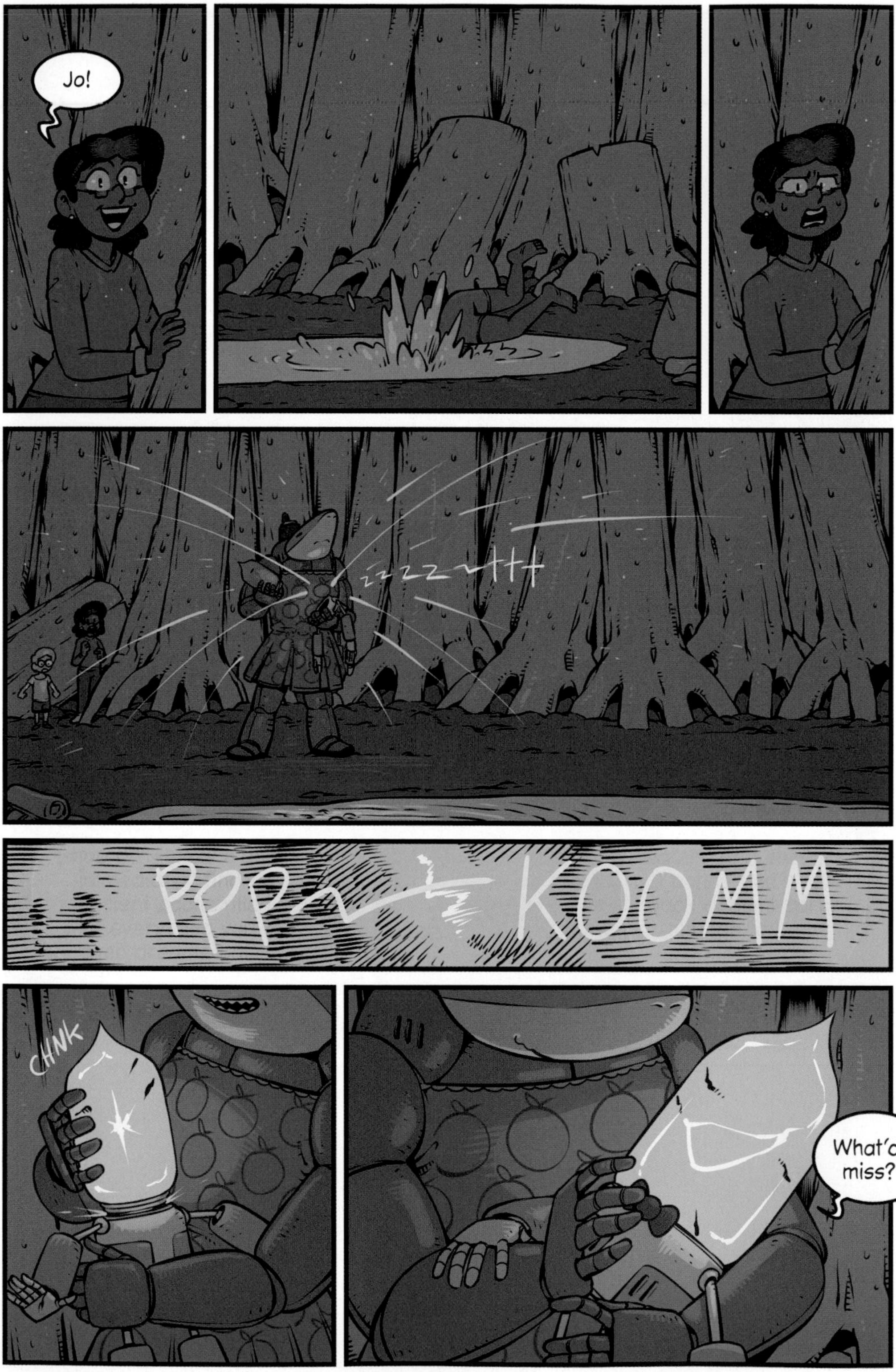
Jo!
zzzzz—ttt
PPPA—KOOMM
CHNK
What'd I miss?

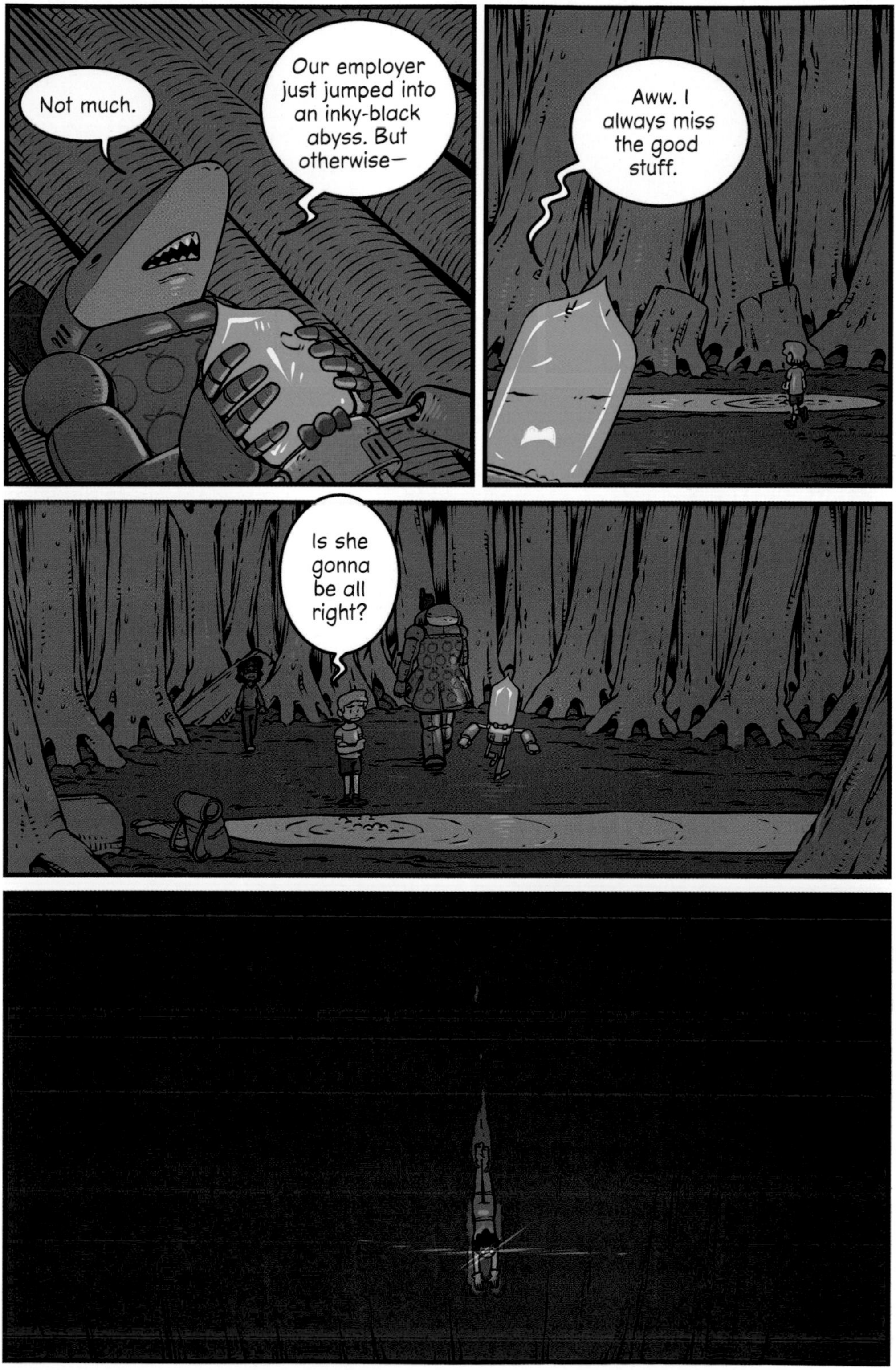
Not much.
Our employer just jumped into an inky-black abyss. But otherwise—
Aww. I always miss the good stuff.
Is she gonna be all right?

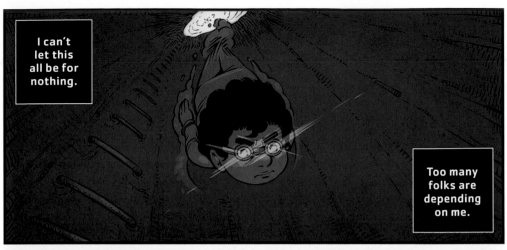

I can't let this all be for nothing.

Too many folks are depending on me.

This is either the way forward—

Or the point of no return.

This is it. What I had hoped for.

It has to be.

I need it to be.

Come on!

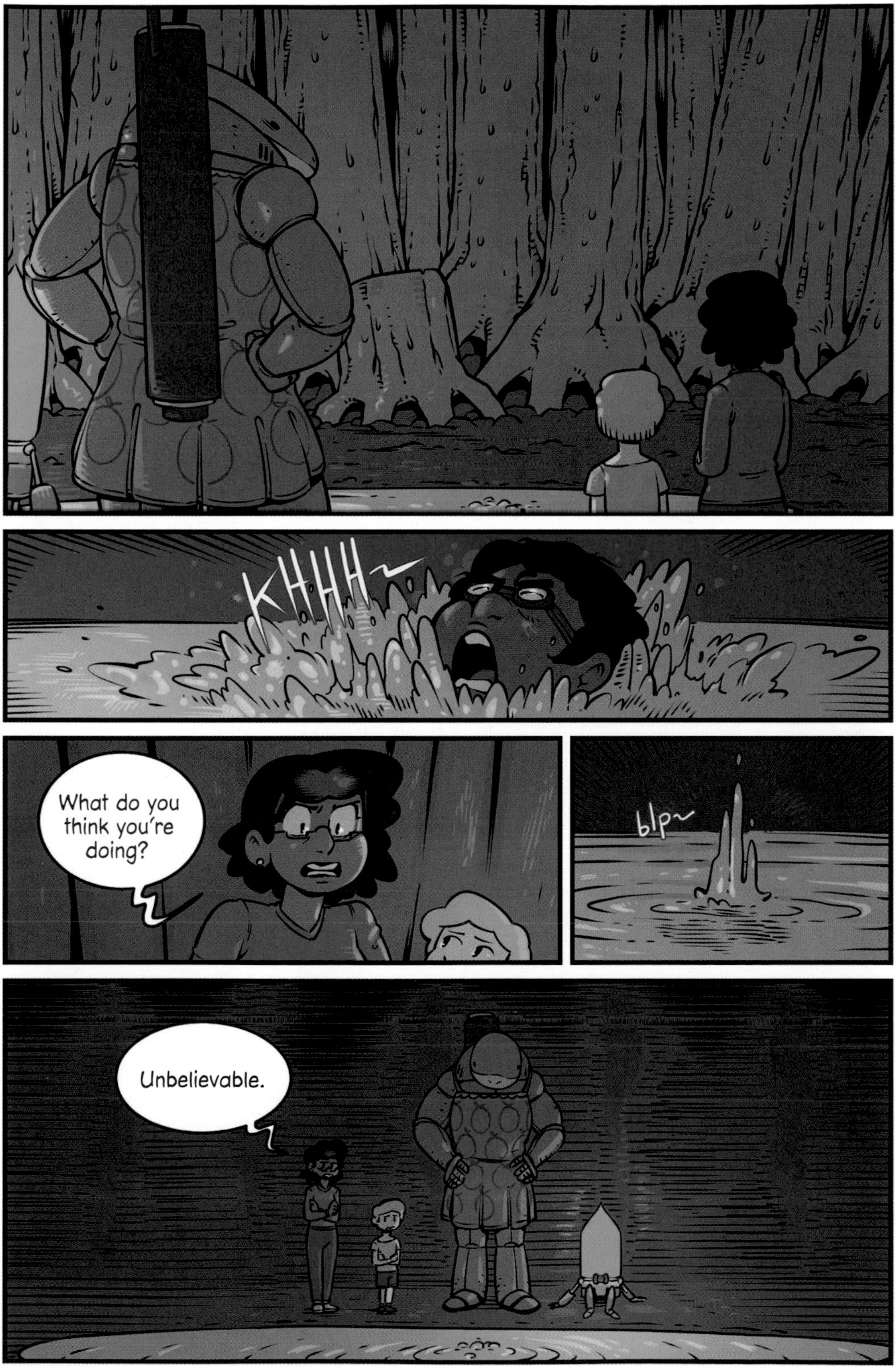
KHHH~
What do you think you're doing?
blp~
Unbelievable.

~VNNN
vt vt vt
~xxxCHK

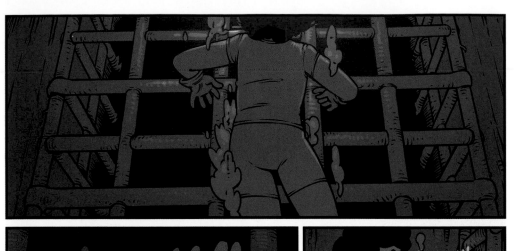

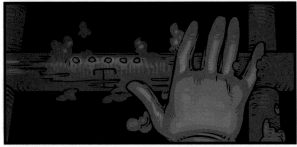

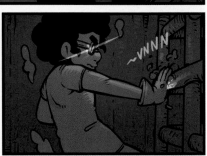

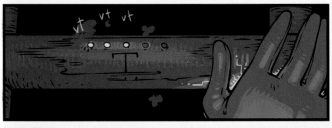

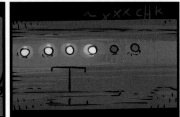

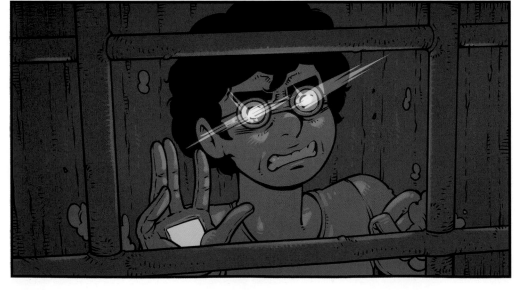

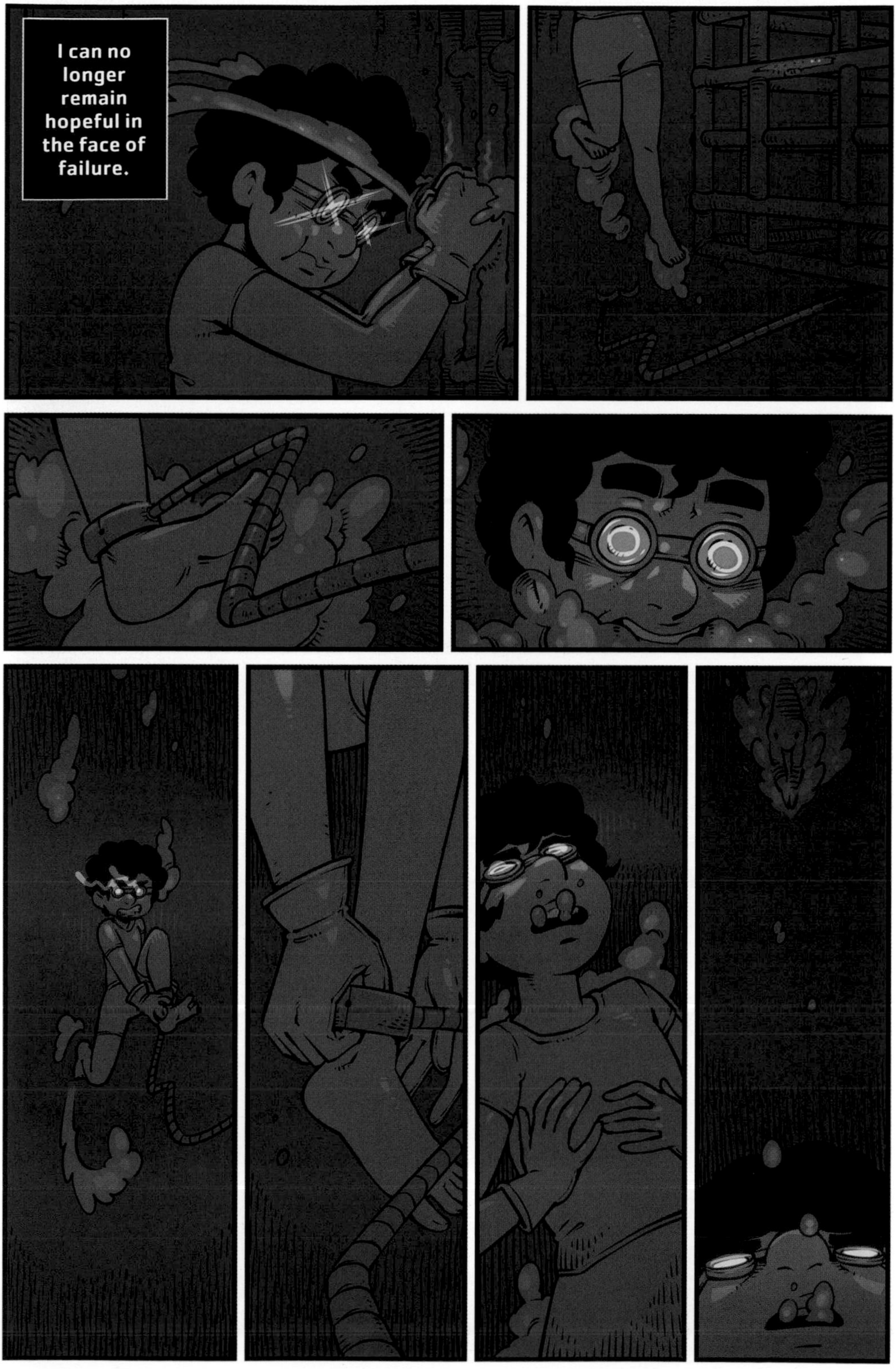
I can no longer remain hopeful in the face of failure.

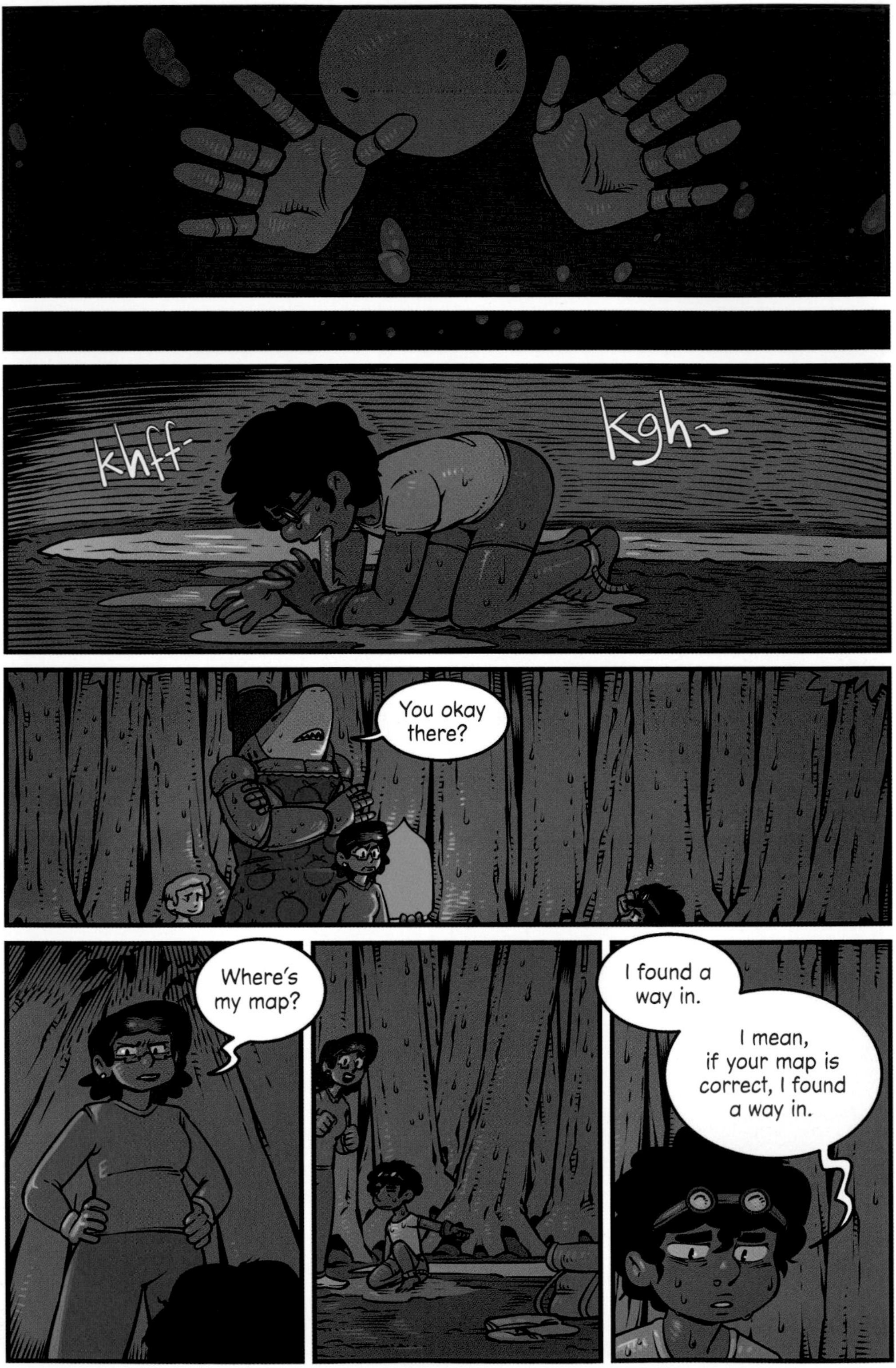
khff-
kgh~
You okay there?
Where's my map?
I found a way in.
I mean, if your map is correct, I found a way in.

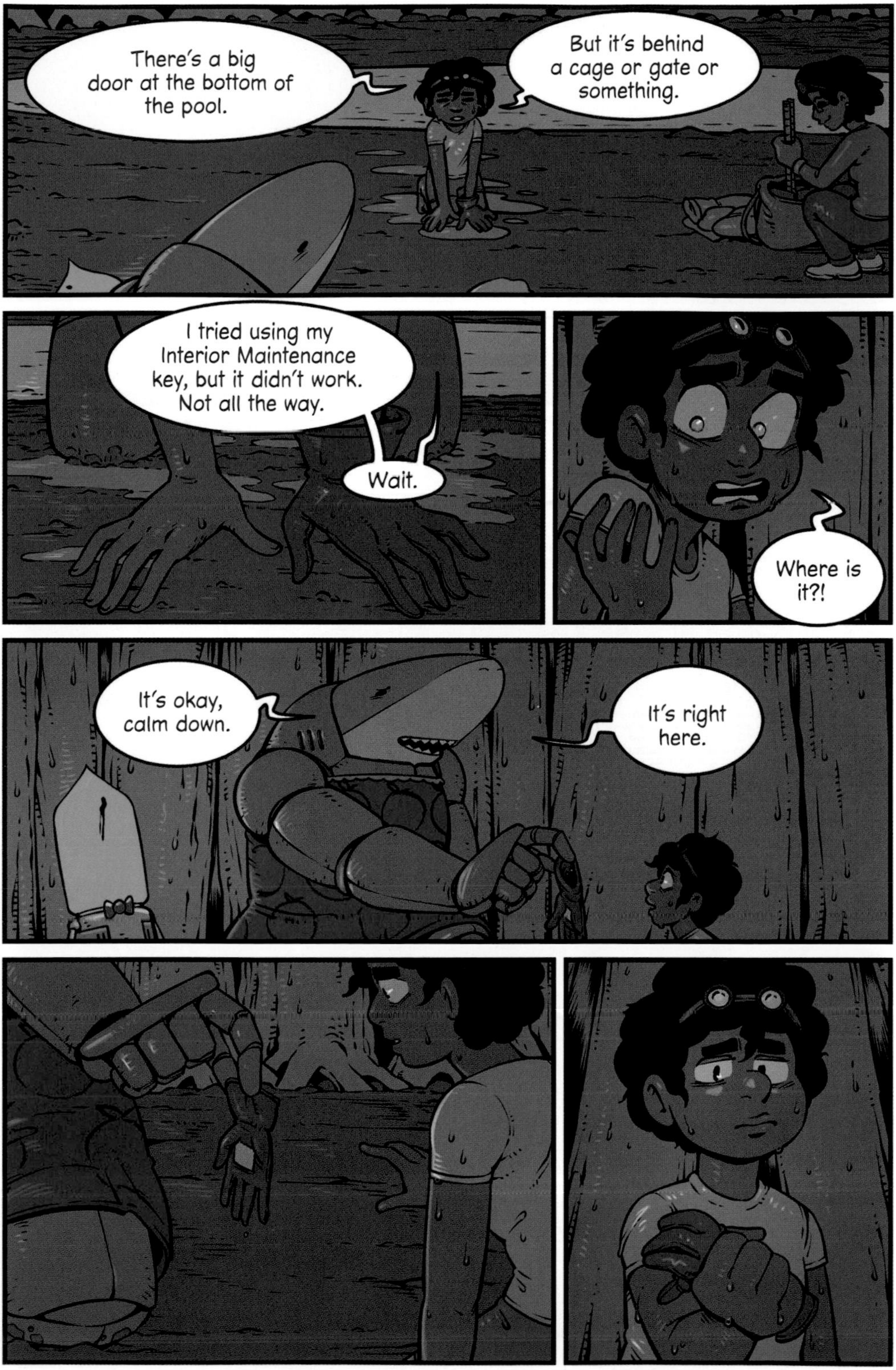
There's a big door at the bottom of the pool.
But it's behind a cage or gate or something.
I tried using my Interior Maintenance key, but it didn't work. Not all the way.
Wait.
Where is it?!
It's okay, calm down.
It's right here.

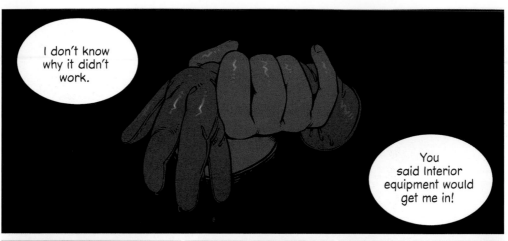

I don't know why it didn't work.

You said Interior equipment would get me in!

Give it here.

C'mon. We don't have all day.

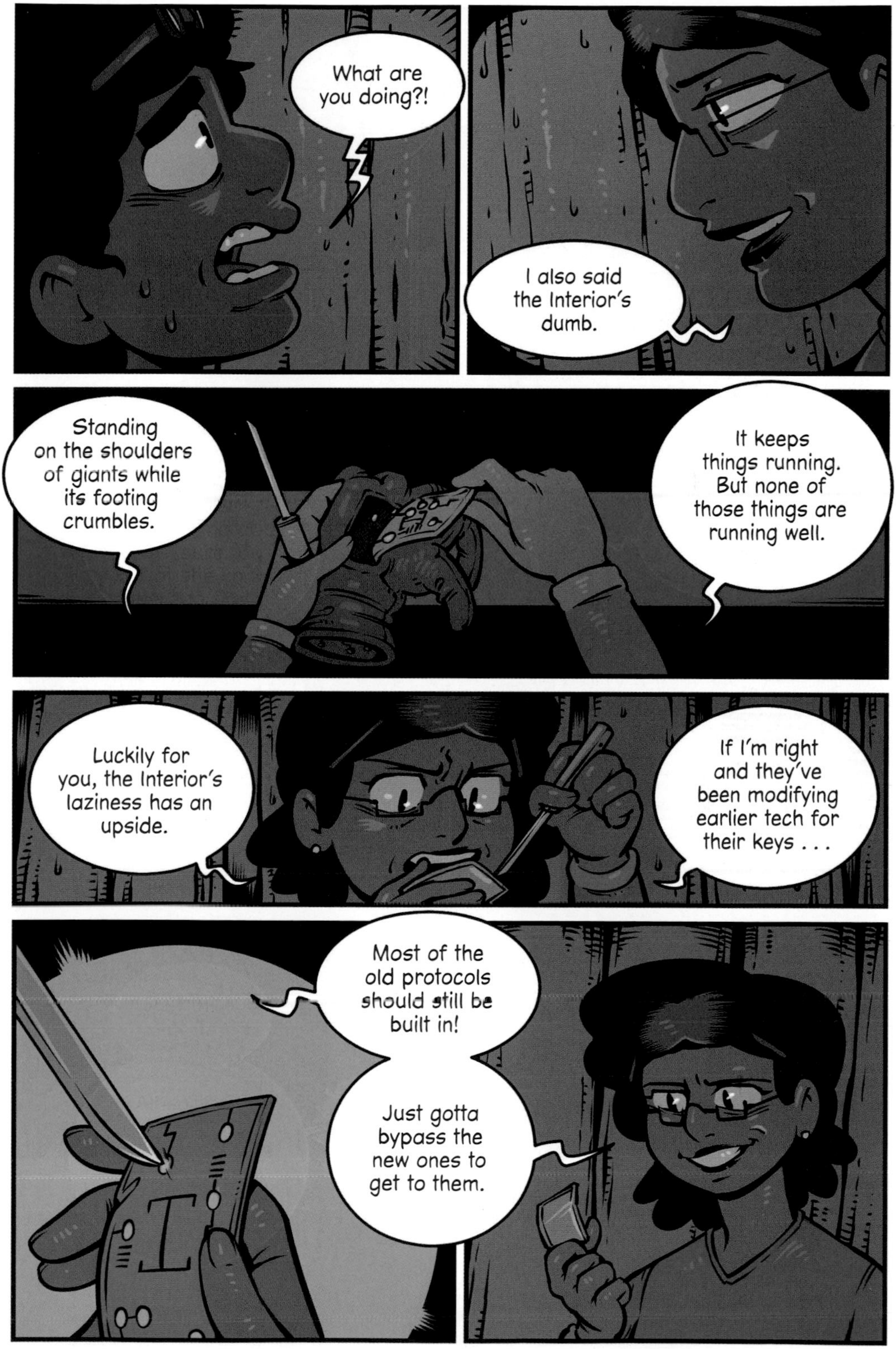
What are you doing?!
I also said the Interior's dumb.
Standing on the shoulders of giants while its footing crumbles.
It keeps things running. But none of those things are running well.
Luckily for you, the Interior's laziness has an upside.
If I'm right and they've been modifying earlier tech for their keys . . .
Most of the old protocols should still be built in!
Just gotta bypass the new ones to get to them.

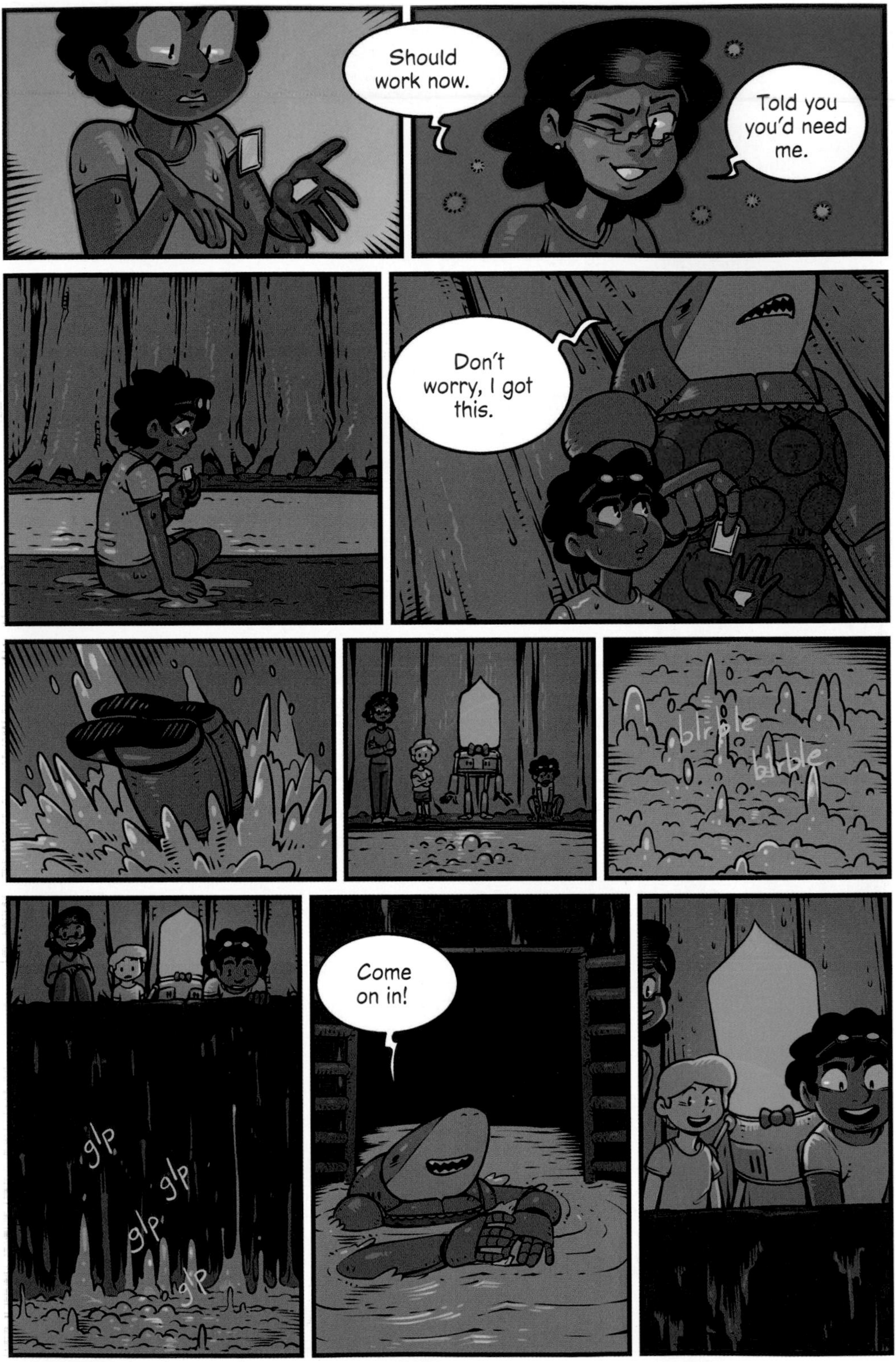
Should work now.
Told you you'd need me.
Don't worry, I got this.
blrble
blrble
glp
glp
glp
glp
Come on in!

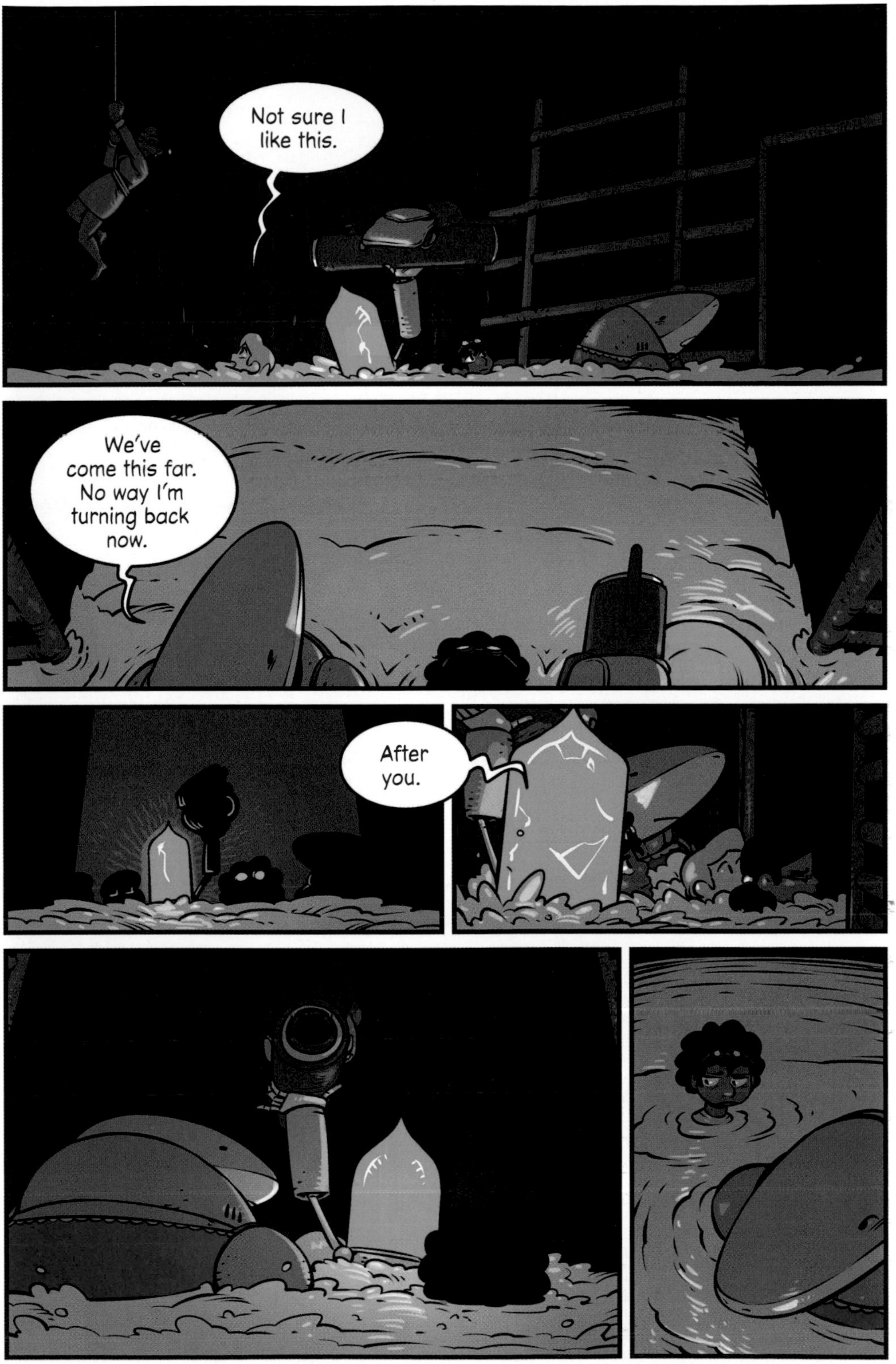
Not sure I like this.
We've come this far. No way I'm turning back now.
After you.

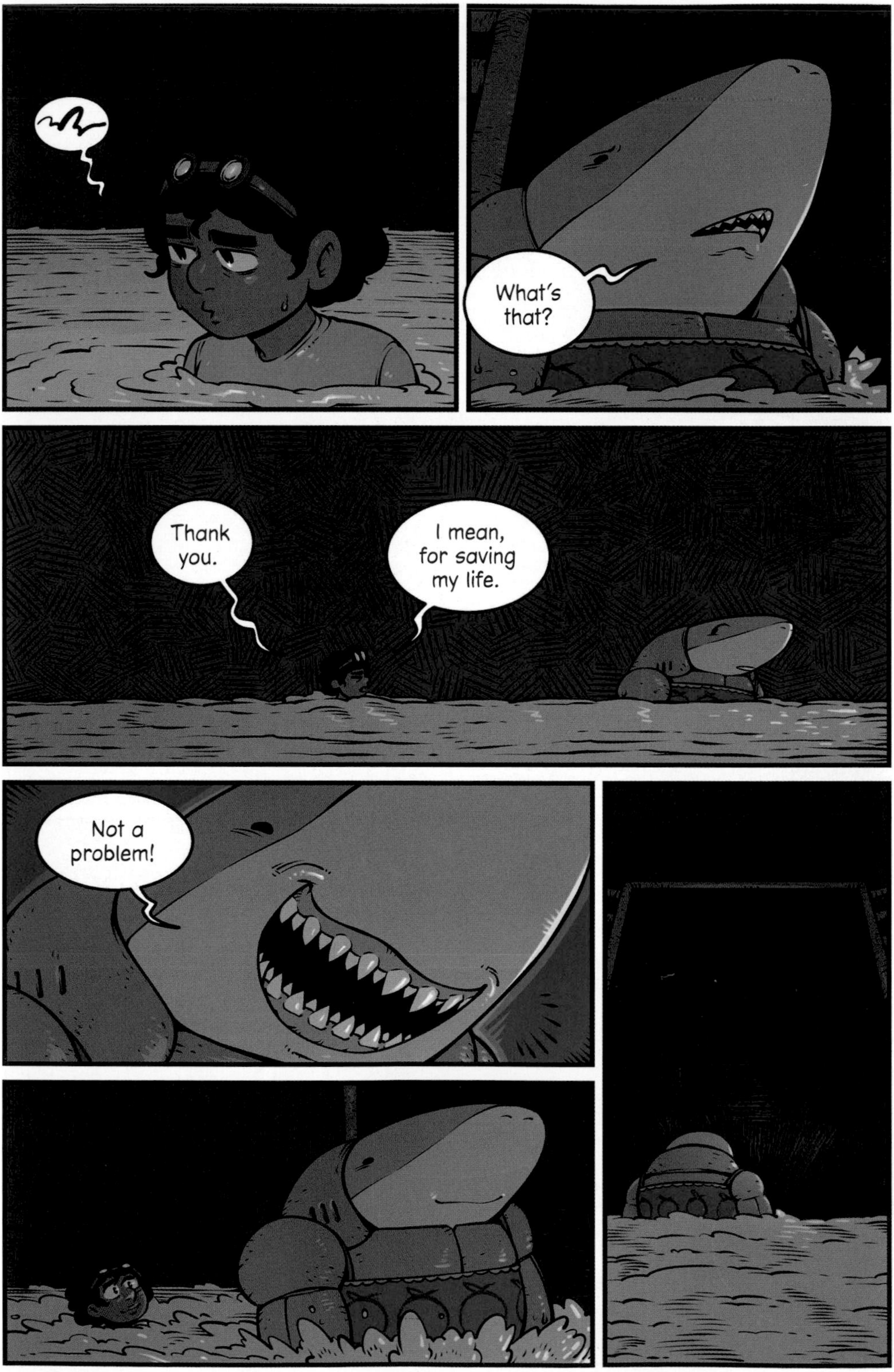
What's that?
Thank you.
I mean, for saving my life.
Not a problem!

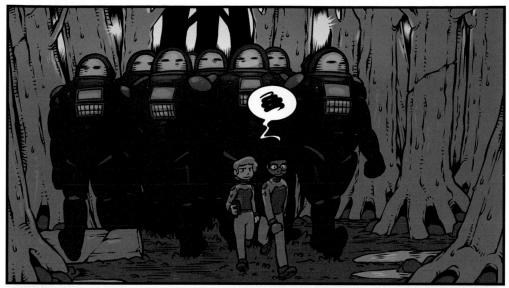

Come on, Vonnegan! We're not doing this here!

I should've just kept my mouth shut.

This whole thing would've blown over eventually.

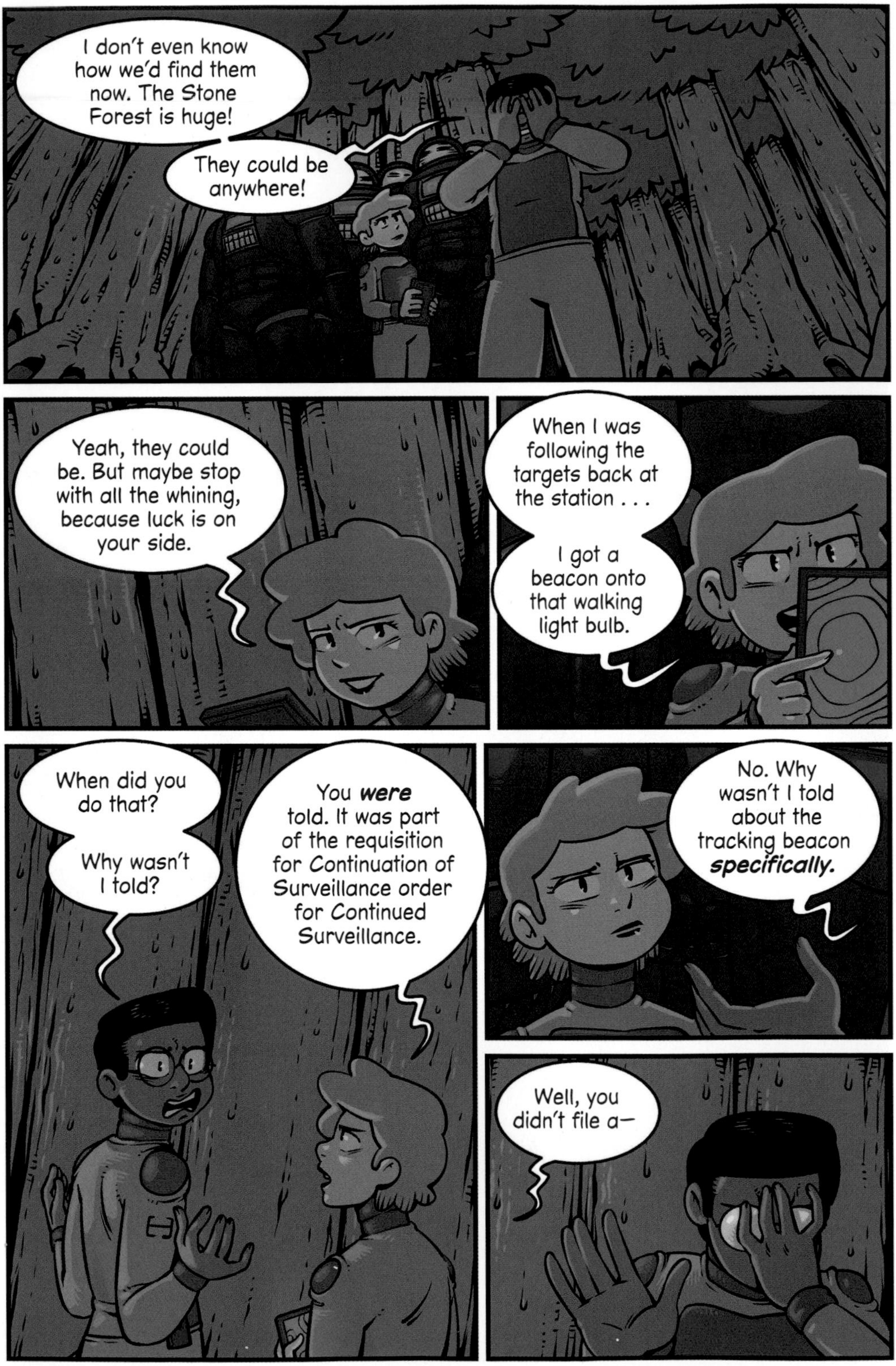
I don't even know how we'd find them now. The Stone Forest is huge!
They could be anywhere!
Yeah, they could be. But maybe stop with all the whining, because luck is on your side.
When I was following the targets back at the station . . .
I got a beacon onto that walking light bulb.
When did you do that?
Why wasn't I told?
You *were* told. It was part of the requisition for Continuation of Surveillance order for Continued Surveillance.
No. Why wasn't I told about the tracking beacon ***specifically.***
Well, you didn't file a—

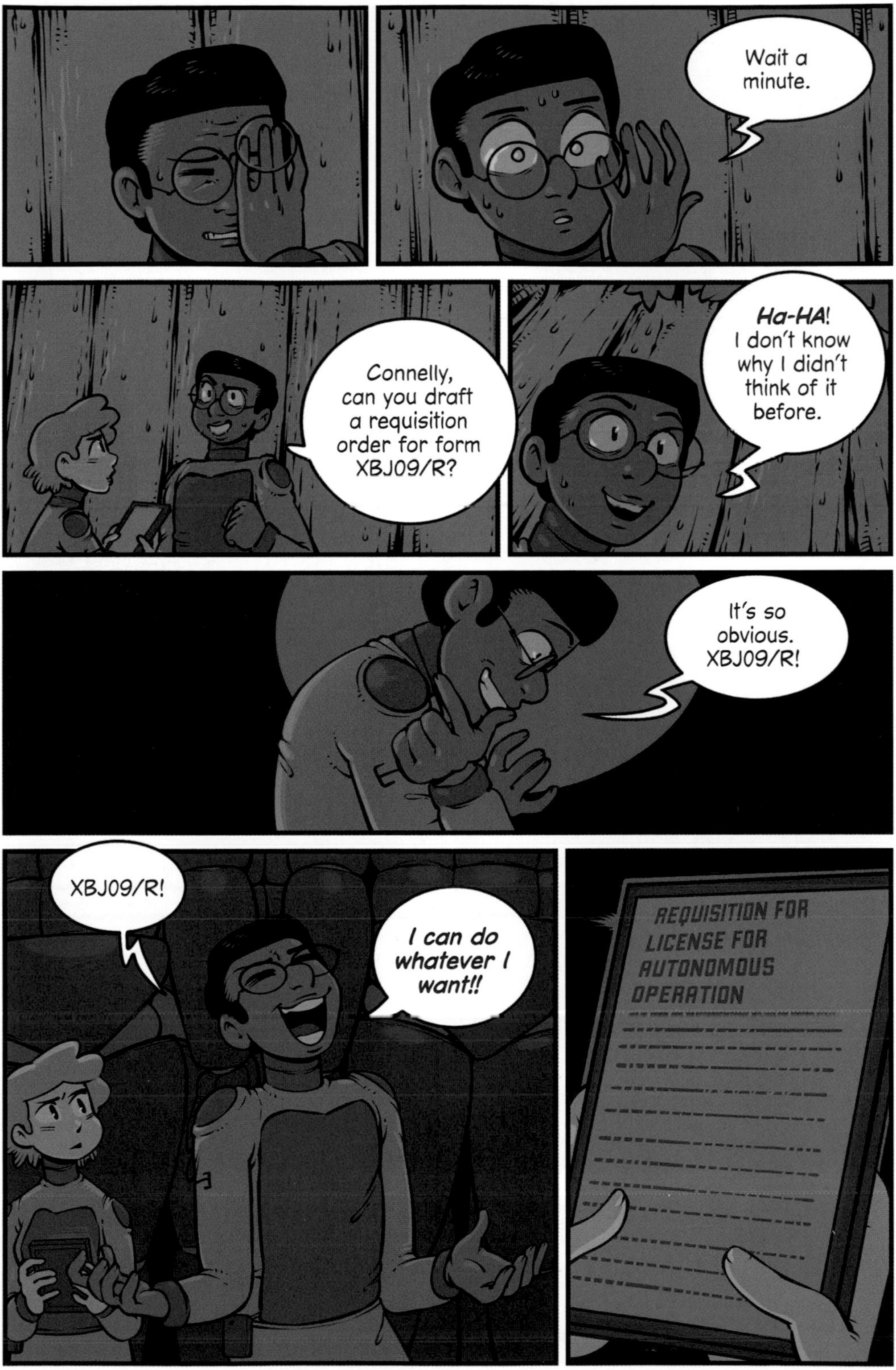
Wait a minute.
Connelly, can you draft a requisition order for form XBJ09/R?
Ha-HA! I don't know why I didn't think of it before.
It's so obvious. XBJ09/R!
XBJ09/R!
I can do whatever I want!!
REQUISITION FOR LICENSE FOR AUTONOMOUS OPERATION

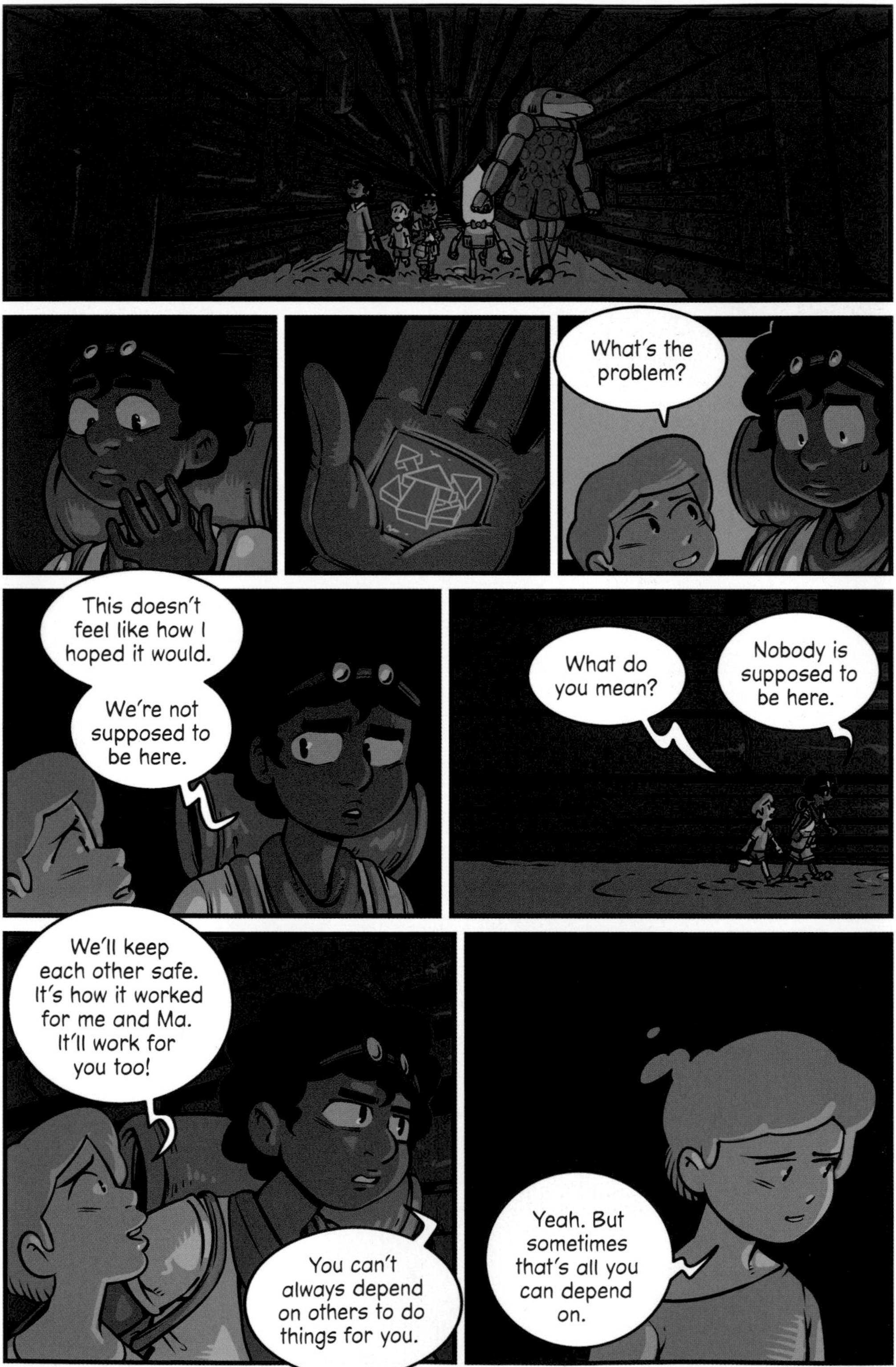
What's the problem?
This doesn't feel like how I hoped it would.
We're not supposed to be here.
What do you mean?
Nobody is supposed to be here.
We'll keep each other safe. It's how it worked for me and Ma. It'll work for you too!
You can't always depend on others to do things for you.
Yeah. But sometimes that's all you can depend on.

I don't understand.
What's wrong?
The map has completely changed.
Well, what's it look like now?
It's basically telling me that we need to be **beneath** where we are now.
But there's no way down.
The only way out is the way we came in!

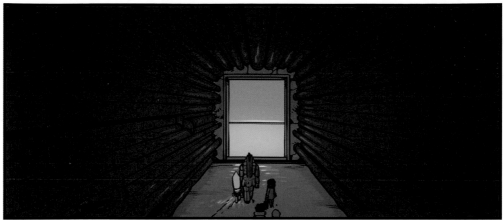

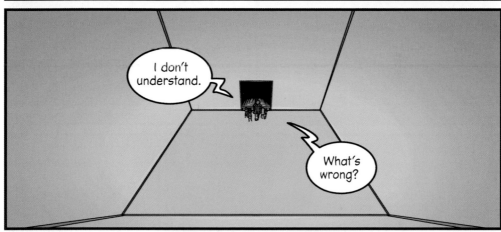

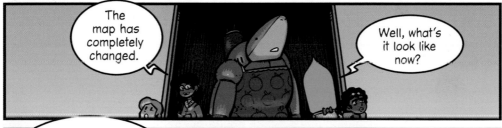

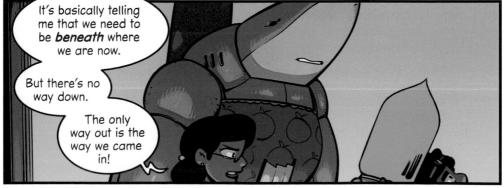

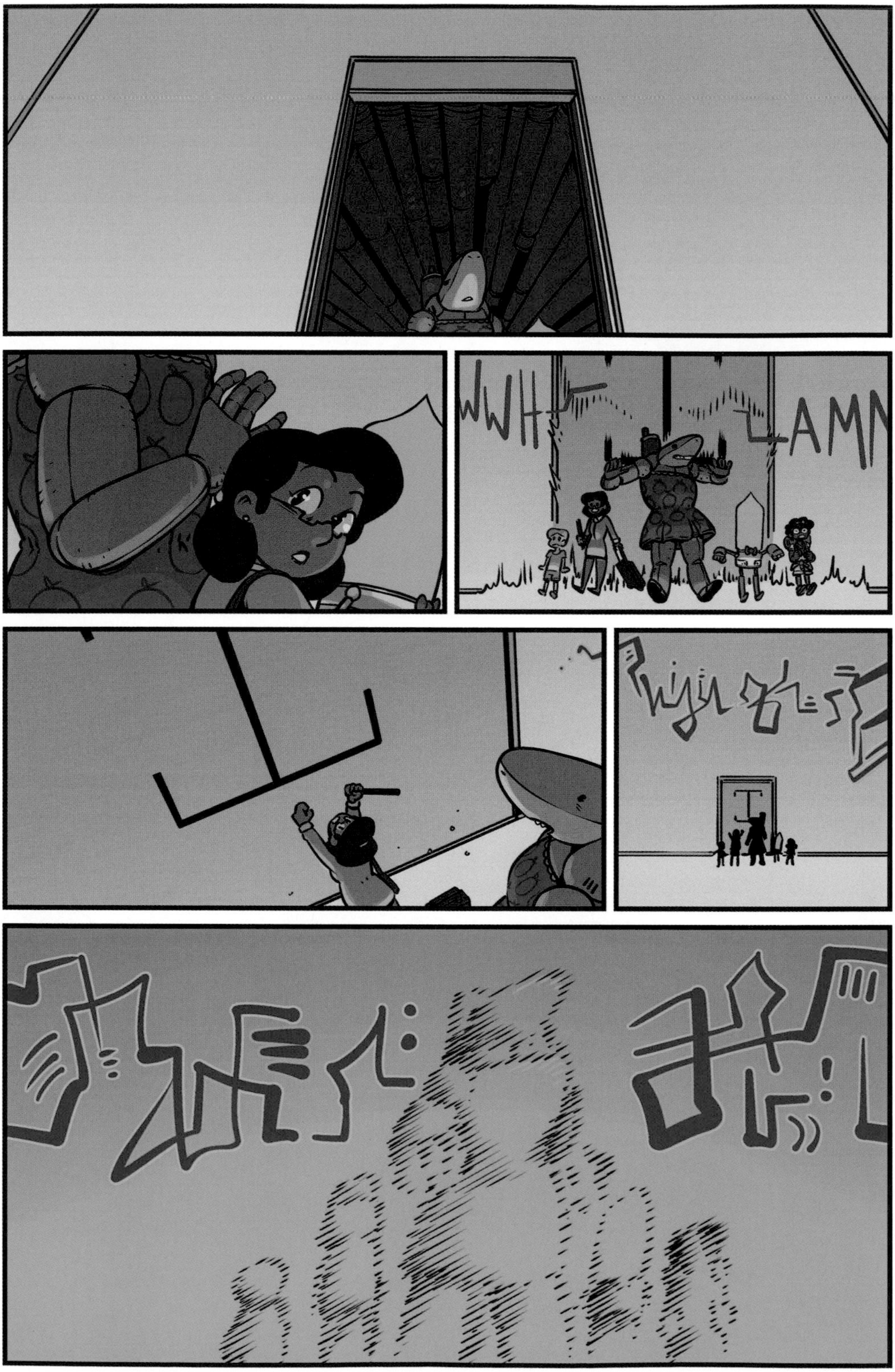

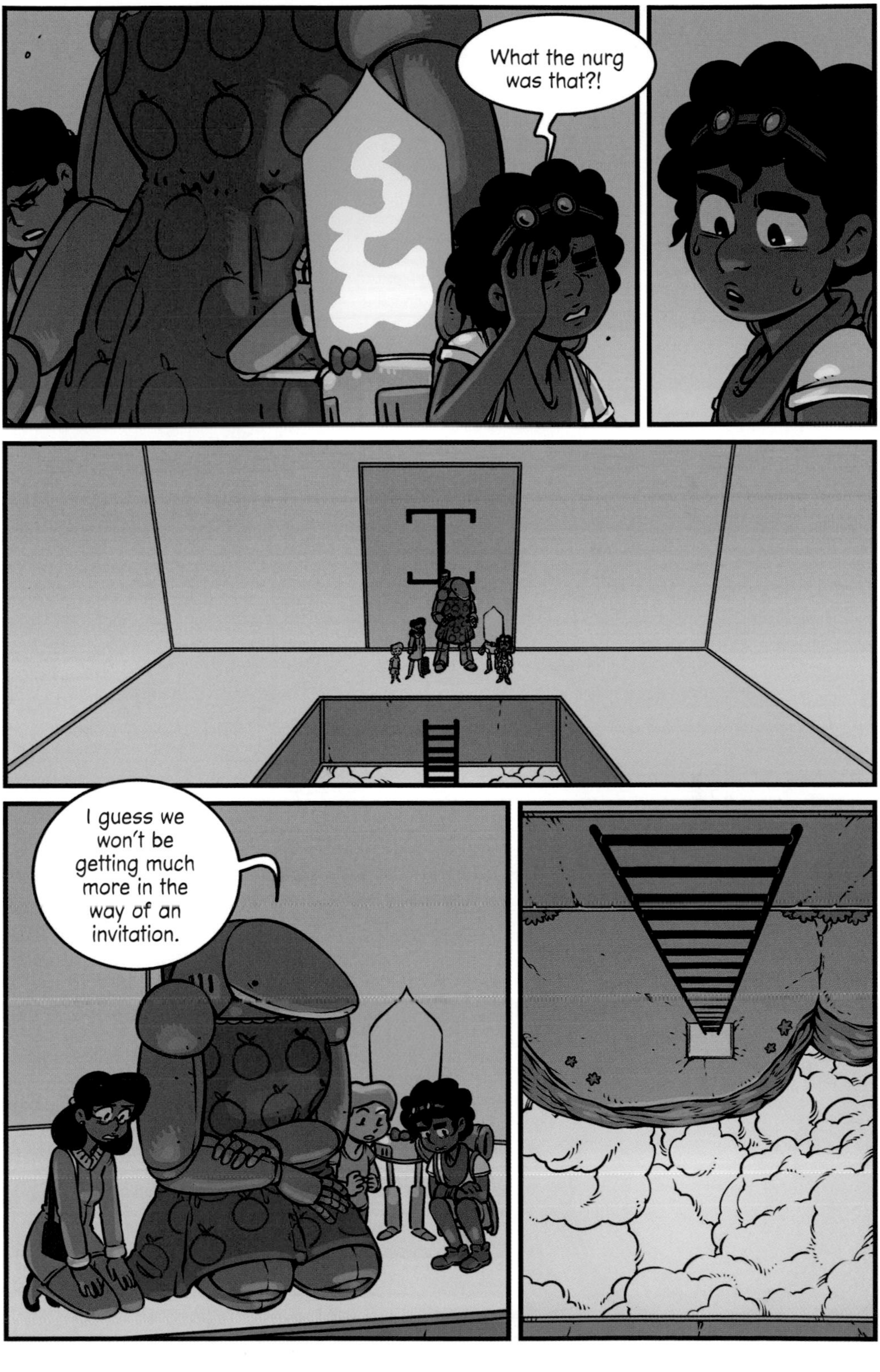
What the nurg was that?!
I guess we won't be getting much more in the way of an invitation.

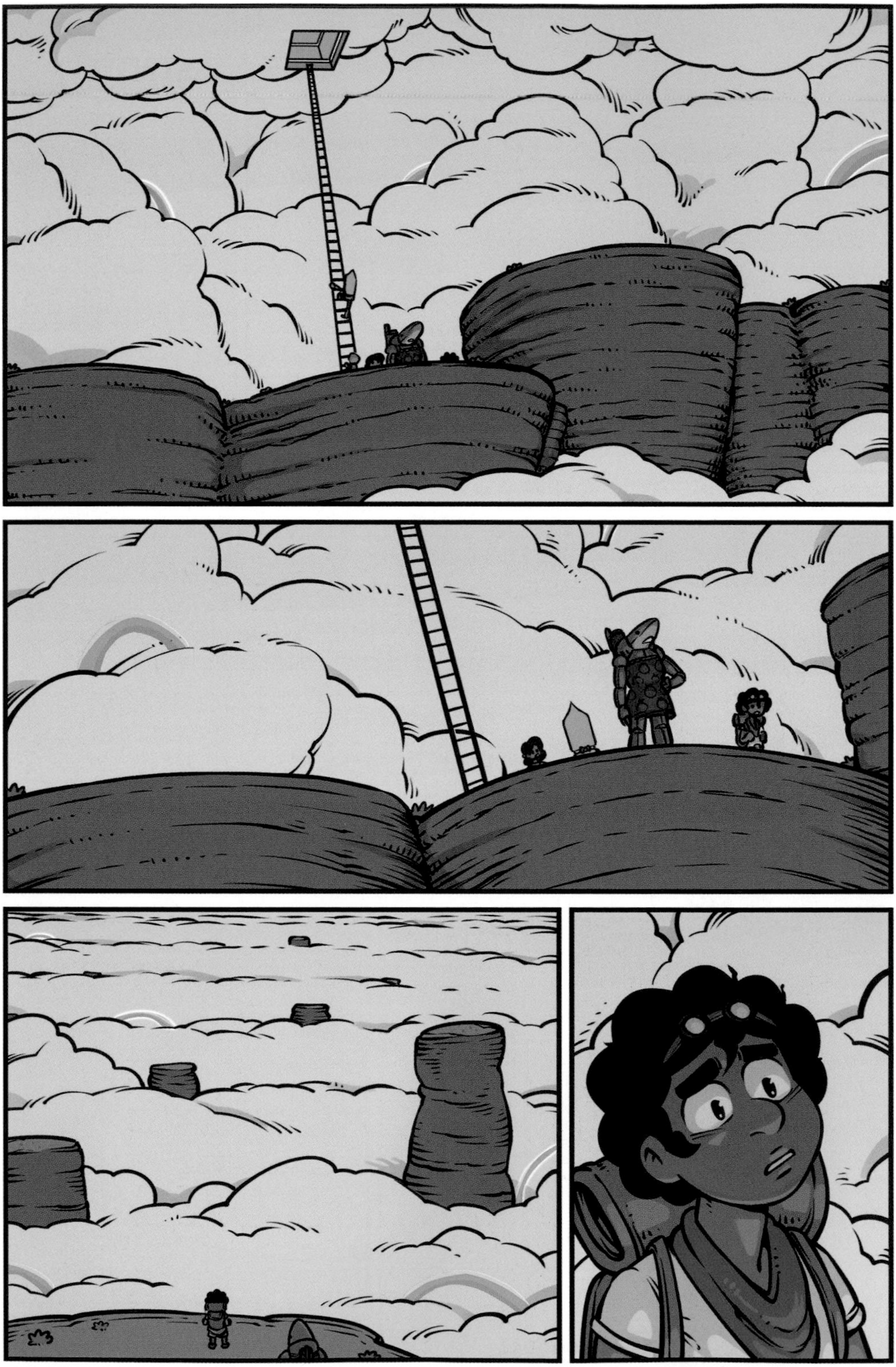

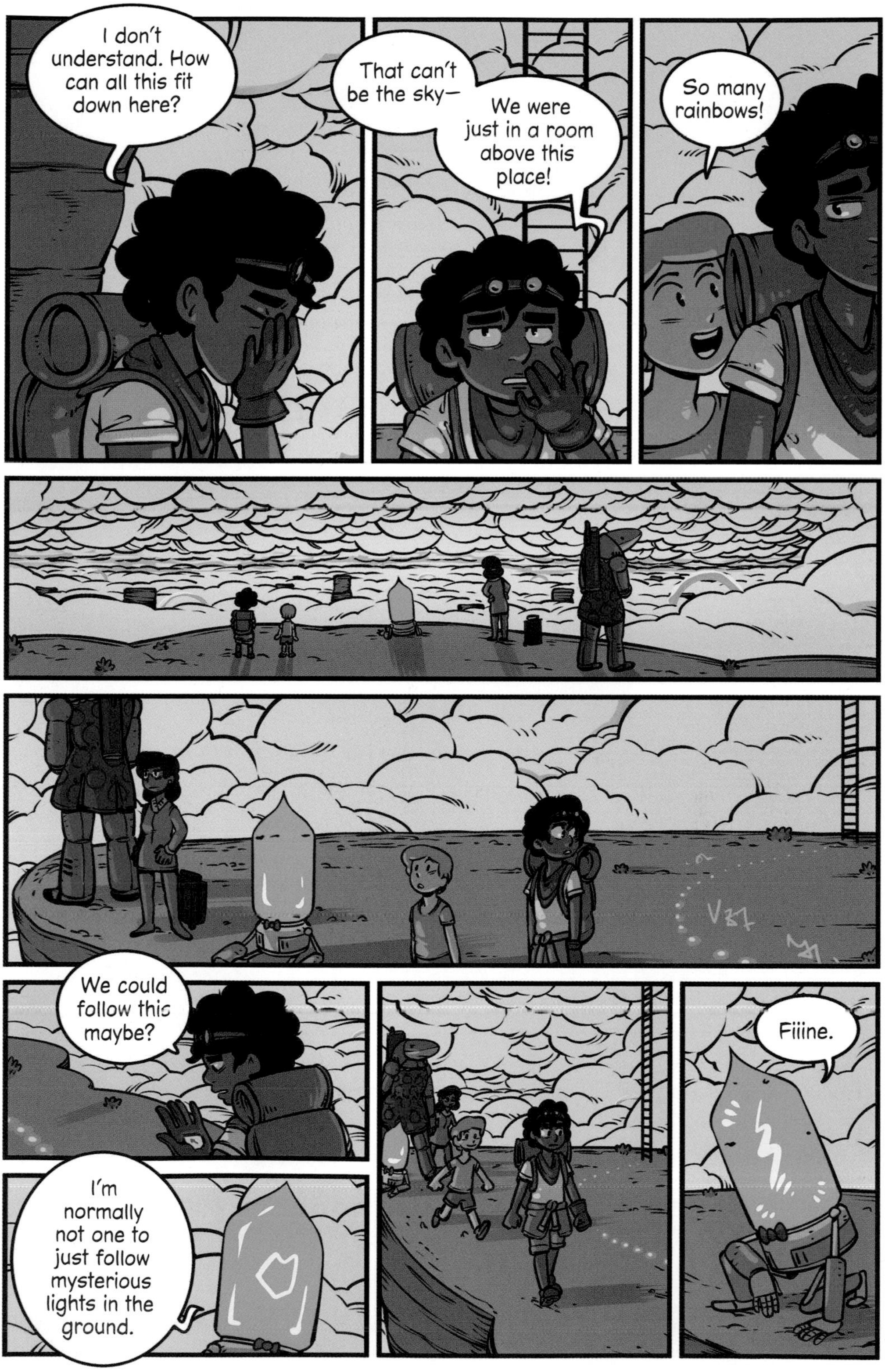
I don't understand. How can all this fit down here?
That can't be the sky—
We were just in a room above this place!
So many rainbows!
We could follow this maybe?
I'm normally not one to just follow mysterious lights in the ground.
Fiiine.

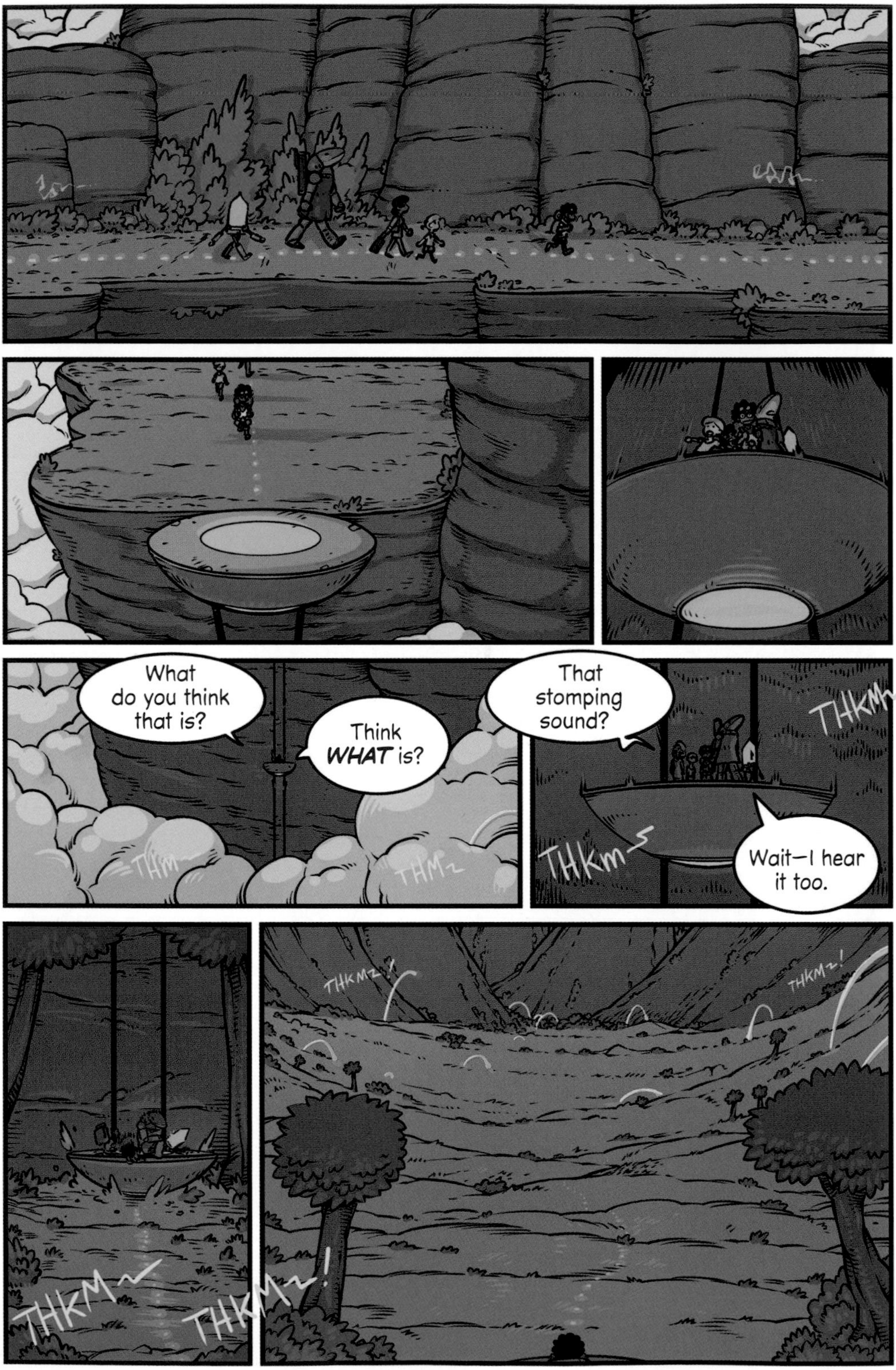

What do you think that is?
Think WHAT is?
THM
THM
That stomping sound?
THKM
THKm
Wait—I hear it too.
THKM
THKM
THKMz!
THKMz!

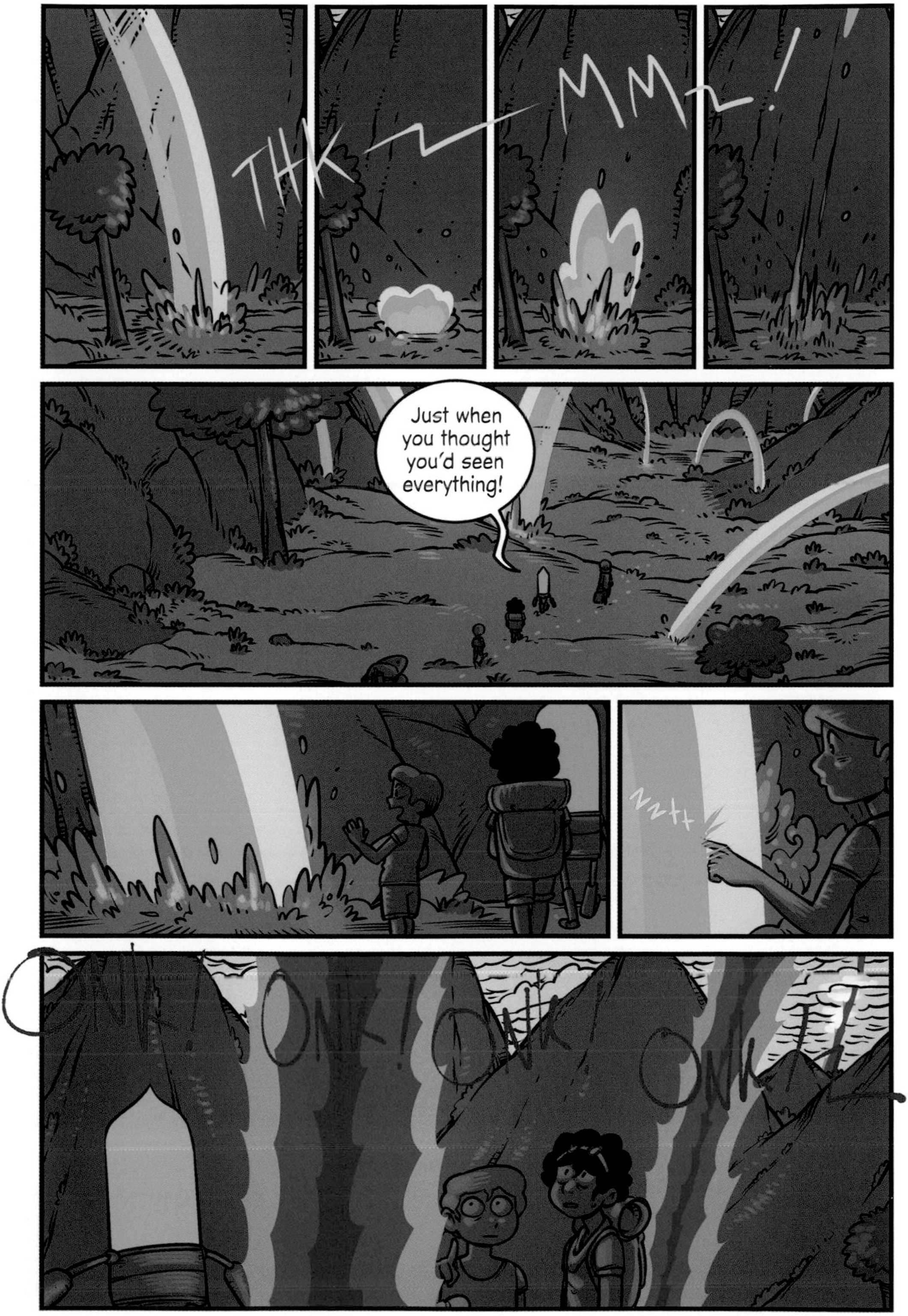
THK
MMz!
Just when you thought you'd seen everything!
Zztt
ONK! ONK! ONK! ONK!

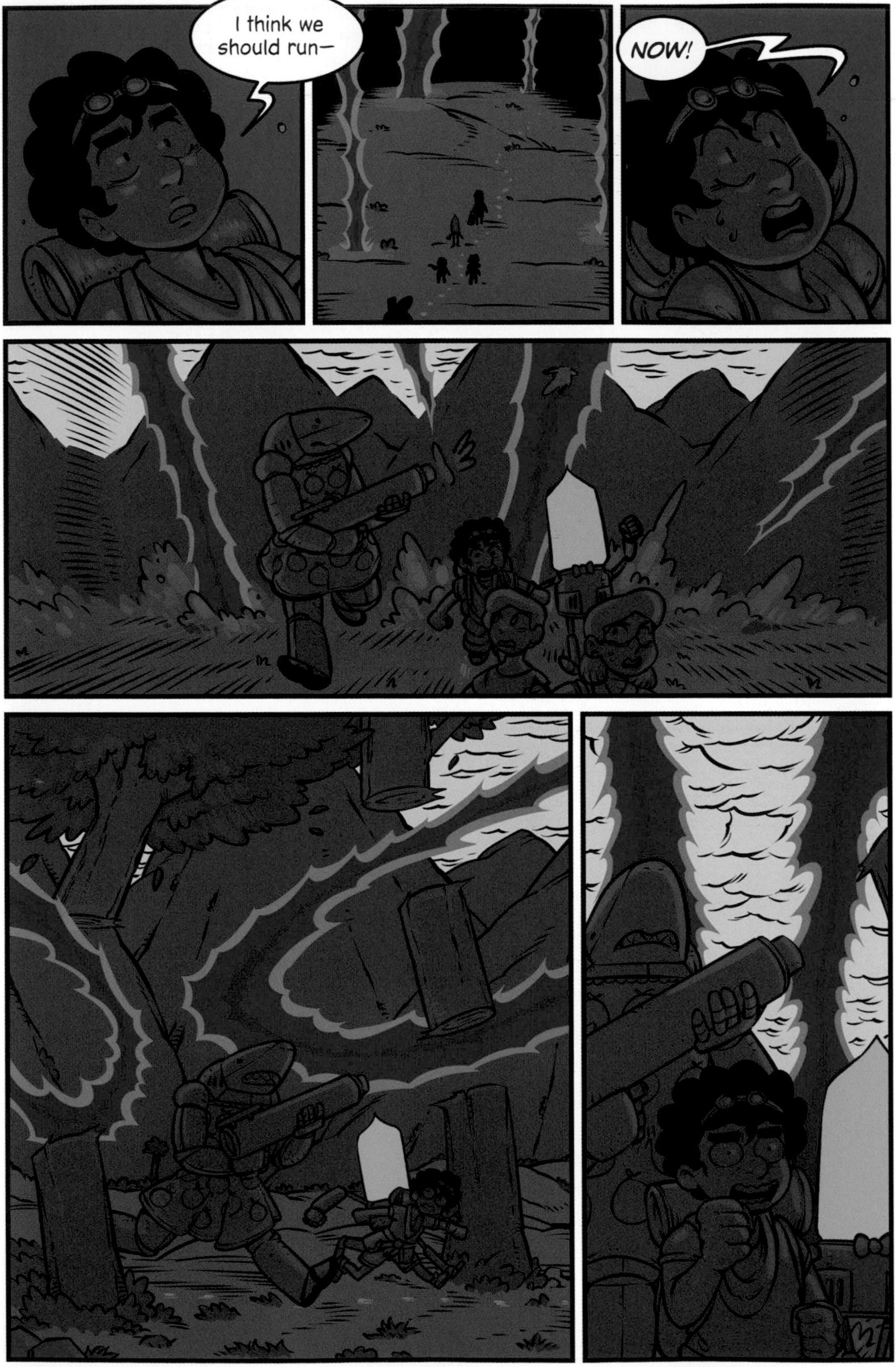
I think we should run—
NOW!

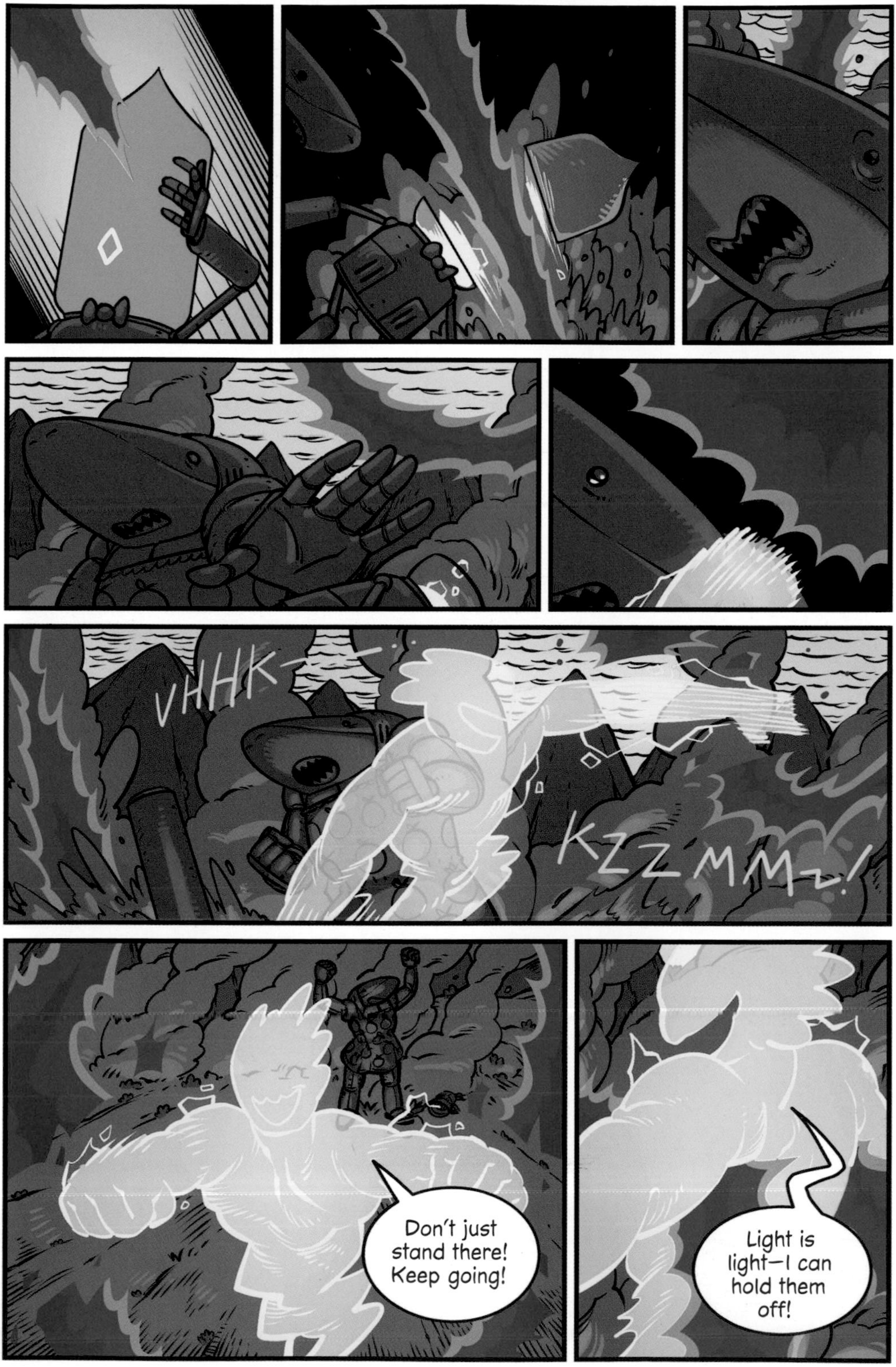
VHHK—
KZZMMz!
Don't just stand there! Keep going!
Light is light—I can hold them off!

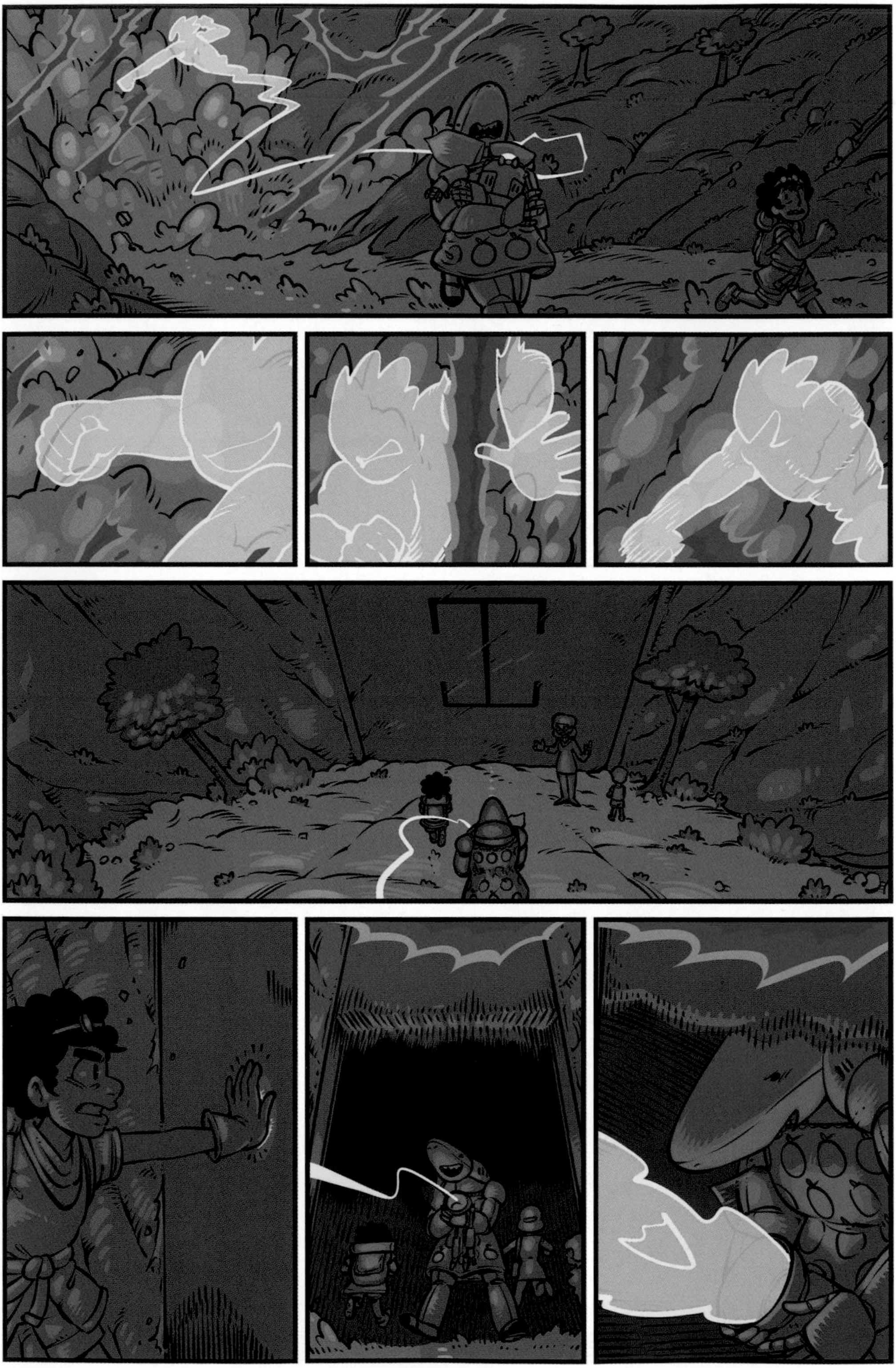

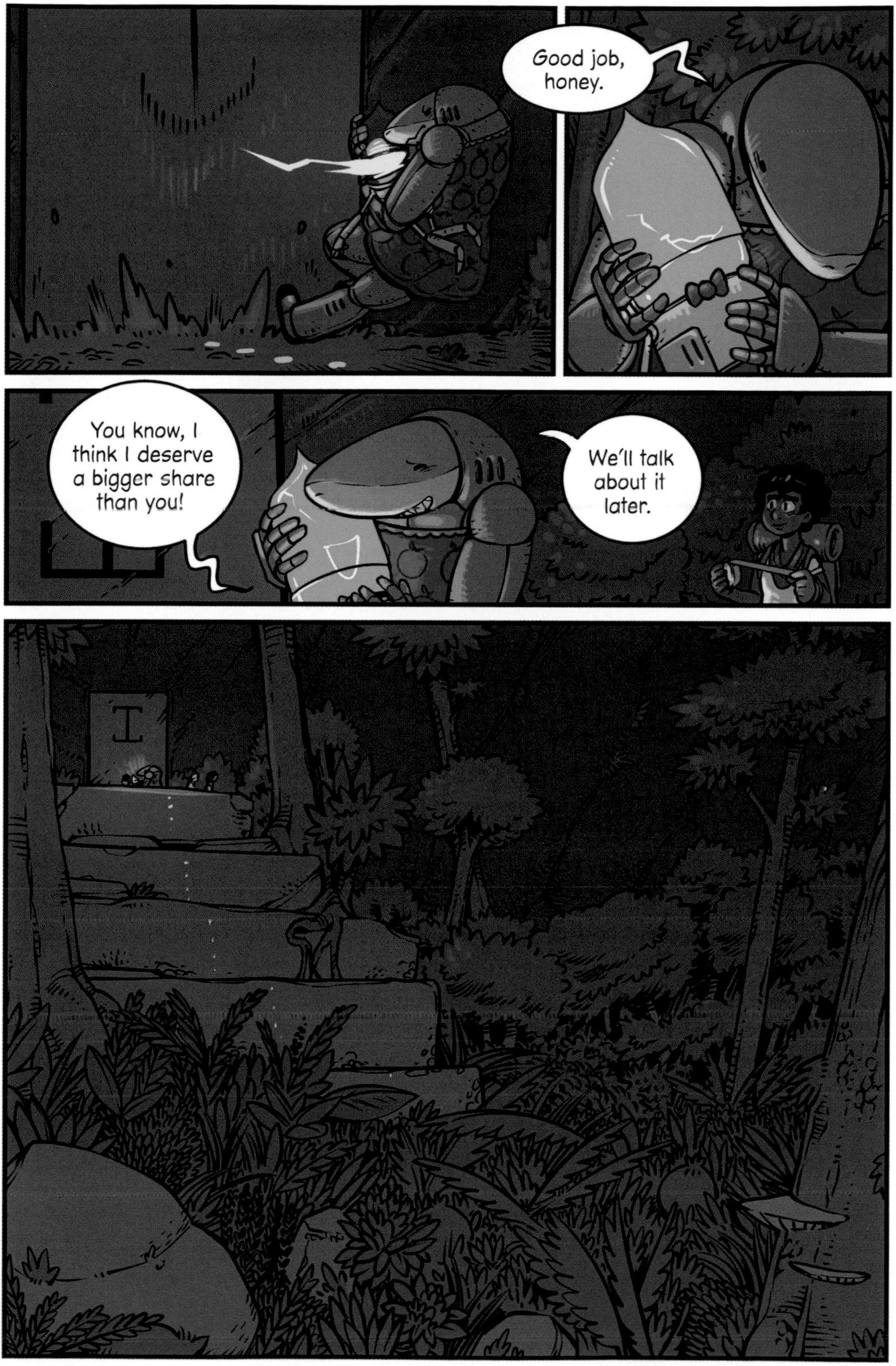
Good job, honey.
You know, I think I deserve a bigger share than you!
We'll talk about it later.

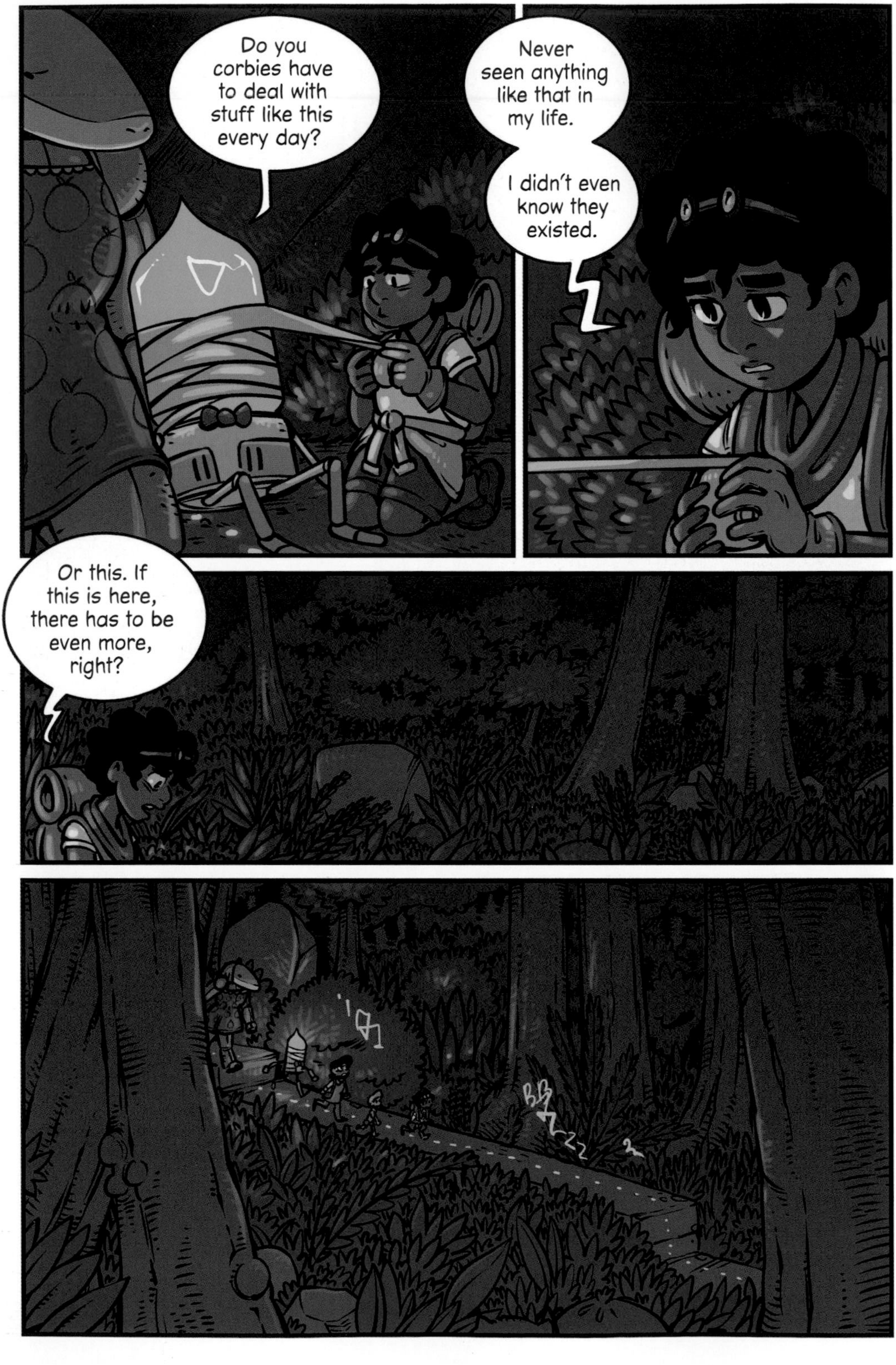
Do you corbies have to deal with stuff like this every day?
Never seen anything like that in my life.
I didn't even know they existed.
Or this. If this is here, there has to be even more, right?

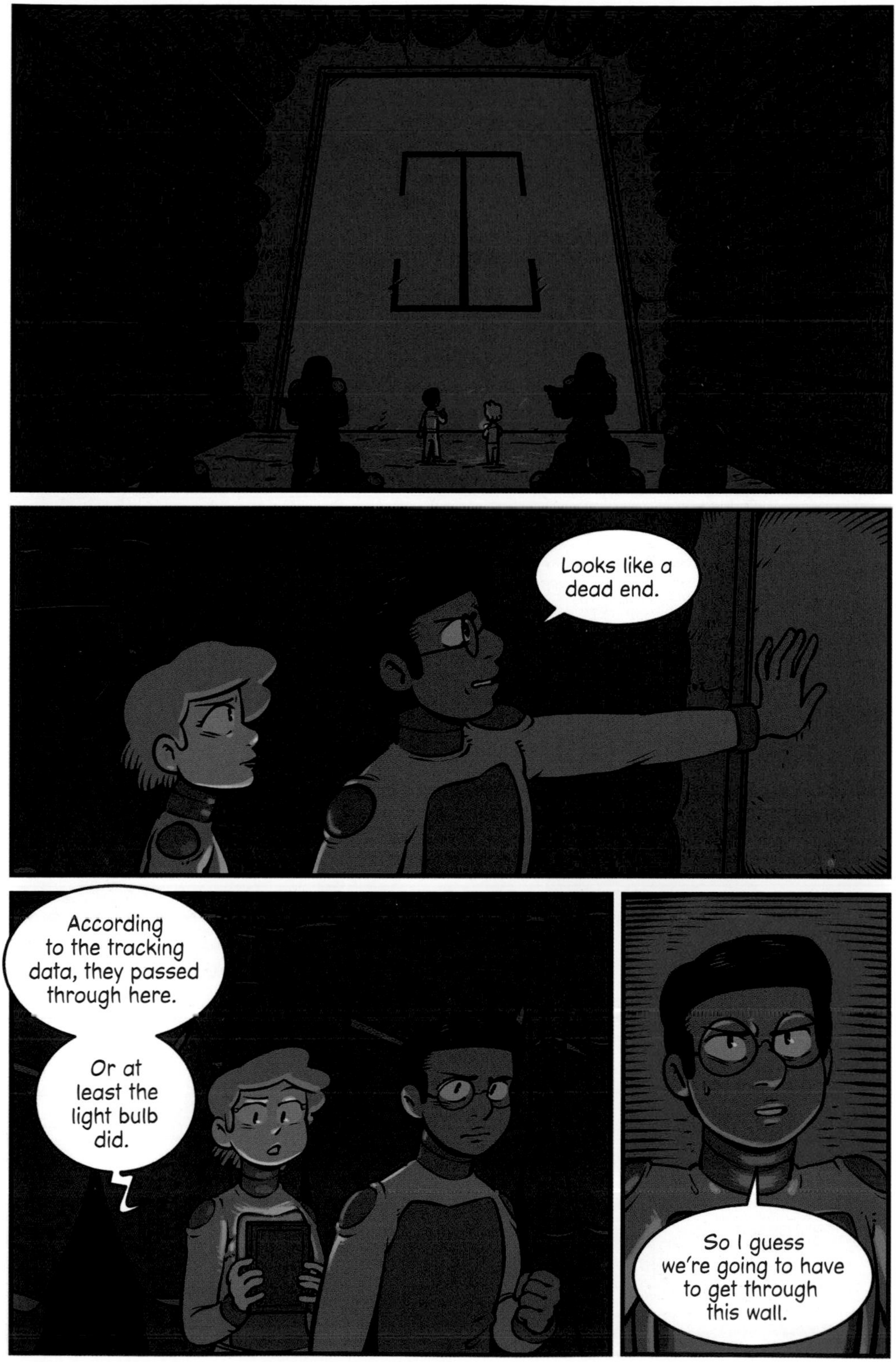

Looks like a dead end.
According to the tracking data, they passed through here.
Or at least the light bulb did.
So I guess we're going to have to get through this wall.

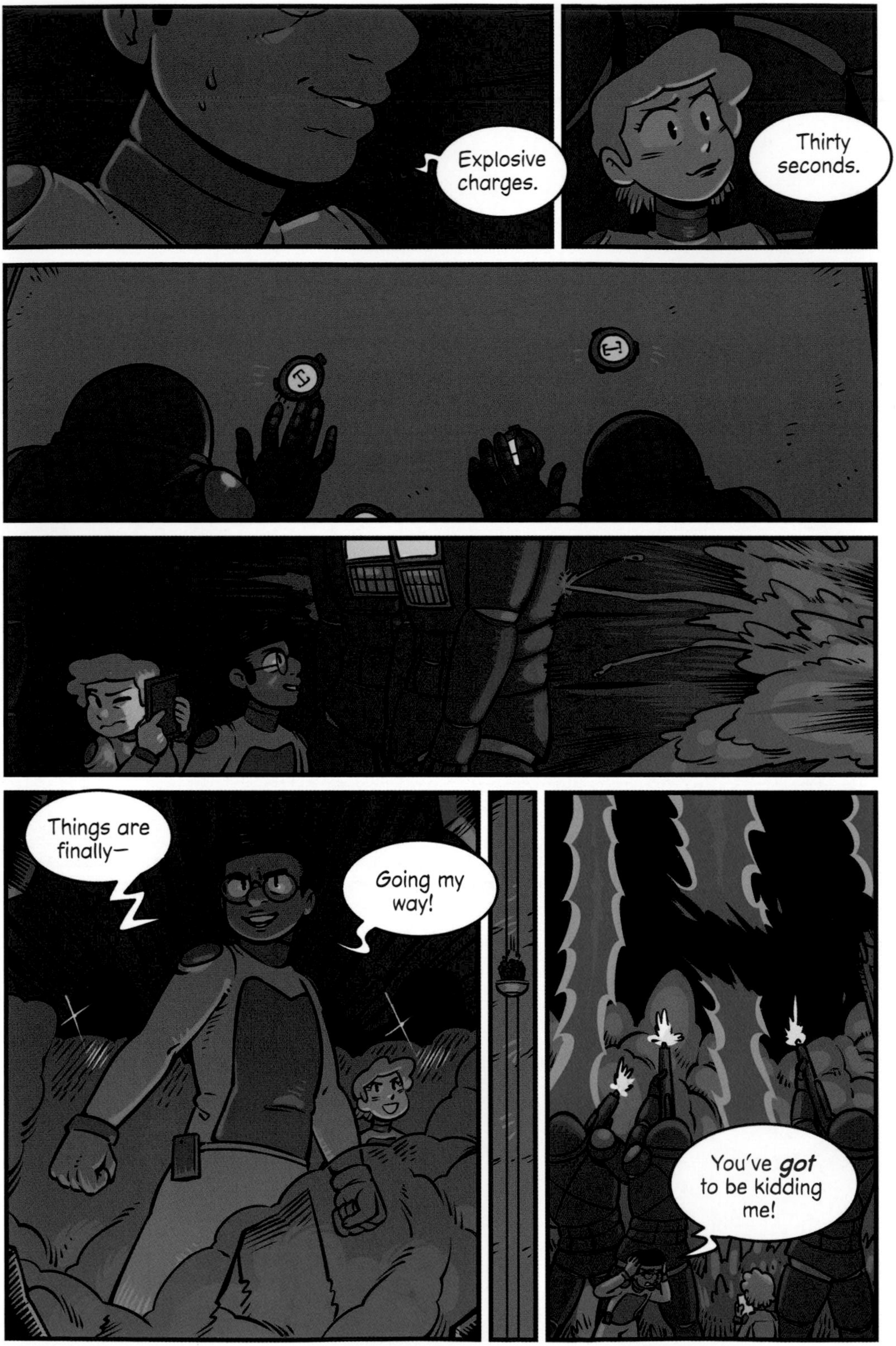
Explosive charges.
Thirty seconds.
Things are finally—
Going my way!
You've ***got*** to be kidding me!

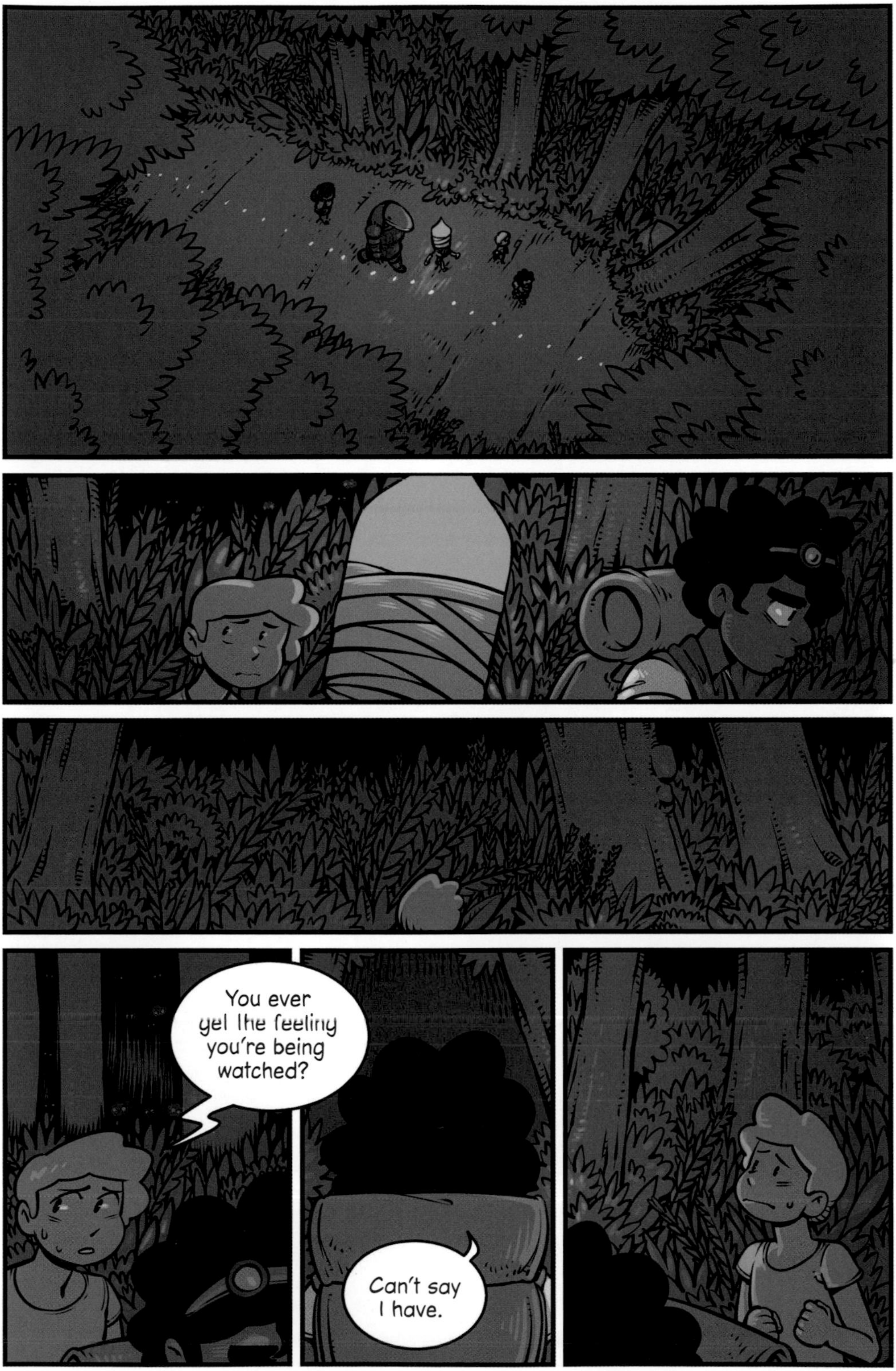
You ever get the feeling you're being watched?
Can't say I have.

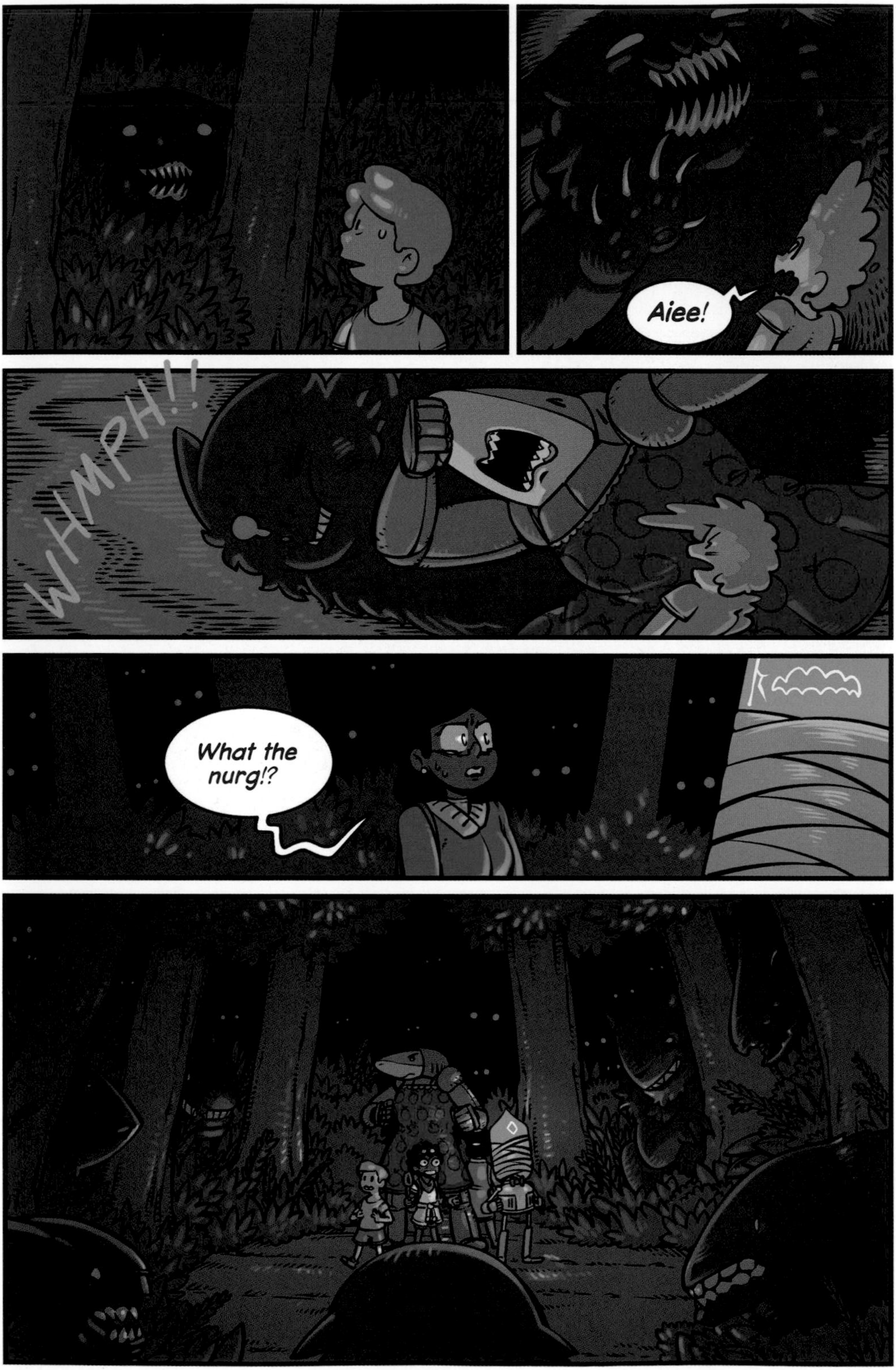
Aiee!
WHMPH!!
What the nurg!?

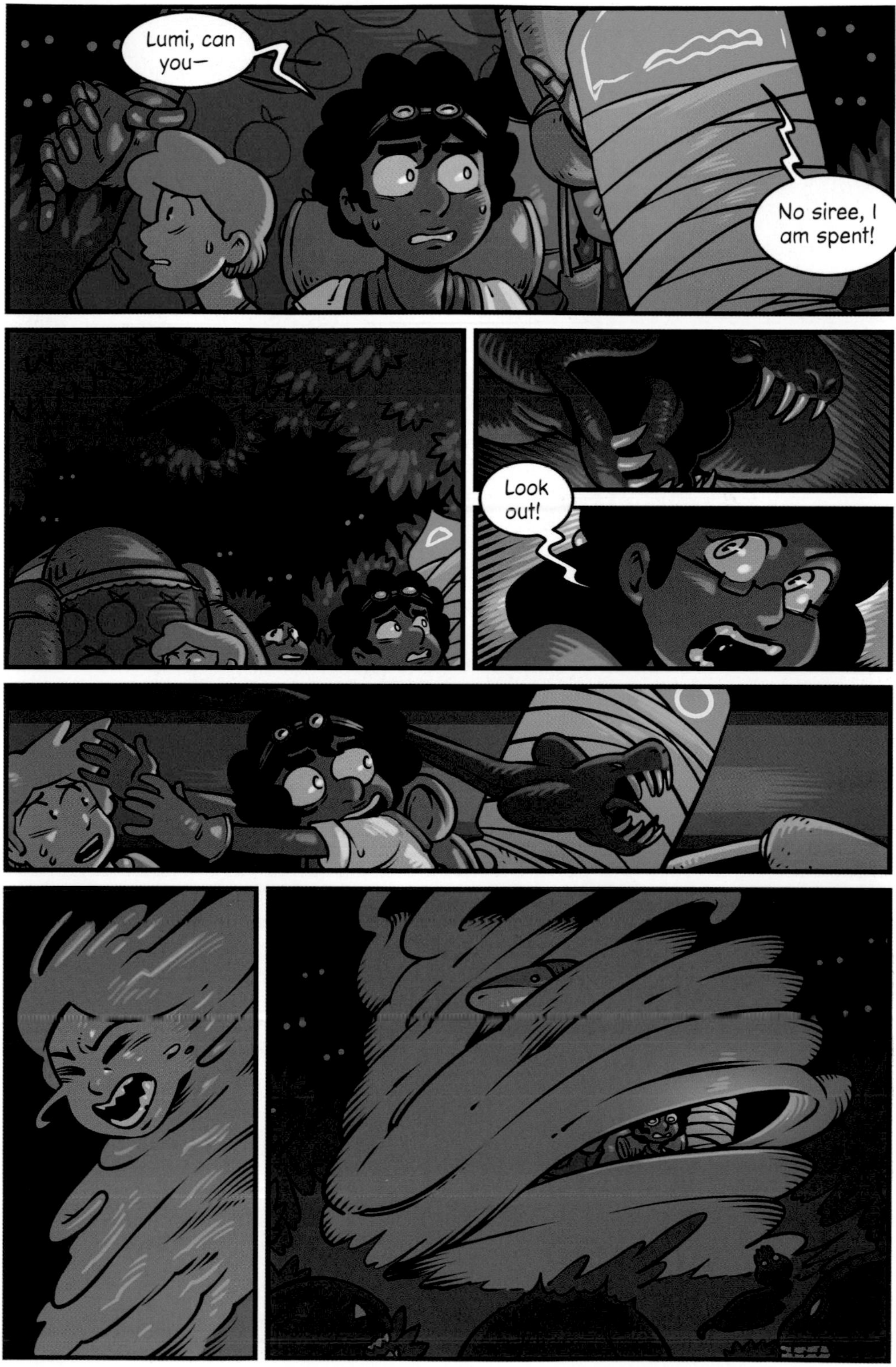
Lumi, can you—
No siree, I am spent!
Look out!

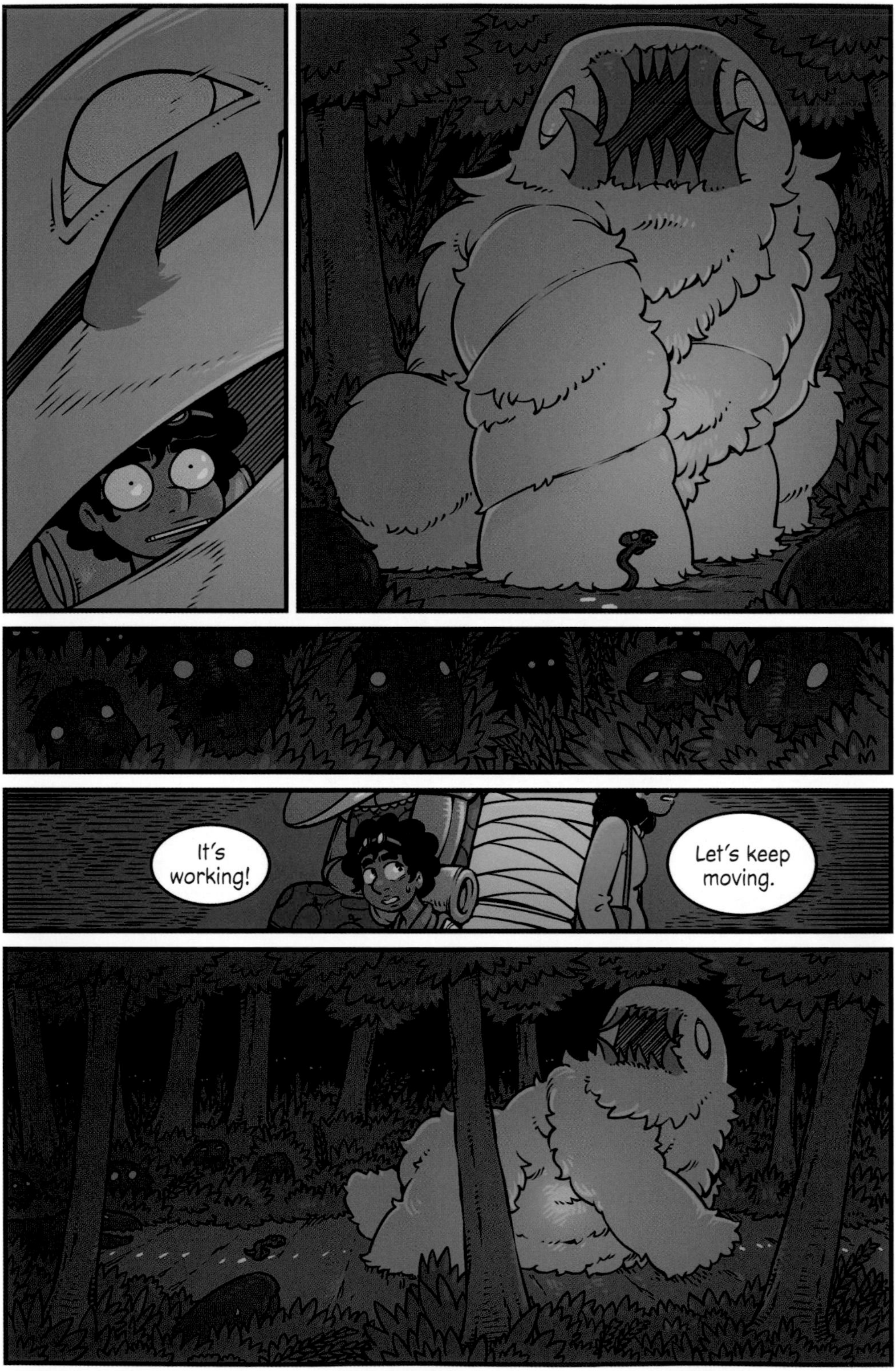
It's working!
Let's keep moving.

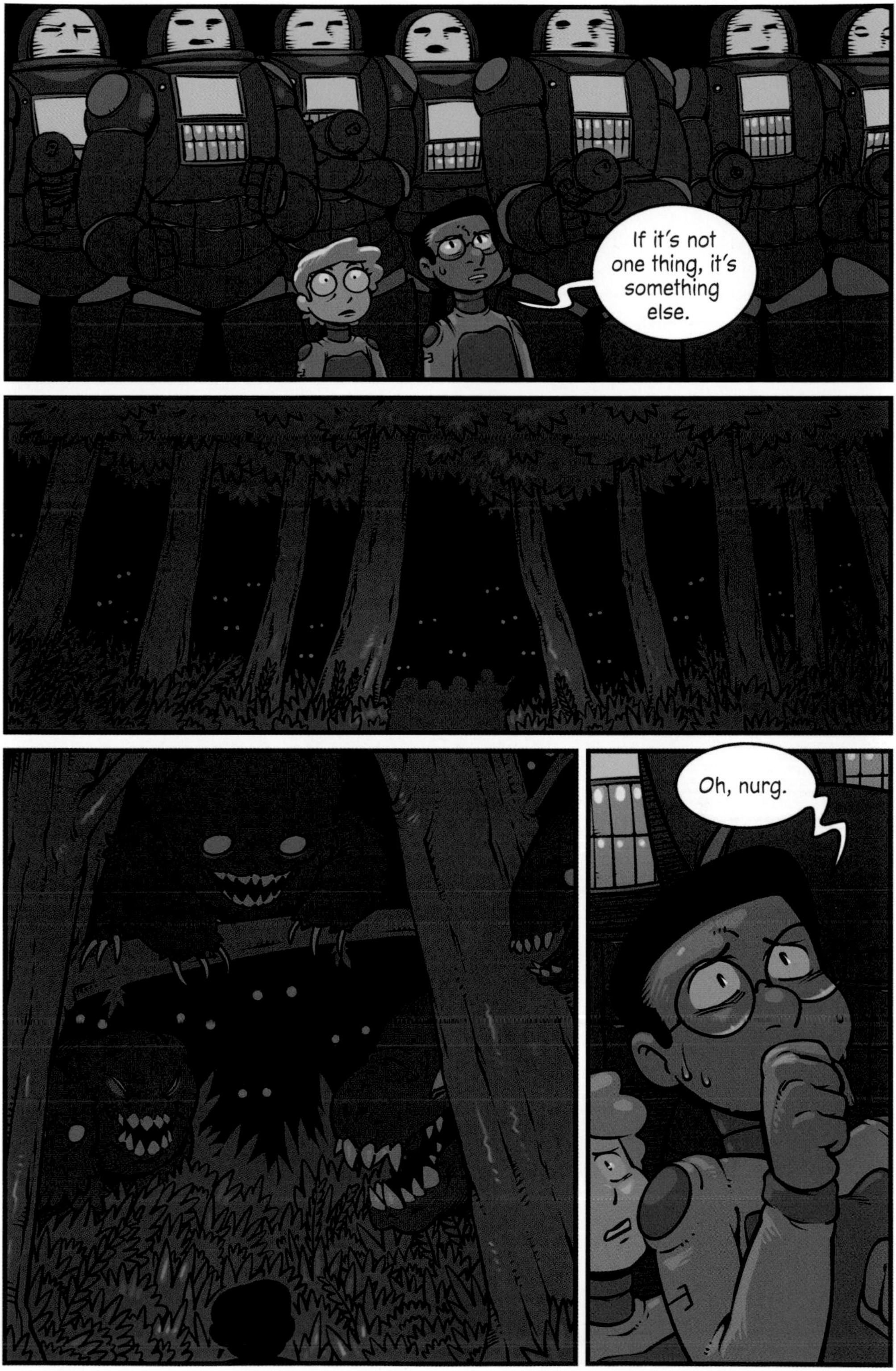
If it's not one thing, it's something else.
Oh, nurg.

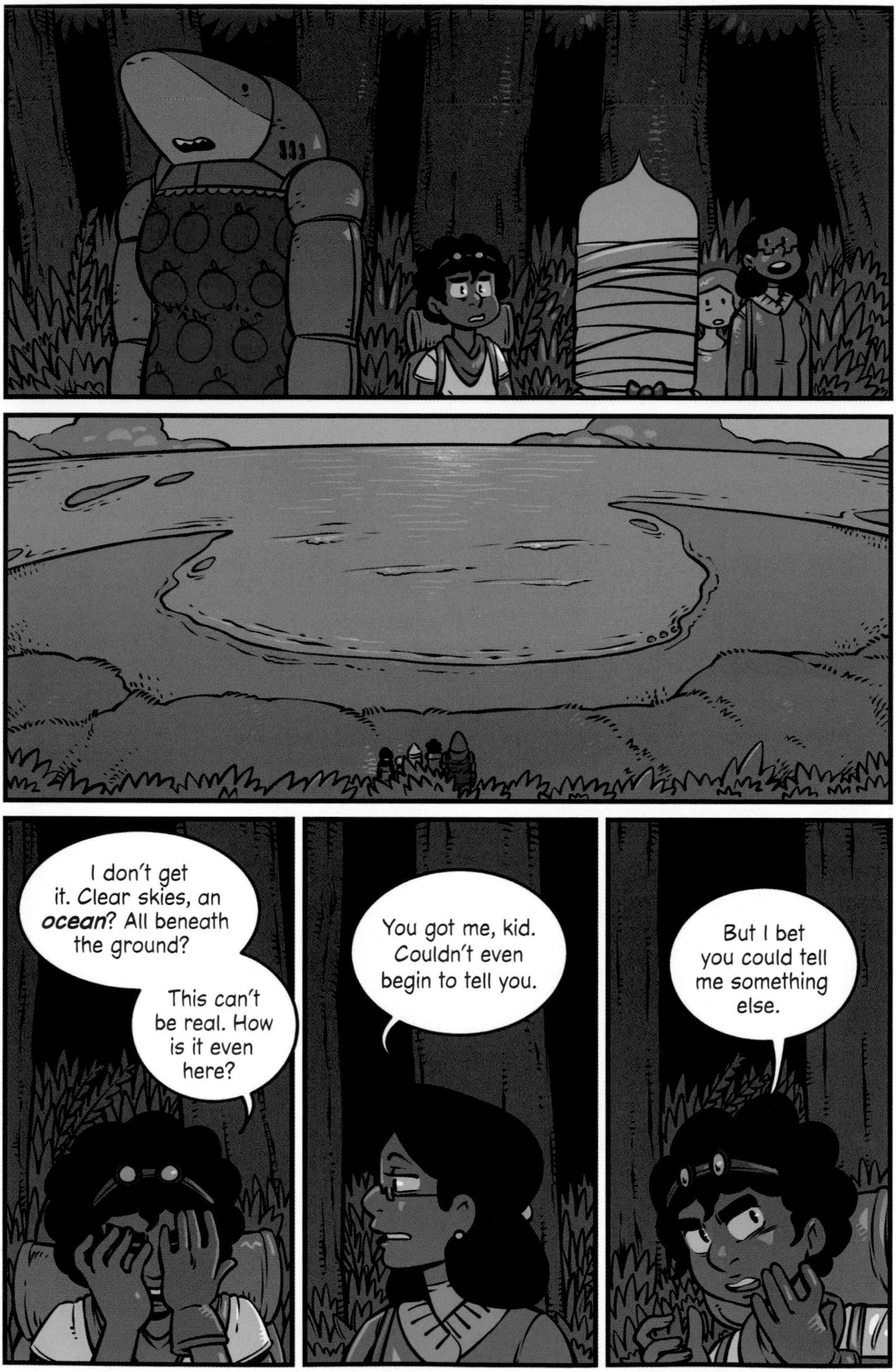
I don't get it. Clear skies, an *ocean*? All beneath the ground?
This can't be real. How is it even here?
You got me, kid. Couldn't even begin to tell you.
But I bet you could tell me something else.

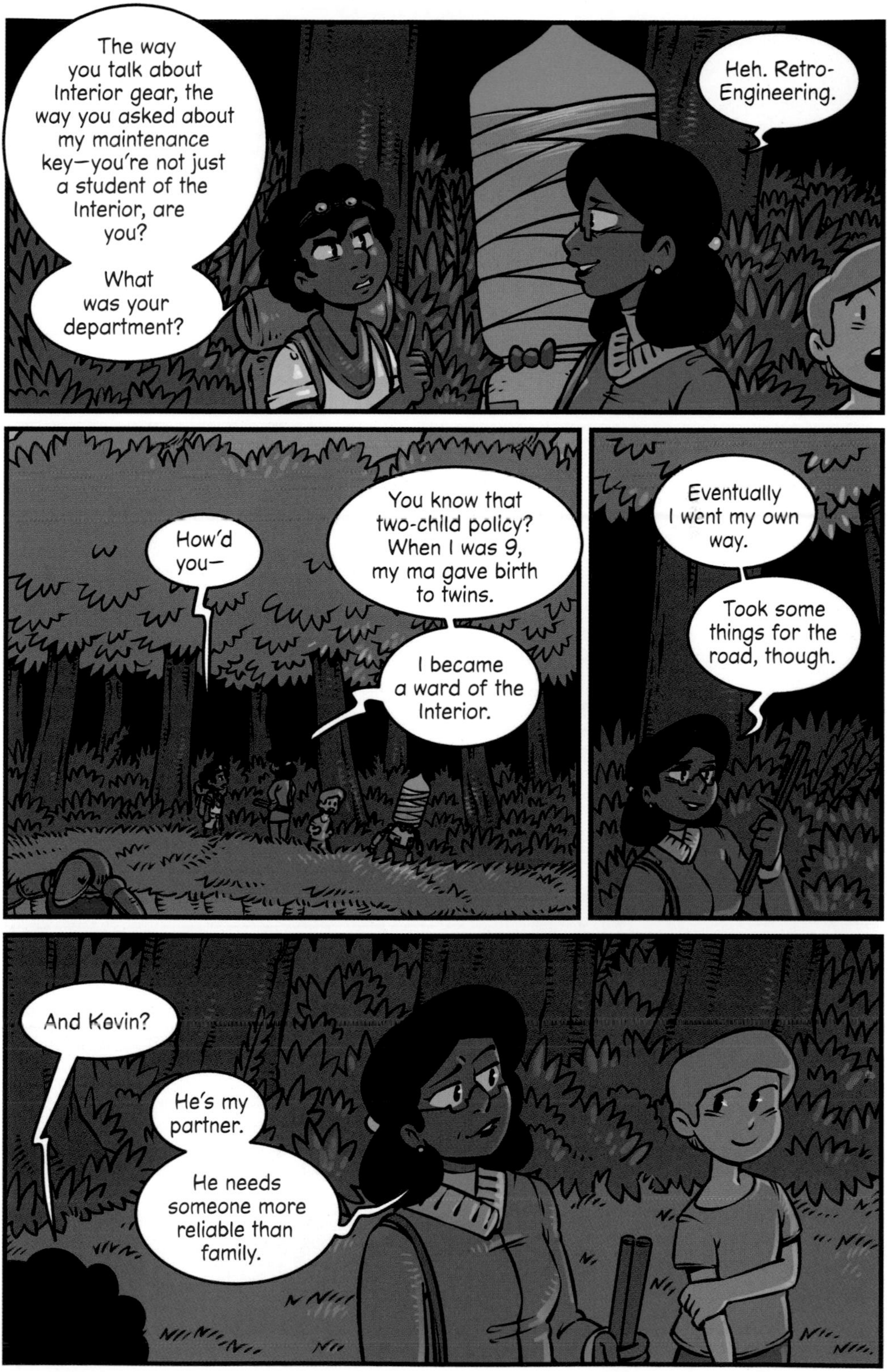
The way you talk about Interior gear, the way you asked about my maintenance key—you're not just a student of the Interior, are you?
What was your department?
Heh. Retro-Engineering.
How'd you—
You know that two-child policy? When I was 9, my ma gave birth to twins.
I became a ward of the Interior.
Eventually I went my own way.
Took some things for the road, though.
And Kevin?
He's my partner.
He needs someone more reliable than family.

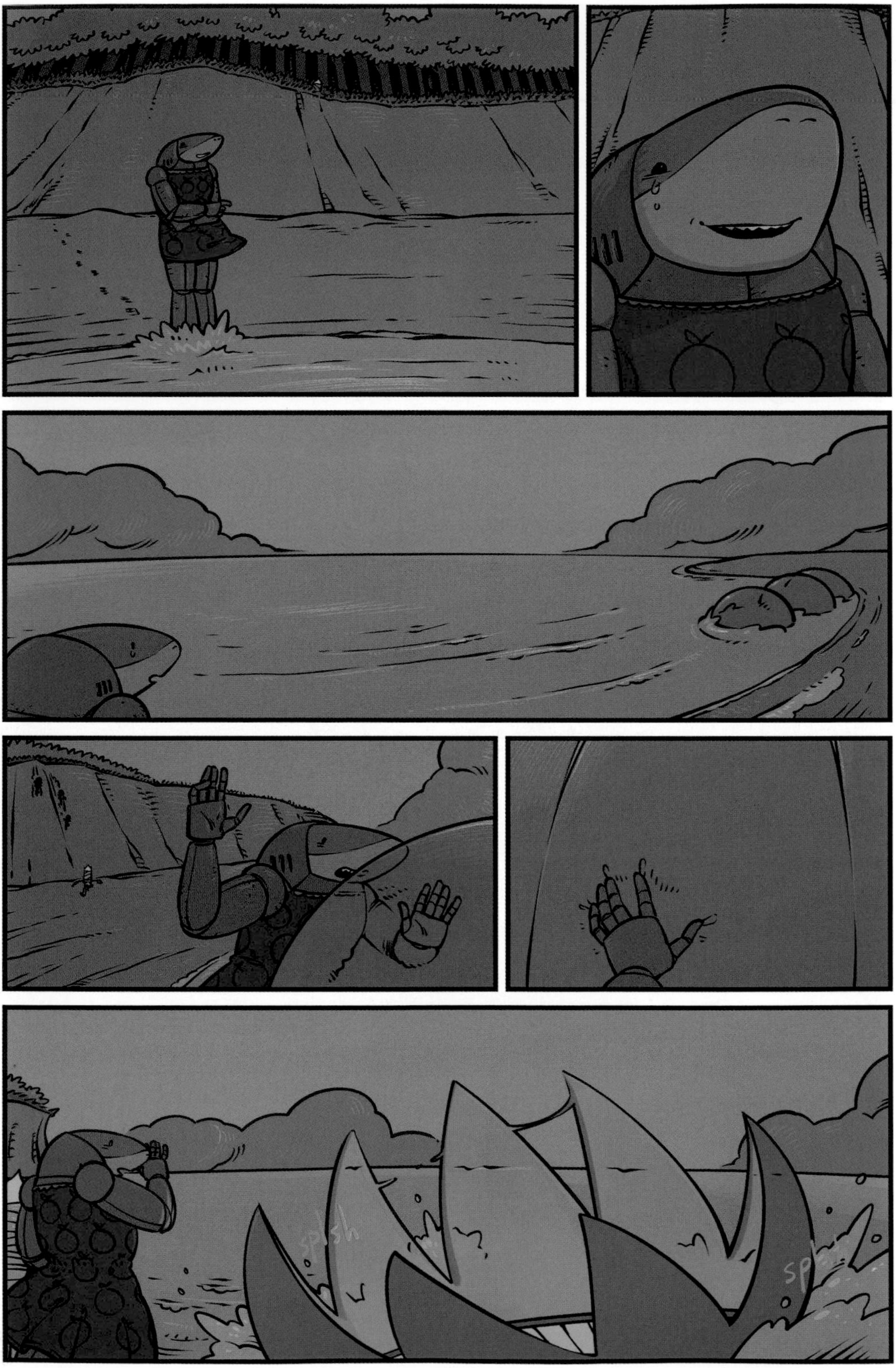
splsh
splsh

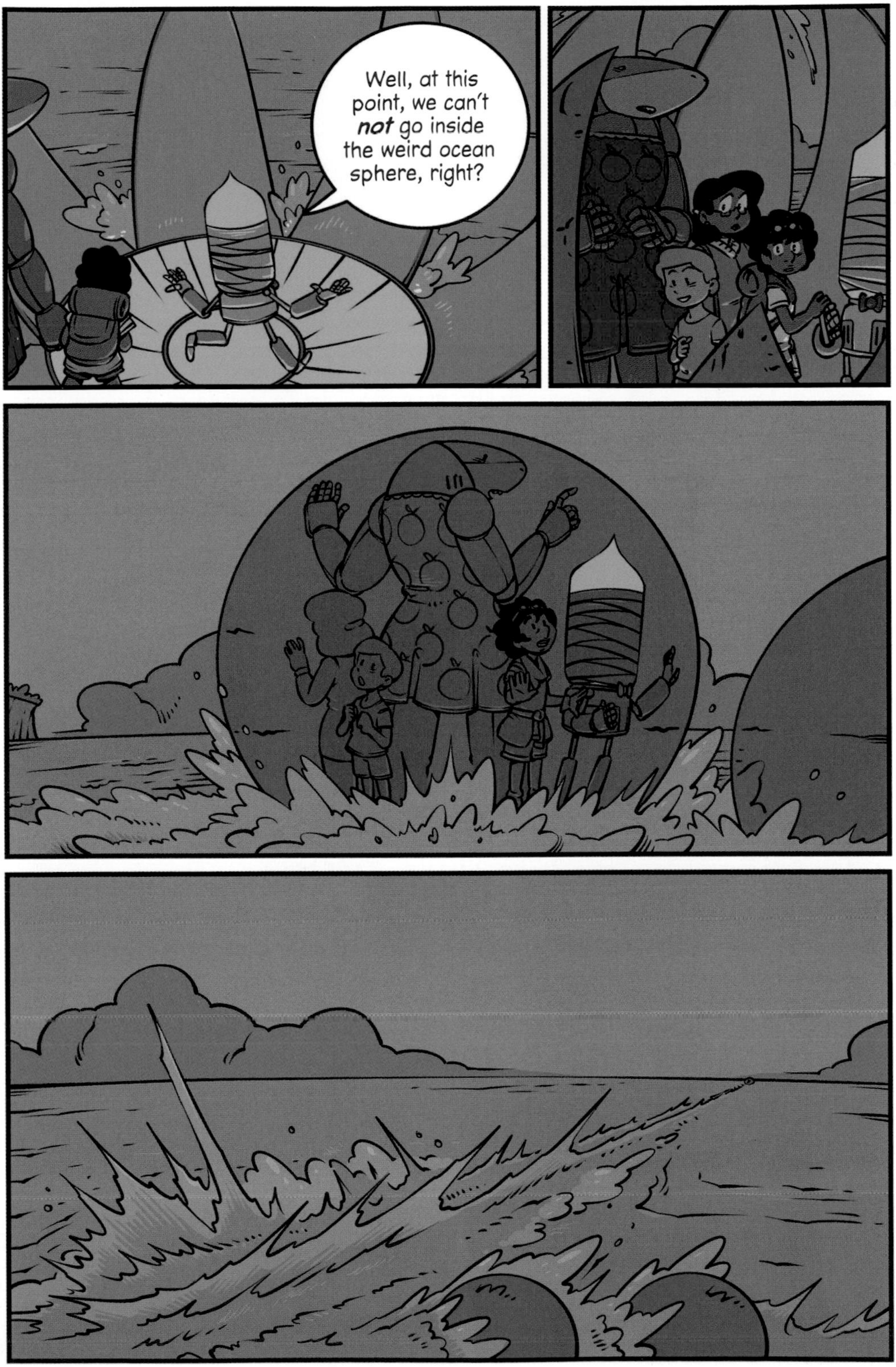
Well, at this point, we can't ***not*** go inside the weird ocean sphere, right?

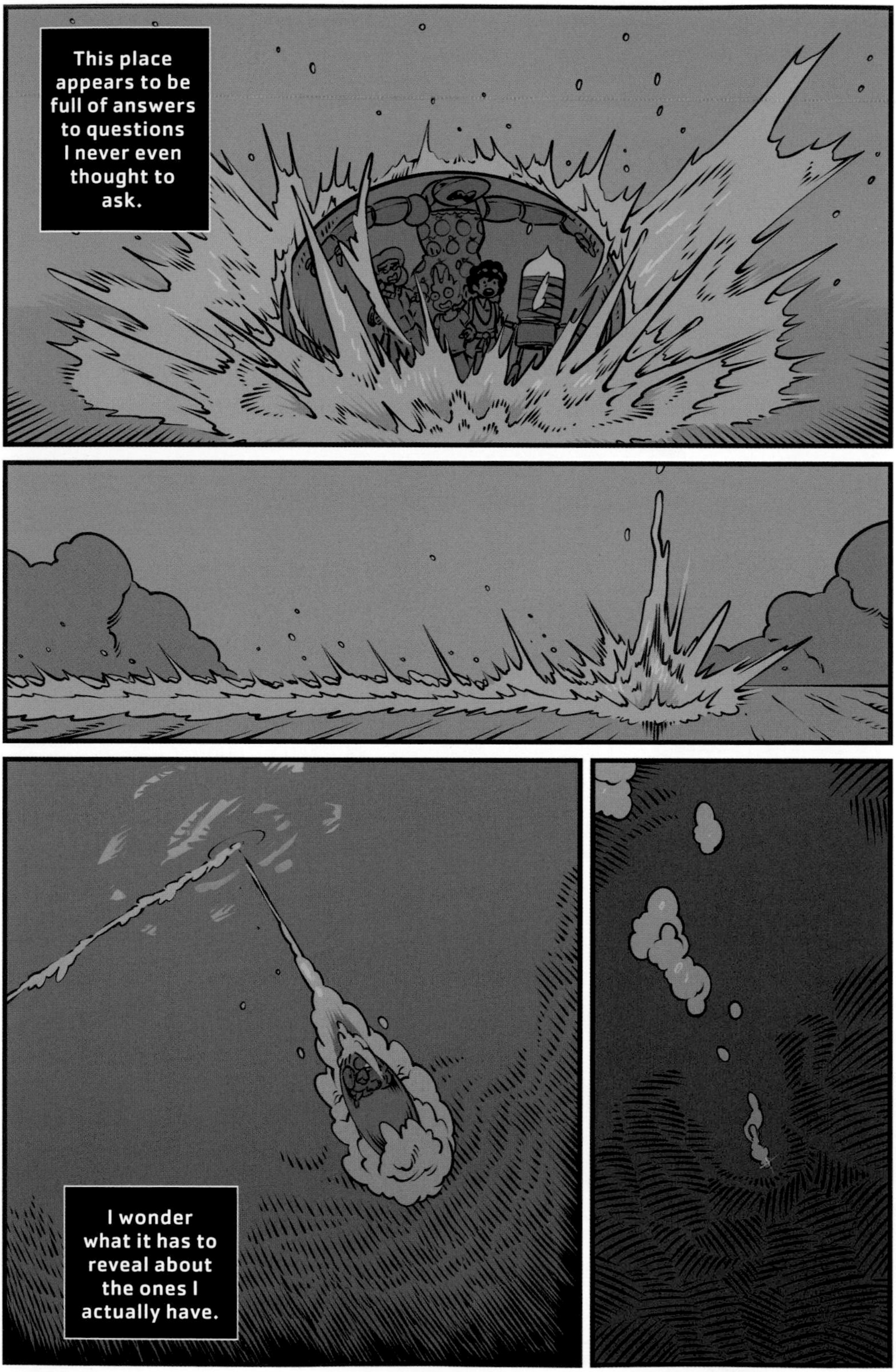
This place appears to be full of answers to questions I never even thought to ask.
I wonder what it has to reveal about the ones I actually have.

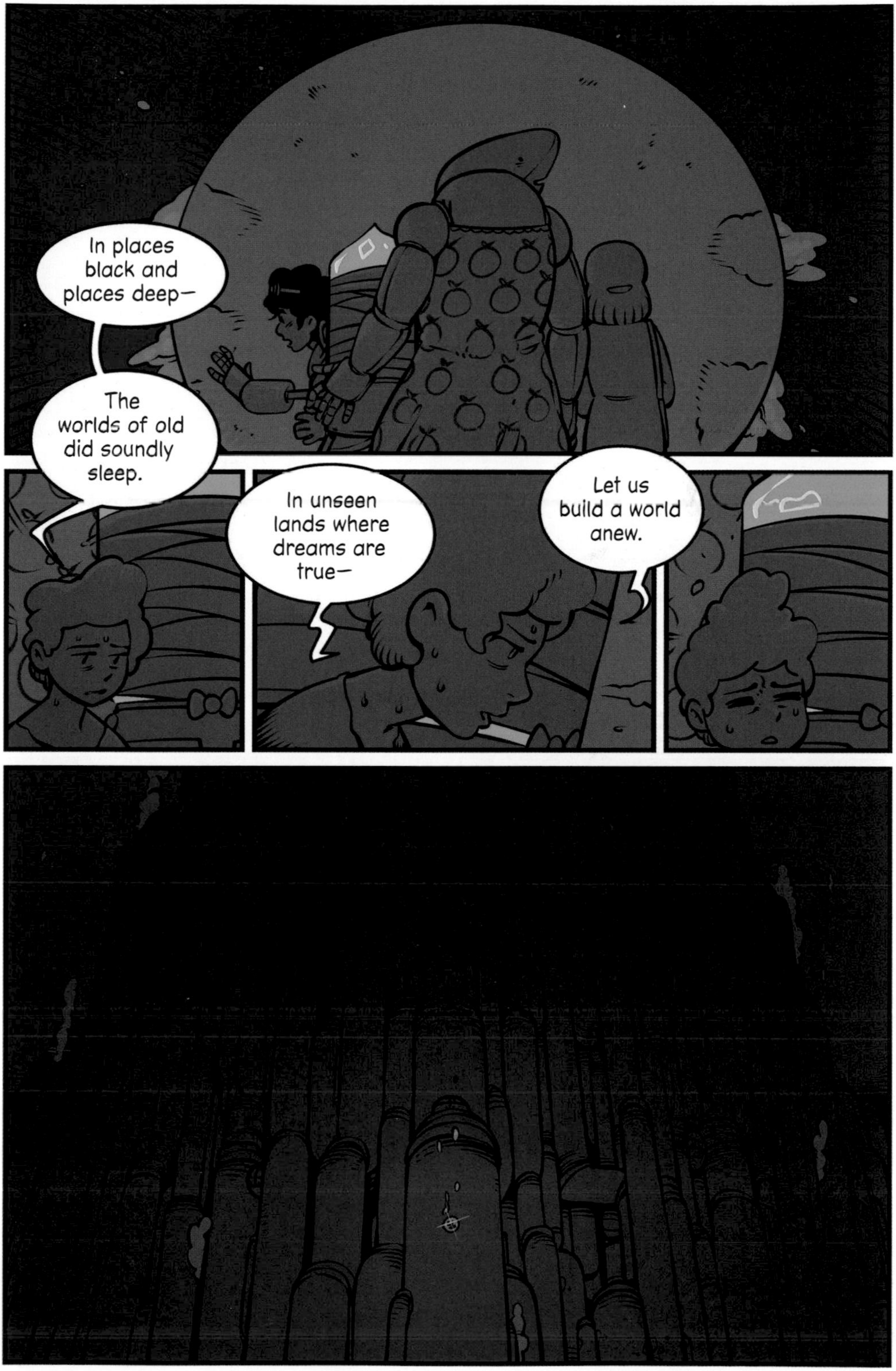
In places black and places deep—
The worlds of old did soundly sleep.
In unseen lands where dreams are true—
Let us build a world anew.

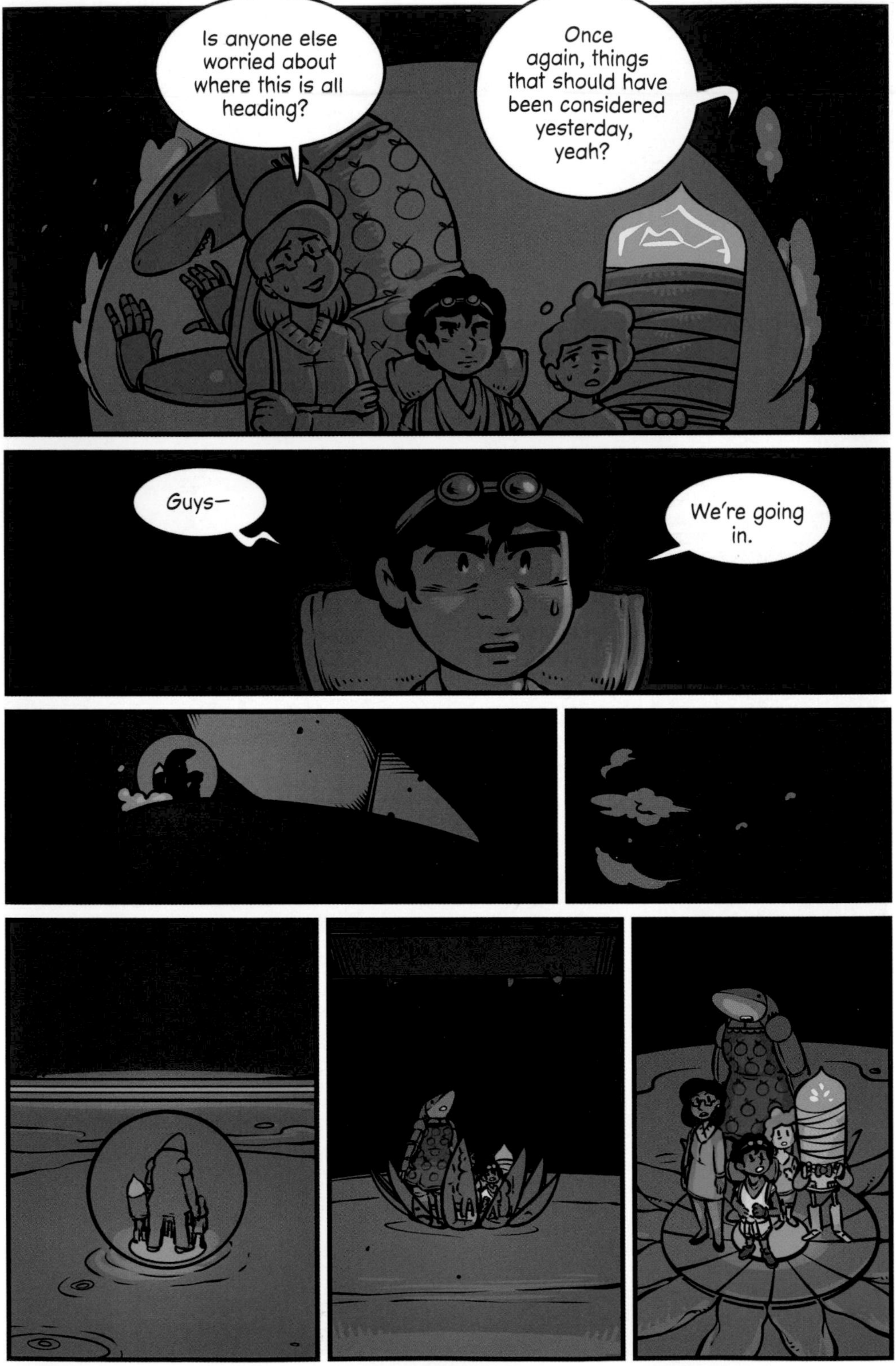
Is anyone else worried about where this is all heading?
Once again, things that should have been considered yesterday, yeah?
Guys—
We're going in.

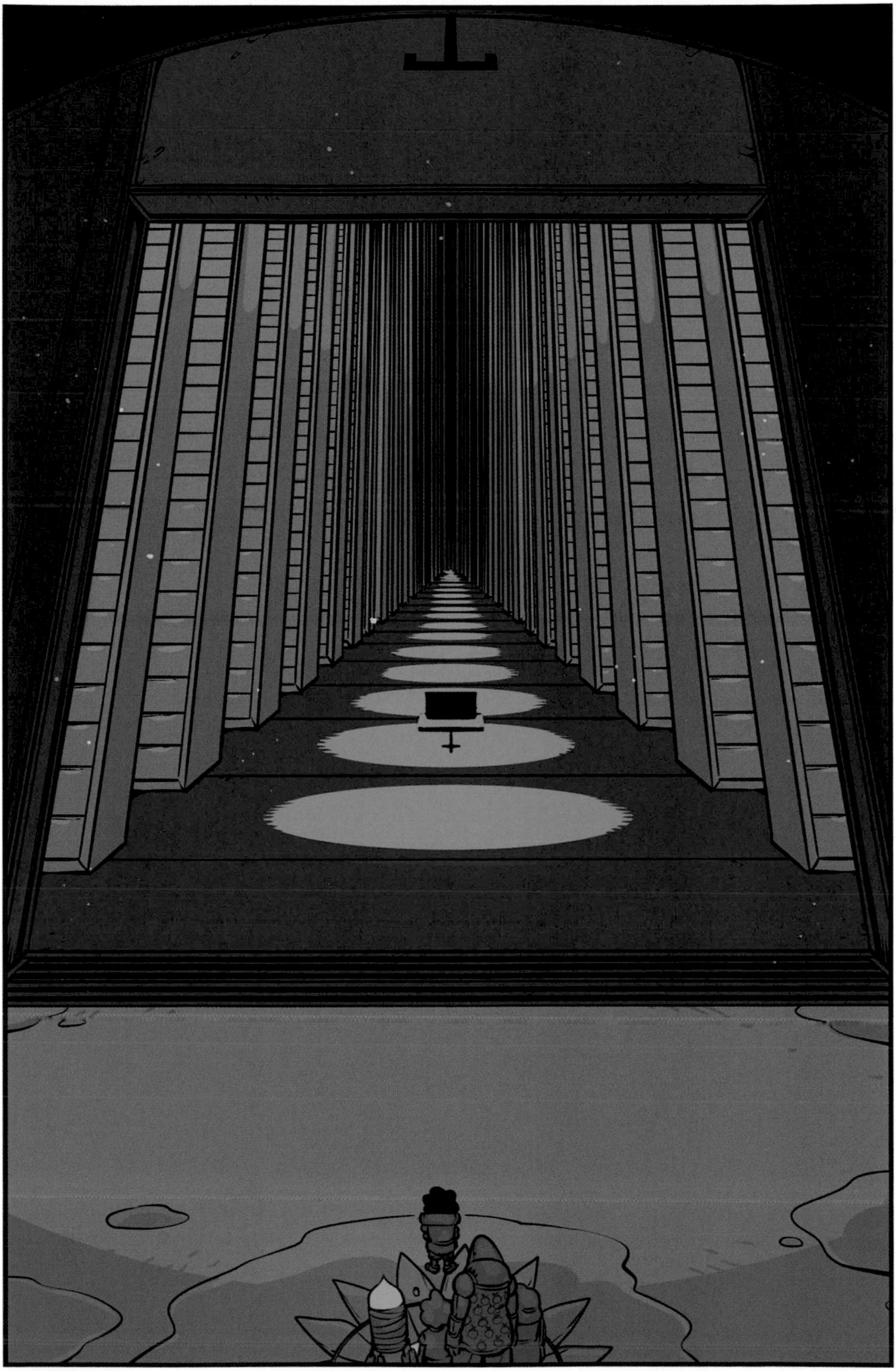

Oh, yes.

We've hit the mother lode!

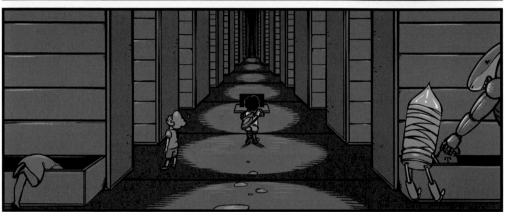

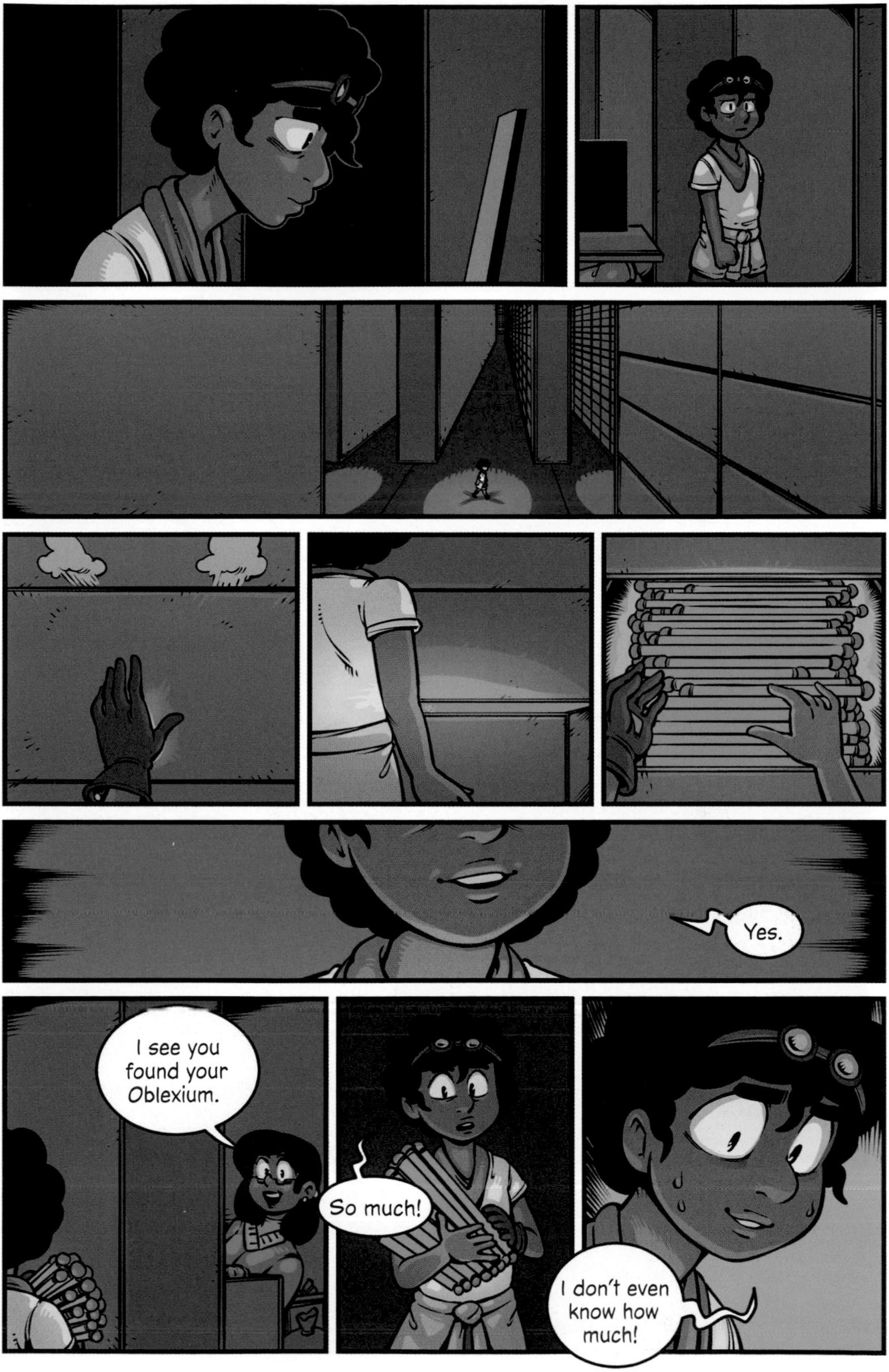
Yes.
I see you found your Oblexium.
So much!
I don't even know how much!

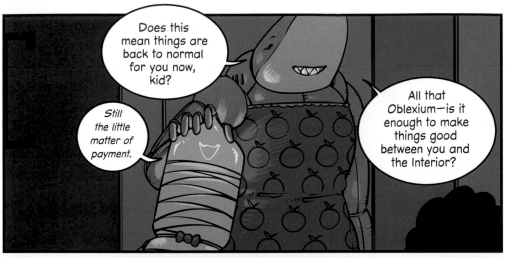

Does this mean things are back to normal for you now, kid?

Still the little matter of payment.

All that Oblexium—is it enough to make things good between you and the Interior?

If this doesn't square me with the Interior, I don't think anything will.

You guys hear something?

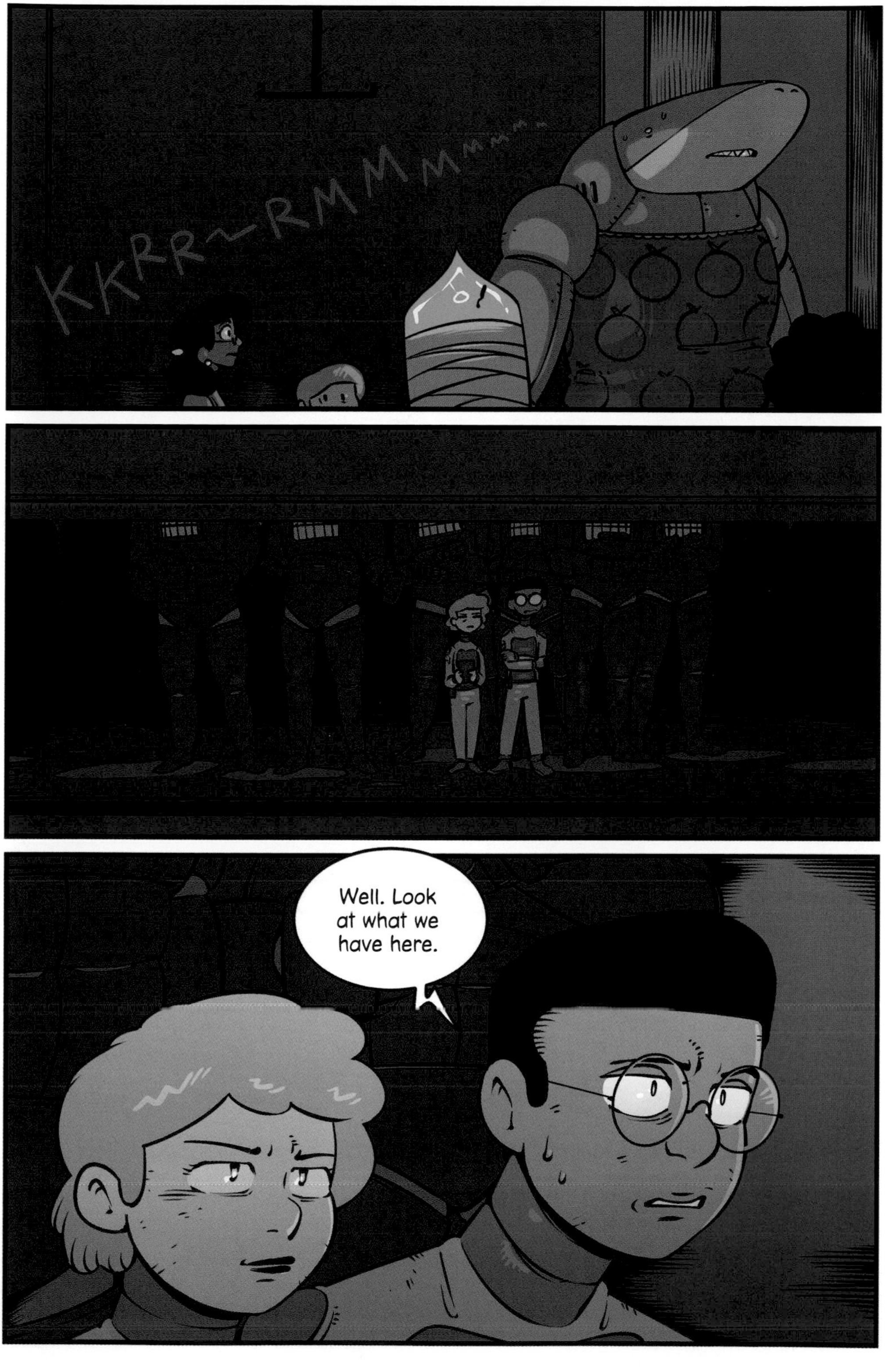
KKRR~RMMMmmmm
Well. Look at what we have here.

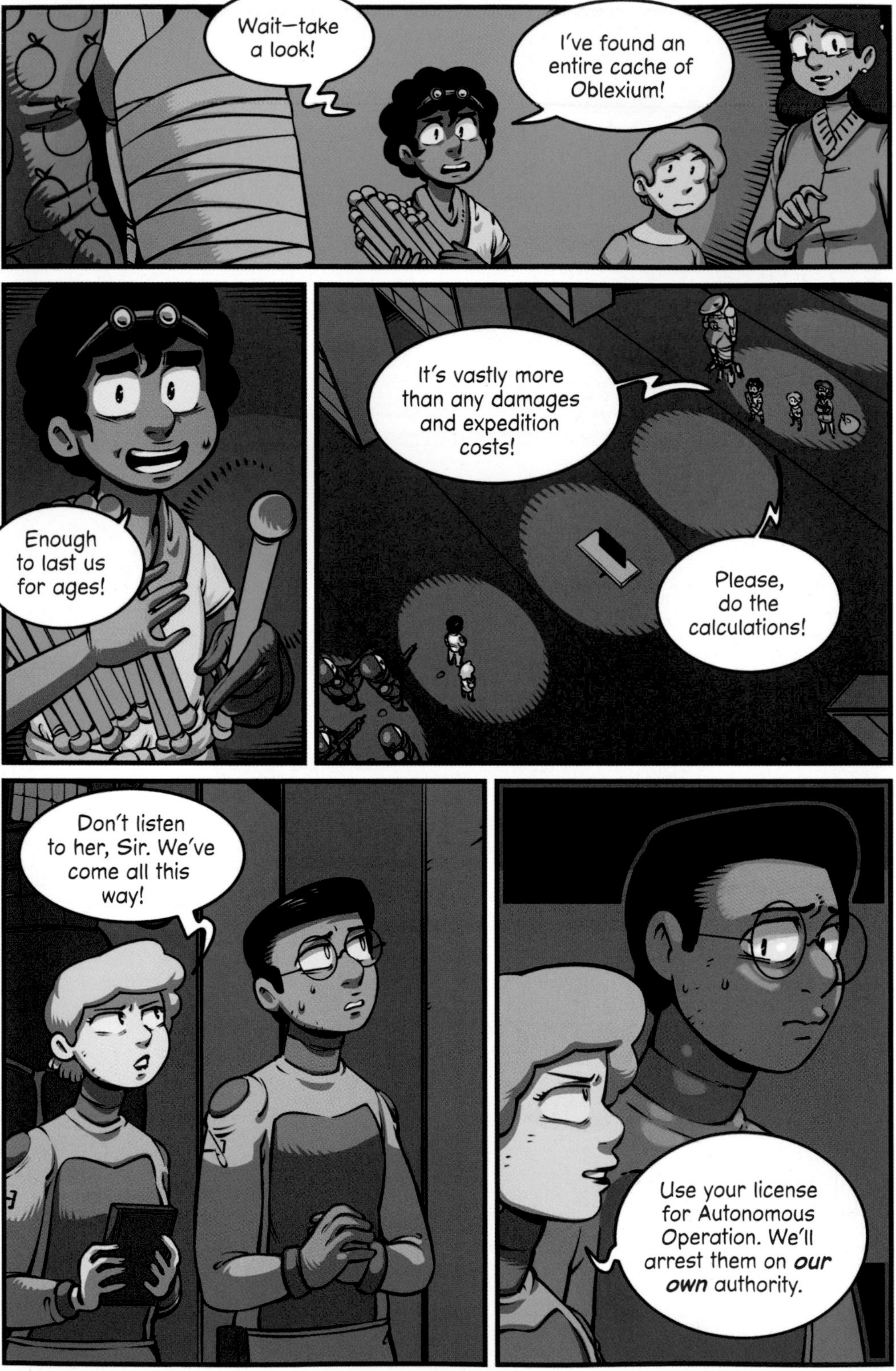
Wait—take a look!
I've found an entire cache of Oblexium!
Enough to last us for ages!
It's vastly more than any damages and expedition costs!
Please, do the calculations!
Don't listen to her, Sir. We've come all this way!
Use your license for Autonomous Operation. We'll arrest them on ***our own*** authority.

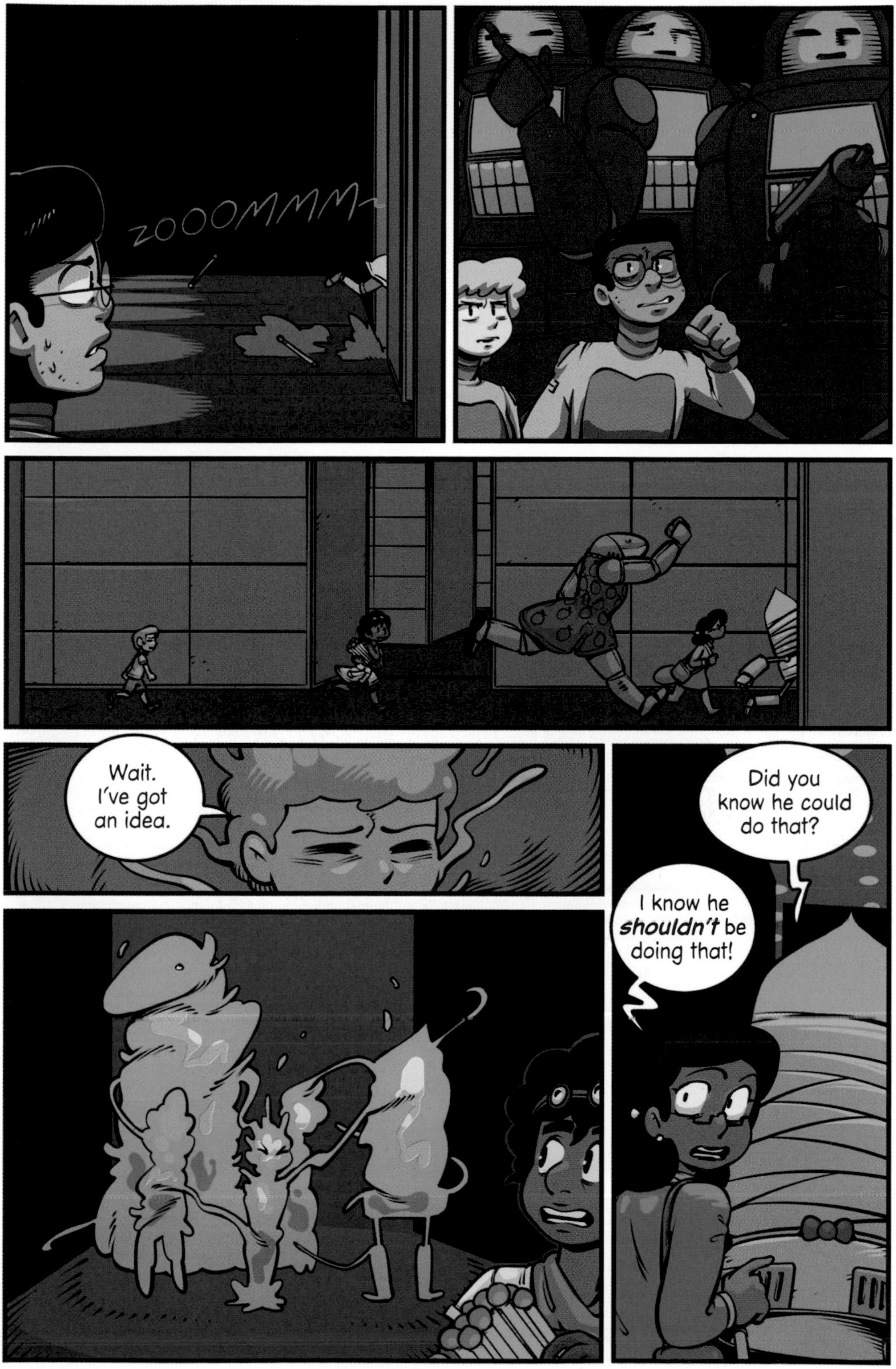
ZOOOMMMM
Wait. I've got an idea.
Did you know he could do that?
I know he *shouldn't* be doing that!

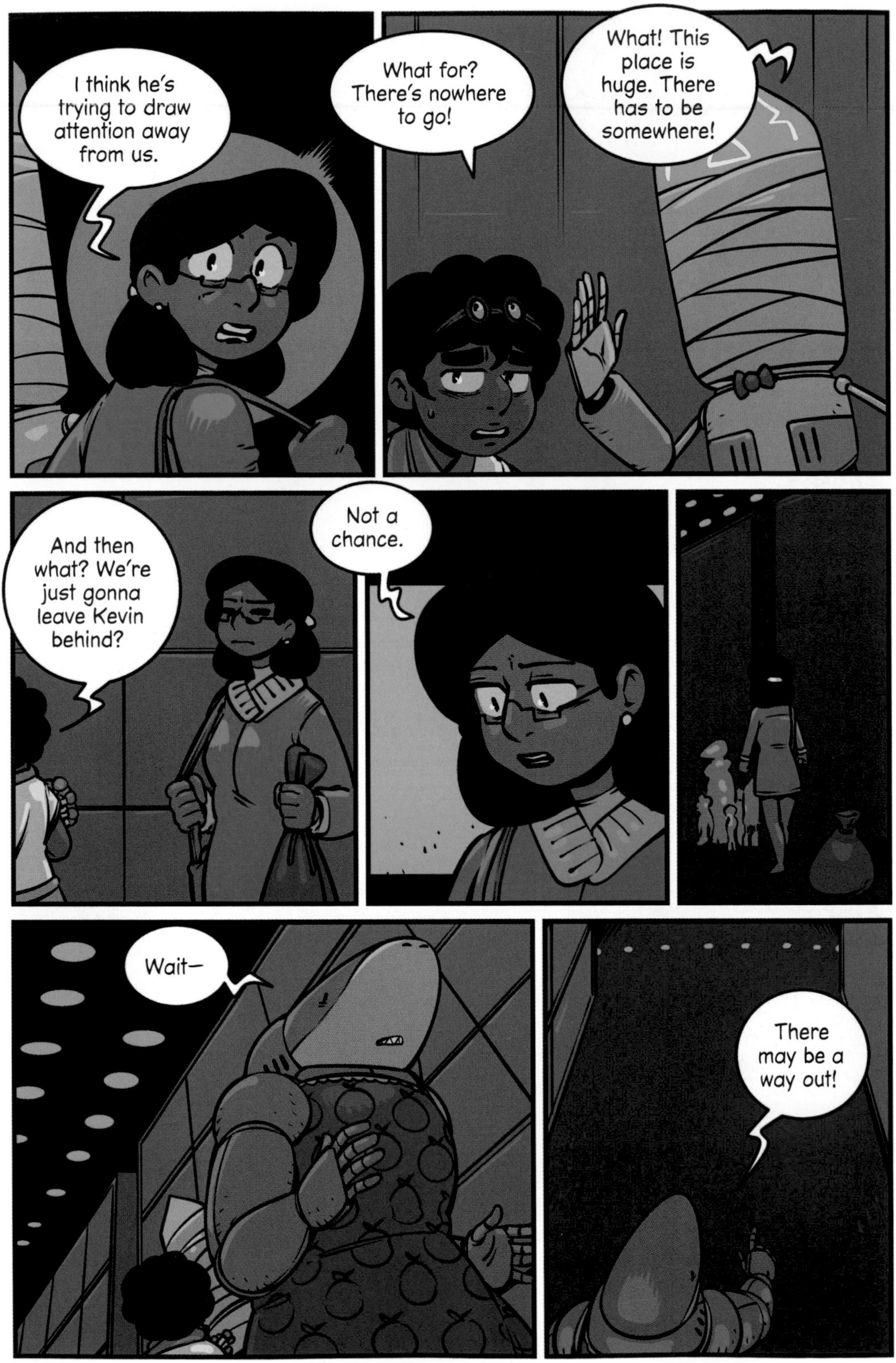
I think he's trying to draw attention away from us.
What for? There's nowhere to go!
What! This place is huge. There has to be somewhere!
And then what? We're just gonna leave Kevin behind?
Not a chance.
Wait—
There may be a way out!

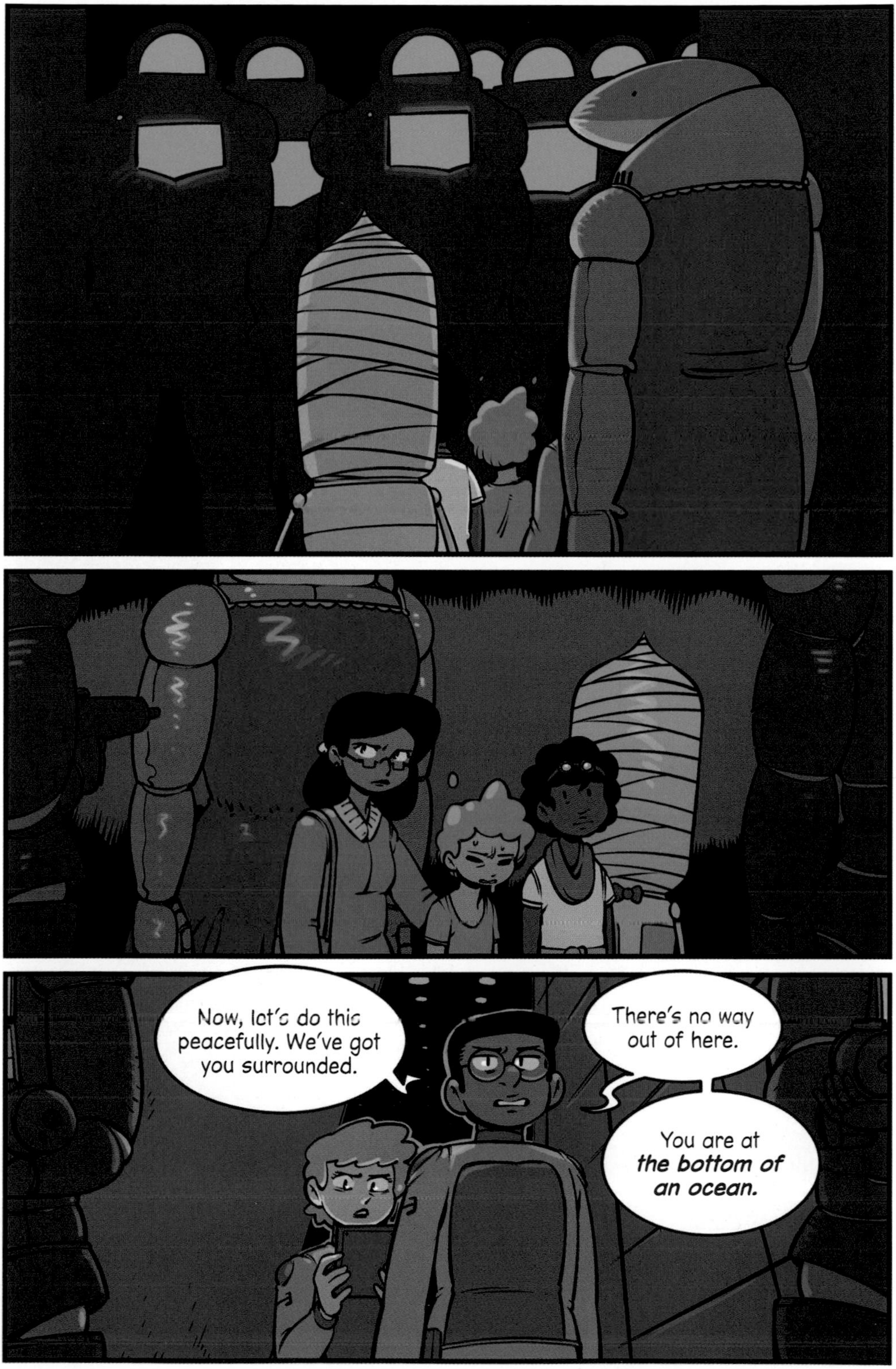
Now, let's do this peacefully. We've got you surrounded.
There's no way out of here.
You are at ***the bottom of an ocean.***

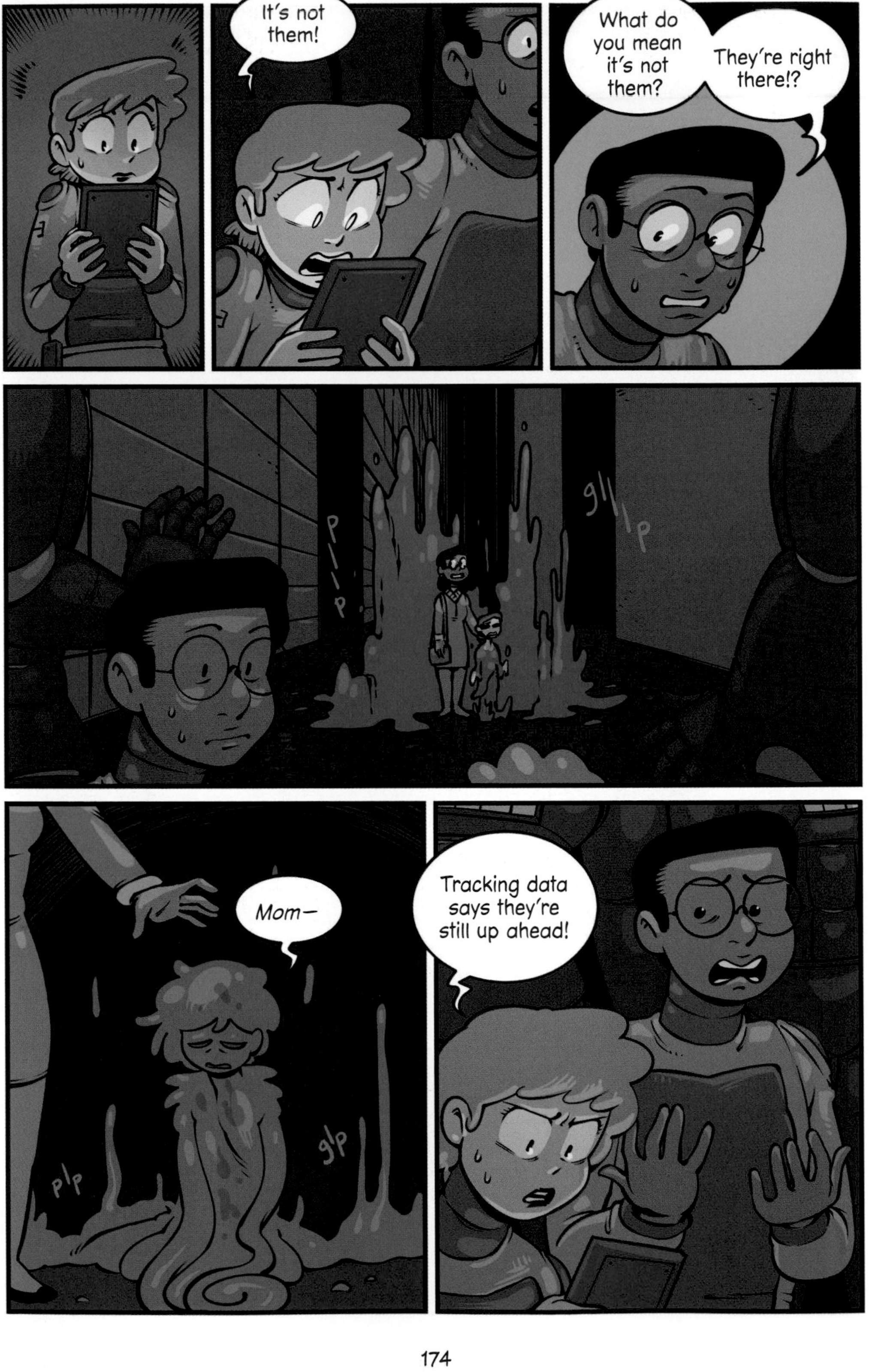
It's not them!
What do you mean it's not them?
They're right there!?
plip
gllip
Mom—
plp
glp
Tracking data says they're still up ahead!

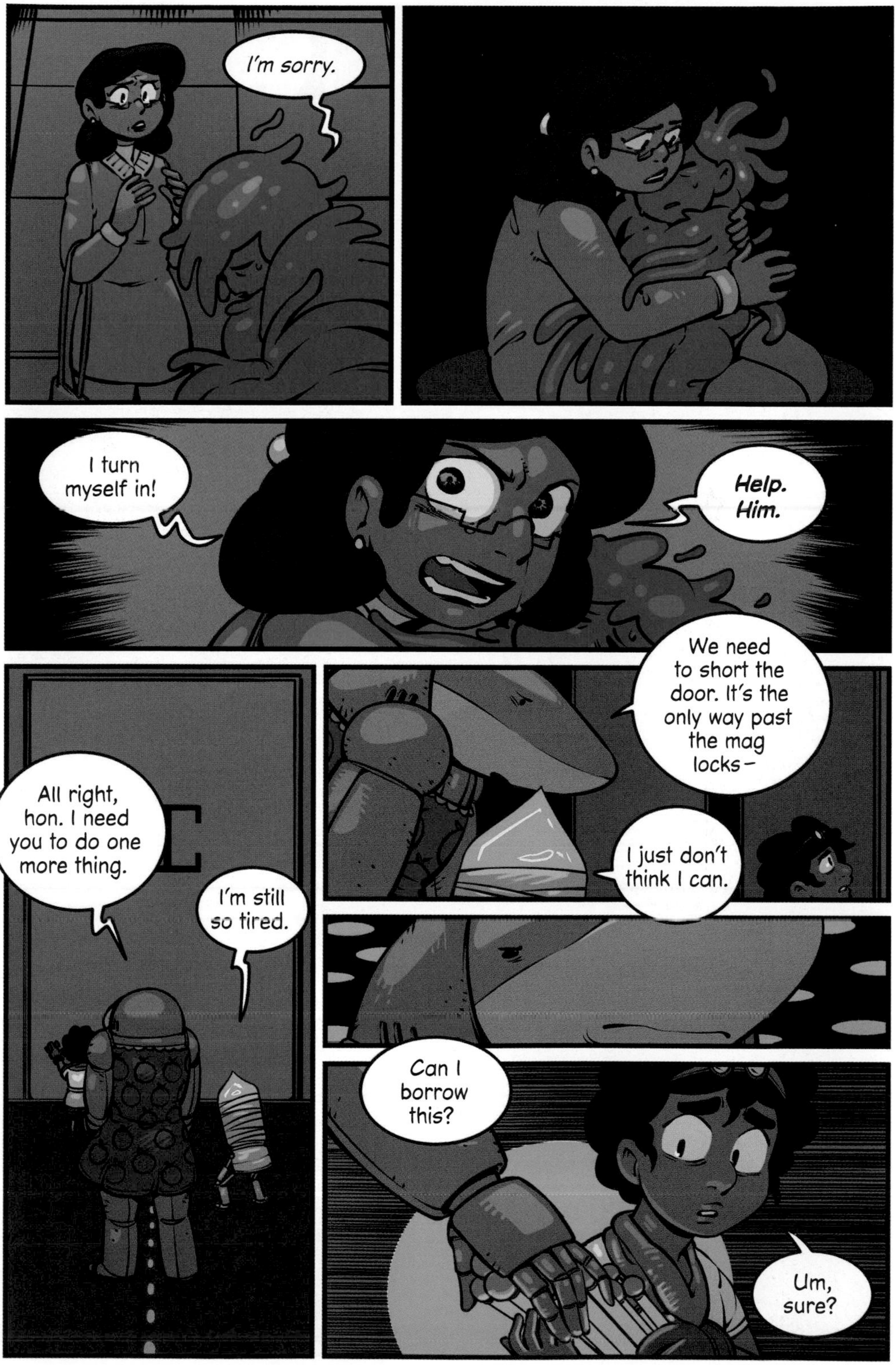
I'm sorry.
I turn myself in!
Help. Him.
We need to short the door. It's the only way past the mag locks—
I just don't think I can.
All right, hon. I need you to do one more thing.
I'm still so tired.
Can I borrow this?
Um, sure?

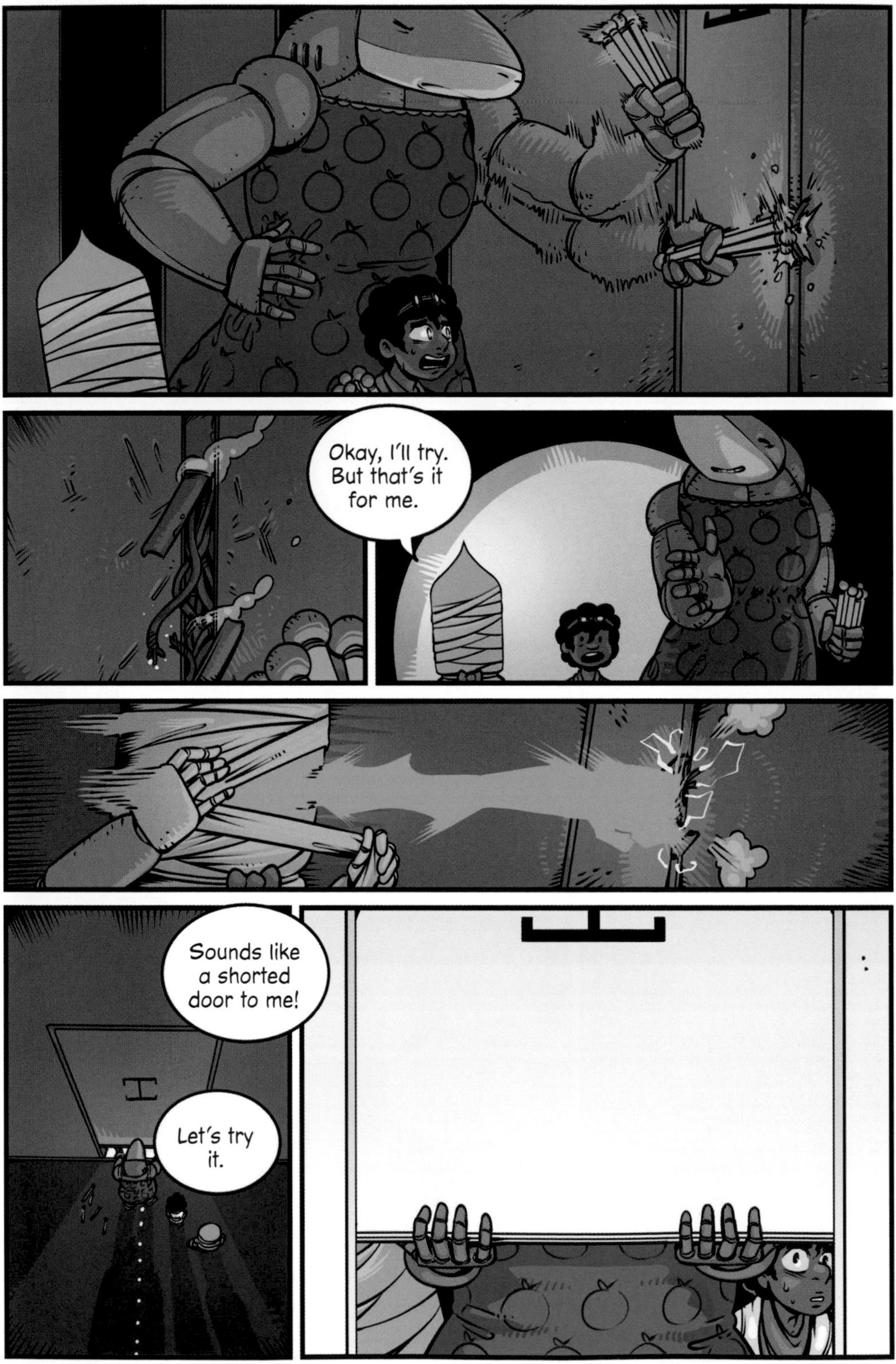
Okay, I'll try. But that's it for me.
Sounds like a shorted door to me!
Let's try it.

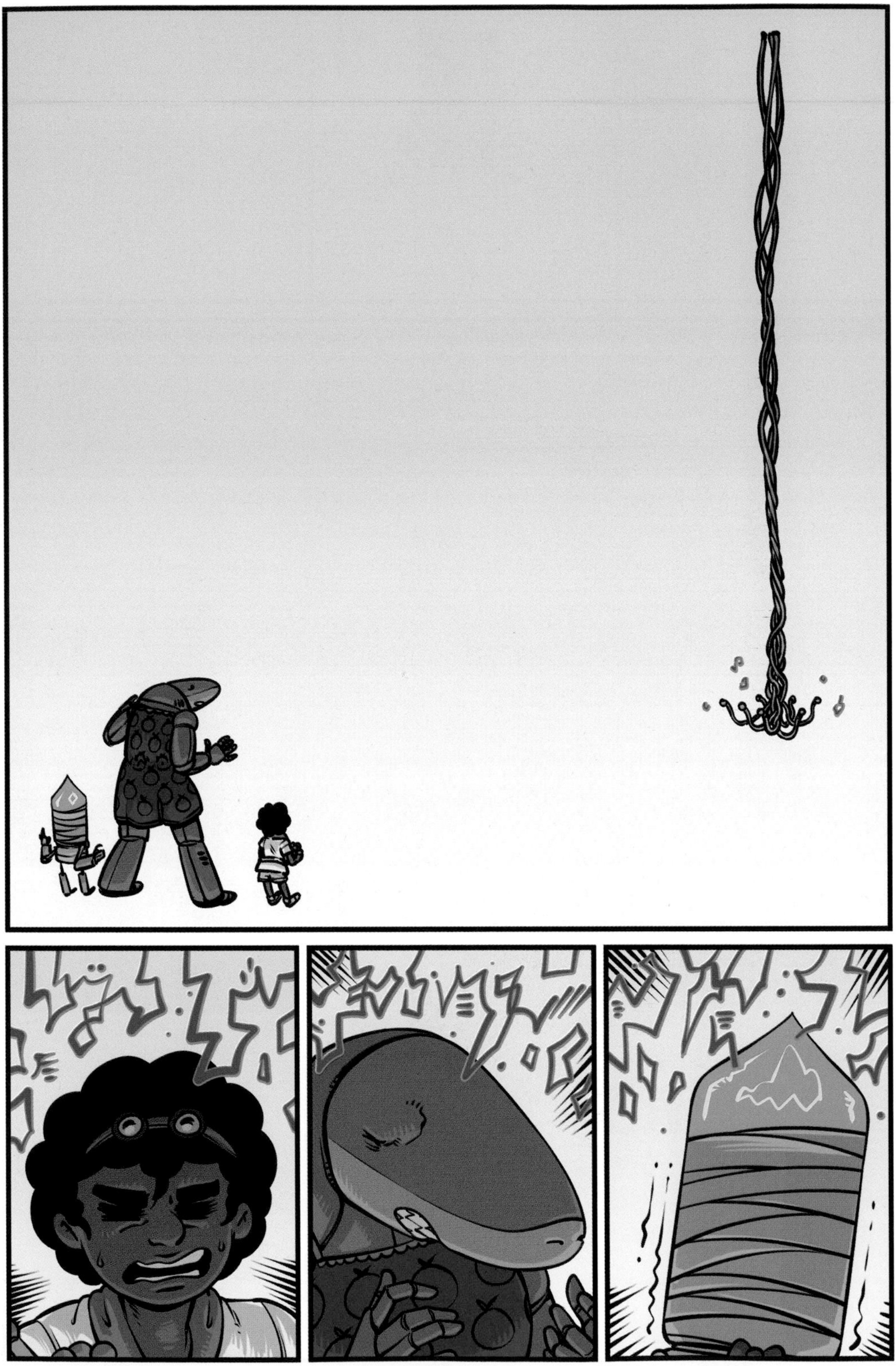

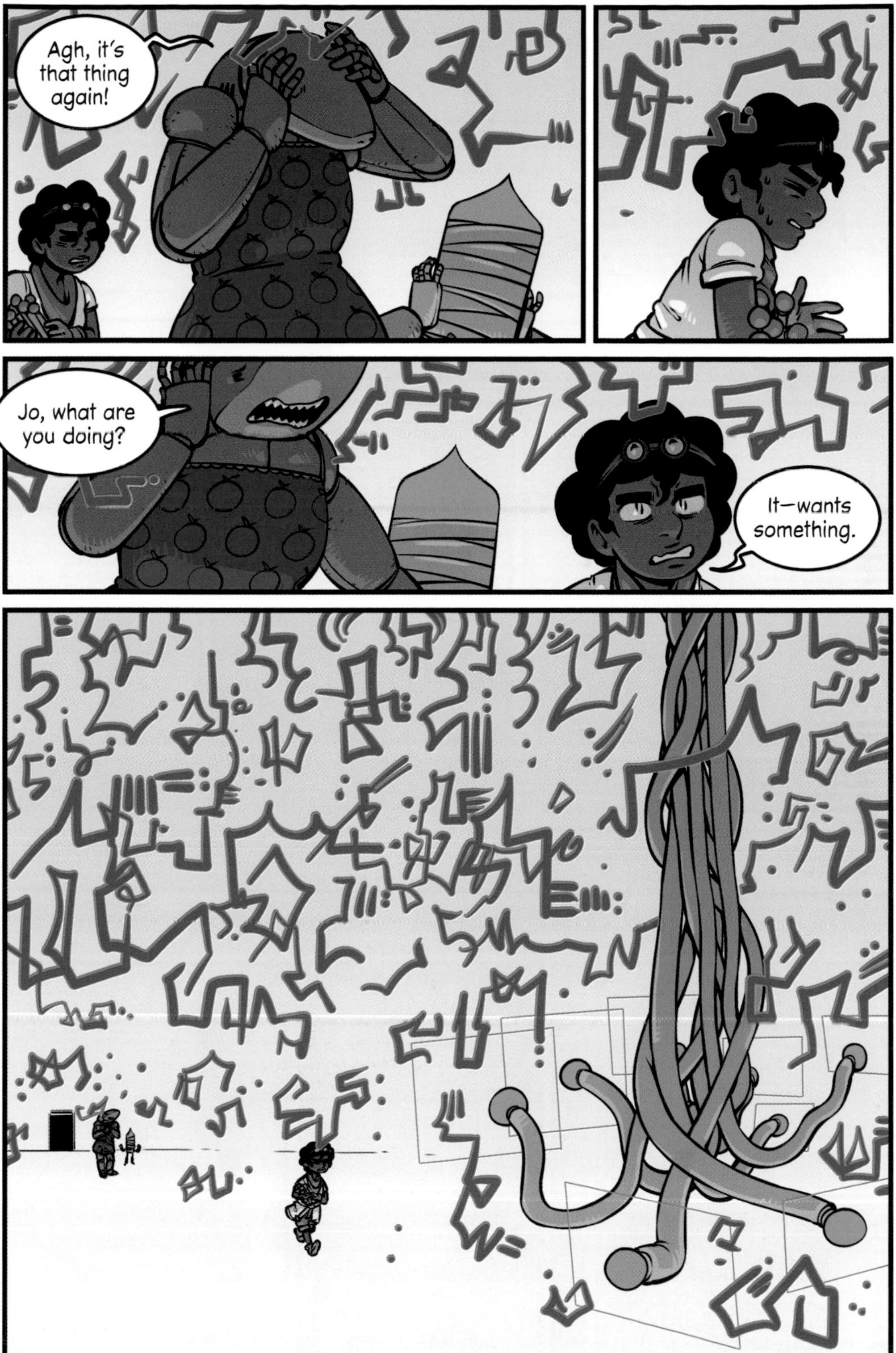
Agh, it's that thing again!
Jo, what are you doing?
It—wants something.

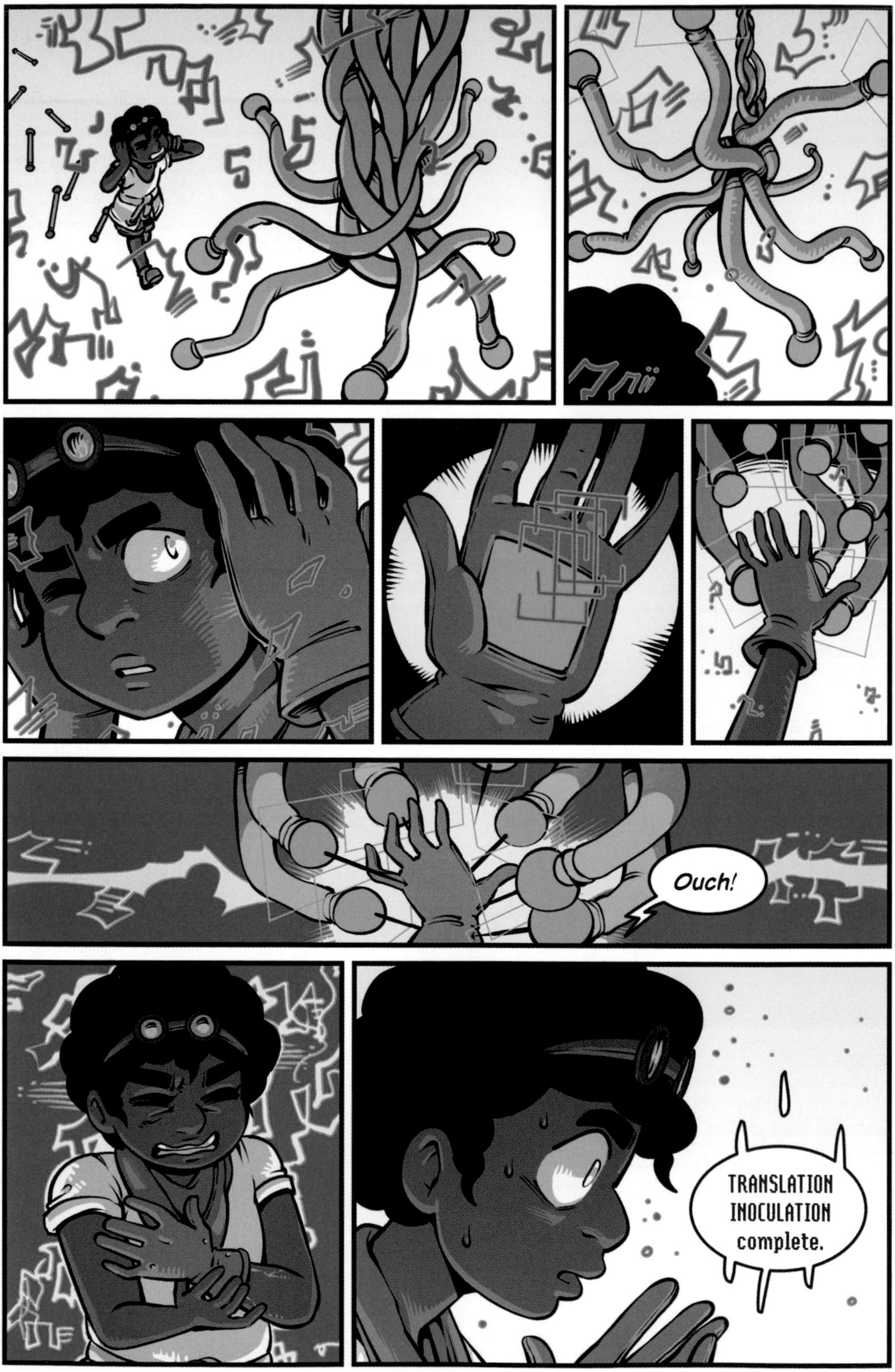
Ouch!
TRANSLATION INOCULATION complete.

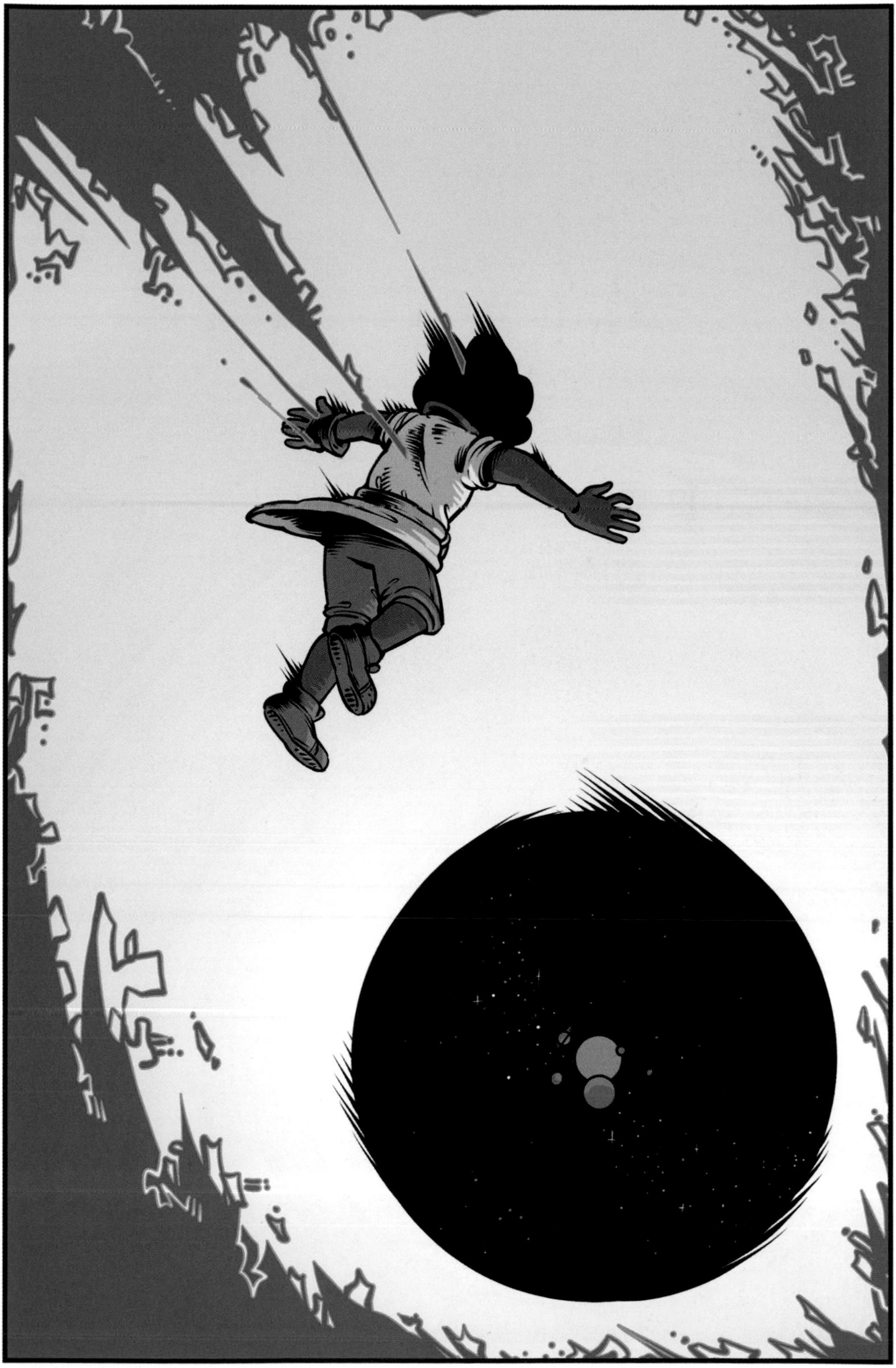

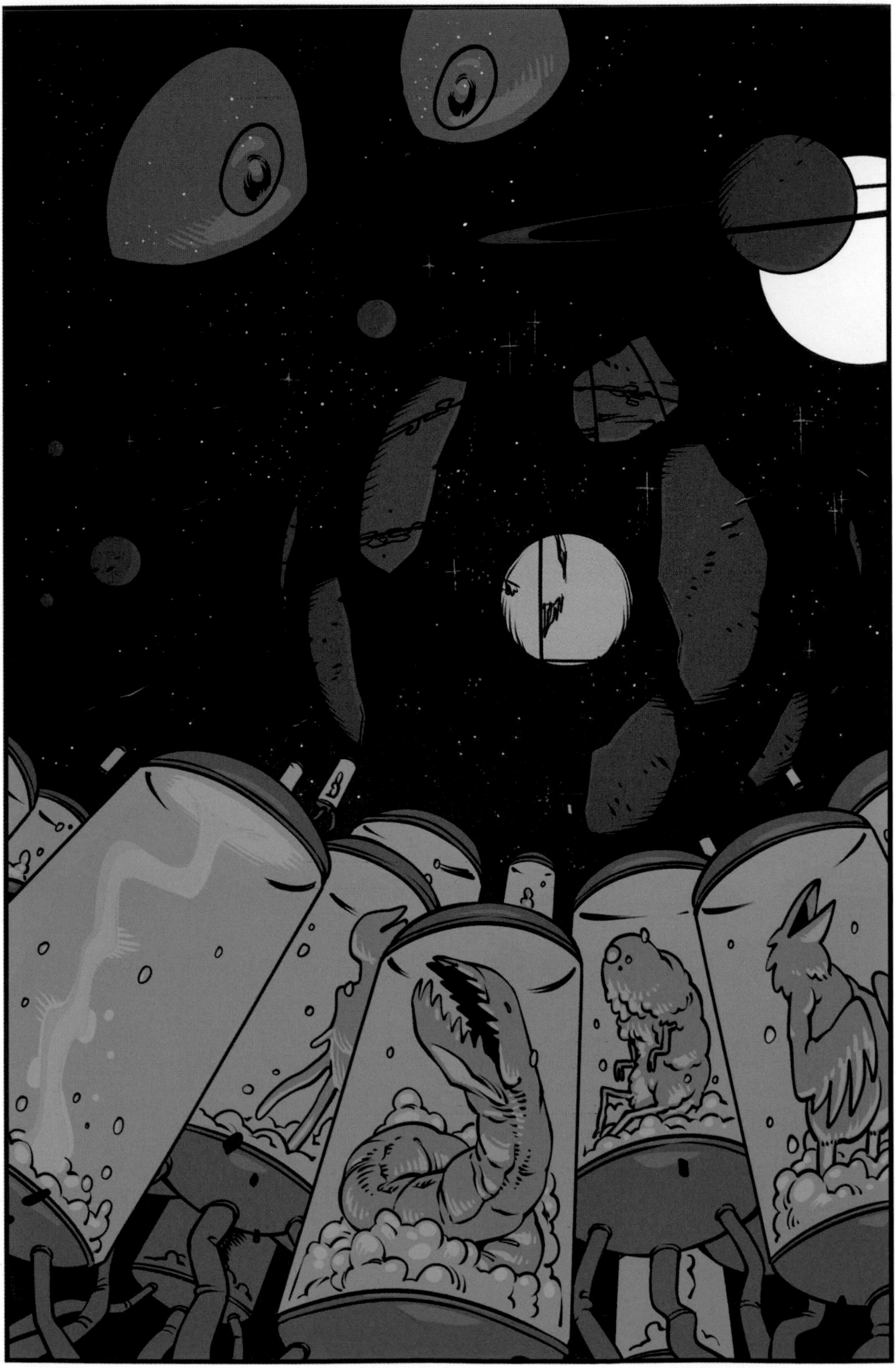

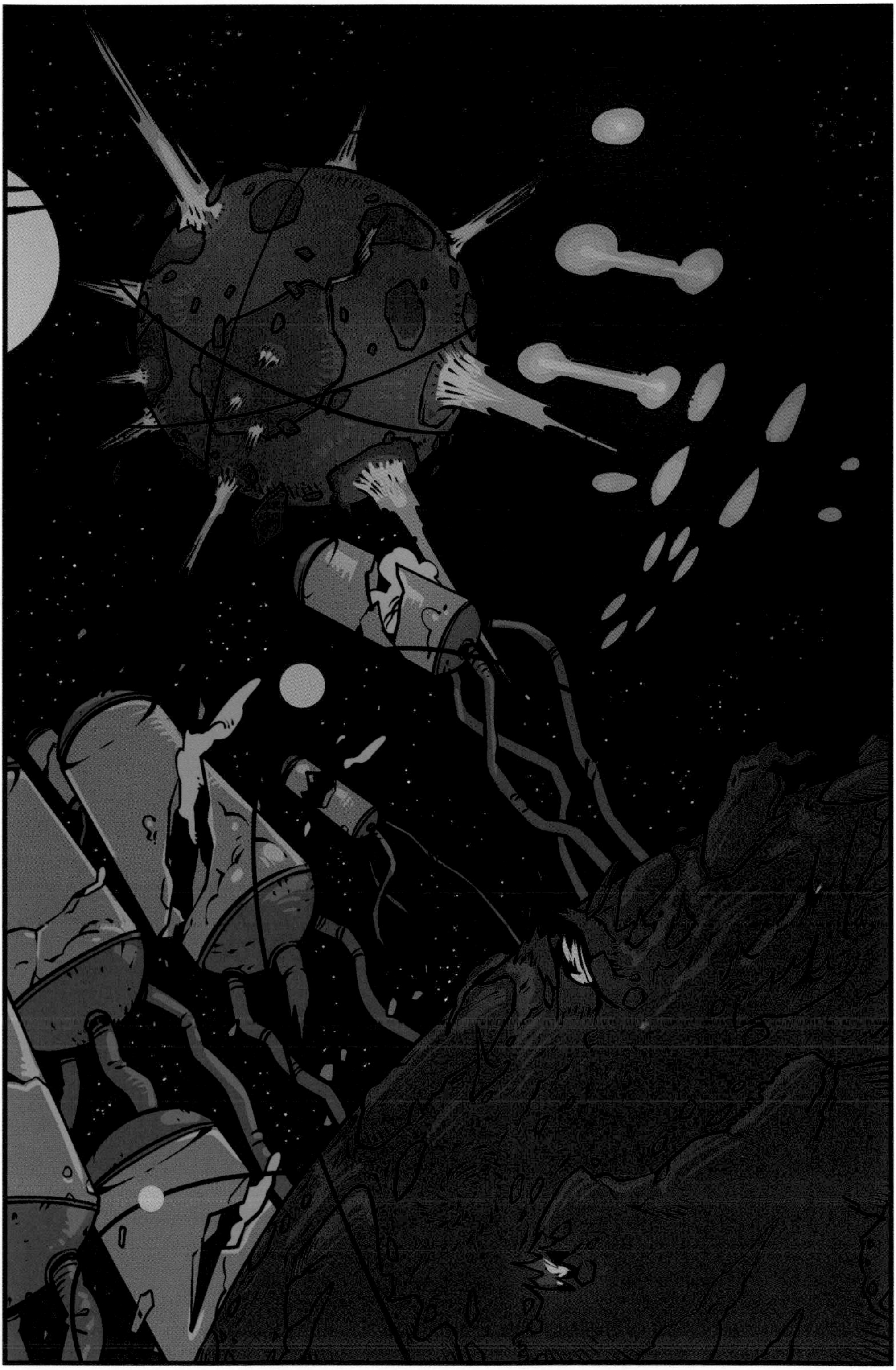

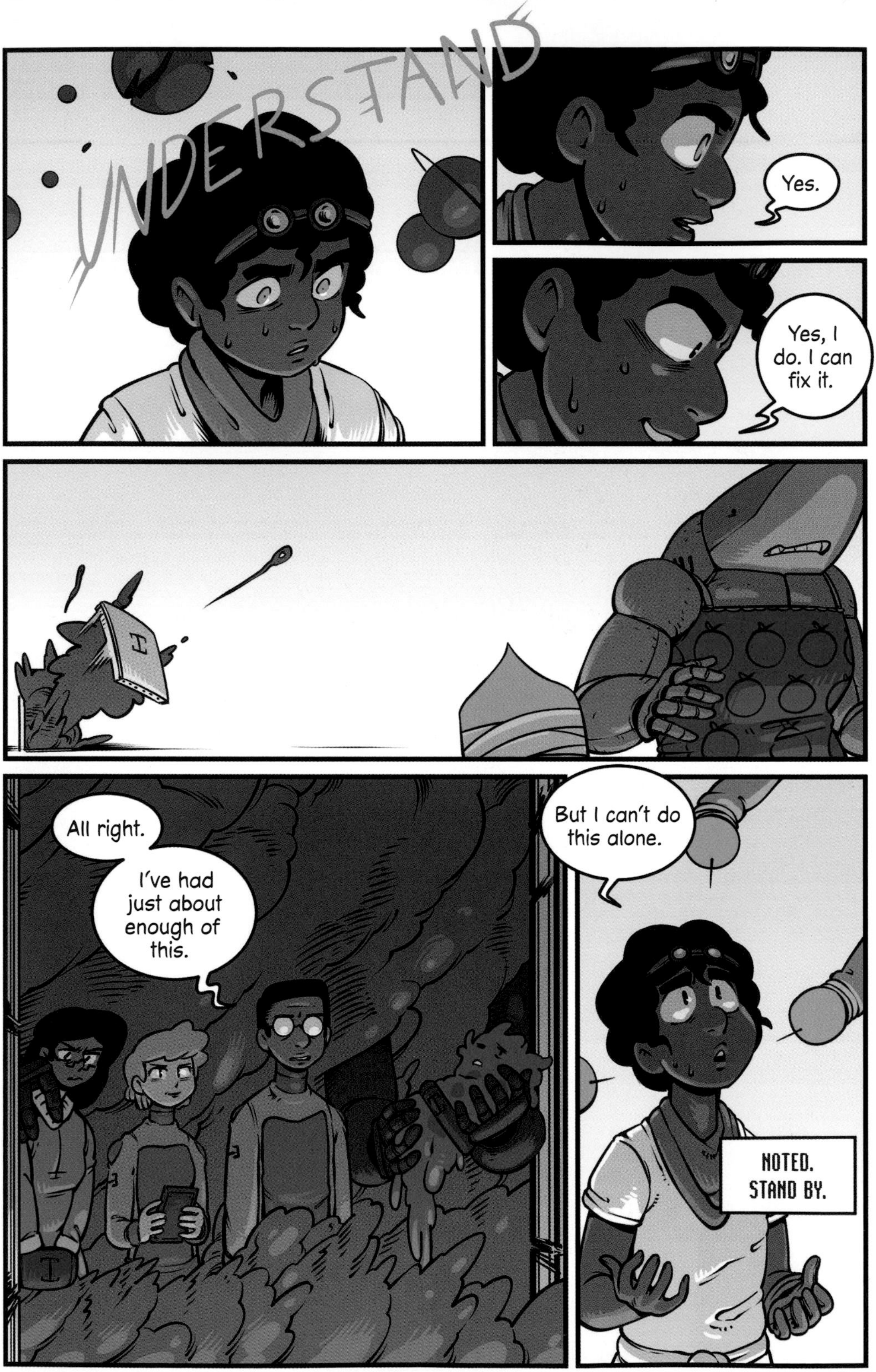
UNDERSTAND
Yes.
Yes, I do. I can fix it.
All right.
I've had just about enough of this.
But I can't do this alone.
NOTED. STAND BY.

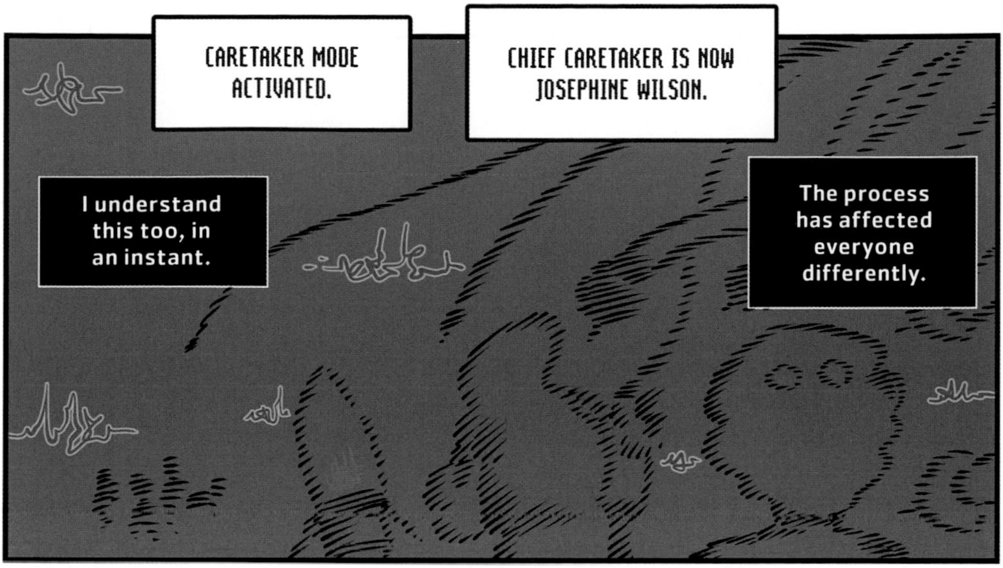
CARETAKER MODE ACTIVATED.
CHIEF CARETAKER IS NOW JOSEPHINE WILSON.
I understand this too, in an instant.
The process has affected everyone differently.

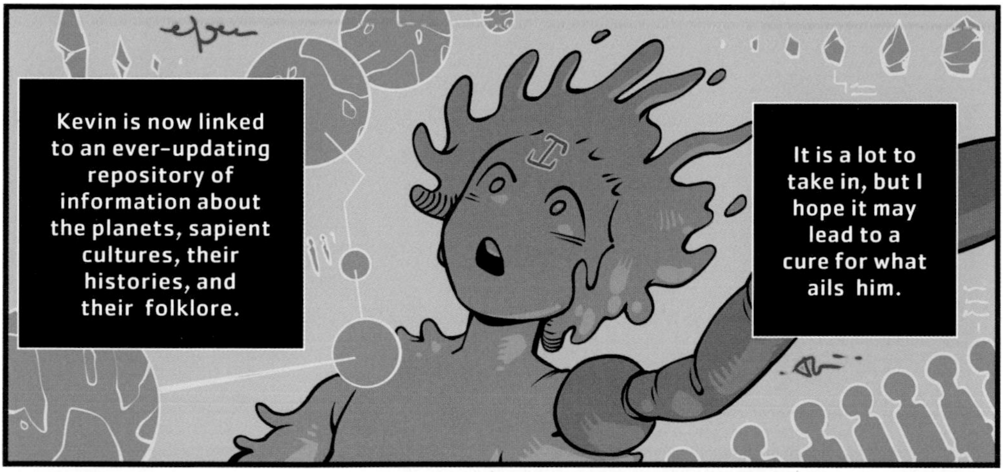
Kevin is now linked to an ever-updating repository of information about the planets, sapient cultures, their histories, and their folklore.
It is a lot to take in, but I hope it may lead to a cure for what ails him.

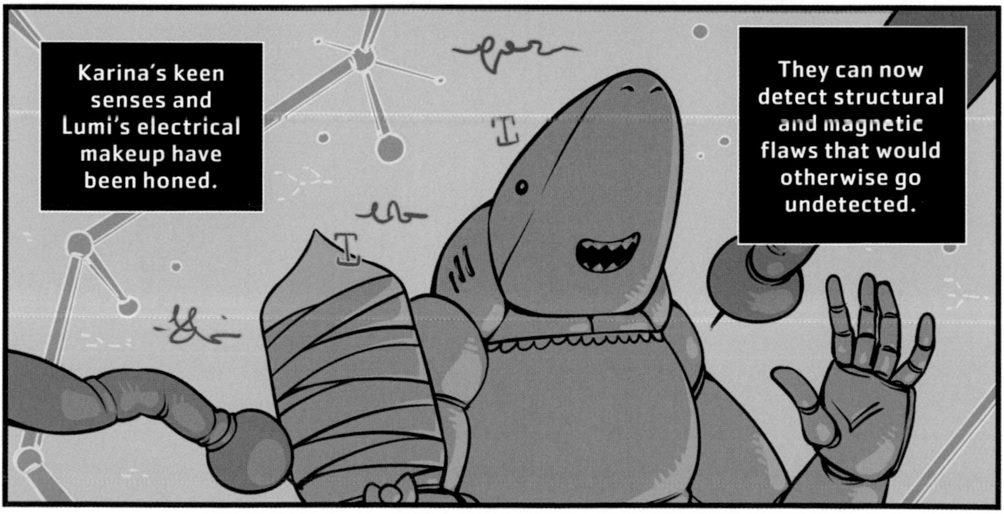
Karina's keen senses and Lumi's electrical makeup have been honed.
They can now detect structural and magnetic flaws that would otherwise go undetected.

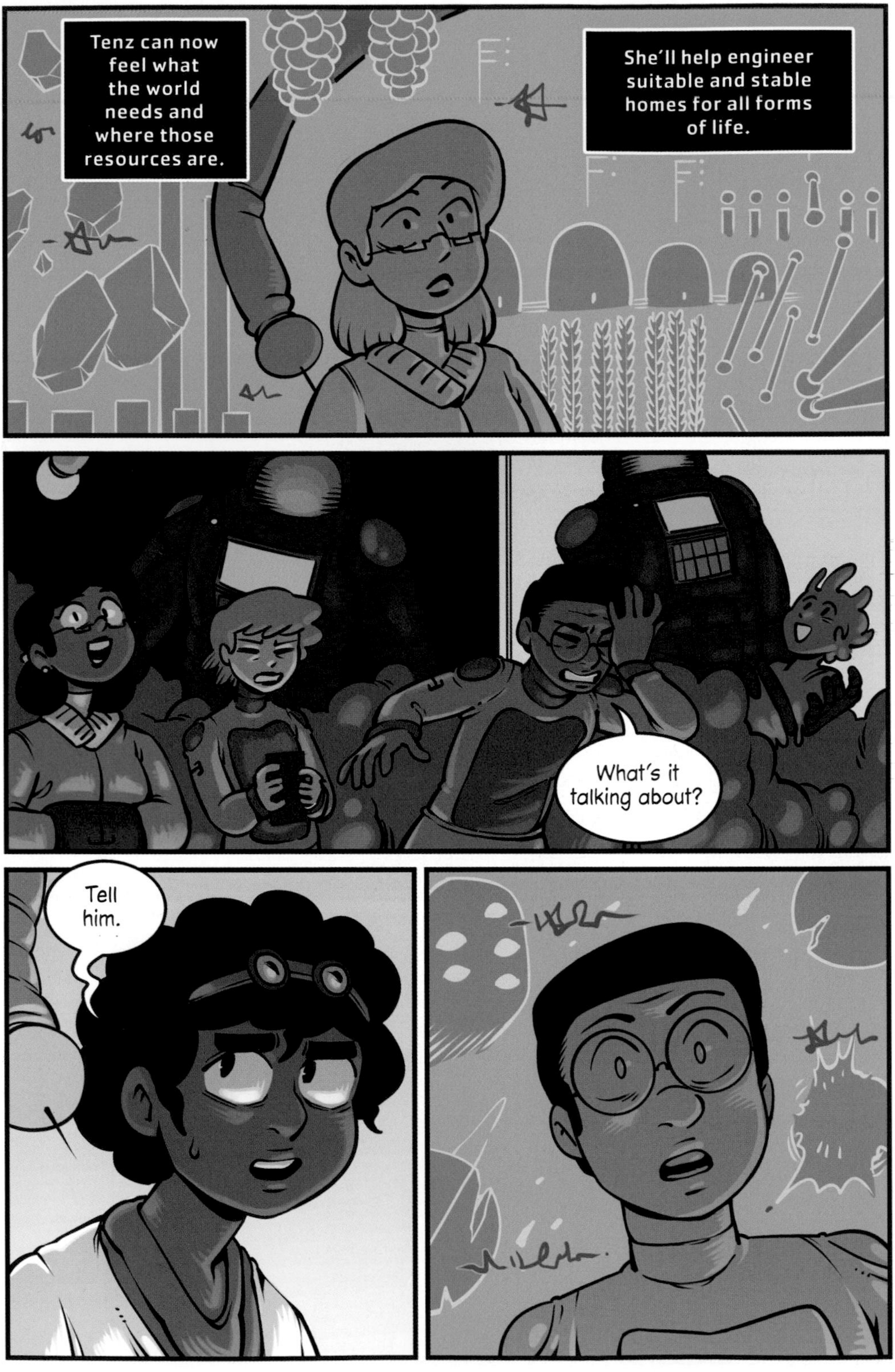
Tenz can now feel what the world needs and where those resources are.
She'll help engineer suitable and stable homes for all forms of life.
What's it talking about?
Tell him.

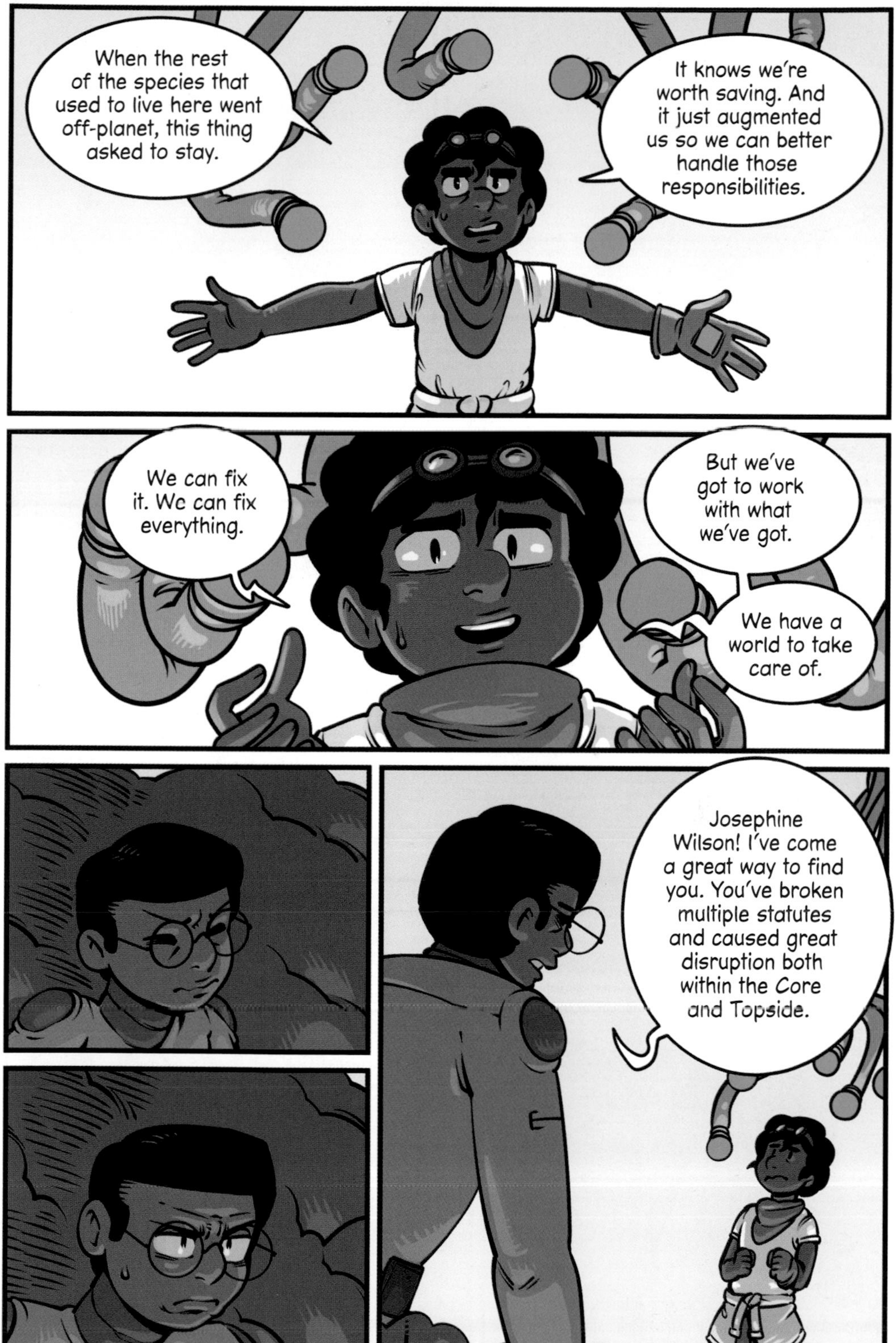
When the rest of the species that used to live here went off-planet, this thing asked to stay.
It knows we're worth saving. And it just augmented us so we can better handle those responsibilities.
We can fix it. We can fix everything.
But we've got to work with what we've got.
We have a world to take care of.
Josephine Wilson! I've come a great way to find you. You've broken multiple statutes and caused great disruption both within the Core and Topside.

I'm afraid I can't let you go until I give you this.

Notice of Resource ...dition Approval

Approved by:
Bram Vonnegan

next time get real approval on your paperwork okay?

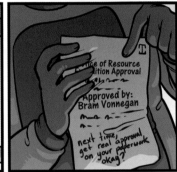

You really gotta have an actual superior sign off on your paperwork, ya know?

But what about the resources? Code violations? Our *report!?*

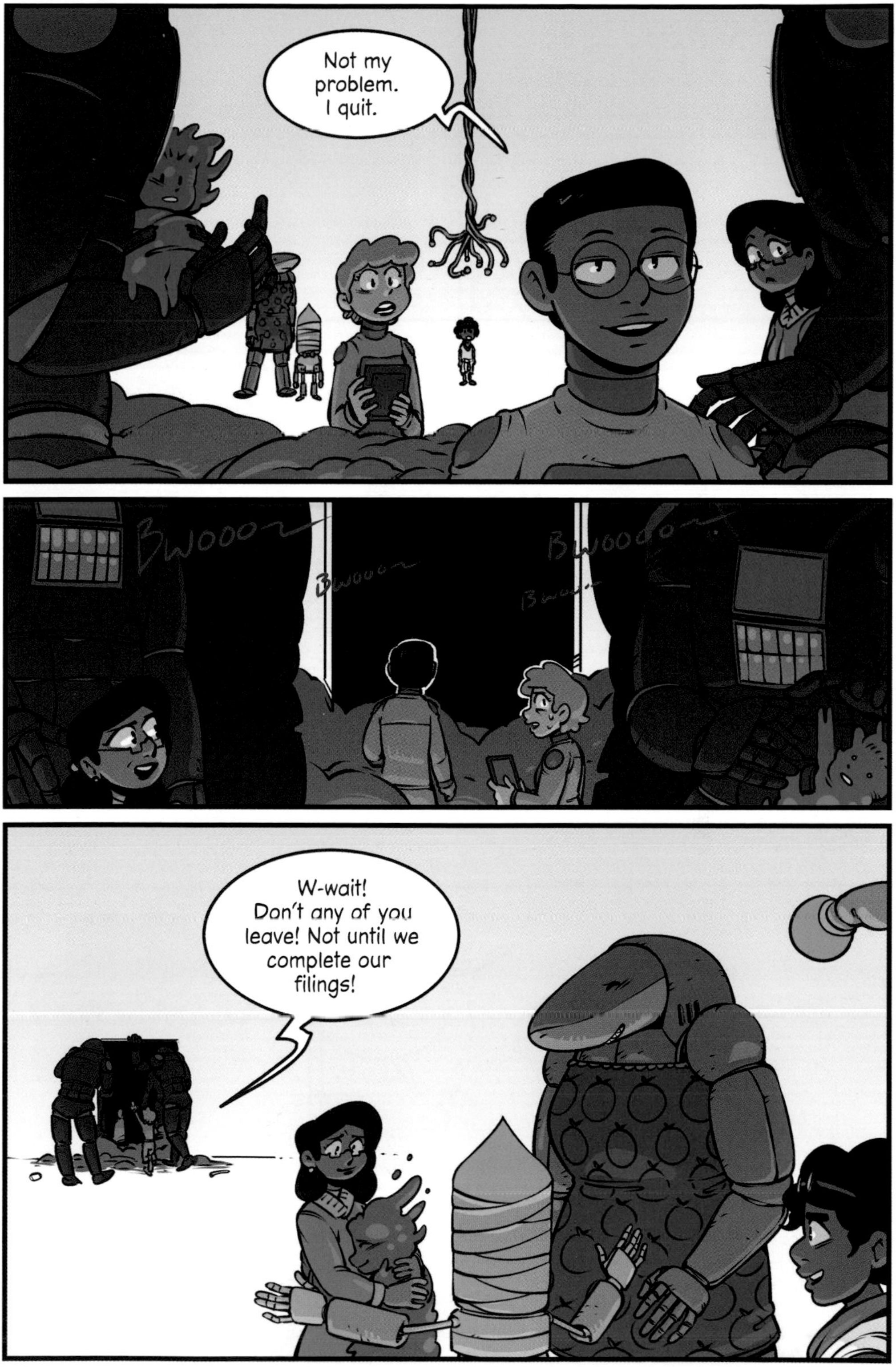
Not my problem. I quit.
BWOOO
BWOOOO
BWOOOO
BWOOO
W-wait! Don't any of you leave! Not until we complete our filings!

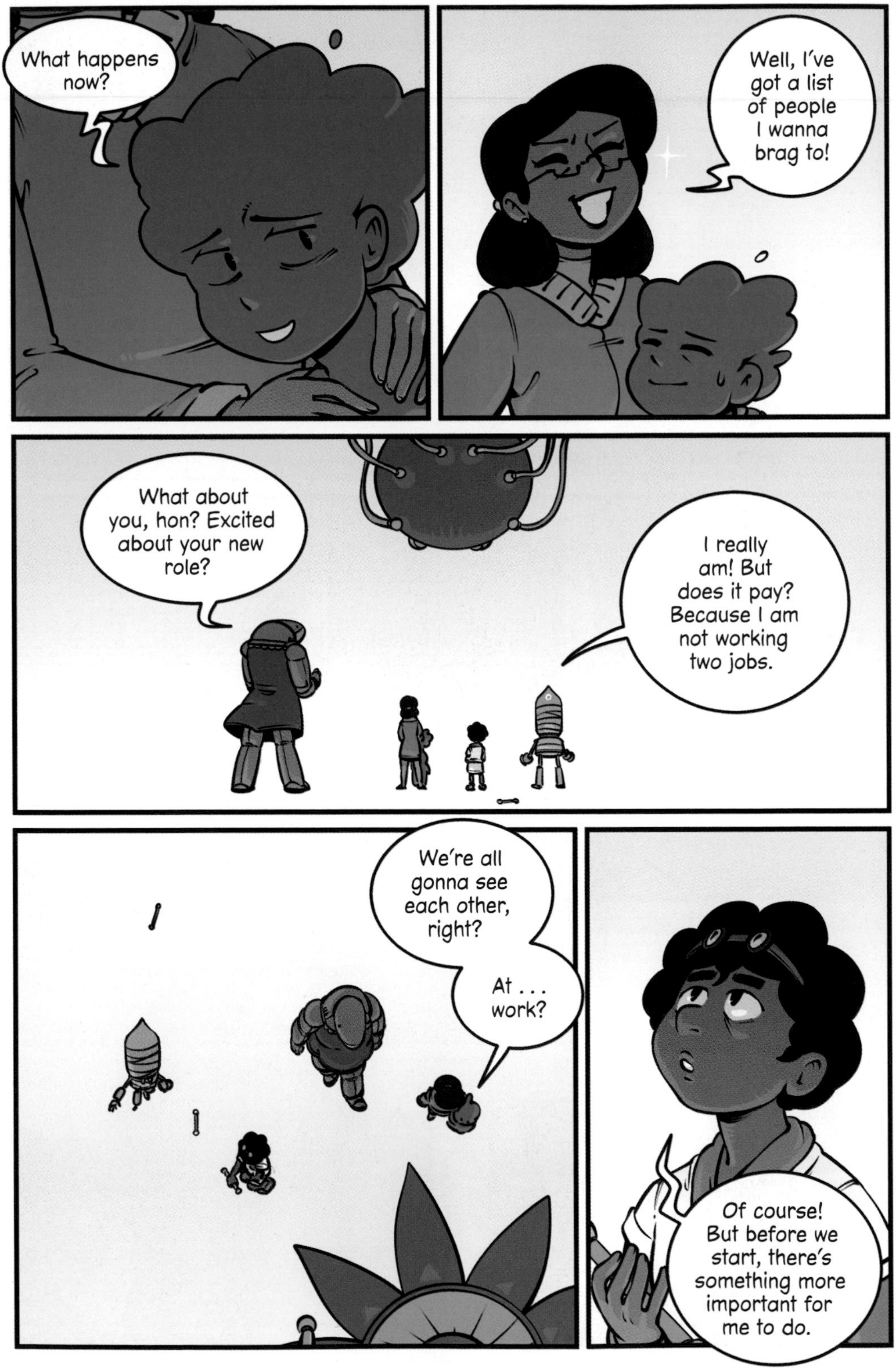
What happens now?
Well, I've got a list of people I wanna brag to!
What about you, hon? Excited about your new role?
I really am! But does it pay? Because I am not working two jobs.
We're all gonna see each other, right?
At . . . work?
Of course! But before we start, there's something more important for me to do.

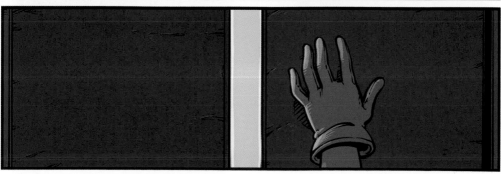

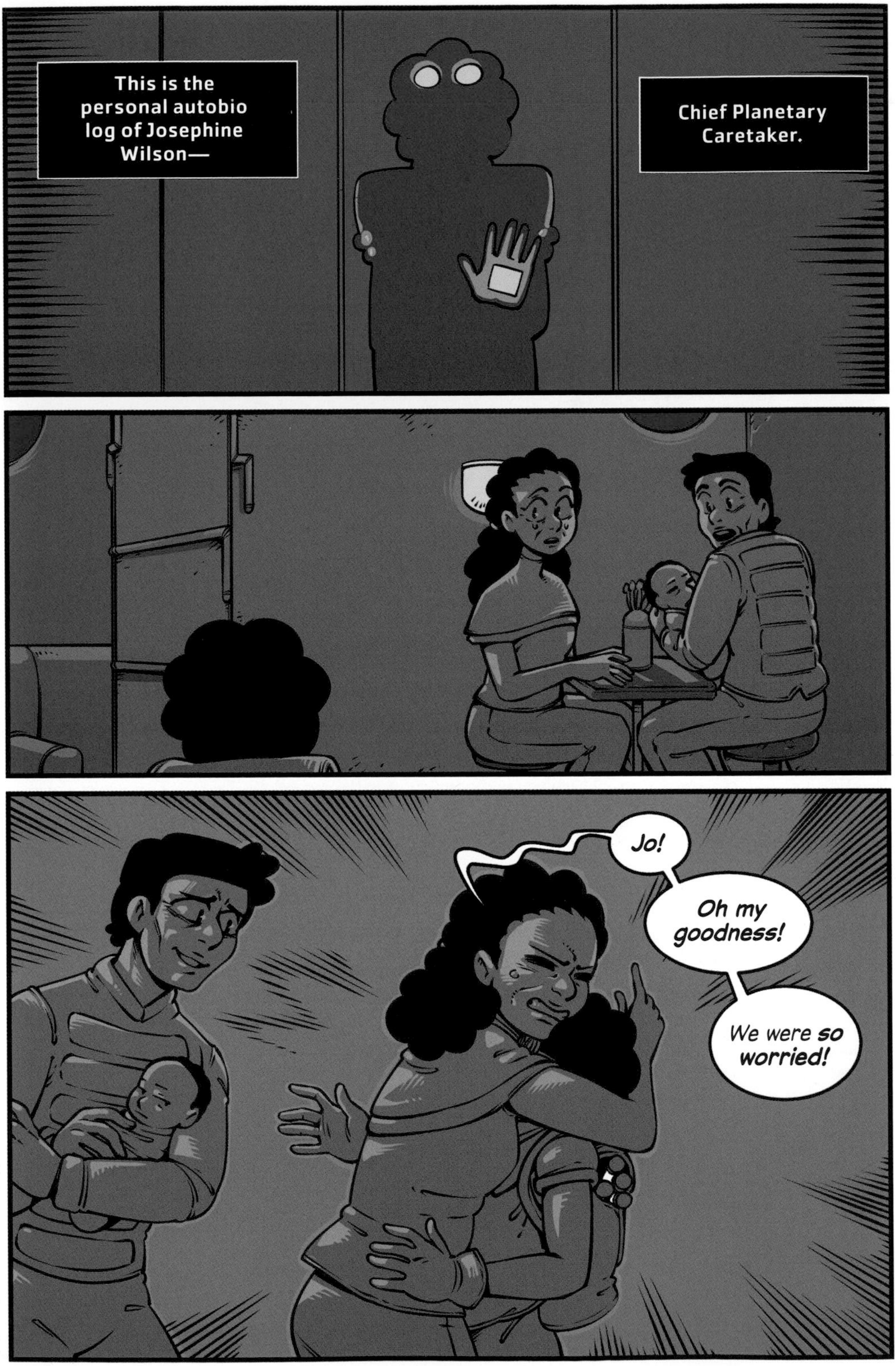
This is the personal autobio log of Josephine Wilson—
Chief Planetary Caretaker.
Jo!
Oh my goodness!
We were so worried!

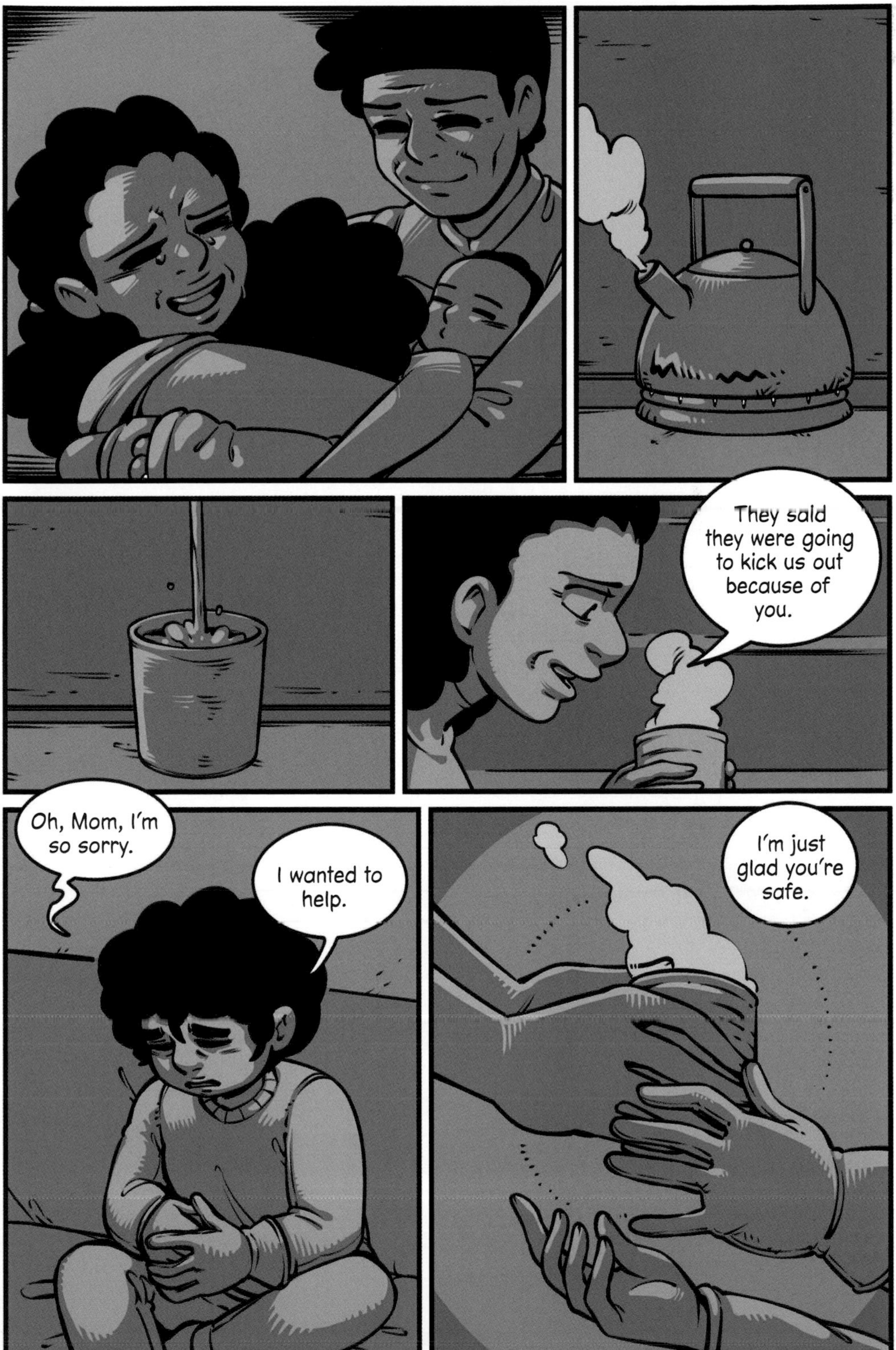
They said they were going to kick us out because of you.
Oh, Mom, I'm so sorry.
I wanted to help.
I'm just glad you're safe.

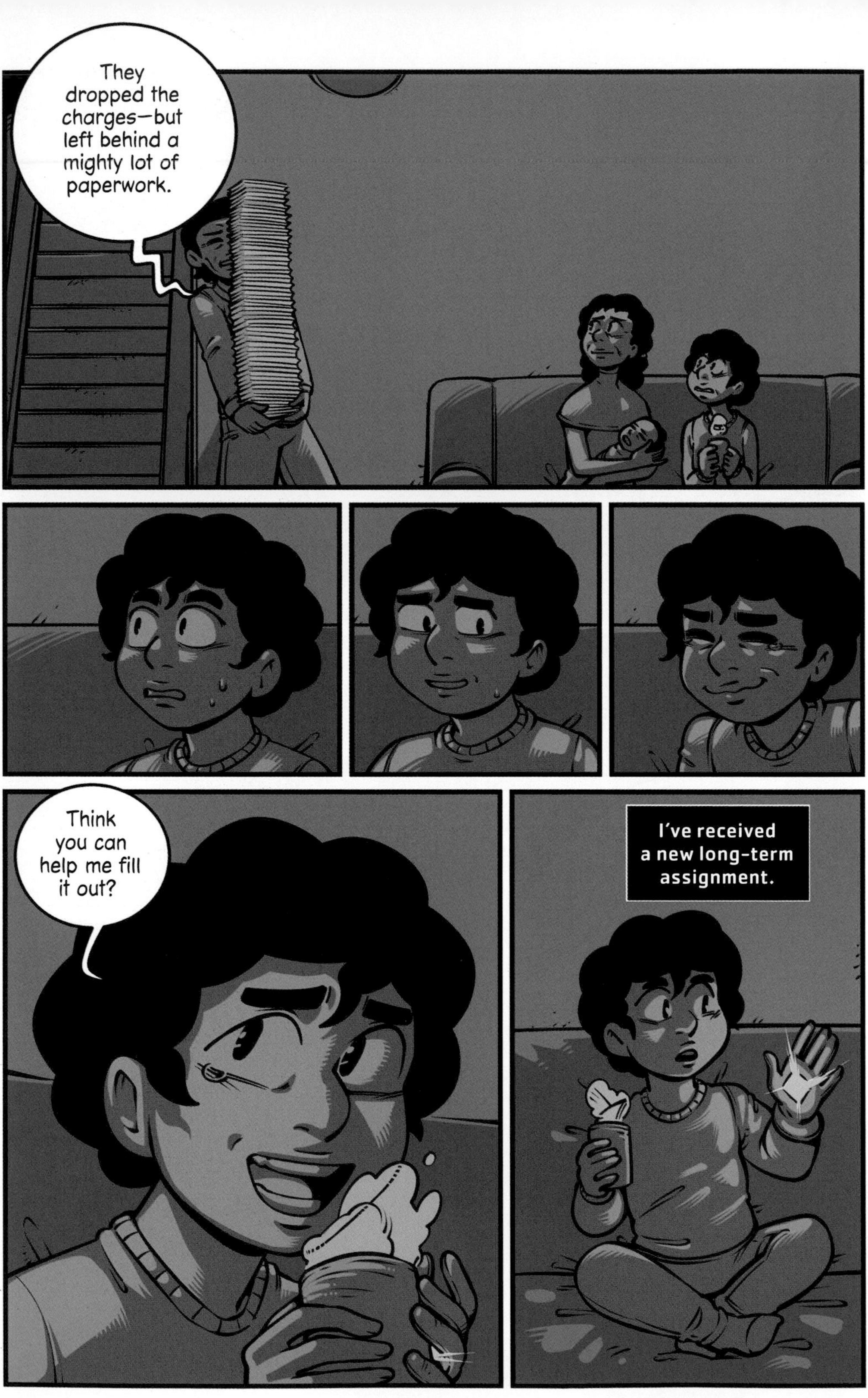
They dropped the charges—but left behind a mighty lot of paperwork.
Think you can help me fill it out?
I've received a new long-term assignment.

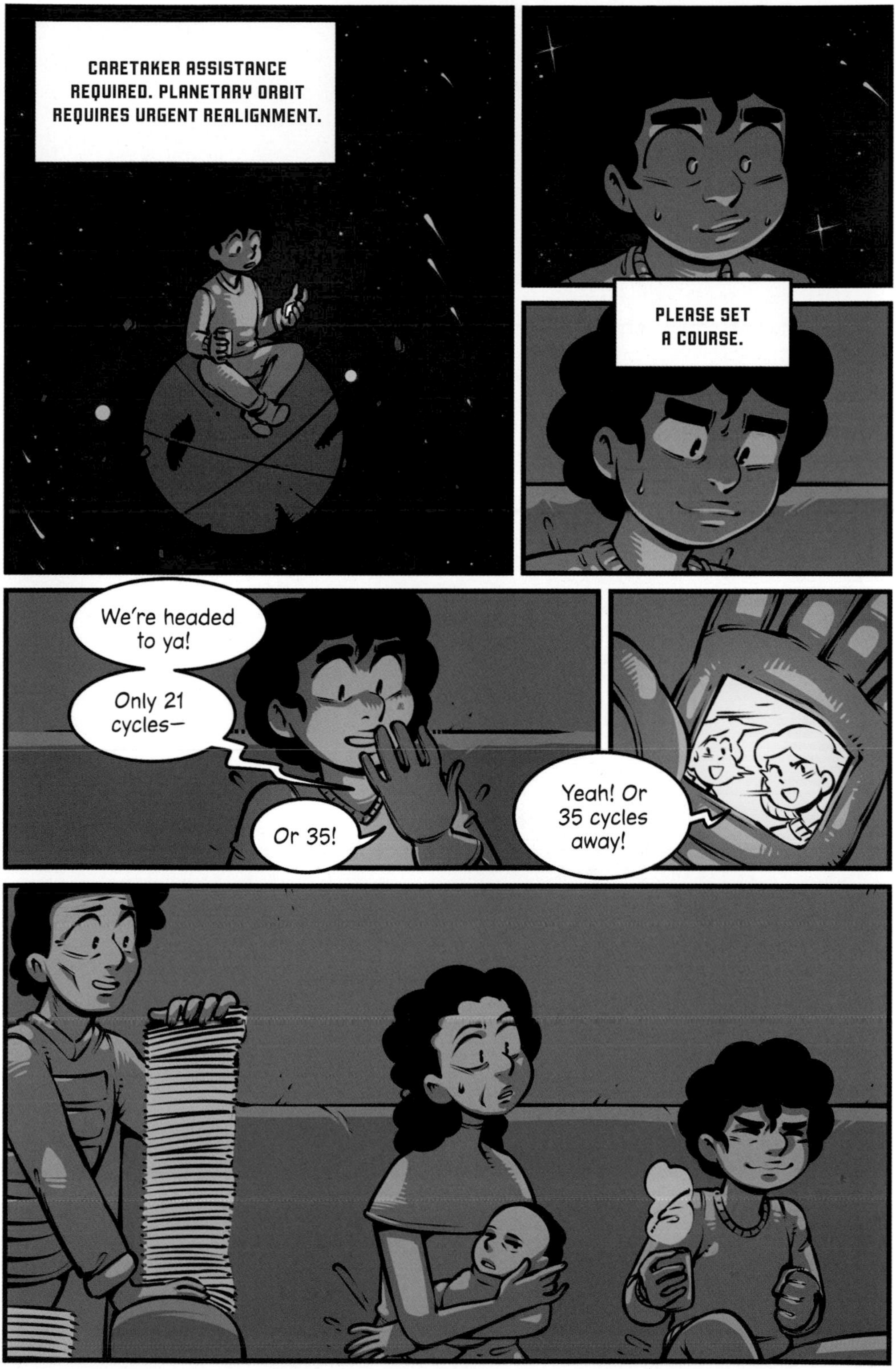
CARETAKER ASSISTANCE REQUIRED. PLANETARY ORBIT REQUIRES URGENT REALIGNMENT.
PLEASE SET A COURSE.
We're headed to ya!
Only 21 cycles—
Or 35!
Yeah! Or 35 cycles away!

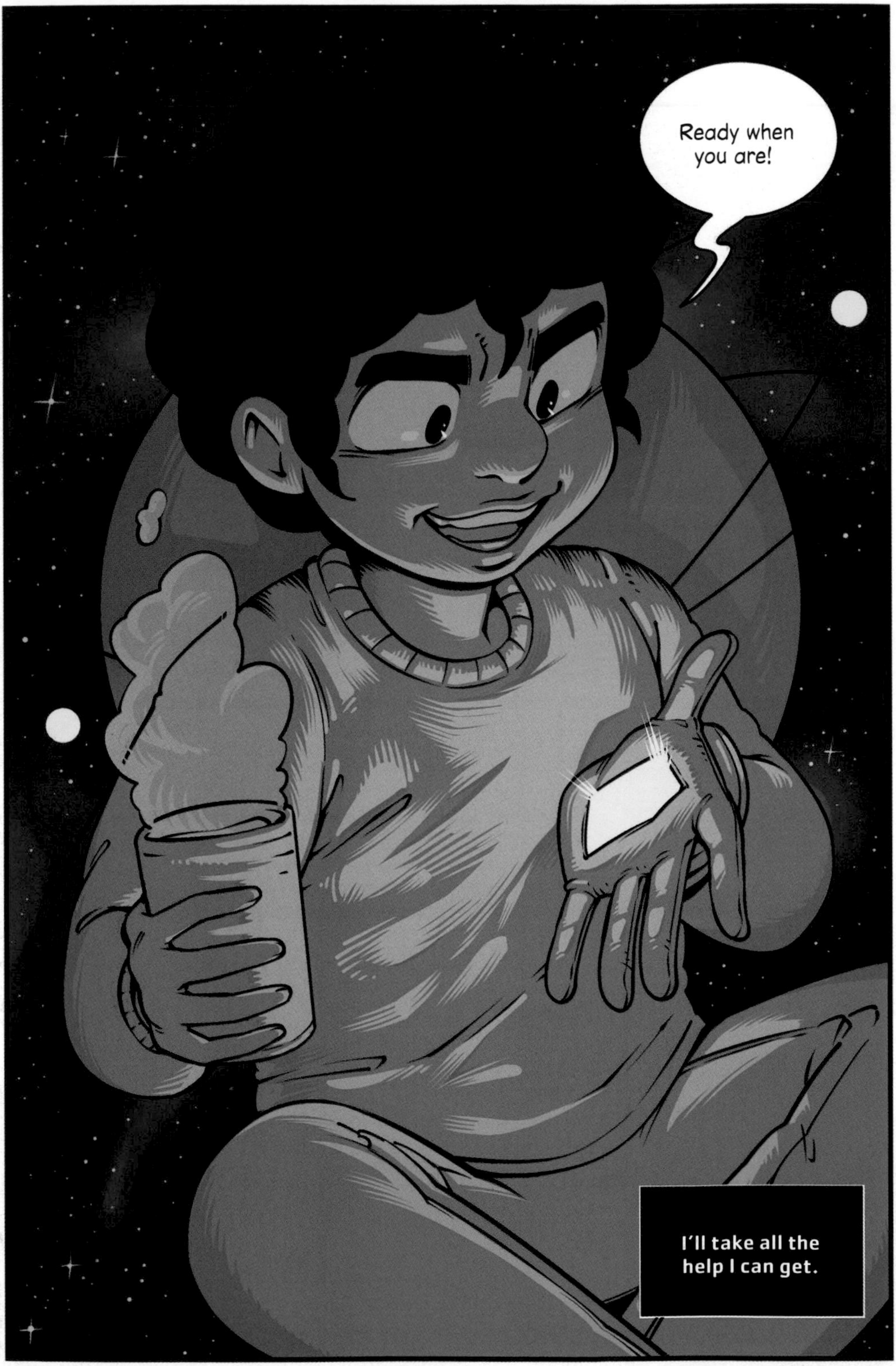
Ready when you are!
I'll take all the help I can get.

CREATING TOPSIDE

JNM: I wanted Jo's appearance to harken back to the early 20th century. Sort of like she had been conscripted into a never-ending Works Progress Administration project.

JNM: Tenz is supposed to evoke a 19th-century huckster if they were reincarnated in the future. To take things a bit further, Harry drew her as if she were a direct descendant of a character from one of our other comics.

HB: Karina is a lovely lady who also happens to be a powerhouse of a shark. I think these two aspects complement each other very nicely, and Karina is sweetness, wrapped around iron.

JNM: The idea of a walking shark has always fascinated me. The idea of a walking shark that wears a dress became a character I had to write someday.

HB: I love the idea of people that are more amoral than immoral—and Tenz is someone who walks that fine line. I want readers to like her even while not trusting her!

JNM: I've always loved the concept of electricity, so it was easy to make electricity a character that others could love.

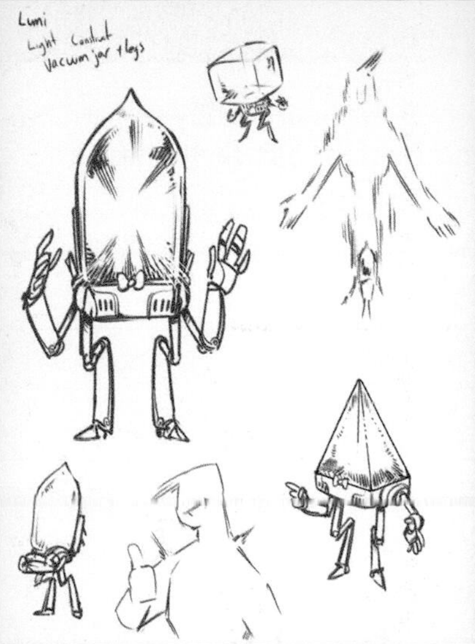
Lumi

HB: I imagined Lumi, as light and electricity embodied, would have a crackling, cheery personality. Not without his potential to zap, if befriended, Lumi will shed warmth and illumination over those he cares about.

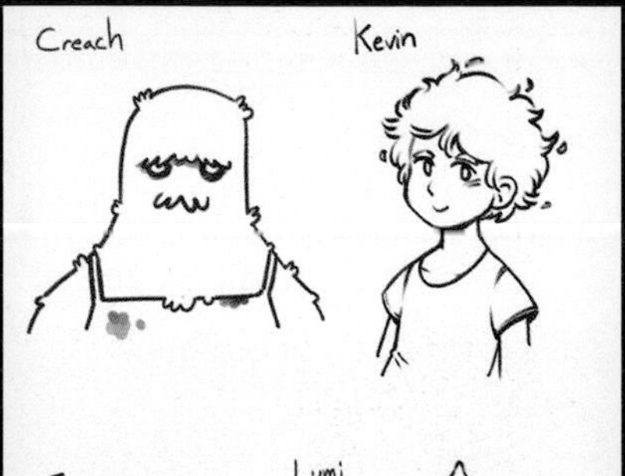
Creach
Kevin
Jo
Lumi

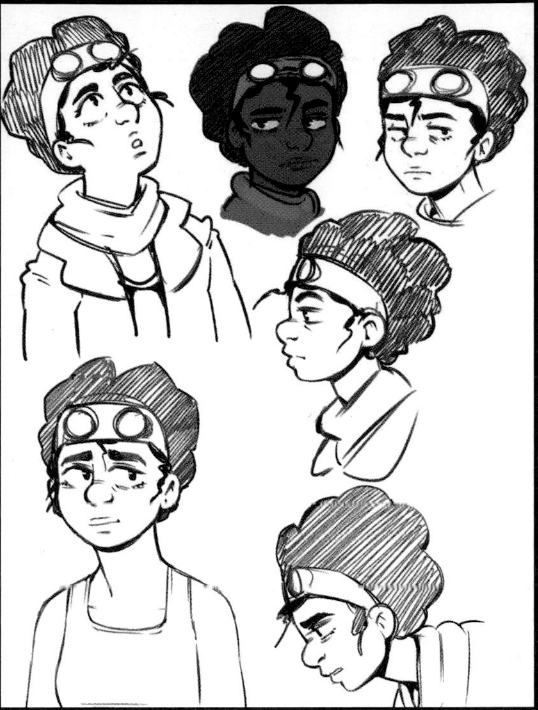

HB: Jo is a character who is always tired and always willing to work harder. From the beginning, communicating a kind of "exhausted determination" was a driving goal!

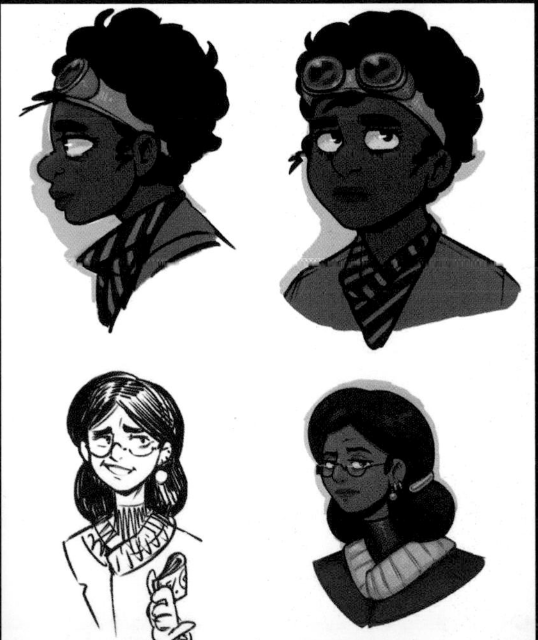

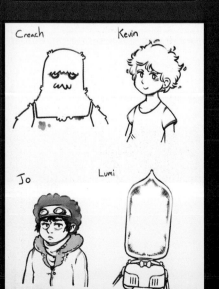

J. N. Monk is a midwesterner with a song in their heart. They've lived in a lighthouse, an active volcano, and Florida, but they always return to the heartland. They love travel, superheroes, food, and cats, and wish that everyone knew the steps to the musical number in their soul. They live in Saint Paul, Minnesota.

Harry Bogosian is a freelance illustrator and comic artist from New York City. Since graduating from Pratt Institute in 2009, he has drawn monsters for video game companies, created freelance work for book publishers, and nowadays primarily makes comics and graphic novels. There is nothing he enjoys more than making new fantastical worlds and filling them with his creations.

Acknowledgments
Endless gratitude to Z, who helped make this all possible; my editor, Greg Hunter, who pushed me to do my best work; McAlister, who never stopped believing in me; my loving parents, Darlene and Maurice, who kept supporting me in my dream to pursue writing comics; Diana and Abby, who offered me places to live while writing this; Kristen, who gave her editorial insight; and finally my cat, Peterbilt, for being all-around great. —**JNM**

I'd like to give my love and thanks to my wife, Shira, who always understands the oddly vast amount of time it takes to do a complete comic page; to my parents, Jo and Eric, for being incredibly enthusiastic whenever I draw a strange monster; to my brother, Travis, just because he's great; and to my cats, Nicky and Scrambles, because it's very helpful to have sentient creatures near you when working alone all day. —**HB**